Ed
P9-CFF-668

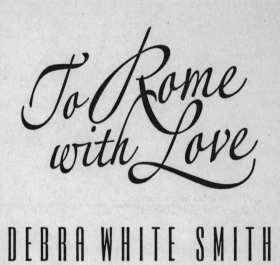

To Rome with Love

DEBRA WHITE SMITH

HARVEST HOUSE PUBLISHERS
Eugene, Oregon 97402

All Scripture quotations are taken from the Holy Bible: New International Version®. NIV®. Copyright © 1973, 1978, 1984 by the International Bible Society. Used by permission of Zondervan Publishing House. The "NIV" and "New International Version" trademarks are registered in the United States Patent and Trademark Office by International Bible Society.

Cover by Koechel Peterson & Associates, Minneapolis, Minnesota

TO ROME WITH LOVE
Copyright © 2001 by Debra White Smith

Published by Harvest House Publishers
Eugene, Oregon 97402

Library of Congress Cataloging-in-Publication Data

Smith, Debra White.
   To Rome with love / Debra White Smith.
      p. cm.—(Seven sisters series)
   ISBN 0-7369-0660-6
      1. Americans—Mediterranean Region—Fiction. 2. African American families—Fiction. 3. Mediterranean Region—Fiction. 4. Ocean travel—Fiction. 5. Courtship—Fiction. 6. Romantic suspense fiction. gsafd I. Title.

PS3569.M5178 T6 2001
813'.54—dc21   2001016946

All rights reserved. No part of this publication may be reproduced, stored in a retrieval system, or transmitted in any form or by any means—electronic, mechanical, digital, photocopy, recording, or any other—except for brief quotations in printed reviews, without the prior permission of the publisher.

Printed in the United States of America.

00 01 02 03 04 05 06 / BC-MS / 10 9 8 7 6 5 4 3 2 1

*Dedicated to Harvest House editors
Kim Moore and Barb Gordon.*

To Kim for lovingly and freely sharing her cruise and travel experiences with me. I could not have written this book without her joyful willingness to repeatedly pass on significant facts and direct me to key websites.

To Barb for all her patience and grace in putting up with a neurotic writer under deadline. Also for her ready laughter at all my corny jokes.

Editors like Barb and Kim are the unsung heroes in the writing world. We authors would be sunk without them! Barb and Kim, you're the greatest!

The Seven Sisters

Jacquelyn Lightfoot: An expert in martial arts, private detective Jac is "married" to her career and lives in Denver.

Kim Lan Lowery O'Donnel: Tall, lithe, and half Vietnamese/half caucasian, Kim is a much-sought-after supermodel who lives in New York City. Mick, her husband, is a missions coordinator.

Marilyn Douglas Langham: Joshua and Marilyn, along with Marilyn's daughter, Brooke, live in Arkansas. Marilyn works as an office manager for a veterinarian.

Melissa Moore: A serious nature lover, Dr. Melissa Moore recently established a medical practice in Oklahoma City. Jilted six years ago, her heart is torn between bitterness and a love that refuses to die.

Sammie Jones: The star reporter for *Romantic Living* magazine, Sammie is an expert on Victorian houses, art, and finding the perfect romantic getaway. She and her husband live in Dallas.

Sonsee LeBlanc Delaney: A passionate veterinarian known for her wit, Sonsee grew up in a southern mansion outside of New Orleans. Now married to her lifelong friend, Taylor Delaney, Sonsee is expecting her first child. They own a ranch in Texas.

Victoria Roberts: A charming, soft-spoken domestic "genius" who loves to cook, work on crafts, and sew, Victoria is married and lives in Destin, Florida.

To Rome with Love Cast

Abby Casper: Pleasingly plump, Abby Casper has exotic, dark eyes that reveal her African-American ancestry and the grace and dignity she's known for. Abby is married to Desmond. Their teenage daughters, Janie and Julie, are twins.

Darla Moore: Melissa's mother, Darla's desire for control and often inappropriate actions plague her daughter. She and her husband, Zeb, live in Oklahoma City.

Desmond Casper: Owner of Casper's Burgers, a large fast-food chain, Desmond is well respected in the business world and in his church. The Caspers live in Dallas, Texas.

Horace Waggoner: A not-so-successful private eye, Horace continually falls short of his father's expectations. He is in love with Sara Murdock.

Kinkaide Franklin: A nationally recognized Christian pianist, Kinkaide resides in Nashville. His dogged determination and strong faith are put to the test as he tries to win back Melissa's heart.

Lawton Franklin: A computer whiz, Lawton travels all over the United States helping blind people gain independence through computer proficiency. Blind since birth, Lawton is Kinkaide's younger brother.

Lenora Osworth: A devious beauty, Lenora worked closely with Desmond at Casper's Burgers' corporate headquarters.

Sara Murdock: Horace Waggoner's fiancée, Sara is also Desmond's secretary.

Shelby Canady: A well-known Christian singer who lives in Nashville, Shelby has close ties with Kinkaide.

One

⌒

"Hello, Mel."

The masculine voice sent a trail of regret up Melissa's spine. She spun from the back door of the children's clinic to face the man who had jilted her more than six years before. Kinkaide Franklin was in town for an extended visit with his parents, but Mel suspected his purpose for the visit lay in hounding her into marriage.

"Are you omnipresent or what?" she snapped.

"Or what." Kinkaide's right brow arched behind black-rimmed glasses. Casually he stroked his dark beard and eyed the doctor as if she were the best-looking woman alive.

"When did you get the glasses?" The question popped out, and Mel squirmed beneath his admiring gaze.

"Yesterday. The doctor says I'm getting farsighted. I'm having trouble seeing things up close."

"You've had that problem a long while, haven't you?" she mumbled.

As a cold February breeze rustled the surrounding oaks, Kinkaide's chin rose a fraction.

"When are you going to take no for an answer?" Mel demanded.

"But I thought—"

Approaching footsteps announced they would soon have company. Mel glanced toward the employee parking lot to see Bobbie Bailey bopping toward them. The nurse's blonde ponytail merrily swung as she sashayed forward. The 25-year-old usually acted as if she were the sole party responsible for spreading sunshine in a dark world. Yet the buoyant demeanor that worked miracles to ease fearful children now grated on Mel's nerves.

Kinkaide crossed his arms and cleared his throat.

Great! Mel thought. *What a morning for Bobbie to be early!* The nurse was usually 5 minutes late. With Kinkaide hovering like Don Juan, Mel would have preferred that Bobbie arrive 15 minutes late.

Energetic and cute, Bobbie didn't lack for male attention. Last fall her male visitors began interfering with her job, so Mel instated a new office rule of no male callers. Shortly thereafter Kinkaide arrived one fine morning. Mel's whole staff, including Bobbie, silently speculated about their boss' mysterious guest.

"Oh, hi, Dr. Moore," Bobbie quipped as she neared. "I didn't see you standing out—" She glanced at Kinkaide and her soft gray eyes gleamed. "Good morning, Mr. Franklin," she added, her lips twitching.

"Good morning." Kinkaide returned the smile.

Mel directed a solemn gaze toward her employee, who lingered as if she were ready to amiably chat about the weather in Oklahoma City or Seattle or China. "I'll be in shortly, Bobbie." Melissa stoically stepped away from the door.

"Oh, sure." Bobbie diverted her gaze. "Don't let me interfere." She hurried into the clinic, leaving behind the faint scent of honeysuckle.

"Look, Mel," Kinkaide began as soon as the white-paneled door clicked shut, "the only reason I'm here is because of the trip."

"What trip?"

"The cruise you agreed to go on with me, remember?" His eyes widened.

Only a month ago, on New Year's Eve, Kinkaide had delivered a bouquet of roses and a mysterious white envelope to

Mel's home. The envelope contained an elegant invitation for an all-expense-paid cruise to the Grecian Islands, along with a tour of Rome. For Mel, that invitation represented the potential for having her heart ripped out all over again. Her spine stiffened. "We haven't even talked about that trip. I never once agreed—"

Kinkaide pulled a postmarked envelope from inside his leather jacket. "This note from you came in the mail two days ago. I've been trying to reach you ever since. I've left three messages on your machine at home and two messages with your receptionist here. I finally went ahead and picked up the tickets—"

"You *bought* the tickets?" Mel's voice broke on an incredible squeak. "You paid for them without even asking me?"

"I asked you, and you said yes." He waved the letter between them. "And I tried to confirm the arrangements by phone, but you wouldn't return my calls!"

A thread of guilt wove through her midsection. Mel grabbed the envelope. "I haven't even seen this." She examined her name and address typed in the upper left corner then pulled out a typed note.

> *Kinkaide,*
>
> > *Thanks for asking me on the cruise. Of course I'd love to go!*
> > *Please keep me posted on the itinerary.*
> > > *Yours truly,*
>
> > *Melissa*

Yours truly! The two words jumped off the page and swarmed through her thoughts, jumbling any attempt to remain coherent. Mel's mouth fell open as she tried to trace the source of the note.

After reading the initial invitation last month, she had crammed it back into the envelope and dropped the whole thing in the trash can. On New Year's Day, when she emptied the wastebasket's contents, the white envelope landed in the top of the plastic bag. Feeling like a heartless ogre, Mel had retrieved the envelope and placed it on the kitchen counter. She never reopened the message, but for some reason she didn't throw it away either. Mel didn't recall seeing the envelope lately, but it had been hectic since her mother and father stayed with her while their kitchen was being remodeled.

"Mother!" she hissed. Her hands shook, her palms moistened, and her shoulders tensed. *When are you going to stop interfering in my life? I'm an adult now!* Mel bit her lips to stop the demand from springing forth.

"You really had no idea about the letter?" Kinkaide queried, a tenor of resignation in his voice.

"None." Mel returned the note and gazed into velvet-brown eyes that made her heart quiver despite logic's insistence that she avoid Kinkaide. As the silence expanded, she absorbed his every feature: the prominent nose that spoke of strong character; the heavy brows that reflected a thoughtful, sensitive mind; the broad, lean shoulders that attested to his physical fitness. His carefree nature, expressed by the collar-length hair, appealed to Melissa as much now as when she first met him. This was the well-tanned man Melissa had painfully dreamed of for the last six years. A man whose charming smile once snared her heart. A man who had never bothered to show up for their wedding.

We planned a quiet, simple affair, Melissa remembered. *Just the two of us and the minister. And then a low-key honeymoon in an Arkansas bed-and-breakfast. Nothing fancy. We didn't need anything fancy; we had each other.*

But Kinkaide didn't honor their commitment. Until last summer when Kinkaide popped back into Melissa's life, none of her six "sisters" knew that he had left her standing at the altar. The betrayal had been too painful for Melissa to discuss even with them.

Kinkaide removed his hands from his slacks pockets to reveal long, slender fingers that turned piano music into warm honey dripping into the soul with a sweet nuance of heavenward praise. Immediately he inserted his hands back into his pockets, and Melissa wondered if the visit unnerved him as much as her.

"So…you think your mother is up to her old tricks?" The lips that had welcomed her with a warm smile now drooped.

"I haven't seen the invitation for quite awhile. She and Father stayed a few nights with me after New Year's Eve. That's the last time I remember seeing it. Five years ago, my sister Monica and her fiancé were on the verge of calling off their wedding. Mother mailed a note, supposedly from Stanley to Monica, and it prompted their reconciliation. Anyway, as you know, she has a long record of interfering. And I know your note was on my kitchen counter. I wouldn't put it past her to—"

"Well, I guess this could be worse. At least you didn't throw the invitation away."

Mel glanced at his loafers. The same voice that insisted she take his letter from the garbage bag now bade her to never reveal she had indeed discarded his request. Despite her attempt to focus on the shoes, images of his face remained with her. The only thing that had changed about Kinkaide in the past six years was the dark, neatly trimmed beard and the few streaks of gray at his temples, streaks of gray that added a gentleman's touch to his demeanor. The older Mel grew, the more ardently she admired distinguished maturity.

"So do I burn the tickets or what?"

"Can you get a refund?"

He gripped the base of his neck and exhaled. "I guess. Probably not complete, though. I had a deadline yesterday to take advantage of this really great deal—slashed rates or business-class plane tickets, two ship cabins side by side, and all that. Sometimes they're really picky about refunds on package deals like this."

"Well, have you thought of taking someone else? Maybe your brother would like to—"

"I guess, but it wouldn't be quite the same." Rivulets of sadness flowed in his inky eyes. "You know, I've never given up on anything I really wanted in life, Mel."

"I know." Mel hardened a heart that threatened to melt.

"But I'm beginning to wonder if—"

The sound of nearing footsteps attested to others arriving for a day's work. Mel and Kinkaide glanced toward the approaching individual—this time, Dr. Nathan McDaniel.

"Hi, Mel!" Nathan called.

The burly doctor resembled a linebacker more than a pediatrician, but children loved his soft voice and kind blue eyes. Nathan observed Kinkaide, then his mouth fell open. "You're Kinkaide Franklin! I can't believe this. I have all your CDs!" Never had Melissa seen the forever calm Nathan McDaniel so excited. "Mel, you didn't tell me you knew Kinkaide Franklin!"

"We're old friends," Melissa muttered.

As the two men shook hands, Kinkaide darted Mel a searching gaze that bordered on jealousy. She suppressed a groan and stopped herself from rolling her eyes. "Dr. McDaniel is one of my partners in the clinic," Melissa supplied.

"I wish my wife were here," Nathan continued, and Kinkaide's tightened mouth relaxed.

A steady stream of employees now meandered from the parking lot. Mel glanced at her watch. "My patients start arriving soon." She gripped the doorknob.

Kinkaide, narrowing his eyes, scrutinized Mel. His jaw clenched as if he were divinely bequeathed a renewed determination. "I'll call you later."

Please don't! she wanted to say. But instead, she nodded, stepped into the clinic, and wove her way toward her office. Resolving to maintain a calm demeanor, Melissa entered her wing of the clinic and swept past the busy staff of four. She stepped into her office, closed the door, and leaned against it. The classically decorated room normally served as a haven of peace, but not today. The stereo system, ensconced behind a walnut-and-glass entertainment center, captured her attention. As if in a trance, Mel stepped forward, inserted a familiar CD, and pressed the appropriate buttons. Kinkaide's fluid rendition of "God Will Make a Way" floated forth. Yet the piano notes that were meant to encourage only heightened Mel's agitation while she transcended the threshold to the past.

As Mel gathered her ankle-length dress and stepped out of her Ford, Kinkaide neared from across the apartment parking lot. Numb from his rejection, Melissa simply watched his approach. A tense silence arrived seconds before Kinkaide stopped only inches from her. The silence spoke a finality Melissa found hard to accept. A silence that increased her confusion.

"I'm sorry," Kinkaide said, his liquid-brown eyes regretful, vulnerable, yet determined. He slipped his hands into the pockets of his suit pants—the charcoal suit he bought to wear to their wedding.

"The least you could have done is call before I left. That way I wouldn't have stayed at the church like an idiot for almost an hour!" The words, full of venom, exploded from Melissa. "I feel like a complete fool!"

"Well, if it's any consolation, so do I," Kinkaide said, his carefree manner replaced by that of a serious stranger.

"So what's the deal?" Melissa snapped. "Do you just not love me anymore or is there someone else?" The mention of a potential rival sent a knifelike pain shooting through Melissa's spirit. Her hands clenched into tight balls, her eyes filled with burning tears, her legs trembled.

"No, Mel, no one else," he rasped. "I just...I..." He glanced past her and Melissa cast a gaze over her shoulder to see a couple of college women who were a tad too interested in their conversation. "Can we go into your apartment and finish this?"

"No," Melissa bit out. Kinkaide winced. She wrenched the simple solitaire ring from her finger and held it between them.

"I'd hate for our relationship to end like this," he said, his eyes narrowing as if he, too, were in pain. "It's not that I don't care for you. I just...I...I couldn't go to the church. I...I...the more I tried to make myself go, the more I panicked." Exhaling, he clasped the back of his neck and hung his head.

As the ring glistened between them, the irony of this moment filled Melissa's stomach with bitter gall. The two of them had met in church. They had prayed together. They had beseeched the Lord about their marriage. Melissa had been filled with nothing but peace all the way to the church. Then Kinkaide didn't bother to show up!

"I'm just not ready for all this, Mel," he said, taking the ring. He shook his head and looked deeply into her eyes. "I couldn't get peace about our marriage." His voice's melodious nuance now rankled. "The whole thing started last night after I dropped you off." Wearily he rubbed eyes marred by dark circles. "I didn't hardly sleep last night. This morning I got up, determined to marry you—despite it all. I even got dressed." He motioned toward the immaculate suit. "But I just couldn't..."

"Despite it all? You don't love me!" Melissa accused, her tormented voice full of disillusionment.

"I don't know." His dark eyes rounded and he slowly shook his head. "I just don't know. That's the whole point. I'm not sure this is God's perfect will for me." He held up the small solitaire, and the diamond produced a merry wink that belied the grim moment.

Melissa swallowed hard. Her world tilted. Her heart was bludgeoned. Her hope crushed. But she determined she would not make a nasty scene. She adjusted her glasses, gripped her handbag, whirled around, and began marching toward her apartment like a soldier retreating from battle.

After that day, Mel wasn't sure if she had ever really seen her heart again. Reality demanded that Kinkaide had taken that part of her with him. The next time Melissa saw Kinkaide was in a Bible bookstore on the cover of his newest CD. Kinkaide's dream had come true. A dream Melissa had longed to share. Driven by an undefined need, Mel purchased his first CD...and every one after that. The discs remained in neat stacks near the front of her office player. Only last fall did she dare open them and listen to the work of what reviewers called "a musical genius."

"Why did I turn this on?" she growled beneath her breath. Gritting her teeth, Mel ground her finger against the stop button. The room was plunged into the hollow silence of a mausoleum. The silence resembled the inner cavity of Mel's heart, a heart once glowing with love, now cold and lonely. Lonely and hard.

Mel bunched her hands and swiveled from the entertainment center. Nothing would ever change her resolve to never trust Kinkaide again. Not even her mother's manipulation. Melissa approached her desk phone. After punching in the appropriate numbers, an angelic feminine voice floated over the line—a voice that defied the very inference that this woman would stoop to such duplicity.

"Hello, Mother," Mel began.

Two

⌒

Kinkaide sank into his Oldsmobile and slammed the door. Lips tight, he wadded the envelope into a ball and hurled it toward the windshield. The paper bounced off the glass and landed in the passenger seat. He slammed his fist against the steering wheel and roared like a thwarted bear. Leaning against the headrest, Kinkaide closed his eyes, relaxed his facial muscles, and forced himself to take several deep breaths. The smell of the new leather interior spoke of his success. Yet the car's emptiness mocked him for the price he had paid.

The musician gazed past the parking lot, toward an empty church playground. The barren tree limbs hung over the equipment as if they were bony fingers awaiting the chance to rip away the first gurgle of laughter. Without warning, an ethereal scene formed. Melissa stood at the base of the slide, her arms outstretched. Kinkaide was perched near the slide's top rung. A four-year-old girl with dark hair and eyes and Mel's smile sat in front of him and clutched the side rails.

"Come on, Whitney! Come on!" Mel called. "Mom's right here."

"Everything's fine, Whitney. You won't fall!" Kinkaide encouraged as the wind blew wisps of the child's peach-scented hair against his chilled cheeks.

With a delighted squeal, Whitney glided down the slide and into her mother's arms. Kinkaide clambered from the ladder and walked toward the two, wrapping his arms around his wife and daughter. Gently he bestowed a kiss upon Whitney's cherub cheek, then his lips lingered against Mel's.

The scene faded, to be replaced by another. A man sitting. Alone. On the end of the slide with his head in his hands. No one to share his life with. Piano music filled the park. Music he had arranged and performed. Music that took on a hollow ring despite the inspirational themes.

Kinkaide, rubbing his eyes, shook his head in an attempt to escape the haunting images. He crammed his key into the ignition and started the engine. A piano rendition of "To God Be the Glory" drifted from the CD player. As predicted, this latest CD was proving a monumental success.

"Too bad I'm bombing in other areas," he muttered as he steered into traffic and headed home.

Seven months ago, Kinkaide arrived in Oklahoma City for one reason: to win back Melissa Moore's heart. After a promising relationship with Christian singer Shelby Canady, Kinkaide at last realized why he could never ask her to marry him. His heart still belonged to the Oklahoma lady he had left standing at the altar. Until this morning, he had never doubted his ability to reclaim Mel's heart. Even though she had foiled his every advance, even though he recognized a seething resentment deep in her eyes, Kinkaide occasionally witnessed a spark of the old flame. A flash that denied her cool rejections. A gleem that suggested she had never stopped loving him.

When he'd received the note, Kinkaide was certain he had finally broken through her icy resolve. So much for that. "Maybe I need to go back to Nashville," he mumbled as he turned up Windsor Drive, a street in Nichol's Hills. The Oklahoma City suburb featured a classic, aging neighborhood lined by majestic oaks with drooping arms. Kinkaide had grown up in the two-story frame home his parents had owned for 40 years. His mother, a genteel lady of Italian descent, was thrilled that her son was home for an extended visit. But in Nashville, Kinkaide had a home. A career. A reputation. And there was Shelby.

But she's not Melissa.

His hands tightened on the steering wheel, and he turned into his parents' circular drive. The events of the last week left Kinkaide the proud new owner of two tickets for an exotic cruise and no one with whom to share the trip. The challenge now lay in getting Mel to change her mind.

"Well, hello Melissa Ann. Why are you calling so early?" Darla's voice oozed with pride and love—a love that could never be questioned. The problem was that she thought love gave her license to control her children's lives.

"Mother…" Melissa picked up a felt-tipped pen from her desk and began methodically tapping her Rolodex. "Did you by chance take a white envelope from my kitchen counter when you and father stayed with me?"

The extended silence answered Mel's question.

"Did you read my mail?" Mel struggled to maintain a calm undertone.

Darla Moore never spoke.

Melissa lowered herself into her leather desk chair. "Do you know anything about a typed letter that was mailed to Kinkaide signed with my name?" *Yours truly.* The words sent a hot flush to Mel's cheeks. No wonder Kinkaide's appraisal had been so warm!

More silence.

"Mother?" Mel prompted as the pen's tattoo increased.

"I find your accusations highly insulting." The angelic tones turned pontifical. "If you're insinuating that I would stoop so low—"

"Well, somebody mailed Kinkaide an acceptance note—supposedly from me—for a trip to the Mediterranean. I certainly didn't send it!" Mel's volume increased a couple of decibels.

"How dare you accuse me of—"

"I'm not accusing, Mother, I'm asking. And the reason I'm asking is because you did something very similar to Monica five years ago."

Darla's prim sniffle preempted her words. "Well, you must admit that it worked. They wound up getting married."

"Right. And Monica is miserable! You should have left well enough alone!"

"She might *think* she's miserable, but there aren't many men who take care of their wives like Stanley takes care of her."

Mel stiffened on the edge of her seat. The pen's steady rhythm escalated into rapid hammering. "There's more to a good marriage than money, Mother."

"Well, financial security goes a long way."

"So does—" Mel stopped herself from blurting "fidelity" and flung the pen to the desk's edge. The last thing she needed to do was breach Monica's confidence because she was too rattled to think straight. "Look, I didn't call to talk about Monica and Stanley. I called to ask you whether you mailed the note to Kinkaide."

"Listen, Melissa Ann, I *am* your mother and I deserve your respect. Furthermore—"

"Mother, I'm your daughter. And I deserve the respect of your allowing me to grow up—once and for all—and to make my own decisions. You can't force me into a relationship that I'm not ready to enter."

"Kinkaide Franklin is a dream-come-true husband for you. I have prayed for years the two of you would get back together."

"But that does not give you permission to go behind my back. Furthermore, I'm not going on that trip, regardless of what—"

"His mother told me—the Franklins are worshiping at our church now—anyway, Rosa told me she thought he was going to marry Shelby Canady. You know, that Christian singer who has a voice just *to die* for. Last spring, Rosa was even starting to shop for a dress for the wedding—expecting any day to have Kinkaide call and tell her they were getting married. Then, low and behold, by June they were broken up—after an 18-month courtship no less!"

Normally, Melissa would have interrupted what she recognized as a potential nonstop monologue. But the more her mother divulged, the more Mel's interest grew. She envisioned Kinkaide with Shelby, the polished blonde who was an acclaimed musician in her own right. The knot in Mel's stomach was in no way an acceptable reaction. Melissa shifted her focus near the desk's edge to the framed pictures of her two sisters and their families. She refused to give brain time to whom Kinkaide Franklin chose to date or marry. Nonetheless, she seized her mother's every word.

"And Rosa said he asked if she minded if he came home for a while. He just finished a new CD and is taking a break from tours and engagements. Anyway, after putting all the pieces of this puzzle together, I came to the conclusion that the man never really got over you. The poor dear has probably pined away all these years."

"Oh, yes!" Mel waved her hand. "He just *pined away* the whole time he was on the verge of marrying Shelby Canady!"

"And I just knew last summer when he asked me for your address at church—"

"If I remember correctly, you *offered* him my address and phone number—"

"What's the difference? He wanted them! Then, when I read that invitation for the cruise, I knew the Lord was answering my prayers—"

"So you *did* read the invitation?"

The phone's decisive click punctuated the truth.

Mel dropped the receiver in the cradle, removed her wire-rimmed glasses, and covered her face with her hands. The faint smell of creamy hand lotion filled her senses, and she tightened her features until she no longer needed to scream. "Oh, Lord," she breathed, "I know I'm supposed to respect her because she's my mother, but some days... Why couldn't you have given me a mother like Kim Lan's or Marilyn's? Neither one of them would dare interfere in her daughter's life!"

She removed her hands and gazed across the office. A poster-sized picture of her and her six "sisters" hung against the striped wallpaper. Kim Lan O'Donnel, acclaimed super-model, sat in the front center. During the years that Kim strayed out of God's perfect will, her petite Vietnamese mother, full of charm and compassion, had silently prayed. Her prayers finally ended when Kim Lan broke off her engagement to actor Ted Curry and married mission coordinator Mick O'Donnel.

My mother would have hired a private eye to spy on me!

Marilyn Langham sat to Kim Lan's right. Her candid brown eyes and blonde hair reflected her mother's honest, straightforward approach. While Natalie Douglas had always inspired her daughter to make right choices, she would never stoop to manipulation. Instead, Natalie stood by Marilyn through a horrible divorce and ultimate recovery.

My mother would have probably thought about paying a hit man to take care of my ex-husband!

The recent newlywed, Sonsee Delaney, sat near Marilyn. Sonsee's mother had died from cancer five years ago. Even though she was no longer in Sonsee's life, Mel never once remembered Sonsee complaining about her mother. Now that Sonsee was married to her lifelong friend Taylor and expecting a child of her own, Mel sensed that Sonsee and her child would be best friends just as Sonsee had been with her mother.

Best friends! What a concept! My mother won't stop trying to control me long enough to be my friend!

Victoria Roberts sat at Kim Lan's left. Her naturally curly hair and finely chiseled features fit her quiet personality. Ever the lady, Victoria possessed a refined air that even the elegant Kim Lan didn't possess. However, Victoria had often told Mel that she wished her mother were less distant and more involved in her life.

Mel sighed. *At least Mother does care enough to get involved.* An unexpected twist of love mingled with Mel's vexation.

Sammie Jones, sitting near Victoria, hadn't seen her mother since she left the family when Sammie was only five. Sammie's grandmother raised her. The six "sisters" knew the subject was taboo—especially on Mother's Day. The fiery, redheaded writer had made up for her mother's abandonment by developing a respected reputation as a novelist and magazine reporter.

My mother would never have deserted my sisters and me. More likely than not, she wishes she could be in three places at once and live with each one of us!

A dry chuckle escaped Mel as she observed her sixth friend who sat next to her in the photo—Jac Lightfoot. Mel and the dark-complected private eye had much in common regarding their mothers. They often joked that their moms should work together as interrogators for the KGB.

Jac would definitely lend a sympathetic ear to this latest episode.

Mel glanced at the phone, then at her brass desk clock. Eight-fifteen swiftly approached. Denver was an hour behind.

Melissa reached for the phone then hesitated. Jac was either just getting up or sleeping in after a long night. Her hours as a private detective proved unpredictable at best.

An upbeat rap on the door altered Mel's deliberation.

"Yes," she answered.

The door opened and Bobbie beamed at her. "Your first patient is in room 3, Dr. Moore. It's Whitney Lowe again. We're squeezing her in this morning. She just can't seem to shake that ear infection."

"Okay, thanks." Mel stood and reached for her lab coat hanging on a peg behind her desk. Another day, another adventure in the world of children.

Mel sighed as an old ache surfaced from the deepest recesses of her heart. She and Kinkaide had planned to have three children. They both agreed to start their family when he established his piano career and Mel finished med school. The first child, they fantasized, would be a little girl who had dark hair and eyes and a bright smile. They planned to name her Whitney.

Now, Mel harbored no hopes of giving birth to a Whitney of her own. Instead, she would spend her life assisting the children of others. If she ever did have children, she would follow Kim Lan and Mick's example and adopt a child from the Vietnam orphanage she visited last year.

Mel walked toward the office door, placed her hand on the doorknob, and hesitated. She swiveled toward the stereo system, and the stack of CDs behind the glass door beckoned her with a silent, hypnotic chant. Mel approached the stereo and picked up the top CD. Kinkaide sat at a black-lacquer grand piano. The ebony tuxedo and starched white shirt with bow tie set off his dark features. But the formal attire contrasted with the boyish charm that had often surfaced during the carefree moments of their courtship.

Their very first date, Kinkaide had kicked off his loafers and dragged Mel into a water fountain—sneakers and all.

Never had she given in so readily to such a lighthearted moment. And with the sounds of summer engulfing them, he had exposed Mel to a fountain full of fervid admiration spilling from sensitive brown eyes.

This morning Mel had been the recipient of the same fervid admiration. She had also witnessed that admiration mix with disillusionment. Disillusionment and despair. Despair and doubt.

Mel's hands quaked. Her throat constricted. A tight sob threatened to escape. She clenched her teeth until the moment of weakness passed. She flung open the CD case and reacted to the primeval need to expel the source of her traitorous yearning. Mel ripped out Kinkaide's picture, dropped the case to her desk, rent his image into tiny bits, then slammed the fragments into the trash can. Yet the spontaneous action, meant to purge the longing that threatened to drown her soul, only increased her torment.

Three

Kinkaide stepped into the entryway of his parents' home. The 1950s house possessed all the charm of the midcentury, replete with an oak banister that Kinkaide and his brother had slid down more times than their mother ever wanted to know. The smells floating from the kitchen validated Rosa Franklin's culinary skill. Kinkaide, his stomach rumbling, succumbed to an unseen force tugging him toward the kitchen.

"Hey, old man!" His brother's familiar voice erupted from the homey den.

Kinkaide halted and pivoted toward the voice. A tall, lithe man, several pounds lighter than Kinkaide, hovered over the Franklin's computer keyboard. His dark hair and complexion, stately nose, and broad cheekbones spoke boldly of his relation to Kinkaide. The shaded glasses and dark room attested that while Kinkaide's brown eyes experienced the world, Lawton's had never seen even a glimmer of light.

"Hey! Whatcha doing here?" Kinkaide's loafers tapped along the hardwood floor as he approached his brother.

"Just passin' through," Lawton replied as Kinkaide affectionately punched his arm.

"Last I heard, you were in Little Rock helping some long-lost damsel in distress find her way around a new computer." Kinkaide tugged on the drape cord. As if the sound of the swishing drapes were witness to the rush of light, an explosion of sunlight spilled through the floor-to-ceiling windows to banish the shadows.

"Yeah, well, we got through sooner than we thought. I took the early flight home this morning. I called Mom from the airport. We haven't been here but about 15 minutes. Now Mom's the latest damsel in distress. She's got some sort of bug in her new word-processing program. I'm trying to bail her out."

Kinkaide dragged a floral armchair closer to the computer and plopped into the cushion. "I could use a little help, too, while you're at it. My new laptop's giving me fits."

"You could probably start by reading the instructions, you lazy bum."

"Why, when I've got you?"

Lawton placed his fingers on the keyboard and began clicking the keys. A small box connected to the computer responded with a warped, feminine voice that detailed the information on the monitor. Although the software spoke in English, Kinkaide was always pressed to grasp what Lawton understood without a hint of struggle.

With a faint smile, Kinkaide rested his head against the back of the chair and gazed at the portrait of his mother and father that hung over the walnut mantel. Last Christmas his father arranged for the painting as a special gift for his wife. Kinkaide Senior took an aging photo to an artist who turned the memory into a masterpiece. The young couple gazed into each other's eyes while sitting on a porch swing. They were in their twenties and in love. In love and oblivious to the world around them.

Kinkaide's vision blurred. In place of his father, he recognized himself. His mother's fine-boned face and thin figure took on the attractive lines of Mel's fuller cheeks. She reached up to stroke his beard, and Kinkaide's gut clenched. He grasped her palm and moved it to his lips then tugged her closer. His lips inched toward hers, and...

"Wake up! I'm talking to you!"

Pain shot up his shin and jolted Kinkaide back into the real world. "Good grief! You don't have to get violent about it!"

"What's the matter with you? Did you go into a coma or something?" Lawton faced Kinkaide as if he were scrutinizing him.

"No, I was just thinking." Leaning forward, Kinkaide placed elbows on knees and clasped his hands. He stared absently at the braided rug that was in the same spot since he could remember.

"Well, while you're doing all that thinking, why don't you *think* about taking me to the grocery store after breakfast. My cupboards are empty. When I heard you drive up I decided you were the lucky one who gets to take me to the store."

Kinkaide's brows rose. "What? Mom still won't let you use her car?"

With a wry smirk, Lawton snorted and focused his energy back on the computer.

The rising smells of eggs, biscuits, and sausage enforced the fact that Kinkaide had skipped breakfast. This morning he'd been too preoccupied with his surprise visit to Mel to bother with food. He gazed across the entryway, through the formal dining room, toward the kitchen door. The occasional clank and sizzle was witness to a morning feast in the making. "I could eat enough for a horse. Do you know if Mom's cooking for me? She may think I ate breakfast out."

"You always did eat a lot when you struck out with the ladies." Lawton punched a computer key, then leaned back and crossed his arms. "From what I've already heard this morning, that cruise idea was a bummer."

"My, my, my, the grapevine seems to be alive and well." Kinkaide slumped back and tapped his temple with his index finger as he gazed toward the ceiling. "Let me guess. Melissa must have called her mother about that note. Mrs.

Moore promptly called Mom. And you must have been privileged to overhear every word."

"Who, me?" Lawton pointed to his chest. "I would never eavesdrop."

"Everybody who believes that, stand on your head!"

"You know, I don't think I heard Mom mention a note. Is there more to this story?" Lawton snickered.

"Oh, yes." Kinkaide rolled his eyes. "Darla Moore mailed me a letter—supposedly from Mel—and accepted my invitation for the cruise."

Lawton whistled.

"We'll just say that Mel *was not* a happy camper when I showed her the note."

"You know, for somebody who usually gets what he wants, you're really bombing big, man." Lawton rubbed a hand over the front of his ribbed sweater.

"Well, do you feel morally obligated to look thrilled about it?"

"Who said I was thrilled?" Lawton shrugged as if he were the personification of innocence. He tilted his head at that odd angle that suggested he observed far more than Kinkaide ever wanted him to realize.

Kinkaide squirmed, uncomfortable with even his younger sibling sensing the tide of desperation that threatened to suck him under. Lawton had known from the start that the sole purpose of Kinkaide's visit home was to win back Mel's heart. In the last seven months, Kinkaide had done everything but throw himself at her feet and beg her to come back.

"If you really want her back, you ought to try sitting on her front porch and howling all night." Lawton's laughter bounced off the knotty-pine walls.

"Oh, so now you're going to try your hand at being a comedian! Back off, will ya?" Kinkaide stood, brushed past his brother, and obeyed the demands of his stomach. He headed toward the kitchen.

"Hey! I've got a few ideas I could share with you if you weren't so defensive about this whole thing." The sound of Lawton's measured footfalls against the braided rug followed Kinkaide. "Maybe if the two of us put our heads together we could come up with a plan or two that might work."

"Since when did you become such an expert?" Kinkaide stopped and turned to face Lawton, who ran smack into him.

"Hey, quit it with the surprise stops, will you?" Lawton grumbled as the two disentangled themselves.

"Sorry." Kinkaide crammed his hand into a pocket of his pleated slacks. "So what kind of suggestions do you have?" he asked, despite a sixth sense that warned him he might be asking for trouble.

"Well…" Lawton hesitated and felt along the top of the nearby rocking chair. The morning sunshine highlighted the room like a christening of liquid gold upon the weighted moment. "My reading has taken an interesting turn lately."

"Oh?" Kinkaide quirked a brow and crossed his arms as his mind spun with how in the world this new reading direction was going to intersect with his present problems.

"The lady I just helped in Little Rock—she's a Christian romance novelist, and…"

"Don't tell me you actually started reading her stuff?"

"I got curious about what she was writing, okay? I mean, you don't meet an author every day, especially not a blind one, and I thought it would be good PR if I read a few of her books. After all, she gave me business, so why not buy some of her books?"

"So you've spent the last three weeks reading Braille romance novels?"

Lawton shrugged and rocked back on his heels. "Sure." He crossed his arms. "Why not! I didn't have anything else to do in the hotel during the evenings."

"So what does this have to do with Mel and me?"

"Well, frankly old man, a few of those heroes have a thing or two on you." One corner of Lawton's mouth lifted.

"Oh, brother!" Kinkaide whipped off his new glasses and rubbed the top of his aching ear. Lawton's features blurred. "I've heard everything now! Why don't you start acting like a normal blind person and get a dog. You need somebody to talk to. You're going wacko! Whoever heard of a computer geek reading romance novels!"

"Hey, don't knock 'em! They're not bad at all. Kinda reminded me of Ruth and Boaz."

"You need to get married. That's the problem." Kinkaide punched his index finger into his brother's chest. "You're losin' it and fast. Why don't you let me fix you up with one of my friends from Nashville—"

"No way! You keep your grimy hands off my love life!" Lawton shoved aside Kinkaide's finger. "The way you're blowing it with Mel, I don't need any help from the likes of you."

Kinkaide replaced his glasses and walked into the dining room with Lawton close behind. He paused by the dining table and gripped the top of one of the high-backed chairs.

"Okay, shoot!" he challenged. "Since you're so smart, tell me what I'm supposed to do."

"Well, what all *have* you done?" Lawton asked in a voice that declared him an expert of romance.

With a resigned sigh, Kinkaide began counting off his attempts, one finger at a time. "I've sent her flowers several times. I've called her. Most of the time I'm forced to leave messages that she doesn't return. I've e-mailed her. I've visited her church. I've popped into her work a few times and even stopped by her house—"

"Have you thought of hiring an airplane to carry an 'I love you' banner over her house?"

Kinkaide blinked. "Uh, no."

"Have you considered arranging a quartet to serenade her?"

Kinkaide shook his head.

"Have you told the woman you've never gotten over her?"

"She won't let me get close enough to tell her. The last full conversation we had was last fall in the yard." Kinkaide pointed toward the front of the house. "She came over for the sole purpose of telling me in person just how serious she really is about our *not* getting back together!"

"Well, you're going to have to get creative."

"You think a cruise and trip to Rome *wasn't* creative?"

"I must admit you do have a point there."

"She's a tougher case than I ever imagined. Last fall she basically told me that I don't stand a chance. For starters, I don't think she's even begun to forgive me for jilting her in the first place—"

"I'm sure you'd be just as hard-pressed if the tables were turned," Lawton said quietly.

"I know, I know." The decision that seemed so right six years ago now hung around his neck like a rotting remnant of the past. "At times I think she still loves me. Then there are times when I feel like she can't stand the sight of me. For the first time this morning, I was tempted to throw in the towel and head back to Nashville."

"What? But I've so enjoyed tormenting you the last few months."

"Ha! All you do is crash land at your apartment for an overnight visit. You haven't been home long enough to torment me. You're too busy globe-trotting!"

"It's a tough job, but—"

"Somebody's gotta do it," the brothers finished in unison.

Kinkaide shook his head. "Romance novels. I've heard of everything now. You seriously need to think about getting a life."

"I'm the one with the life, old man, and don't forget it." Lawton began his steady trek toward the kitchen.

"Okay, you've got a life. Maybe you need a *wife*."

"No, *you're* the one who needs a wife, remember? I'm perfectly content the way I am," Lawton shot over his shoulder, then he stopped and raised his head as if he were just aware of something his senses had detected minutes before. "When'd you get the glasses?"

"Yesterday, and they're driving me nuts. My ears are really sore. Doctor says I'm getting prematurely farsighted. I can't see my music or anything else up close, for that matter."

"Bummer. That's a particularly terrible state to be in—especially when you're thick-skulled on top of everything else."

Kinkaide gently shoved his brother. "You need to watch your attitude. This cruise is going to get long and tedious with you acting this way."

"Who says I'm going on the cruise?" Lawton crossed his arms.

"*I* do. I've spent hard-earned money on these tickets, and I'm not letting them go to waste. You've got three months to arrange your schedule and save some money."

"What if I decide I don't want to go?"

"Since when have you ever turned down a trip to any-where?"

"Okay, okay. You know me well." Reaching forward, he gripped Kinkaide's forearm. "But I've got to warn you, I'm not nearly as good a kisser as Melissa probably is."

"Oh, stop it, will you?"

Lawton's abandoned laughter exploded as the two entered the spacious kitchen. While the tranquil taupe-and-white decor fit his mother's penchant for taste, it drastically contrasted with Kinkaide's mood. Indeed, if the interior were to reflect his emotions, the walls would have been a psychedelic confusion of neon colors.

"You know, on second thought, I'm not certain I'm so ready to give up on Mel. I'm just wondering what would happen if I put to good use some of your advice." Kinkaide stroked his beard and eyed his mother dishing up a mound of scrambled eggs with sausage on the side. "Plus, if I told her you were going and even got her to invite a friend, she might reconsider."

"I think that sounds like a much more logical idea, Kinkaide," Rosa Franklin said. Her dark eyes widened with her approving nod. "I think it's an insult for a gentleman to ask a lady on a cruise alone. What will people think?"

"Nobody's going to think anything," Kinkaide protested. "It's the twenty-first century, and I arranged for us to have separate cabins. The whole thing is at the most discreet level possible."

"I'm sorry to be prying, Kin, dear. And I haven't said a word since you came home about any of this business with Mel. But I've got to tell you that there are a lot of people who would agree that going on a cruise alone with a woman just doesn't look good. And you've got to watch your reputation. It's not like nobody knows who you are now. What if somebody recognized you and snapped a picture? The next thing you know, there'd be a magazine article somewhere speculating about your lack of discretion."

Rosa's dark, bobbed hair, attractive application of makeup, and chic pantsuit made her look more like Kinkaide's elder sister than his mother. Once he arrived in his adult years, Rosa had indeed been a friend and confidant—unless Kinkaide or Lawton dared traipse across the boundaries of proprietal norms. Then she graciously unveiled her motherly opinion.

"I didn't even know you'd asked her until a few minutes ago when Darla called. If you'd told me about this whole thing, I could have told you that no lady who has any inkling about what's proper would ever agree to go alone on a cruise with a man."

"Take my word for it," Kinkaide groused as he joined Lawton at the breakfast table covered in navy cloth, "the reason she turned me down has nothing to do with her worrying about what's proper." Absently he toyed with the wooden saltshaker.

Rosa placed two plates, laden with breakfast, in front of her sons. "Actually, I'm struggling with feeling a bit annoyed about all this." Her frown accented the laughter lines around her eyes. "You've certainly put a lot of time and effort into winning Melissa back. It would seem to me that she might have the inclination to respond a little more favorably."

"So you *did* want her to go on the cruise with me?" Kinkaide paused, fork posed over the eggs.

"No, certainly not *alone*. It's just that—"

"I think Mom's trying to say that she's hacked at Mel for not falling at your feet and begging you to marry her," Lawton inserted.

A slight huff escaped Rosa and she eyed her younger son. "Your eggs are at three o'clock. Your sausage is at nine o'clock. Your biscuit is at the top. And your coffee is to your right."

"Okay, okay. I get the hint. Just eat and mind my own business, right?"

Rosa's frown increased as if she didn't quite know how to handle Lawton.

The same expression had been directed at Kinkaide as many times as not. Looking back, he wondered how his proper mother had survived raising the two of them with her sanity intact. Certainly the firm hand of Kinkaide Senior had proven a needed remedy on more than one occasion.

"If it's any consolation, Mom, I figure that by now Mrs. Moore is just as aggravated at Mel as you are." He sighed.

"I never said I was aggravated..." she paused for a pointed gaze toward Lawton "...or even hacked. It's just that my heart breaks every time you come home like this." Rosa twisted a button on the front of her wool pantsuit. "I'm beginning to wonder if perhaps Shelby—"

"Shelby isn't the one for me."

"But you have so much in common, and she always seemed to be crazy about you."

"I know." Kinkaide tackled a fork full of spicy sausage and thoughtfully chewed. The problem was that the closer he got to Shelby the more he focused on Melissa. As the courtship wore on, the very thought of marriage to any woman but Mel left him in a panic.

"You know, there are some parts of this whole business that make some of those romance novels seem boring." Lawton, suspiciously straight-faced, reached for his steaming coffee.

"Just wait." Kinkaide narrowed his eyes. "Your time's coming, and when it gets here I'm going to laugh you to scorn!"

"No way! I don't think I'll ever be the victim of 'my ex-fiancée's mother just forged a note to me' syndrome." He sipped the black liquid.

"What?" Rosa looked from Lawton to Kinkaide, her tiny diamond earrings sparkled with the movement.

"Oh, Mrs. Moore didn't tell you about *the note?*" Kinkaide's voice fluctuated with sarcasm. "That figures."

"No. All she told me was how disappointed she was that Melissa had turned down your invitation for the trip. She is so afraid you're going to back off. I'm not the only one who thinks Mel is being a little..." Rosa deliberated, as if trying to choose the softest yet most truthful word.

"Hardheaded?" Lawton asked.

"You always did have such a way with words." Kinkaide dumped two teaspoons of sugar into his hot coffee and stirred.

"The letter?" Rosa prompted, never once giving Lawton even a sideways glance.

Kinkaide reached for the stoneware mug. "Mrs. Moore somehow got her hands on my invitation to Melissa and mailed me an acceptance letter, supposedly from Mel."

Rosa gasped. Her eyes widened.

"I think we can safely say that that was *not* a polite move," Lawton said with an impish grin.

"Please behave." Rosa tapped her son's arm. "This is dreadful. I honestly can't believe that Darla *actually* interfered on this level. I've known for years that Mel's mother can be, well, difficult, but this is quite..." She shook her head and placed her immaculately manicured fingers against her cheek. "Well, quite alarming."

"You can say that again," Kinkaide grumbled.

Four

Private detective Horace Waggoner peered through the binoculars and adjusted them until the images of identical teenage girls came into view. With skill, Julie and Janie Casper sailed across the park's skating court, as surefooted on rollerblades as if they were running. Horace shifted in the driver's seat and scanned the tree-lined Dallas park until he spotted the ever-present bodyguard. The brawny youth was Desmond Casper's nephew, the girls' first cousin. Horace lowered the binoculars and reached for a bag of sunflower seeds in the passenger seat of his dilapidated Ford.

Desmond, the owner of a national chain of burger joints, employed numerous family members. According to Lenora, they were a tight-knit clan. As former Casper CEO, Lenora Osworth knew as much about the Caspers' operation as Desmond. She also knew as much about Desmond as did his wife, Abby. That proved to be a problem—especially when Desmond ended his affair with Lenora, who promptly vowed vengeance.

"Hell hath no fury like a woman scorned," Horace quoted. He once again raised his binoculars and attempted to manage the bag of sunflower seeds with his free hand. The bag rattled, protesting his invasion.

According to Lenora, this job would be easy. Horace would kidnap the girls. He and his fiancée, Sara Murdock, would take their part of the ransom, get married, and disappear. Horace lowered the glasses and glanced at the overdue electric bill lying on the dashboard. Even though

37

making a big break involved transgressing the law he had endeavored to preserve, Horace decided reversing his precarious financial situation deserved drastic measures.

But what if we get caught?

He grappled with the bag of shelled sunflower seeds on his unsteady thigh and managed to grasp a few bites. His cell phone's ring sent a zip through his gut, and he dropped the binoculars. The bag tipped sideways and a cascade of sunflower seeds spilled across the seat and onto the floorboard.

"Oh, great!" Horace groaned, eyeing the girls as they rolled from the skating court toward his vehicle. He scrubbed his palm against his sweat pants, grabbed the phone, and pressed the talk button.

Before he could utter a greeting, Lenora's voice broke over the line. "Where are you?" she demanded.

"I'm still at the park." The Casper girls were heading toward the car. Horace eyed Julie and Janie as they rolled up the sidewalk. They neared the gap where they would skate across the narrow road in front of the car and into the parking lot.

"Well, what's going on?" Lenora demanded.

He conjured an image of the polished dame pacing her apartment's plush living room.

"Janie and Julie have just been skating, and I've been watching. That's all."

Horace ducked his head as the girls whizzed across the winding road about 100 feet in front of his gray sedan.

"You've been watching all week!" Lenora snapped. "When are you going to make a move?"

Horace brushed the scattered sunflower seeds from his seat, crumpled the empty seed bag, and hurled it toward the passenger floor. The balled plastic bag plopped in place amid a collection of refuse.

"We're talkin' kidnapping here," Horace snapped. "You can't just go in and snatch 'em without some strategy. I already told you, we need to get a good grip on their schedule then try to find a time when that hulk isn't at their beck and call. We'll meet tonight as planned and decide when to make our move."

"Good! I'm tired of waiting! I *hate* those brats."

Lenora reminded Horace of Jane Seymour. According to Sara, Lenora's engaging smile, long slender legs, and striking figure had been a large part of the reason for her rapid upward move at Casper's. Too bad Mrs. Casper didn't appreciate Lenora's talents.

The girls sat on a bench near the parking lot, removed their skates, and replaced their shoes. "They're getting ready to get in the car now. I need to follow them. Maybe tonight Sara will have some new inside information."

"Yes. Tonight," Lenora said before beginning another tirade against the Caspers.

Last week, Desmond promoted Sara. Now she served as his secretary. Lenora had been ecstatic. Sara was privy to enough inside information to ensure the kidnapping's success. The promotion had resulted in a significant raise. With some self-discipline, he and Sara could now afford to get married—despite Horace's failing business. Yet the increased pay paled in comparison to a cold million dollars.

But what if we get caught? Horace gripped the cell phone as Lenora's outburst diminished. Both Sara and Lenora acted so sure. Lenora often said, "Nobody's going to get hurt." *But is that true?* Horace wondered.

Janie and Julie tumbled into the blue Cadillac. Their cousin, Steve the Brute, slid behind the steering wheel and cranked the car.

"They're pulling out," Horace reported. The Cadillac purred toward him, and Horace scooted down in his seat.

He started the engine. The car protested then came to life with the chugging of a dysfunctional muffler.

"Okay, okay. Don't lose them," Lenora urged. "We'll talk tonight."

Horace disconnected the call and tossed the cell phone toward the passenger's seat. The phone tumbled to the floorboard accompanied by the crunch of discarded paper. He glanced toward the Cadillac, now picking up speed. As the car neared, Horace stretched for the phone, hoping the move would conceal him. But his foot, pivoting with his stretch, slammed into the accelerator. The decrepit vehicle protested with a resounding backfire then died. Horace sat straight up as if he had been shot.

A wide-eyed glance to his left revealed that the Cadillac was slowing, and Cousin Steve stared straight into Horace's chilled face. The Cadillac's window lowered. Horace gulped against the knot in his throat and snatched several shallow breaths.

"Are you okay?" Steve hollered, his black eyes pools of concern.

Horace, still staring, debated what to do. He could roll down the window and amiably respond, tell the kid to get lost, or crank the car—if it would start—and speed away.

An impatient honk behind Steve prompted the baby-faced giant to glance in his rearview mirror. He cast one last gaze toward Horace, shrugged, and the Cadillac eased forward.

Horace reached for the ignition, but his hand shook so violently all he could do was rattle the keys several seconds before getting a grip on the switch. With protest and sputter, the engine came to life. Horace decided not to mention this episode to Sara or Lenora. Neither would appreciate Steve's noticing him. And Lenora, no doubt, would detonate in an ugly emotional explosion. As he gripped the gearshift, a surge of hot panic rushed to his head. *What if Lenora is setting me up? What if she somehow gets her hands on the ransom then leaves me and Sara to take the rap?* Horace had worked with criminal minds. Someone depraved enough to arrange a kidnapping would not blink at double-crossing him. The dragonlike vengeance forever glinting in Lenora's black eyes seemed to bore into his psyche.

Perhaps he should consider telling Lenora he wanted out. A cold dagger of terror pierced his heart. If Horace backed out, Lenora would make certain he paid. As long as he was awake and standing, Horace didn't fear the spike-heeled vixen. He could readily defend himself. But she just might break into his duplex while he slept and do something really unneighborly, such as driving a stake through his temple.

On Sunday morning Melissa clutched her hands in her lap as Kinkaide took his place behind the church's baby grand piano. The lights dimmed. The congregation seemed to take a collective breath. And Kinkaide, erect and sure, placed his fingers on the keyboard. The first notes of "Jesus Loves Me" flowed forth like silken threads.

The pastor, short and stocky, stepped off the platform and walked in front of the podium. "At this time, we will be closing our service with a special dedication. I'd like to ask the Petersons and their parents to come forward."

Mel angled her legs to the side as her sister Michelle, clutching baby Justin, walked into the aisle. Michelle's husband, Todd, followed close behind; after him, Mel's parents and Todd's parents. By the time they all filed past, Mel was questioning her sanity when she chose to sit so close to the aisle. At last they all walked toward the minister, and Mel resumed her normal position.

As Kinkaide continued playing "Jesus Loves Me," Mel glanced toward him then darted her attention back to her sister. Yesterday's phone conversation between Melissa and her mother ricocheted through her mind.

"Don't forget, Melissa Ann, we're expecting you at Trinity tomorrow," Darla admonished.

Mel hadn't heard from her mother since their confrontation over that forged letter. Now Darla acted as if nothing in the least bit negative had transpired between them. Her "let's pretend all is well" tactics usually left Mel frustrated. Due to the level of her mother's recent duplicity, Mel had gripped the kitchen counter and locked her knees to stay her rising emotions.

"Is Kinkaide going to deliver a miniconcert again?" she asked, her cool voice no indicator of her inner turbulence. During the last few months, Kinkaide had occasionally performed numerous pieces at Trinity Church of the Nazarene. Every time Darla tried to coerce Mel into attending, the answer had been no. The answer remained no. Mel poised her lips to deliver the edict when Darla continued.

"No, he isn't. But Michelle and Todd are having Baby Justin dedicated tomorrow, and they did request that Kinkaide play a few children's tunes during the dedication. You promised to go. Remember? Monica and Stanley are driving in. If you're not there, just think how it would look."

Mel, massaging her forehead, leaned against the kitchen counter and noticed the water faucet's steady drip. "Mother, I said I'd go, so I'll go. I just forgot the dedication was scheduled for tomorrow. You don't have to force me into keeping my word." Melissa marched toward the faucet and pressed down on the single handle. The drip stopped.

"Great," Darla hummed like a satisfied salesman.

Mel squirmed in the pew and frowned, wondering if her mother had somehow arranged this whole baby dedication in order to throw her into Kinkaide's path. But that was ridiculous. Michelle and Todd were members at Trinity. The natural thing was to ask their pastor to perform the baby dedication. Although her common sense dictated she rivet her attention on the touching ceremony, Mel dared steal another glimpse of Kinkaide. His gentle eyes returned her appraisal. As if he were oblivious to the rest of the crowd, an impish grin accented the smile lines around his eyes. Before Mel could turn away, he winked.

A flush, warm and pleasurable, assaulted Mel's face, and she inched down in the pew. With great resolve, she focused on her white-knuckled fists clenched in her lap. Yet her hands blurred, and the image of the man she once adored swam before her eyes. Kinkaide sitting at the piano. Dark suit and tie setting off his near-black hair. Dreamy eyes behind those black-framed glasses. His beard giving him a distinguished air. Hands on the keyboard, making even the simplest childhood tune sound like music straight from the hearts of angels.

He winked at me! The man actually had the audacity to wink at me in front of a sanctuary full of people! Mel's panicked gaze dashed from side to side. Everyone nearby focused on the baby dedication. Even the elderly lady next to Mel appeared oblivious to the flirtatious moment.

Then she glanced at Mel. The lady leaned toward her, and a fog of heavy perfume swirled across Mel's senses. "You must know Kinkaide Franklin," she whispered, a trace of mirth stirring in her eyes.

Melissa, her heated face cooling, looked squarely into the woman's fading gray eyes. She had never met the lady before, but the church was so big there were numerous people Mel didn't know.

"He's going to make somebody a fine catch one day," the lady continued. Mel wondered if her mom had paid the woman to voice that opinion. "Rumor has it that he's here on an extended visit. Someone said Darla Moore's daughter is the reason." The twinkle in the old woman's eyes suggested that, if no one else saw the wink, she did, and she knew exactly who Darla's daughter might be.

Mel's toes curled in her low-heeled pumps, and she turned her attention to the baby dedication. Yet her mind barely registered the minister's moving comments as he held her nephew. *Does the whole church know Kinkaide is chasing me?* She slouched down a few more inches and squelched the urge to crawl under the pew. Mel imagined her mom's furtive whispers as she "discreetly" informed a few choice friends—probably three or four dozen—about her daughter's recent suitor, their background, and how desperately she hoped Mel would come around. "This is an urgent, urgent prayer request," Darla undoubtedly concluded, as she always did when presenting gossip in the form of "spiritual concern."

Mother, if this weren't my nephew's dedication, I'd walk out of the service and never come back. Why did I begin my practice in Oklahoma City in the first place? Botswana would have made more sense—halfway around the world, far from Mom's interference! She sighed. *But I wanted to be near my family.*

Her stoic father stood next to his plump, dark-haired wife, his features forever schooled in a bland expression that suggested his complete indifference. Although his demeanor rarely changed, Mel saw through the mask. She could read his eyes in an instant; eyes that spoke approval during Mel's childhood; eyes that sparkled with glee when she announced her acceptance into medical school; eyes that clouded with ire every time Darla meddled in Mel's affairs. Yet her father never said a word against his wife. And despite their differences, Mell occasionally witnessed a glimmer of the old affection when they looked at each other.

The congregation members began shifting in their seats. Papers rattled. The people in front of Mel stood. She glanced toward the lady at her side to see she was standing as well. Mel hurried to her feet and dashed one more glance toward Kinkaide. To her amazement, he no longer sat at the piano. After the brief benediction, Mel strained to see her sister and family moving from the front of the church toward her pew. They had all planned to eat out for lunch, but Mel wasn't certain of the chosen restaurant. In order to retrieve her Bible lying on the pew, she purposefully turned her back on the prying lady who shuffled away. When Mel stepped into the aisle, Kinkaide awaited her.

"Hello, Melissa," he said, her name rolling off his tongue like a lover's melody.

Melissa glanced into beseeching eyes. Kinkaide's audacious wink seemed to tug them together, and her stomach lurched. Unable to tear her gaze from his, she relived the first time Kinkaide had winked at her—right before a college English exam at the University of Texas. Even though they attended the same church growing up, the congregation had been so big that the two barely knew each other. Ironically, they both chose to attend the University of Texas and, for the first time, really got acquainted. After a semester of friendship, they began studying together. The evening before the big test, Mel suspected Kinkaide's esteem involved more than friendship. His flirtatious wink the next morning underscored her discernment.

By Christmas Eve, what started as a wink matured into a kiss. The two college kids settled on a park bench in the Franklins' front yard. Kinkaide urged Mel closer, stroked her cheek, and his lips brushed hers with aching sweetness. The sun itself, dipping low on the horizon, showered the moment in fiery sparks.

Mel's mouth tingled with the remembrance of that breathless moment that began their lengthy courtship. But another memory came upon the heels of that one. A memory as potent in its bitterness as the kiss was sweet. A memory of the lips that once caressed hers explaining why he had abandoned her.

Never again. Never! Mel mentally accused. *No matter how charming you are or how much you chase me, I will never trust you again!* Yet the heart that had once beat in synchrony with Kinkaide's yearned to feel him close once more. Mel caught her bottom lip between her teeth, directed a cool nod in Kinkaide's direction, and attempted to rush past him.

Five

⌒

"Mel, please don't go." Kinkaide, desperate for a word with her, stopped himself from dropping at her feet and begging her to stay.

She paused, and he gently laid a hand on her shoulder. "You remember Lawton, don't you?" he asked.

Mel pivoted toward Kinkaide and acknowledged his brother nearby. "Yes, of course." She hesitated. "Hello, Lawton. It's been awhile."

"Hi, Melissa." Lawton's mischievous smile made Kinkaide a bit uneasy. No telling what his brother might come out with. Dragging Lawton along for moral support had seemed logical only minutes before, now he doubted the wisdom of that decision.

The crowd meandered around them, and Kinkaide groped for an appropriate way to apologize for the awkward misunderstanding over the cruise. But every comment that entered his head proved more than inappropriate.

You look great!

Will you have lunch with me?

I want to kiss you.

Will you marry me?

Mel shifted, cleared her throat, and glanced toward the back doors.

"So, how 'bout them Red Sox?" Lawton quipped. The church's recessed lights reflected against his dark glasses as he tilted his head and chuckled.

47

Even though Lawton couldn't see him, Kinkaide shot his brother a warning glance that appeared to only encourage him.

"Kinkaide told me about the cruise," Lawton continued as if they were all the best of friends.

"Oh?" Mel's brows rose and she leveled a challenging gaze at Kinkaide.

"Yep. He's convinced me to go. You ought to bring a friend and—"

Grinding his teeth, Kinkaide deliberately placed his heel on the toe of Lawton's loafer and pressed.

"Yeow!" Lawton pushed at Kinkaide. "Here I am, trying to help you out, old man, and you—"

"Look, don't you have somebody you need to talk to?" Kinkaide shoved his brother up the aisle. "There's Carrie O'Brien. I'm sure she'll be thrilled to chat."

"Somebody deliver me," Lawton groused. "She thinks she's my mother."

"Hi, Carrie," Kinkaide called. A petite redhead, amiably chatting with friends, turned to spot Kinkaide and Lawton. "She's on her way," Kinkaide said under his breath.

"I'm going to get you for this," Lawton muttered back. "Just wait. I owe you big."

While Carrie claimed her prey, Kinkaide touched Mel's elbow and nudged her out of the mainstream traffic and into the space between two deserted pews. All the while, he held his breath, afraid she would bolt and run. Finally they were out of hearing distance, and Kinkaide rushed into his pre-planned speech.

"I'm really sorry about—about that cruise business."

"Oh?" She schooled her expression to hide what her eyes revealed—a spark, a twinkle, a suggestion of what once had been. For the first time in days, Kinkaide's plummeted hopes soared.

"I…" *Have you told the woman you've never gotten over her?* As the silence stretched, Lawton's question from days ago exploded into Kinkaide's mind. His hands clamped together, and he pondered the day Shelby Canady discovered Mel's photo on his grand piano. Initially the accomplished singer thought Kinkaide was two-timing her, but she soon came face-to-face with reality. Her competition was a ghost from Kinkaide's past—a ghost who was still alive and well.

Just as his heart had been stirred by that photo once stored out of sight, a corridor of his soul now ached to hold Melissa close. "Heaven help me, Mel," Kinkaide gasped, taking in her features. "The older you get, the more attractive you are." The unexpected words bounced between them like an echo from the past, an awakening of what might have been.

Mel's eyes widened. She sucked in a quick breath.

Kinkaide, uncertain of the impact of his honesty, plunged forth like a warrior of love, ready to battle all odds to convince the lady of his unyielding devotion. "I know this isn't the time or place to tell you all this." He waved his hand to take in the massive, modern sanctuary. "But you haven't given me much of a chance to tell you before…" He hesitated and prayed for the power to measure his words despite his heart's wild palpitating.

"I love you, Mel. I never stopped loving you." Kinkaide stroked his beard and shoved his hand into his slacks pocket. "I've regretted walking away from you more than you can ever imagine." He had harbored these words for months, hoping to share them at exactly the right moment. Whether or not this was the right moment still remained to be seen. However, Kinkaide pursued his intent, never once glancing from her eyes, misty with tears.

Sniffling, Mel looked down.

Kinkaide, spurred onward, continued spilling forth the essence of his heart. "Mel, all I'm asking for is a second chance. Honestly, I thought that convincing you would be easier, and that you would—"

"Whatever gave you the idea that I would?" she blurted. Mel looked fully into his eyes. This time, the mist had vanished. Vanished, to be replaced with bitterness. Bitterness and pain. Pain and distrust.

Kinkaide removed his glasses, and her features took on a faint blur. "Mel, I—"

"You seem to have no idea how much you hurt me. *None!* You just walked out of my life and rode off to Nashville and made your dreams come true without me. Now you have the arrogance to think you can just pop back in six years later, and I'm supposed to fall at your feet. You *devastated* me, Kinkaide!" With every word, Mel's cheeks flushed all the more. "For all you knew, I could have jumped off a cliff, and you wouldn't have even known about it. You didn't call to see if I lived or died after the day you left me standing at the altar. I'm just glad we didn't have any guests. Standing around a church with an embarrassed minister was enough humiliation for a lifetime!"

"Melissa, I—"

"No! *You* listen!" she demanded, her voice low and firm. "I'm not interested in being the object of your amusement."

"This is not about amusement!"

"I told you last fall, standing in front of your parents' house, that there's no chance of our ever getting back together."

"I think that's mostly because you're eaten up with unforgiveness," Kinkaide accused, all the while despising the turn of their conversation. What started as an attempt to draw her closer was disintegrating around his feet, and he possessed no power to stop the downward spiral.

Her features tightened into a mask he recognized. A mask that spoke of her ultimate control over her emotions. Mel never let herself get too far out of hand. A time or two, Kinkaide pushed her to the limits just to see if she would ever really let her temper fly. Not once. Not ever did he remember Melissa Moore losing control. Some puckish urge to shove her over the edge overtook Kinkaide.

"Nothing about me is any of your business anymore." Mel's soft words held the virulent undertow of a deadly current. "Whether I've forgiven you or not is immaterial to—"

"Yes, but you do still love me," he said with an assured smile.

"What?" she demanded as if he'd spoken in Russian.

"You still love me."

"I never said—"

"And I can prove it." Kinkaide cast a glance around the sanctuary. The few remaining individuals paid them no heed. He dropped his glasses to the pew, gripped Mel's arms, pulled her close, and lowered his face to only inches above hers. All the while, some warning voice deep within suggested that he was trampling all boundaries and should back off. But the reckless side of him surged forward.

He looked deeply into Mel's hazel eyes, all the while expecting her to fight. But she didn't. Instead, she stared back at him as if he were a lion and she were a mesmerized lamb, a prisoner of his gaze. In that moment he recognized, deep in the shadows of her soul, the flame that had once burned with passion. The flame that Kinkaide had kindled. The flame that never went out.

The old sparks exploded anew. Kinkaide, fully expecting to maintain control, felt as if he were being hypnotized by the power she held over him. While their breath mingled, he could almost taste the sweetness of her lips against his. If he kissed her, she would mold into his arms, and the old magic would engulf them once more. Yet Kinkaide sensed that, when the moment passed, she would have one more reason to despise him. His breathing uneven, he eased his hold and inched away.

Mel jolted backward as if released from an indomitable magnetic clutch. Her wide-eyed appraisal suggested that they had indeed kissed. In the following seconds, fraught with tension, Kinkaide debated whether to verbalize yet another apology. But Mel's abrupt departure ended any chance of voiced regrets. Without a word, she rushed up the aisle, through the sanctuary door, into the foyer, and out of sight.

With a sigh, Kinkaide sat on the pew's edge, propped his elbows on the pew in front of him, and covered his face with his hands. He massaged his eyes then gazed at the oversized, wooden cross hanging above the baptistery. Lawton's recent words, frank as always, punctuated his failure, *For somebody who usually gets what he wants, you're really bombing big, man.* The words "bombing big" no longer fit the level of destruction his and Mel's relationship had undergone.

"If you could call this a relationship," he muttered. Shoulder's sagging, Kinkaide retrieved his glasses from the pew. He shoved them on his face and stood. *So much for apologizing.*

Heart heavy, he began the slow trek up the aisle. Kinkaide needed to find Lawton and head home. By now, Carrie O'Brien had probably cornered the poor man. The cute redhead had a thing for Lawton and everybody knew it. However, Lawton wasn't interested in any woman who felt sorry for him or thought she was going to somehow rescue him from the throes of being blind. He often said, "I'm not looking for a mother."

"Well, neither am I," Kinkaide mumbled. "I just want Melissa."

But if you really love her, are you willing to set aside your wants for her best?

The thought barged in upon Kinkaide's disgruntled mind. He stopped. A verse from the famous love passage challenged his motives: *Love is patient, love is kind. It does not envy, it does not boast, it is not proud. It is not rude, it is not self-seeking....*Kinkaide pivoted and once more peered upon the giant cross. All the while, Lawton's humored jeer taunted him. *For somebody who usually gets what he wants...*

Kinkaide reflected over his adult life—a life indeed typified by getting exactly what he wanted. Not that he hadn't worked hard for what he got. Thanks to their parents, both Kinkaide and Lawton made life happen for themselves despite any and all setbacks. Their parents refused to allow Lawton to think he was handicapped and impelled him to a life of independence. They also prohibited an adolescent Kinkaide from abandoning classical piano lessons just because all his friends thought Beethoven wasn't cool. As adults, the brothers were dubbed geniuses. However, Kinkaide maintained that much of their genius was more a willingness to work ten times harder than most and to never—absolutely never—give up. That was exactly the mind-set with which Kinkaide had won Melissa's heart in the first place. He assumed the process would work the second time around.

"But I'm bombing." He shook his head. "I am bombing big." Kinkaide rocked back on his heels. "This ain't workin'," he muttered, recognizing the tenor of Lawton's voice in his own. "I've got to figure out a new tactic. There's got to be a way to make her come around."

If you really love Melissa, why not give her the freedom to reject you, once and for all?

The cross loomed before Kinkaide. His brow wrinkled, and he stroked his beard. The passage from 1 Corinthians swirled into a tormenting mantra that stirred the waters of his soul like a whirling gale.

Love is not self-seeking...not self-seeking...not self-seeking.

Kinkaide ripped off his glasses and rubbed the crest of his sore ear as if to expunge the thought from his mind. The litany continued, and the cross seemed to grow with every repetition. The weight of Kinkaide's desires increased tenfold.

At last, his limbs stiffened and he stumbled backward. *No. I want Mel. Period*. He tore his gaze from the cross and spun on his heel, all the while feeling as if the cross' arms beckoned him to step into their invisible grasp. Nevertheless, Kinkaide determined to achieve his goal at all costs. He strode toward the foyer like a dogged sea captain who refuses to change course in the face of a typhoon.

He spotted Lawton in the glassed-in foyer, near the exit. Carrie, close to his side, hung on to Lawton's arm as if she were afraid he'd topple over. Kinkaide picked his way through the dispersing crowd.

"Ready to go, Lawton?" he asked, too grim to even smile at the relief trailing across Lawton's face.

"Sure." Lawton's casual tone contradicted all hints of impatience.

"Let's go, then."

"See you tonight?" Carrie's charming smile and upturned nose had probably caught many a man's eye. Too bad for her that Lawton needed an equal, not a matriarch.

"Yes, tonight," Lawton called over his shoulder. "If you ever leave me with her like that again," he muttered under his breath, "I'll personally place a virus in your PC *and* laptop."

"If you ever do what you did with Mel again, I'll sneak into your house when you're gone and rearrange your whole closet. You won't be able to find your shoes for days." Kinkaide steered his brother out the door, across the parking lot, toward the ebony Oldsmobile. "Then, I'll put sand in your sugar, and—"

"Oh, get real," Lawton chided while Kinkaide opened the passenger door. "You don't have the heart to be so mean."

"And you do?" Kinkaide rounded the vehicle, opened the car door, and plopped into the smell of new leather.

"I'm meaner than a junkyard dog." Lawton climbed into the passenger seat and slammed the door.

"Everybody that believes that, stand on your head!" Kinkaide growled.

"Oooh. We are not in a good mood, are we? I take it you bombed with Melissa…yet again, folks!" Lawton added like a circus announcer.

Kinkaide scowled, and the cell phone's ring cut short any retort. Before starting the vehicle, he reached for the phone and pressed the answer button. After his brief greeting, a beloved voice floated over the line.

"Hey, man, where are you? I've been calling for the last 30 minutes."

"Desmond!" Kinkaide exclaimed. "What's up, my friend?" He inserted the keys into the ignition and started the car.

"Listen, I'm here in OKC," Desmond Casper explained.

"No way! You're in town? Where are you? We'll meet for lunch. Oh, wait just a minute." Kinkaide covered the mouthpiece. "Did Mom cook lunch for us?"

"Roast beef," Lawton said as if he were salivating over the very words.

Kinkaide removed his hand from the mouthpiece. "Hey, Desmond, Mom has cooked her killer roast beef. Why don't you plan to meet us at my parents' house? I can give you directions."

Desmond hesitated, and Kinkaide sensed that this phone call involved more than a friendly chat and a quick visit. "Listen, I'm in big trouble. I really need to talk." Desperation, like a dreadful alarm, underscored his every word.

"Is everything okay with Abby and the girls?" Kinkaide rushed, picturing the attractive family as they were the last time he saw them—Desmond and Abby standing hand in hand on their front lawn with the twins, Janie and Julie, sitting in the oak swing.

"The girls are fine, but Abby…"

Kinkaide's heart felt as if it dropped into his lap. "Oh no, did she d–d–"

"No. She's alive and healthy. I think she just wishes *I* were dead about now. Listen, I really need to talk."

"Sure, sure." Kinkaide put the car into reverse and backed out of the parking place. Within seconds, he and Desmond had arranged to meet at a local steakhouse that featured strategically placed alcoves for diners desiring privacy.

Sounds like I'm not the only one with lady troubles, Kinkaide thought as he steered the vehicle toward his parents' home.

Six

Melissa parked her Toyota in her garage and entered her home through the utility room. She traipsed through the kitchen, into the living room, and cast a cursory glance at the answering machine on the end table. The message indicator light blinked, and Mel approached the machine to retrieve the message. Her finger hovered over the button. What if Kinkaide had already left a message? The memory of his melodic voice sprang upon her, and Mel stiffened. At the moment she didn't think she could endure even the slightest hint of his tones.

She paused to absently gaze across the home she had purchased the year before. The acquisition of the renovated house on Mantle Drive had been the result of her mother's urging. Melissa had balked at the price and size of the homes in Green Hills, where her mother had originally suggested, so Darla had begrudgingly hinted at this street. She insisted that the young doctor would be more deeply respected as a member of the community if she owned a home. At last Melissa had grown accustomed to the idea and decided to look at houses.

Something within Melissa was reawakened when she inspected this classic home...something that died when Kinkaide jilted her. Something that insisted she needed a "nest." A haven. A home with a mailbox at the street, flower beds, and a garage. Melissa fell in love with this house—and fell hard. Her mother relinquished and stopped pushing about the bigger homes. Although this house was the smallest, most understated of the ones lining the street, the inside had been transformed into a designer's paradise.

Owning her own place created a new sense of accomplishment within Mel, a fresh awareness of roots. She admired the balance created by the decorator's hands: the muted shades of mauve and green mixed with touches of burgundy, the elegant lines of Queen Anne furnishings, the classic paintings hanging here and there. If Kinkaide thought she was going to ditch everything she had worked for, swoon at his feet, and follow him to Nashville, he was out of tune—way out of tune.

Screwing up every ounce of courage she could muster, Mel rested her knee on the mauve sofa and pressed the message button. Jac Lightfoot's voice came over the line, and Melissa shoulders relaxed. "Hi, Mel. The crew is wondering what you're up to these days. You must not have checked your e-mail in two weeks. We've been chatting on that new e-mail loop Marilyn started for us. There's probably about 100 e-mails waiting on you."

She leaned against the sofa's armrest and groaned.

"Anyway, all the sisters were wondering if you had fallen off a cliff or something. We're all speculating whether or not you changed your mind about the cruise. So I volunteered to call. What's up?"

Melissa glanced at her watch. In celebration of baby Justin's dedication, her whole family had reservations at a restaurant at one o'clock. Mel had stopped home to change into a comfortable windsuit. If she hurried, she had time to check her e-mail before heading out the door. Jac was right. She hadn't been on the internet lately.

A large part of the reason for her cyber-delinquency revolved around Kinkaide Franklin. His perpetual hovering left Mel so distracted that e-mail from her six friends never entered her mind. All the sisters were particularly impressed with Mel's travel invitation, hand-delivered by Kinkaide during their New Year's bash at Mel's house. They lovingly teased Mel when she vowed not to go on the cruise or to Rome. In retrospect, she marveled that one of the sisters hadn't called before now. They jokingly decided to crown Kinkaide the king of romance and Mel the queen of mean.

But he didn't jilt you. Mel's lips quivered. Then her thoughts went back to the anticipation of the kiss that never happened and the emotional turmoil of their heated encounter at the church. She scrubbed at her lips, smearing every trace of the earth-toned gloss from them. Mel rushed to her bedroom as if she could outrun the latent desire that gushed from the caverns of her heart. The last time she was kissed, the man had been Kinkaide Franklin. The night before their wedding. Before they vowed a lifetime to each other. Before they would consummate their vows. The kiss had been long and sweet and laden with the promise of full physical expression. That very morning when Kinkaide lowered his face to Mel's, the memory of the last kiss consumed her, and the ardor, still smoldering, flamed into an inferno.

She yanked off the blue suit, panty hose, and slip, and left them amid the tumble of covers on her poster bed. She didn't have time to make the bed this morning any more than she had the time now. Mel rifled through her closet, wrenched the windsuit from the hanger, and put it on. She pulled on a pair of socks and crammed her feet into her canvass shoes, then tied them. After stomping to her corner computer, she booted up the machine, tapped her foot, and waited. With precision, Mel clicked the appropriate icon and brought up the e-mail program. While the computer connected to the internet, she tromped toward the kitchen, grabbed a plastic tumbler, and yanked open the freezer. Mel slammed ice into the oversized glass, filled it with water, and downed the liquid. Her head ached with the rush of cold fluid, and she welcomed the pain—anything to blot out the needs that demanded requital.

Mel looked out her kitchen window over her sink and observed her Great Dane, Bernie, as he made his rounds in the backyard. She once joked that Bernie was the only masculine companionship she would ever need. *I was out of my mind.*

"Blast men! Blast them all! Blast *you,* Kinkaide Franklin!" she shouted. "Why don't you just go back to Nashville?"

Mel, massaging her temple, flicked her wrist and checked her Timex. The second hand showed no mercy as it deliberately ticked off the time. The family would be at the steak house in 15 minutes. That left Mel 5 minutes for e-mail. She marched back into her bedroom and clicked the icon that downloaded all her cybermessages. As Jac predicted, Mel had nearly 100—93 to be exact. She plopped into the desk chair and shook her head.

"Sorry, ladies," she whispered, then glanced at her watch. "There's no way I have time to read every one of these." Melissa skimmed the subject lines of each one, deleting the junk-mail messages. Then she came upon a series of notes titled, "Where's Mel?"

Kim Lan: Anybody heard a peep from Mel since New Year's?

Marilyn: Not me. Do you think she eloped with Kinkaide?

Jac: Not on your life. My guess is she killed him and is now doing time.

Sonsee: Give her a break, Jac. Everybody doesn't have a criminal mind like you. :-) I figure she's probably drowning in patients. It's winter and children get sick.

Victoria: I vote for the elopement story. Sounds like fun!

Jac: Not to me.

Victoria: Just wait. One day you'll get bitten by the love bug.

Jac: No way.

Sammie: That was once my motto. I should have stuck to it. Mel, on the other hand, will probably have kissed Kinkaide's whole face by now—if the look in her eyes when she read that invitation is anything to go by. Helloooooooo, Mel! Are you out there? Tee Hee.

Mel blinked. Sammie Jones, author and magazine columnist, had offered a few hints over the last year that all was not well in her marriage. While the six sisters had collectively pondered Sammie's problems, none of them had pried into the redhead's family issues. Mel, feeling particularly impish, hit the reply button and responded privately.

"So what gives, Sam? Is all not well at home? Care to share?" She signed, "MM," hit Send, and continued reading the sisterly banter.

Kim Lan: Rolling on the floor laughing!! Sammie, you are just toooo funny!

Marilyn: Ditto!

Jac: Somebody needs to call the poor woman before we all write too much and get her mad at us.

Sonsee: You go, girl! Call her! See if she's still speaking to us.

Marilyn: Are you kidding? I'm not worried about Mel— Mouth of the South—Moore. The way she interrogated me when Josh and I met, she's got it coming!

Victoria: Do I sense a little tension there?

Marilyn: Are you talking to me?

"Ha, ha," Mel said aloud. Shaking her head, she produced a genuine chuckle. Before Marilyn decided to give Joshua Langham a chance, Melissa had called her one fine day and asked one too many questions. Marilyn, stressed over the potential relationship, had told Mel to mind her own business then hung up on her. Of course the two friends had mended their differences, but Marilyn obviously wasn't going to extend Mel any mercy.

Melissa glanced at her watch. Without hesitation, she clicked the "respond to all" button on the last e-mail and typed in a quick note:

> Hi! I'm here. No, I did *not* fall off any cliffs. Jac, I got your phone message. Just for the record, you're all going to get it. I haven't eloped or kissed anybody's whole face. I've also not gone to prison for any murders, *Jac!!* I'm heading out the door to eat lunch with my family. Baby Justin was dedicated today. Honestly, I wish you all would pray that Kinkaide would back off. He's driving me nuts! So is my mother. Groans. More details later. Ciao! MM

Mel hit the Send button and waited but a few seconds before getting off the internet and logging off her computer.

The screen blurred as Mel considered signing back on and requesting that her friends pray specifically for her. When she weighed her hit-and-miss prayer life, a twinge of regret stabbed her conscience. Like every other logical concept in her life, Mel's father taught her to accept God as a fact. But Mel had never been adept at connecting the certitude of His existence with the realities of her life. Marilyn, Sonsee, and Kim Lan had certainly undergone their share of troubles, but the three seemed far more in touch with God than she was. Jac, on the other hand, confessed Christ as her Savior but at times seemed almost uninterested in the things of God—to the point that she attended church about once a month. Although Mel was a regular at worship services, she had spent most of her adult years wondering if God even cared about the small details of her life. Sammie and Victoria, both married for years, seemed almost as preoccupied with their families as with any relationship with their heavenly Father. Mel suspected that even they were more in touch with the holy Creator than she was. Out of guilt, she muttered a prayer for each of her six friends and hoped they returned the favor.

The phone on the nightstand broke into Mel's musings and she cringed. Would this caller be Kinkaide? She checked her watch and groaned. One o'clock had arrived—she was going to be late at the restaurant. Mel stood, braced herself, and grabbed the receiver.

"Hello, Melissa Ann." Darla's angelic voice had never been so welcome.

"Hi, Mom, I'm on my way," Melissa rapped out.

"Well, we're all here." The sounds of voices and clanking silverware underscored Darla's words. "We were just wondering if we should wait on you or—"

"Just go ahead and let them seat you and place your order. I'll order when I get there. I'm about to leave."

"Great. And..." Darla hesitated, "you're never going to believe this, dear, but Kinkaide is here."

"What?" Mel shrieked, feeling as if she were living in the twilight zone. No matter where she turned, Kinkaide appeared like some specter who couldn't be shaken.

"Yes. They just seated him. He's with that friend of his who owns all those restaurants. What's his name?"

"I have no idea. I didn't know he had a friend who owned restaurants."

"Oh, yes...you know...uh..."

"Desmond Casper. Casper's Burgers," Mel's father's voice floated over the cell phone.

"I didn't know he knew the man who owned Casper's." *And I couldn't care less!*

"Well, you could tell Kinkaide was looking for you."

Mel rolled her eyes and noted the brass-trimmed ceiling fan looked as if it were growing fur. She had resisted the need for a housekeeper because her mother kept insisting she should hire one. "Mom, I'm sorry, but I really don't care."

"But we all saw the two of you talking after church—"

"Well, you can tell everybody I told him to get lost!"

Darla emitted a huff. "You're imposible!"

"Toodles, Mom," Mel said. "I'll see you in about 15 minutes." Without waiting for a response, Melissa hung up the burgundy receiver and stifled the need to scream.

"My own mother is going to send me to an early grave!" Mel envisioned herself popping tranquilizers in order to function and took several deep breaths. "It's either that or move to Australia," she grumbled.

Melissa grabbed her keys and purse-organizer from the dresser then started toward the garage. All her life she had lived under the cloud of her mother's manipulation. Even when Mel began considering a career choice, Darla had made her opinion known. Early in her exploration of the medical profession, Melissa had expressed a vague interest in pediatric medicine. Darla suggested that Mel would make a better nurse, which only fueled Melissa's determination to answer God's call to become a children's doctor. Now that she had succeeded, Darla oozed to anyone who would listen about her daughter the doctor. Only last year did Melissa learn from her younger sister, Michelle, that their mother had really wanted her to be a pediatrician all along. She tried to steer Mel toward nursing because she knew her daughter would be all the more determined to enter medical school. Even now, Mel's teeth ground with the memory, and she wondered if her mother would ever learn to take her hands off situations and allow God to do His work. Melissa knew she would have become a pediatrician without her mother's stratagem, but she didn't know if Darla ever saw that truth.

Mel paused at the utility room's door, one foot in the garage, one foot still inside the house. Gradually, she pivoted to stare through the utility room, into her kitchen. A sickening reality sank into her soul. For the first time since purchasing her home, she put the whole puzzle together. Her mother had suggested the high-dollar executive houses in Green Hills, probably knowing Mel would balk, just like she balked about nursing school. After Mel's resistance, Darla had begrudgingly accepted the smaller home on Mantle Drive. Mel fell in love with the house, thinking she was actually making up her own mind about her choice of home. Mel pictured her mother having looked at the house days before Melissa asked the realtor for a tour. And she knew without ever asking...she knew just as sure as she knew about her mother sending that note....Darla Moore had orchestrated the purchase of this home—the exact home she wanted Mel to buy.

"This has got to stop," Melissa said, her mind grappling for some means to break the cycle of lifetime control. "And it's got to stop now."

Seven

Kinkaide took the proffered menu from the waitress and leaned back in the booth long enough for her to deliver the glasses of water. The rustic steakhouse featured checkered tablecloths and waitresses and waiters dressed in overalls. "I'll be back to take your order," the middle-aged woman said.

"Okay. Take your time," Kinkaide said. For once, his appetite failed him. Even the smell of aged steaks cooking on a grill did little to stimulate his interest.

"Same here," Desmond said. "Actually, could you bring me some coffee right now?" The bags under his eyes spoke of numerous sleepless nights.

"That sounds good for me, too," Kinkaide added. "Just coffee for now."

"Sure thing," the waitress said.

"So, what's going on?" Kinkaide asked, skipping all pleasantries, as he eyed his distraught friend. He and Desmond Casper met in Nashville when they landed on the same church basketball team. Their height and fire for winning assured the team's success three years in a row. Then Desmond moved the Casper's Burgers headquarters to Dallas, and the two maintained their friendship long distance. Despite the facts that Desmond was ten years older than Kinkaide and married, they shared much in common. Their love for the Lord and drive to succeed bonded them as brothers.

"I had an affair." Desmond's hand, lying atop the table, curled into a tight fist.

"What?" Kinkaide's eyes bugged, his mouth dropped. When Desmond said that Abby was dissatisfied with him, he had expected news more in the line of financial decline or perhaps overworking—anything but an affair.

The successful restaurant owner was widely known for his dedication to the Lord. Several times a year, he even spoke at men's retreats. His testimony of how the Lord brought him from a childhood of poverty to a successful college completion and entrepreneurship of a nationwide food chain invariably inspired and encouraged other men in their walk with the Lord. And Desmond always—absolutely always—gave glory to God for the strength and wisdom to build a financial empire from nothing.

Desmond's dark eyes stirred as if he were chained to a tormentor's rack. "I didn't plan it. The whole thing just happened."

With a low whistle, Kinkaide leaned back and gazed toward the open-beamed ceiling. "Does your pastor know? And what about your board position? Good grief! You're a Sunday school teacher! And Abby is the women's ministries director." Kinkaide blurted the facts as they entered his mind. "How long has this been going on?"

"It started the first part of last July—just over seven months ago." Desmond placed his elbows on the table and rested his forehead in his palms. His fingers dug into his short, springy hair as if he wanted to rip it out in clumps.

"Are you still involved with—"

"No. I ended the whole thing two weeks ago."

The waitress arrived with the steaming coffee, and Kinkaide scanned the nearby tables. None of the other patrons gave them even a second's heed. "Did Abby find out, and—"

"No," Desmond insisted. "She never knew until I told her. No one knew. I just couldn't continue...like that...and I finally had to confess."

Kinkaide's toppling respect for Desmond's integrity righted itself somewhat. "So, this isn't about being sorry you got caught?"

Desmond, shaking his head, peered into Kinkaide's eyes like a man about to drown in despair. "I would have probably never gotten caught. The whole thing started at work and stayed at work. The woman involved knew how to cover our tracks, and nobody even suspected."

"Who is she? Did I ever meet her?" When Desmond's headquarters were located in Nashville, Kinkaide had visited numerous times. Even though he lacked comprehensive knowledge of the whole staff, he had met some of the upper management.

Desmond cradled the mug of coffee in hands, dark and capable. His designer sweater and understated gold watch spoke of a material quality that didn't touch the quality of his reputation. A reputation now at stake. "Her name is Lenora Osworth. Lenora Osworth," he repeated. The name, tainted with scorn, fell from his lips as if laced in hemlock. "I don't know if you met her or not. She started out in Tennessee and moved to Dallas when we moved headquarters."

Kinkaide wrinkled his forehead in thought as he added two packets of sugar to his coffee. "Seems like I might have met her at the Christmas party you invited me to about four years ago. Wasn't she really tall, thin, and—"

"Drop-dead gorgeous—"

Kinkaide snapped his fingers. "I remember. Wasn't she one of the executives?"

Desmond nodded.

"I recall thinking she reminded me of Jane Seymour."

"You've got it. She's got looks to kill, more business sense than three men put together, and a disposition that would put most boa constrictors to shame." Desmond swallowed a mouthful of inky coffee and winced. "We had to work together quite a bit, and she...she made a pass at me." The cadence of Desmond's words resounded with the methodical chant of a mourner's mantra.

Kinkaide shook his head. "What happened?"

"Well, I got a call from her late one night. She said it was an emergency. I knew she'd been working late that night on a new restaurant we were trying to open. There had been some trouble over the city ordinances and permits." He waved his hand. "I'm not even going to get into all of it, but the bottom line is she called me that night. Frankly, things had been a little uptight between Abby and me for quite awhile." Desmond gulped his coffee. "If you ever decide to get married, get down on your knees and pray that God will give you a woman who understands your sexual needs." He shook his head. "It's like for years Abby couldn't care less most the time. We were arguing when Lenora called."

"Go on."

"When I arrived at the office, I felt like Abby was scorning me. Lenora was dressed in something I don't even want to talk about. She had the wine poured. The music was on and—"

"But you don't drink," Kinkaide said.

"I usually don't!"

"But you did?"

"I did. And one thing led to another. After that first night, the whole thing snowballed. I've never been so miserable in my life. Do you know how hard it is to teach a Sunday school class on Sunday morning after being with another woman all week?" The lines between his black brows deepened.

"And Abby didn't suspect?"

"Oh, Abby seemed relieved. I almost never bothered her with my needs anymore," Desmond spewed.

And I only thought I was having problems. Kinkaide shook his head.

"Finally, Lenora started talking about me leaving my family for her. I was already about to die from the guilt and conviction. After Lenora started hinting about marriage, I knew I had to stop." His forehead wrinkled. "I love my kids too much to leave them. And the truth is, I love Abby, too."

"So how'd Lenora take the breakup!"

Desmond snorted. "She went into orbit." He leaned against the padded booth as if hoping he could dissolve from existence. "I told her I wanted to call the whole thing off, and that we couldn't work together any more. I offered to move her back to Tennessee, closer to her family, and even give her a long-distance position with the company with a nice raise to top it all off."

"But that's not the same as marriage," Kinkaide observed.

"Those were exactly her thoughts. She told me she was quitting Casper's, and she wanted a million-dollar severance package."

"Yikes!"

Desmond's dark eyes rounded, and he nodded. "Right. She also said if I didn't agree, she'd tell Abby about the affair. When I told her I was already planning on telling Abby, it was like pouring gas on a fire." He twisted his diamond-studded wedding band and watched the sparkles as if he were mesmerized by the irony of what the ring represented. "I did offer her a hundred-K severance package, and she wound up taking it. I figured that was more than generous, considering—"

"Feel free to offer me that kind of package any day," Kinkaide snickered, and Desmond joined him.

"I will—just as soon as you start wearing lipstick."

"No deal."

The friends' mutual laughter mingled together, then all vestiges of humor faded in the face of panic. "What am I going to do?" Desmond begged. "Abby is beyond furious. She wants a divorce. Every time she asks me—or rather demands to know—why I stooped so low, I try to explain my needs and how our marriage lacked in that area. Then she starts yelling that I'm blaming her for my sins and goes off on a tear about how I don't understand her needs, either. And I've about decided she's right. I don't understand her—not in the least!" Desmond picked up a packet of sugar and tormented it with quivering fingers.

Kinkaide stared at the man who epitomized success. A man whose shoulders now sagged with the weight of his sin. A man at a crossroads who might fall to ruin if he made another wrong decision. And Kinkaide felt like a preschooler trying to teach a college chemistry class. He had no advice to give whatsoever. He was royally botching his attempts to reach Mel, and they weren't even married yet. *How in the world am I supposed to come up with any solutions for this problem?* "Uh…have you tried marriage counseling?" Kinkaide's suggestion sounded contrived, even to him.

Desmond shook his head. "Right now, I'm staying at a hotel. She won't even go to dinner with me, let alone a marriage counselor. All she says is she wants a divorce. Period. I have betrayed her in the most horrible way known to womankind, and she never wants to see me again—*ever!*" He flung his hand to the side and almost toppled a water glass.

Kinkaide caught the cold tumbler and the icy liquid sloshed onto his hand. The chill seeping between his fingers reminded him of the rocklike resolve in Mel's eyes. He glanced over at the Moores as they rose to be lead to their table. Mel still wasn't with them. He had exchanged greetings with her parents when he and Desmond followed the hostess to their booth. The last thing he wanted to do was get into a discussion with Darla Moore. A discussion with her might lead into an argument over that forged note. Kinkaide was still a little sore over that whole deal. While he appreciated Mrs. Moore's championing his efforts, he didn't enjoy being made a fool of—no matter how well-meaning the gesture.

Kinkaide, determined to focus on his friend, decided to be honest. "Well, I hate to tell you, but I'm not going to be much help. I have gotten nowhere with Melissa in seven months. Zero. Zip. Nada. I'm completely at a standstill. I've done everything I know to convince her to reconsider our relationship, and she's only getting farther away. I don't have any advice. I'm afraid I'll only make matters worse."

"I understand. Really, what I need right now more than anything is just somebody to talk to." Desmond rested his head on the back of the high-backed booth. The shadow along his jawline intensified the dark circles under his eyes. "All I know is I want my family back—like things used to be. I don't want a divorce. I don't want to leave my daughters. I love them."

"Do they know about—"

"No!" A shroud of horror clouded Desmond's dark eyes. "All they know is that their mother and I aren't getting along right now."

"So who else knows besides Abby?"

"Just my pastor. God made me the most miserable man on the face of the earth. I had to confess to Pastor Waits, or I was going to *die* of conviction. Of course, I also resigned all my positions in the church. Right now, nobody knows why. I'm sure time will change that. But for the present, only Pastor Waits and Abby know."

The waitress reappeared, and both men placed their orders for steaks, potatoes, and iced tea. Kinkaide's stomach, forever the betrayer, rumbled despite the crisis moment. Amid the sounds of clinking silverware and the conversation of diners, several minutes passed. Minutes in which Kinkaide reviewed Desmond's precarious circumstances. Minutes in which he thanked God for giving him the grace and wisdom to overcome his past and escape such a terrible mess. More than once, Kinkaide had been offered the opportunity to fall flat on his face. While he didn't consider himself a celebrity by any means, his well-known status guaranteed more feminine admiration than he'd ever imagined. Even a few Christian women could have easily been as big a nemesis as Lenora was to Desmond.

Wishing he could dispel Desmond's demons, Kinkaide finally quipped, "Well, I guess I could mention what Lawton suggested to me about Melissa. Why not sit at her door and howl all night?"

Desmond burst into an eruption of unconstrained guffaws that turned a few heads at nearby tables. "Oh, yes, now that would probably go over really great."

"Those were my thoughts exactly."

"So, how is that brother of yours?" Desmond asked.

"Ornery as ever."

"Still no lady in the picture?"

"None."

"Maybe he's the smart one." The waitress reappeared with their iced tea, and Desmond squeezed his lemon over the ice until no drops were left.

"Looks like we're in the same boat," Kinkaide observed. He squinted as an unexpected idea sprang upon him. "Hey! In three months, I'm going on a cruise to the Grecian Islands then on to Rome. There are supposed to be some vacancies. Do you think Abby would agree to go with you? Maybe it would be a step toward rebuilding your marriage."

Desmond's blank stare was followed by a hint of speculation. "I don't know...she always *did* want to go on a cruise."

"And you've never taken her?" Kinkaide asked as if he were scandalized.

"Maybe if I suggested that the whole family goes—and if I tell her you're going as well. She always *did* like you."

"At least *somebody* of the female persuasion likes me."

"Hey, keep your mind on your own woman, okay?" Desmond's upturned lips and quick comeback made him seem more like the same old friend Kinkaide had grown to love.

"So what do you think?"

The entrepreneur stroked the thin black mustache that gave him a certain distinguished appeal. "I'll ask her." He nodded. "Yes. I'll ask her and let you know. Maybe she'll at least consider it."

"Don't forget to howl after you ask. That just might do the trick."

Melissa, her shoulders hunched, stepped into the steakhouse and scanned the waiting area. No sign of Kinkaide. She relaxed a fraction. That black Oldsmobile out front was either his or one identical to his. Mel eased toward the vacant hostess podium. Dining rooms, lined with decorative balusters, graced each side of the foyer. Mel cast a furtive glance to her right. She perused the dining room and saw no signs of either her family or Kinkaide.

Next, she peered through the balusters that lined the dining area to the left and scrutinized the patrons until she noticed a pair of men in the corner booth. Mel's eyes widened, and she gripped the edge of the podium. Kinkaide, his dark hair gleaming in the dim light, talked with the friend her mother had mentioned. The friend looked about as distraught as Mel felt. Kinkaide, on the other hand, appeared at ease, confident, and…and as appealing as usual.

Mel swallowed hard, and the windsuit that offered warmth against the winter breezes now suffocated. The longer she observed Kinkaide, the more riveted she became. Of their own volition, the years rolled away and, from somewhere in the shadows of her mind, a scene played out before her. A scene in a restaurant similar to this one. A scene that Mel wished she could expunge from her psyche.

They had met in their favorite booth at the burger joint where other college students gathered. Their budget was tight, as usual, and they had precious little money to go anywhere else. Kinkaide, always in need of a haircut, brushed at the bangs that fell into his eyes. Mel reached to stroke the dark hair she adored.

With an expectant smile, he handed her a present wrapped in white with a nondescript red bow atop. "Happy Valentine's Day." His brown eyes shrouded her in a mist of love.

A surge of joy bubbled up within Mel as she took the present. Expectantly she tore away the paper, opened the cardboard box, and pulled out a heart-shaped, cut-glass jewelry box. A slip of white paper against red velvet caught her eye, and she removed it. The note said, "Look under the passenger seat of my car."

Amid mutual laughter, the two rushed past the approaching waitress and out to Kinkaide's car parked near a grove of trees in the city park across the street. He hovered nearby as she retrieved another present from under the car seat. Mel plopped into the car and tore at the red ribbon that matched the first one. White paper fell away to reveal another box—this one blue velvet. Her heart palpitated. Her eyes watered. She held her breath as she gazed at the telltale box.

"Go ahead. Open it," Kinkaide prompted.

Mel, tears spilling onto her cheeks, popped open the lid and gazed in wonder at a modest solitaire diamond ring.

Kinkaide knelt in front of her, took her hands in his, and asked, "Will you marry me?"

"Yes!" Mel whispered. "You know I will."

With a sigh, Kinkaide pulled her into his arms, stroked her cheek, and sealed the moment with a kiss that promised a lifetime of joy, the euphony of love, the fervor of two hearts beating as one.

As if he sensed someone watching him, Kinkaide scanned the crowd. The voice of reason insisted that Mel dart from sight, but the specter of their past still held her captive. In an instant his gaze collided with Melissa's. She sucked in a lungful of air. Kinkaide's eyes, silken soft and pleading, beckoned her forward, into his waiting arms. Mel, tangled in the emotions of the reminiscence, took two steps toward him then stopped.

Kinkaide, never shifting his attention from Mel, spoke briefly to his friend then picked his way through the maze of tables. Her heart's gentle pounding intensified, and she stumbled backward. The closer he came, the more violently her heart raced. Her legs tottered, and she locked her knees. She was spinning...spinning in a whirlpool of sweet agony and remorse and confusion. Longing...longing for the fulfillment of a love that had never died. Groping...groping for the heart that once plighted to be her mate.

Kinkaide continued his steady approach, and Mel gasped. No matter how fast she breathed, there was never enough air.

His eyes, adoring and sincere, seemed to repeat the words he had uttered an hour before: "I love you, Mel. I never stopped loving you. I've regretted walking away from you more than you can ever imagine."

"Excuse me? Are you ready to be seated?" a female voice broke in upon Mel's enchantment.

As if the chains of love snapped, she swiveled to face the smiling hostess then lurched backward. "No...no. I've...I've changed my mind." She bolted toward the door.

"Melissa!" Kinkaide's urgent cry stroked her spine and wove its way into her heart, yet she forced her feet to carry her out of the restaurant and into the parking lot.

"Please wait, Melissa!"

Without a backward glance, she raced to her white Toyota halfway across the spacious parking lot. *Don't look back. Do not look back. You might very well do something foolish— something you'll regret. Keep running...keep running. Oh, Lord, if You're watching, help me keep running.*

"I love you!" Kinkaide's words reverberated across the parking lot, mingling with the sounds of traffic, with the gusts of wind, with the mellifluous memories that tantalized Mel's mind.

While her heart beckoned her to stop, to fling herself into his arms, to declare a love that never waned, Melissa heeded her common sense. She wasn't ready, she simply was not ready, to take the chance. While the yearnings of a lonely heart bade her stay, her will demanded she unlock the car door, collapse into the seat, and crank the engine.

As she pulled out of the parking lot, she glanced into the rearview mirror. Kinkaide stood by the restaurant door, hands in his pockets, shoulders sagging. Mel choked on a sob that burst from a musty closet hidden in the corridors of her soul—a closet where spurned love implored release.

Eight

⌒

"It's time to stop sitting around and take some action." Lenora Osworth paced in front of the townhouse's fireplace. "I'm ready to get this over with and go back to Tennessee." She drew on a long brown cigarette, then threw the butt in the crackling fire.

Horace Waggoner exchanged a glance with his fiancée, Sara Murdock. He shifted his wiry frame against the settee's plush pillows and debated their options. The Sunday meeting with Lenora had been planned for three days now. Last night, Horace debated whether this meeting should end their participation in this subterfuge or remain a time of stratagem as originally planned. However, he had never expressed his reservations to Sara.

"What's the brats' schedule like on Mondays?" Lenora's question jolted Horace back to the problem at hand. Lenora lowered herself to the sofa, stretched her arms along the back, and crossed her shapely legs. Her slinky red pants flopped with the effort.

Horace cradled his cup of hot tea and nodded at Sara who dug through her purse. She retrieved the oversized glasses that made her look like a little girl playing dress-up with her mom's eyewear. Sara strained against her bulging midsection to reach the leather-bound organizer near her feet.

While Sara fumbled for the appropriate page, Horace gazed around the townhouse and considered the contrast of his and Lenora's world. The ultramodern apartment, nearly stark in its decor, screamed of success. Even the extensive collection of crystal cats atop the brass-trimmed mantel probably cost more than he made during the last six months. The rooms he leased in downtown Dallas, near his dingy detective agency, looked like a slum reject compared to the opulence of this home. But his drab existence did sparkle with the light of freedom—something not guaranteed if he were caught in the act of kidnapping.

"Okay," Sara began in her nasal tone, "on Monday afternoons the twins go to piano lessons in Plano. After that they usually go home. The best we can tell, given what Horace has observed and what I picked up from Mr., um, Mr. Casper..." Sara's eyes shifted, and her index finger paused upon the schedule. The last time she mentioned Mr. Casper, Lenora had digressed into a three-minute tirade.

The businesswoman jumped up and grabbed the silver cigarette case from the mantel. As Sara continued, Lenora narrowed her eyes, lit the cigarette, and inhaled deeply. The acrid smoke floated around the room like fumes from flames of fury.

"Um, after the piano lessons, which are at 4:30, they eat. They usually stay in the house until around 6 or 6:30. Last Monday night a couple of older girls arrived, and the four of them went to the Town East Mall until about eight. Then they went home. All lights in the house were off at ten."

"The mall, huh?" Lenora's eyes narrowed. "The perfect place for a kidnapping."

"Actually, I was thinking more in terms of church Wednesday night," Horace said.

"Church?" Lenora quizzed.

He shifted on the couch then stood. His tea sloshed onto the cream-colored carpet, marring the pale pile in a collection of tiny puddles.

With a huff, Lenora marched toward the kitchen and came back with a barely used dishtowel. She dropped the cloth on the tea and pressed her square-toed shoe against it. Even though she didn't voice a word, the look in her eyes was familiar. Many times Horace's father had put verbal force behind such an attitude. *If you can't even hear gunfire without jumping, how are you supposed to be a successful detective!* Horace never scraped together the nerve to tell his father he would have rather been an accountant. Instead, he floundered as he tried to fulfill his dad's expectations. Despite his father's recent death, Horace felt as if the old man were peering over his shoulder.

A slow burn manifested itself in Horace's gut, and he fumbled in his shirt pocket for a chewable antacid. The movement jostled the tea, and new droplets splashed onto Lenora's leather shoe. She glared at Horace as if he had dashed the whole cup into her face.

"Sorry," he mumbled.

"You know, Horace has excellent options for our strategy." Sara took the tea from him, and her cool fingers closed around his hand. Her high-pitched voice held a twinge of challenge, so faint he wondered if Lenora perceived it—until her eyes narrowed.

Horace managed to fish one of the individually wrapped tablets from his shirt's ink-stained pocket.

"Last Wednesday Horace followed Janie and Julie to church. Their church is huge."

"Yes, I know," Lenora stated, her right brow arched as if she detested the very mention of the Caspers' place of worship. "Desmond always insisted on our not meeting on Sundays because of that horrid place."

Sara deposited the tea mug atop a silver-trimmed coaster on the end table.

"After the service, people were everywhere," Horace said. "Julie and Janie were hanging out with a group of teenagers. Mrs. Casper wasn't there. The last two Wednesday nights, she hasn't attended."

"We're thinking that she doesn't go on Wednesdays," Sara added.

"So did their father take them?" Lenora's jeer left little doubt about the hatred those images stirred.

"No." Horace tore the pill wrapper, popped the medicine into his mouth, and squeezed the wrapper into a tight ball. "The best we can figure, it was the pastor's wife who picked them up."

"Mr. Casper moved into a hotel room last Thursday. He hasn't seen his girls since, that we know of, Sara said."

"Good," Lenora purred. Her flawlessly made-up eyes twitched at the corners.

"There were so many people milling around that Horace could easily lure the girls away."

"Oh? And how do you plan to do that?" Lenora's calculating tones held the hint of disdain that surfaced after their last meeting.

"You know, Lenora," Sara said as if she were privy to some unspoken secret, "I think we all know too much to afford to be anything but trusting." She pulled her opened beige sweater tight around her bulging midsection.

As the silence stretched, dread crept along Horace's shoulders like a vengeful scorpion. The daggerlike hatred gleaming in Lenora's dark eyes reminded him of a rabid wolf.

"Of course." A smooth smile tugged at the corner of Lenora's mouth—a smile that belied the devious glint in her eyes.

"Tell Lenora your plan, Horace," Sara said, her voice steely.

Horace glanced from Sara to Lenora and back to Sara. "I was thinking about approaching the girls Wednesday night and telling them there had been an emergency with their father. Church is one of the few places where that hulk cousin Steve isn't trailing close behind. I could flash the girls my badge and tell them their mother told me to come get them."

Lenora crossed her arms. Her flawless face, the color of heavily creamed coffee, relaxed. The disdain vanished, and she nodded. "I think that just might work."

Melissa entered her home to the accompaniment of the telephone's ringing. She glanced at her watch to see that 30 minutes had lapsed since telling her mother she would meet them for lunch. Undoubtedly, Darla Moore had been kept waiting long enough. Melissa stepped into the living room and turned up the answering machine's volume. After that encounter with Kinkaide, she possessed no endurance to deal with her mother. Guilt, sharp and unyielding, spiraled through her chest, and she imagined Darla's reproof over the absence. Three times Melissa's fingers hovered over the receiver, but she backed off. Finally, the machine answered, and her father's voice floated over the speaker.

"Melissa, I was worried—"

She grabbed the receiver. "Hi, Dad. Sorry for the delay in answering."

The sounds of clinking silverware and a baby's cry accompanied Zeb Moore's voice. "Is everything okay? I started worrying that you might be having car trouble."

"No. Everything is fine. Listen…please don't tell Mom— but I got to the restaurant and ran into Kinkaide. Things weren't, uh, exactly peachy. I left the restaurant almost as soon as I got there. I'm really sorry, Dad, but I just don't think—"

"It's okay. No need to explain. You're a grown woman with a life of your own."

Melissa warmed with her father's words. "Please ask Michelle to call me after lunch so I can explain. Tell her I'm sorry about missing lunch. I think she'll understand."

"Will do."

Mel bid her father adieu and hung up. She rubbed the tiny lines between her eyebrows and acknowledged her pounding head. "What a day," she breathed.

On impulse, Mel opened her purse–organizer and flipped to the "L" section of her address book. Her finger ran down the line of names until she came to Jacquelyn Lightfoot. She punched in Jac's number; an immediate hello rewarded her.

"Hi. It's me—face-kisser, mouth-of-the-south, fell-off-a-cliff, doing-time Melissa."

Jac snickered. "So, I guess you checked your e-mail?"

"About 30 minutes ago. I must say that you guys don't mind talking about a woman behind her back."

Jac's companionable laugh instigated a round of sisterly banter.

Melissa settled into the love seat and picked up the framed 5 x 7 photo of her and her six friends taken last summer at Marilyn Langham's wedding. All the sisters wore tea-length Victorian dresses the color of rich sapphires. Jac Lightfoot stood behind Mel, a hand draped affectionately on Melissa's shoulder. The private detective's dark complexion and hair spoke of her mixed racial heritage. She boasted of Native American, African-American, and Caucasian ancestors. Mel had occasionally teased that if Jac went far enough back in her family tree, she would undoubtedly find a pit bulldog. The private investigator possessed more grit than all the sisters put together.

"Listen," Melissa finally asked, "I was wondering if you could tell me what grounds I need to file a restraining order against Kinkaide."

"What?"

"He's driving me crazy, Jac."

"Is he doing anything criminal—threatening you or—"

"No, nothing like that. He just won't back off. Don't tell anybody—this is really embarrassing—but he just chased me out of a restaurant calling 'I love you' across the parking lot." Mel managed to cover the shakiness in her voice and refused to ponder exactly how she might have revealed her weakness if Kinkaide had caught up with her.

Jac burst into a chorus of laughter.

"Listen, Lightfoot, this is *not* funny!"

"Sorry," Jac said through diminishing snickers. "It's just that the last time I advised a restraining order it was because a woman was afraid her ex-husband was going to kill her."

"Okay, okay." Mel plopped the framed photo on the end table. "So this isn't life threatening. But the fact still remains that the man won't back off. He just won't take no for an answer. In the last seven months, I've tried everything— *everything*—and he can't seem to get it through that thick skull of his that I'm just not interested. He even bought tickets for that cruise."

"And you aren't going?"

"No!"

"Come on, Mel, why don't you give the poor guy a break?"

"Give him a break?" Mel rested the heel of her hand against her forehead. "What's the matter—are you going soft on me? If I'd wanted somebody to tell me to give him a break, I'd have called Victoria."

"No, I'm not going soft." Yet the underlying tones of Jac's firm voice attested to a vulnerability that Mel had never heard from the tough private eye.

An awkward silence extended between the two friends. Mel, eyes narrowed, closed her purse-organizer and placed it on the love seat cushion. "Okay, what's going on?" she queried.

Independent to a fault, Jac seemed the most distant of the friends. While all the sisters knew she was available if needed, Jac often let her career slip in the way of contacting them. As far as Mel could calculate, Jac's phone call, plus her e-mail interaction, along with her vulnerable tones, pointed to a potential problem.

"Well, I've been a little down lately," Jac confessed. "And I can't pinpoint why."

Mel nodded. "Hmmm. This isn't like you. I've never known you to even have much trouble with PMS."

"Right."

"Do you feel like you're into full-blown depression or is this just the blues?"

"How do you tell the difference?" Jac's voice dropped several decibels.

"Did you wake up feeling low today or is this something that's been going on awhile?"

"Awhile."

"How long?"

"It started about a year ago, I'd say."

"A year ago? And you haven't said anything?"

"I didn't really think I needed to say anything. I'm so busy, I just kept thinking it would go away."

"And it hasn't?"

"No. It's getting worse. I was wondering what you thought. Should I see a doctor?"

"Hmm." Mel considered the private eye's fast-paced life. Jac was always hopping on a plane to somewhere. She usually had callers beeping in from all directions. The few e-mails Melissa received from Jac the last year had been at odd hours. Mel kept the strenuous hours of an in-demand pediatrician, but she did make time for herself. She couldn't remember the last time Jac mentioned taking an extended vacation.

"Depression can be caused by a number of factors," Mel said, attempting to keep the professional edge from her voice. "Stress is one of them. Might be that you're just exhausted. You *do* work like a Turk."

"And now you're starting to sound like a Dr. Seuss book," Jac quipped.

"I sense some resistance," Mel said through a smile.

"Okay, okay, maybe I do work hard—at times a little too hard. My mother has been really riding me lately about taking a break."

Mel groaned. "Don't start talking about mothers."

"Oh, boy—is yours acting like a KGB agent again?"

"Again? She never stopped! Did I tell you about the note?"

"Note?"

"She actually forged a note from me to Kinkaide accepting his invitation for the cruise!"

Jac whistled. "Holy smokes. My mother has *never* gone that far!"

"You think *you're* depressed? I'm beginning to wonder if I'll be on nerve pills by the time I'm 40!"

"Sounds like you *need* that cruise."

Mel waved her hand. "Right, Lightfoot, right! A week with Kinkaide Franklin on a ship, and I can just skip the nerve pills and go into a straitjacket." She envisioned the magnificent boat's gentle rocking, the smell of the sea, the moonlight, the mild zephyr, the warmth of Kinkaide's arms, and her toes curled.

"You know, I think the lady doth protesteth too much."

"Don't start throwing Shakespeare into this!"

"At least he's more sophisticated than Dr. Seuss." Jac snickered.

"That's a matter of opinion!"

The doorbell's ring interrupted their repartee. With the ringing came the echo of Kinkaide's haunted admission reverberating across the parking lot. *I love you, Melissa!* She swiveled on the love seat, and tugged aside the window sheers. A black Oldsmobile, glistening in the winter sunshine, claimed the curb in front of the house.

"What's the matter?" Jac asked. "You got quiet." She turned in her rolling chair and propped her feet on the edge of her computer desk.

"Kinkaide's at the door," Mel hissed.

"Oh, really?" Jac responded in her most inquisitive "private eye" voice. "Then I would deduce that he's come to visit you."

"You're just *full* of insight today, aren't you?"

"Today and always."

"I'll call you back." Melissa's wary voice preempted the phone's click.

Jac pulled the receiver away from her ear and stared at it. "Thanks for the farewell," she said with a twisted smile.

All the sisters agreed that Mel was still in love with Kinkaide—as in eaten up with it. They also agreed that the woman would probably decapitate him before she kissed him. "She's got a grudge going there about the size of South Dakota," Jac echoed the friends' general consensus.

Nine

Jac stood, stretched, and grabbed her coffee mug from the end table. The sofa beckoned her to collapse against soft cushions, but she resisted and padded toward the kitchenette. Jac awoke this morning at five, as usual, went for her usual jog, ate her usual whole-grain cereal, and spent her usual hours in the office. If she wasn't on an assignment, Sunday morning was the time she caught up on paperwork. If she didn't have paperwork, she went to church. Her schedule drove her mother crazy.

But she doesn't hold a candle to Mel's mom. Jac shook her head, picked up the empty coffee carafe, frowned at the eight-cup decanter, and shoved it under the water faucet. This had been a long morning.

While the coffee brewed, Jac exerted a halfhearted attempt to straighten her apartment. Her sparsely decorated quarters, functional and convenient, served every need. She required only a place to land when she wasn't on the road or in the office. Jac considered herself the antithesis of Victoria, that domestic genius who could almost turn water into wine. However, during the last four weeks Jac had spent more time at home than she had in three months combined. Furthermore, she couldn't seem to get enough sleep, no matter how long she stayed in bed. Little did Melissa know that Jac's comments about depression had been mere hints of what was becoming a huge problem.

Jac, her hands shaking, poured herself another cup of coffee—the ninth one since five o'clock. The smell of the rich brew tantalized her to drink the whole pot, and she took a swallow of the stinging liquid. Caffeine seemed the only means to keep herself awake. But at times even caffeine didn't work. She walked into her bedroom and deposited the steaming mug on the nightstand. The simple pine bed, covered with a tightly tucked spread, summoned her and she could resist no longer. Yawning, Jac plopped onto the bed, kicked off her running shoes, pulled up the blanket, and snuggled under it. Outside, the wind blowing snow clouds across the Rockies lulled her to sleep....

Jacquelyn, pigtails flailing, ran through the dank woods. Her bare feet slammed against the forest floor, and with each step the angry briers snaked out to snare her tender flesh in their unrelenting grasp. Jac whimpered, clawed at the unforgiving briers, and pushed forward. Footfalls, heavy and near, crashed behind her. She dashed a frantic glance over her shoulder, but the dense foliage concealed any signs of the beast. Every breath erupted from her lungs with a painful burst. Every step brought her closer...closer...ever closer to the blinding beams that penetrated the edge of the forest. Every second empowered the dragon to come nearer... nearer...ever nearer to his cringing prey. His impatient roar echoed through the forest, and a cackling vulture, twice Jacquelyn's size, swooped down to clasp her in his bony talons. She clamped childish hands over her ears and emitted a scream that exploded from the rends in her soul. The dragon's fiery breath seared through the trees and scorched Jacquelyn's back. The smell of singed hair hovered over her head like a cloud of doom, and the vulture released a triumphant squawk. She hunkered down, gritted her teeth, and braced herself for the consumption of her tender flesh.

Yet the light on the forest's edge bid her step into its revealing rays. Jacquelyn, salty tears christening her lips, edged forward and placed one cautious foot into the glow. The vulture screeched. His talons slipped from her hair. His wings pulsated in a panicked tattoo. The faintest of glistening beams shot up Jacquelyn's leg and penetrated her soul—a soul ravaged by bloody wounds. Wounds and heartache. Heartache and devastation. Jacquelyn lunged back into the forest's shadows, back toward the monster, back through the brier's arms. The internal pain eased. As long as she couldn't see the wounds, the agony diminished to a dull ache.

"No, no, no," she whimpered as the vulture descended upon her shoulder then nibbled her ear. "No. Not the light. Anything but the light. I don't want to know. I don't want to know."

The dragon's feet hammered ever closer. His labored breathing rasped in and out of oversized nostrils, and he halted behind her. The beast and the vulture merged into one being, and Jacquelyn covered her eyes. The fiend's warmth penetrated her back. His foul breath brushed the top of her head, stirring her bangs against her forehead. He chuckled over her, as if savoring the moments before he gorged himself. Jacquelyn's skin prickled with gooseflesh. Her stomach rolled with nausea. Sweat trickled down her spine.

She had met the dragon before. She had spoken with the dragon. She had even embraced the dragon.

An explosion of fairylike tinkles, rolling ever nearer, bade Jacquelyn to open her eyes. The ethereal beams on the forest's edge exploded with sparkles. Sparkles that swirled like a thousand tiny stars released from the corridors of heaven. Sparkles that called her name in voices laden with love. A path amid clouds of swirling gold dust opened before the girl. The dragon's claw raked across her back. She jolted toward the light, but the glow illuminated her soul's gaping wounds. With the illumination, the bloody ulcers pulsed, as if the light fueled their agony.

"No, no, no...I don't want to know. I don't. I don't. Don't make me remember. Don't. Don't. Please, please, don't."

The dragon's scaly palm settled across her shoulder. Jacquelyn stiffened. Then a scream, garbled and soul-rending, erupted from the core of her being.

The scream continued in short bursts like the reverberations of a tormented soul chained in a dungeon. Jac sat up in bed, gathered the blanket to her, and kneaded it. Drenched in sweat, she gazed around the spartan bedroom. She glanced from one corner to the next in search of the dragon. Her pulse, hard and unrelenting, pounded against tender temples.

"No, no, no," she croaked. "I don't want to know. I don't. I don't."

Run, run, run! The edict floated up from the internal wounds pulsing with pain. Jac obeyed. She dashed aside the blanket, plunked her feet on the floor, and raced for the bathroom. After flipping the light switch, she hurried to the sink. Hands atremble, Jac twisted on the cold water and splashed her fiery face. The frigid liquid stunned warm flesh and jolted her into the real world. A world where she was in control. A world where no dragon would ever terrorize her again.

"Because I'll knock your teeth in, you beast," she growled into the mirror. The cold water, glistening on bronze skin, dripped from her nose and chin. Her chin-length hair clung to her cheeks, and Jac shoved it back. She snatched a worn hand towel from next to the basin and scrubbed her face dry. The years of taekwondo flashed before her eyes. Yes, she could demolish the dragon now. As a child she was at his mercy. But now...now...now...

Images of that recurring dream crashed upon Jacquelyn anew. The briers. The vulture. The smell of burnt hair. The light—coaxing, wooing, promising. A low sob swelled up her throat. She shoved a wad of towel between her teeth and clamped down. A moan, low and guttural, tore through the towel. Jac slammed the towel against the counter. "I don't want to know!" she yelled. She shook her fist at the ceiling. "Just stop it! Stop it! I don't want to know!"

Jac raced to her bedroom. She jammed her feet into her running shoes, tied them, and reached for her keys on the nightstand. The backs of her fingers brushed the mug of coffee—still warm. Jacquelyn looked at the clock. Only 30 minutes had lapsed since she'd sunk into the bed. Only 30 minutes. This time the dream came sooner. The nightmare raced upon her more swiftly with every attempt at sleep. A whole month had lapsed since she had experienced a full night's rest. Never had she so desperately craved sleep. Never had sleep so eluded her.

The office. The office beckoned. *I can lose myself in the Wilson case.*

Jacquelyn rushed into the living room and grabbed her parka from the back of her trusty recliner. Tammy Wilson, at age six, disappeared two years ago. The family had hired Jac as a last attempt to find the child. This afternoon the detective could do some research on the internet. Jac pulled leather gloves from her coat pockets, stuffed her hands into them, and stepped onto the apartment landing. The dragon once again receded to the far recesses of her mind, to a place where he could no longer torment her as long as she consciously denied his existence.

Ten

~

Kinkaide, heart in his throat, held his breath as Melissa opened the beveled glass door. Her wary gaze flicked across him as if she were a lamb in the face of a starving wolf. He cleared his throat and shifted. *This could be worse,* he reminded himself. *At least she didn't pretend to not be home.*

"Can we talk?" he asked, feeling like a 16-year-old on his first date.

Mel peered past him, as if she didn't want to look him straight in the eyes. For an instant her teeth clenched and the muscles in her jaw tightened. Kinkaide braced himself for rejection. Then she narrowed her eyes and stepped away from the entry. As she swept open the door, the beveled glass produced an array of cheerful colors that belied the anxiety swelling up within Kinkaide.

"Yes, I think we need to talk," she confirmed.

He inserted his sweaty hands into his overcoat pockets, and his left hand encountered a velvet box. Kinkaide had locked the box in his glove compartment several months ago. A whimsical nudge had suggested that perhaps he might have the opportunity to present the remnant of the past to the lady of his heart. As days blurred into weeks, Kinkaide had almost forgotten about the box. But today, on the way from the restaurant, it nudged into his mind and he had placed it in his pocket.

Stroking the plush velvet, he brushed past her. Perhaps his and Mel's conversational agendas were antithetical. Nonetheless, Kinkaide had gotten farther than he thought he would on the way over. She didn't slam the door in his face. Miracles would never cease.

He gazed around the classically decorated home. Nothing in the elegant room surprised him. Mel always had exhibited the best in taste even though she often joked that she couldn't create the look—she just knew what she wanted.

One wall lined with framed photos attracted Kinkaide more than any other element. He meandered toward the photos and stopped to examine them. Each picture featured an up-close shot of a particular flower. Daisies, daffodils, irises, roses. Bluebonnets, spider lilies, geraniums. Dogwood blossoms and apple blossoms. Each bloom exhibited a different stroke of nature, a different spoke of Mel's interest. Her penchant for photography melded with her love of nature to produce some breathtaking shots. Kinkaide focused on one photo in particular—a bloodred rose covered in droplets of dew. The sunlight burst upon each droplet, turning them into liquid diamonds.

From across the room, Mel cleared her throat and Kinkaide turned to face her. "Have you ever shot a bougainvillea?"

"A what?"

"Oh, come on, Ms. Nature Lover," he teased, "you don't know about bougainvillea?"

Mel adjusted her glasses. "No, afraid not."

"It's a beautiful flower that grows in the Greek Isles. The blooms can be various colors from fuchsia to red. They creep any place they can climb—over walls or even archways—you get the picture. You'd have a heyday with your camera."

"So I should go on the cruise with you—just for the photos alone, is that it?" She folded her arms, and the nylon windsuit swished with her movement.

Kinkaide held her gaze. *My, my, my aren't we feisty,* he wanted to say, but for once he held his tongue. Memories of those charged moments at church denounced her defensiveness. Melissa Moore, practical and self-possessed, was more affected than she wanted to admit.

"Of course," Kinkaide said with a pleading smile. "I'll try anything. I'm a desperate man."

"The reason I invited you in is because it's time we had a serious talk." Like a soldier with a mission, Melissa marched toward him and stopped a few feet away.

He vacillated between reaching to embrace her and backing up. His index finger pressed against the opening in the velvet box, and the lid expanded enough to pinch his fingertip.

"Kinkaide, what we had six years ago can never be repeated. You need to understand that nothing you can do or say is going to change my mind. I don't know why you followed me home, but—"

"I'm not really sure either, Mel." Kinkaide shrugged and scraped his right hand through the base of his neck-length hair. "It's just that, I guess we've had a rather eventful day—"

"You can say *that* again," she mumbled.

"And, well, I really am sorry that everything turned out like it did." Kinkaide's gut clenched with the recent manifestation of their old magnetism. In the restaurant, she looked as if she were transported to another year, another moment, another memory. A memory that included him. And love. And promises. "I shouldn't have pushed so hard, it's just that—"

"You aren't used to taking no for an answer." Melissa tilted her head in the angle that spoke her dogged determination to stand her ground.

A cold fist of steel settled in the pit of his stomach. *Go back to Nashville and get on with your life*, a defeated voice urged. *This is a waste of time.* He pulled his hand from the velvet box and crossed his arms.

"It might interest you to know," she said in measured tones, "that I feel strongly enough about all this that I inquired about a restraining order against you."

The metal fist pummeled Kinkaide's midsection.

"Against me?" he squeaked.

"Yes."

"And?" His chin rose a fraction.

Mel's gaze faltered. "It would appear there aren't grounds."

The fist relented. "But you wanted me to know so I would understand that you really are serious about us—or rather about the lack of us."

Melissa swiveled and paced toward the window covered in lace sheers. The lightweight pantsuit rustled with her every move, and a faint, powdery smell followed in her wake.

Kinkaide ached to hold her. Mel's reactions to him that day only heightened his memories of the love they once shared. He inserted his hand back into his pocket, and the velvet box snuggled into his palm, as if it were begging to be removed from darkness into light.

Last spring Kinkaide found the plush symbol of their love when he'd rediscovered Mel's picture in the attic. He'd searched for the mementos from his relationship with Mel because of a snag with Shelby. A snag named Melissa. Soon, the memories haunted him, propelled him to reflect upon that day he walked away from the only woman he ever loved. When he removed the plastic lid from the storage bin, he connected with his heart for the first time in six years. Kinkaide rifled through the various memorabilia from their relationship. Old love letters. A dried wedding boutonniere. Reservation confirmation from that Arkansas bed and breakfast. Kinkaide hadn't been able to throw away any of the stuff, despite what his common sense insisted.

And the other items...He gripped the ring box tighter. That day Kinkaide had left the attic and stashed the ring in his dresser drawer then placed Mel's photo on his grand piano. He had lowered himself onto the stool and his fingers flowed over the keys as he sang "Can't Help Falling in Love," the song he had planned to sing to Mel during their wedding ceremony. The melody was going to be a surprise—a gift from his heart.

As the song floated across Kinkaide, Melissa swiveled to face him. Her hair, wispy and windblown, shifted around her cheeks, and Kinkaide rubbed his thumb along his fingertips as he longed to caress the tresses.

"Exactly why did you jilt me?" The question burst forth like a long-imprisoned captive locked in the musty confines of a dungeon.

Kinkaide, startled from his reverie, spoke the first words that came to him. "Because I was a fool." He tilted his head to one side and observed Mel's defensiveness diminish to speculation.

"But was there ever a logical reason?" she challenged. "Or was it some foolish whim? You never—never really explained it to me." She waved her arm as if she were fighting off a swarm of noxious flies.

"I tried to explain that day, but you refused to listen."

"So talk," she insisted.

He gazed past her, out the window, toward a male robin hopping across the yard. A lone robin. A robin who neared a female so much like him. But she flitted away, as if she couldn't care less whether the bird was lonely...yearning... aching. Kinkaide shifted his attention back to Mel. Shining through her determined antagonism flickered the rays from the love they once shared. As their gaze lengthened, Kinkaide pressed his index finger against the box's opening. This time he touched the ring of gold that sat therein.

"I got scared...or, rather, terrified." He grimaced.

"Yes, you mentioned that."

"All I could think was that I had somehow deviated from my dream. I wanted to pursue my music, and my first goal had been to stay single until I achieved the level of recognition I sought. The day of our wedding, all I could think about were bills and babies and never getting to cut the first CD because—"

"But we had decided to wait awhile on the family." Mel's words, full of passion, sounded more like a wail than a statement of fact.

"I know," Kinkaide rasped. "I know." A silence, cumbersome and strained, gripped them like an unrelenting vise.

Kinkaide's attention trailed to the landscape painting above the love seat. An exquisite sun hovered on the horizon, either instigating a new day or placing a glow on the day's end. The verdict rested with the viewer. Likewise, Kinkaide felt as if his fate with Mel hung in the balance. Today's interaction might mean a new beginning or an end. An absolute end, indeed, if Mel was serious enough to consider a restraining order. Kinkaide withdrew his finger from the ring, and the box snapped shut. Perhaps he really should just pack and return to Nashville. His booking agent would be thrilled. And maybe Shelby would be, too.

Images of the polished blonde floated through his mind. For many men, Shelby was a dream woman. Beautiful. Talented. Smart. Great figure. Yet Kinkaide couldn't focus on her. Another lady blurred her image—a practical woman whose beauty was understated. Her talents, not as flamboyant as Shelby's, manifested themselves with children and cameras. And Mel's figure…well, Mel possessed a few curves Shelby's had never known. Her full figure suited Kinkaide just fine. He always had preferred a woman with some meat on her bones. Furthermore, Melissa held his heart. Shelby never had.

The longer Kinkaide thought of Mel's endearing qualities, the more he longed to stay in Oklahoma City. Again, he glanced toward the painting and decided that the sun was rising. *It has to be. I won't accept any other option.*

But are you more interested in what's best for you or what's best for Mel? Kinkaide stiffened and gripped the velvet box.

Melissa, chewing her bottom lip, crossed her arms then shoved her hands into the pockets of her loose jacket. "So let's just pretend I decided to…to…" she narrowed her eyes, "to agree to another engagement. How can I be sure you won't do the same thing to me again?"

Kinkaide removed the ring box from his pocket and placed it on the nearby end table. Mel's gaze followed his every move, and he watched her from the corner of his eyes. When she recognized the box, her eyes widened.

"I have suspended my career for the last seven months in order to win your heart; and I have made no pretense regarding my intent. Because of you, I broke off a long-term relationship—"

"With Shelby Canady?" Mel's hazel eyes demanded his indubitable honesty.

"Yes." Kinkaide didn't flinch from her dauntless scrutiny.

"So if you loved me so much, why did you start that relationship in the first place?"

"I didn't realize I still loved you when I met her."

"Oh? And it took an *18-month* relationship with her to figure it out?" she challenged.

"You certainly have your facts straight, don't you?" Kinkaide teased, pleased that she cared enough to search out the truth.

"I don't have a choice. My mother is the sleuth of the century. She gets all the facts and passes them on to me whether I want to hear them or not." A smile teased the corners of her mouth.

"And did you want to know?" Kinkaide peered into her eyes. This time she didn't move.

"What do you think?"

He shrugged, and his all-weather coat seemed to whisper the answer he longed to hear. "I think..." Kinkaide took a step toward her, but Mel retreated. He stopped. "I think that I would really like to kiss you, if you—"

"No." She gulped and leaned against the windowsill.

"Okay." Kinkaide rocked back on his heels and put every ounce of charm he could muster into his smile. "That's a disappointment. But I'm all grown up. Perhaps I can deal with it."

"Perhaps you'll have to." Mel choked like a woman drowning in her own emotions.

"I guess I should have taken my chances at church. But I must admit that was highly inappropriate. If my mother had discovered that I kissed you standing between the third and fourth pews, she would have dissolved into a heap of humiliation."

"My mother was probably spying from the balcony, cheering you on."

"You know, I always did like that woman."

"Then why don't you ask her to live with you? She's driving me nuts."

"She's always driven you nuts, Mel. And she'll probably drive you nuts until the day she dies."

"The way things are going lately, she'll probably drive me to an early grave. I'm not sure I'll be around the day she dies."

Kinkaide sighed. "I know I blew that apology this morning, but I really am sorry about the way the cruise business turned out. I should have never assumed anything until I talked with you personally."

"Well, you *did* try." Mel shrugged. "I'm sorry I didn't return your calls. It's just that..."

He held up his hand. "It's okay. Really." This interaction had already progressed about a thousand times further than he'd ever imagined and in exactly the opposite direction of Mel's staunch claims. At this point, Kinkaide would agree to eat leeches in order to keep the conversation in the present vein.

"Will you be able to get a refund on the cruise?"

"Probably not. I haven't inquired, actually. Lawton is interested in going, and Desmond Casper—he was the man with me today at the restaurant—anyway, he's thinking of taking his whole family and joining us."

"Sounds like a regular fun-filled excursion." A wary note crept into her voice, and Kinkaide took the hint.

A raucous bark followed by the squeak of claws on a window erupted from the back of the house. Mel glanced through the broad entryway and brushed past Kinkaide. "That's Bernie. He thinks he's supposed to come in as soon as I get home from church. Sounds like he's at the end of his patience."

Kinkaide, strolling toward the dining room, observed Mel as she opened the patio door and allowed a dog the size of a small horse to enter. He whistled. "Now that's what I call a dog."

Tail wagging, the Great Dane rushed toward Kinkaide, halted, sniffed his outstretched hand, then approved with a friendly lick. Kinkaide squatted and scratched the canine's ears.

"That's a switch." Mel snapped the patio door shut. "He usually takes quite a while to warm up to people, and if they make one false move…" She drew an imaginary line across her neck. "A few months ago Bernie clamped down on a man he thought was attacking me."

"Oh?" Kinkaide prompted.

"Yes. The man was asleep on the couch, and when I tried to wake him up, he tackled me because he thought I was an intruder. Bernie took a nice bite out of the man's leg."

"So you're letting men sleep on your couch?" Kinkaide joked.

"He was a friend of a friend, and he was in a bad situation. He just needed a safe place for a few days. Actually, he and my friend wound up getting married. Oh, wait, you would have met him briefly New Year's night. He and his wife—that's my friend Sonsee—were standing on the porch when...you...delivered..." She trailed off, but the unspoken words "delivered the cruise invitation" floated between them and ushered in another bout of silence. A silence brimming with questions. Questions and expectations. Expectations and persuasion.

Kinkaide braced himself against beseeching her to go. The brochures had convinced him that if there were ever an atmosphere to awaken an old love, it was a cruise to the Grecian Islands and a visit to Rome. If only Mel would agree.

For once in his life, Kinkaide chose to control his spontaneity. The visit had gone so well, he didn't want to push too hard. He gave Bernie's ear one last scratch and stood. "Thanks for your time, Mel."

"Oh. You're leaving." She blinked as if the realization had taken her quite by surprise.

Well, I don't have to. Want me to stay until dinner? We can go out for Chinese—your favorite.

Yet the old shadows clouded Mel's eyes.

"I can let myself out," he said. "You tend to this horse of yours. He looks hungry." Kinkaide, not waiting for her response, walked toward the front door.

"Just a minute. You left something." Melissa sped past him toward the end table and picked up the blue velvet box.

His hands, already cold, produced a thin film of sweat. Kinkaide had fully intended to leave that symbol of their love right where he'd placed it. With that steely glint back in her eyes, Mel extended the ring box. Kinkaide, caught on the brink of indecision, glanced from the ring box to the painting and back at Mel. The sun was rising on their relationship. It had to be. Kinkaide refused to believe anything else.

"No. I want you to keep it," he insisted and accomplished a hasty exit.

Melissa, eyes stinging, gripped the box and stared at the closed door. Her legs quaked, and she stumbled toward the love seat. Deliberately, she placed the blue box on the polished coffee table and tightened her face in an attempt to stay the tears. But this time she possessed no control over her emotions. Mel ripped off her glasses, cast them on the cushion, and covered her face. The emotional storm swirled upon her like a hurricane prohibited from coming ashore. But alas, the hurricane did bluster onto land and annihilated every scrap of dignity.

Despising herself for her weakness, Mel coughed against the sobs. Not since the day after Kinkaide walked out of her life had she given full rein to her emotions. Instead, she had directed all negative feelings into the seething pool of animosity that fermented in a recessed cavern of her spirit. Mel pounded the love seat's armrest and a resentful roar surged from her heart. She snatched the ring box from the table and hurled it across the room. The velvet box smashed against one of the framed photos, and the picture collapsed to the floor.

"I don't want the ring," she yelled. "I don't want the ring! Don't you understand? All…I…want…is…" She hiccupped on the diminishing sobs. "All I want…" Mel gulped. "I want your love." She slumped backward, and scrubbed at her cheeks.

I want your love. I never stopped wanting your love— despite what you did to me. I still love you…even now…even now.

A heavy sigh marked the end of the tears, and Mel reflected upon her words and actions. While she repeatedly told Kinkaide and everyone else that she would never awaken their former relationship, Mel found herself gravitating closer to a renewed commitment every time she interacted with him.

She often told herself that if he would just go back to Tennessee, she could get on with her life and everything would go back to normal. But was that the truth? While her external life had rocked on with all the trappings of normalcy, Mel wasn't certain her life had been normal since the day Kinkaide walked away.

Legs unsteady, she stood and stumbled across the room. The ring box lay beneath the fallen photo, and Mel bent to retrieve them both. While the box revealed no sign of abuse, the picture glass sported an unsightly crack across the center of the rich red rose sprinkled with diamond-like dew. Of all her flower photos, this one was Mel's favorite. With a sigh, she rehung the photo and made a mental note to purchase a new frame. The rose's dew, so brilliant and pure, reminded her of the diamond that once reflected Kinkaide's love. As if moving on their own volition, Mel's fingers popped open the velvet box. The solitaire winked up at her, and her left thumb stroked the inside of her ring finger.

Put on the ring. The thought rose from that hollow place within her heart—the place that had been vacant since Kinkaide. She reached for the ring then stopped. Pursing her lips, Mel snapped the lid shut. She strode to the end table where Kinkaide had left the box, tugged on the narrow drawer, and dropped the ring inside.

She prepared to shut the drawer, but the ring box had landed on a familiar book, a private book she hadn't opened in years. She didn't even know how the thin journal had landed in this drawer. Perhaps during the move last year one of the hired workmen had been responsible for its placement.

Mel, attempting to recall her last entry, pulled the journal from the drawer and thumbed through the pages. About three-fourths of the way through, the pages were blank. Mel flipped backward and arrived at the final entry, separated into the different categories she used as a system to cover all elements in her life: Personal, Practical, Spiritual. Her eyes blurred as she read the words that sent a knife through her soul.

Personal

Well, this is the night before the big day. I can't wait to say I do. I know Kinkaide's love is forever. Every day our love grows and I can't wait to begin our new life together. I am a little nervous. Okay, I'm a lot nervous. This is a big step, a once-in-a-lifetime deal, the biggest day of my life.

Mom has called three times in the last hour. She wants to come down, but I insisted we'll be just fine. Kinkaide and I want this to be simple and private—something between me and him. Honestly, I'm already a nervous wreck. Having Mom here would just make matters worse. I know she loves me, but at times I wonder if it's too much!

Practical

The button popped off my wedding dress. I've poked my index finger three times trying to sew it back on. Here I am, learning to sew up patients and I can't even sew a button on. I've packed and repacked so many times I've lost count. The honeymoon has to be perfect, and I want to make sure I have all the right stuff together. I'm nervous about our first night together. Now I'm back to personal stuff. Oh, well, my index finger is stinging, and the button still isn't on the dress.

Spiritual

I feel closer to God than I ever have. My father taught me that God is a fact. All I need to do is believe He exists because He does. But experiencing Kinkaide's love is opening a new realm for me. As mentioned yesterday, I've started a new Bible study—one Kinkaide and I plan to continue together after we're married. The Word of God is really coming to life for me. I've noticed that the New Testament talks about Christ as the bridegroom and the church as the bride. Yes, I believe that God is a fact, but I'm also beginning to sense a new dose of grace and love that I never really connected with before. Kinkaide has encouraged me in my spiritual growth. I thank God that He has put such a godly man in my life.

Melissa turned the page. The entry for the next day was a collection of bold black slashes accompanied by a scramble of scribbling. The rest of the pages were empty. She snapped shut the journal.

For the first time in her life, Mel had given her heart wholly and completely to another...another who pointed her toward Jesus Christ and a closer walk with Him. Now, Mel reminisced about those months of spiritual growth. Looking back, she wondered if she had been on the verge of some spectacular spiritual breakthrough. A breakthrough that never happened. When Kinkaide turned his back on Mel, she distanced herself from everything he held dear—including God.

Just because Kinkaide turned his back on me, doesn't mean Christ did. The thought rushed upon Mel like the sweet waters of a sparkling mountain brook. Her spirit longed for the knowledge of God's presence. The weeks before her wedding she had been close, so close, to believing that God's factual existence did indeed intersect the realities of her life with a grace, love, and mercy far beyond her human comprehension. But the rancor that invaded her soul after Kinkaide's desertion had obliterated all sensitivity about the things of God.

Mel searched for a means to journey back to the green pastures and still waters, a place where her soul would find restoration. She sensed that the path back to that land was narrow—so narrow there wasn't room for any excess baggage. In order to feel the Lord's green pastures beneath her feet and experience the freshness of His calm waters, Mel would have to shove her bundle of bitterness off a cliff and never return for it. Yet the bitterness was bound to her back by unyielding cords of unforgiveness. To release the pain, Melissa would have to forgive Kinkaide.

She clenched her fist, dropped the journal atop the ring box, and slammed the drawer shut.

Eleven

Horace Waggoner pulled his Ford into a parking place on the church's east lot. He put the car in park, turned off the ignition switch, then eyed the megachurch, aglow with lights that penetrated winter's darkness. Several clumps of people ambled from the parking lot and entered through glass doors. The Wednesday night activities started in 15 minutes.

A group of laughing teens neared from behind his car, and Horace swiveled to scrutinize the group. As they passed, he gripped the steering wheel with unsteady hands and searched for the Casper twins. Sure enough, the two girls hung at the back of the group and shared a furtive whisper. Horace's pulse increased; his mind raced. His thumbs, resting against the horn, spasmodically flexed, and the horn produced a brief blare. Horace jumped and uttered an oath. The band of teens squealed then giggled. A few of them glanced toward Horace, and he slumped into the seat.

"Great," he griped as he added this goof-up to the list of details Lenora would never learn.

Lenora and Sara awaited him at a nearby hotel. All Horace had to do was convince the girls to go with him. Simple enough. But his stomach's telltale burn did little to convince him of his pending success. Horace pulled an antacid from his shirt pocket, unwrapped it, and popped the medicine into his mouth. He tossed the wrapper onto the floorboard then chewed the mint-flavored pill.

When Julie and Janie Casper were about 50 feet from the glassed entry, Horace opened the car door, climbed out, and glanced toward the backseat. The dome light cast an eerie glow across the tattered interior. A glow that sent a shiver down Horace's spine. The floorboards and seats were now clear of all clutter. The girls had plenty of room. Horace checked to make sure the doors were unlocked. With a faint click, he pressed the door shut. A swift glance behind the car verified that no vehicle blocked a speedy exit.

All is in order.

Horace sucked in a lungful of the frigid air and slowly expelled a white cloud of breath that hovered as if it were a specter bidding him to retrace his steps. He stopped and glanced toward the twins. They reached the glass doors. Fingers trembling, Horace fumbled with his keys. They fell from his grasp and clattered onto the asphalt. Janie and Julie stepped into the foyer. The doors closed behind them, and the girls paused to speak to a couple of teenage boys. Horace bent, scooped up the keys, then crammed them into his pocket.

He lunged forward and quickly spanned the distance to the glass doors. Horace turned up the collar of his denim jacket, stepped into the spacious lobby, and began weighing his options. Perhaps he should bide his time. If he waited until the service was over, his plan had a better chance of success. The twins would undoubtedly be missed if he pulled them away now. Furthermore, in the confusion of the crowd's dispersing, no one would notice his bundling the girls into his car.

Surrounded by animated teenage interaction, Horace skulked past Janie and Julie toward the sanctuary. A scrupulous glance through swinging doors attested to the sanctuary's vacancy. Horace slipped through the windowed doors and into the dimly lit meeting place. A hallowed shimmer bathed the padded pews, fresh flowers, and grand piano in a reverent radiance that challenged Horace's detestable deed.

Crossing his arms, he leaned against the wall by the doorway and tried to use the podium to block out the glimpse of the baptismal cubicle. When he was 11, Horace had made a profession of faith. At age 12, he had been baptized to the accompaniment of his mother's gentle weeping. His mother, rest her soul, would have grieved his present choices. His teeth on edge, Horace peered through the windows and picked out Julie and Janie in the crowd. From this vantage point, he could remain undetected then follow the twins as they went to their designated meeting place.

As if fighting an unseen force, Horace peered at the baptismal. The cubicle riveted his gaze while a sense of dread scampered across rigid shoulders.

I can still back out.

The thought pierced his schemes, and Horace mulled over the concept. But there was Sara to consider. Sara and Lenora. Lenora...Lenora...Lenora. The reverberation of her name evoked images of a serpent's deadly eyes. If she would arrange to kidnap the daughters of her former lover, no telling what she might do to him or, even worse, to Sara. Then there was his father. His death hadn't swept away the lifetime of censure heaped upon Horace. His face heated with the shame of a child who could never please his dad. The ransom money would surely prove Horace's worth once and for all. The baptismal's spell disintegrated.

Horace steeled himself against further diversions and focused solely on Janie and Julie Casper.

"I hope this is the right move." Desmond slammed the door on the gold Mercedes and peered across the top at Kinkaide.

Kinkaide closed the passenger door and produced the most assuring smile he could muster. "You've got to start somewhere," he said, then gazed past the lighted parking lot toward the large church in an attempt to hide his own misgivings.

Desmond had stayed in Oklahoma City Monday and most of Tuesday. This morning, Kinkaide followed him to Dallas to provide moral support for the strategy they had mulled over for two days. The plan was simple. Desmond would take his girls home from the Wednesday night service, then convince Abby to talk with him about the cruise and, perhaps, a reconciliation. Both friends hoped that Kinkaide's presence would influence her acceptance. The two men had prayed over the plan and agreed that Desmond needed a miracle.

As they traipsed across the lot, a winter's chill crept up Kinkaide's spine. The traffic's omnipresent roar seemed to echo that Desmond wasn't the only one who needed a miracle. Mel once again was not returning Kinkaide's phone calls.

In deference to Desmond's plight, Kinkaide shoved all images of Melissa from his mind. He peered toward the church's glassed foyer and noticed a familiar pair of teens. "Hey, I think I see your girls just inside."

"Where?" Desmond asked like a man starved for the faintest glimpse of his daughters.

"Right there." Kinkaide slowed, grabbed Desmond's forearm, and pointed toward Janie and Julie. "They're talking to that tall, blond boy."

"Should I approach them now?" Desmond asked.

"Sure. Why not? That way they'll know you'll be waiting for them after church."

The cluster of teens, as if by group consensus, walked from the foyer and disappeared around a corner.

"Let's go," Desmond said, rushing toward the entryway.

Kinkaide joined his friend and jogged to the lobby. They swept through the doors and into the church's welcoming warmth. The familiar smells of hymnals and furniture oil urged Kinkaide forward as he followed Desmond toward the corner. The hallway, curving around the octagonal sanctuary, was empty. Distant conversation attested to the group's nearness.

"They're usually in the gym on Wednesday nights," Desmond said. "It's around the corner, fifth door on the left."

"Let's go," Kinkaide urged.

"Desmond?" a deep, male voice thundered from behind.

The two swiveled to face a wiry man whose frame in no way matched his voice. With a welcoming smile, he approached Desmond and extended his hand. "Great to see you."

"Same here." Desmond pumped the man's hand then turned to Kinkaide. "This is my pastor, Henry Waits. Brother Waits, my friend, Kinkaide Franklin."

"Nice to meet you," Kinkaide said.

Pastor Waits acknowledged Kinkaide with a brief handshake then focused on his parishioner. He adjusted his stylish tie and pointed a thumb over his shoulder. "I was just heading to the hearth room where we're having our Wednesday-night Bible study. Care to join us?"

"Actually..." Desmond hedged, "I was trying to track down my girls."

"Ahh." The minister nodded as if he understood all too well. "I haven't seen you around in a week or so, although I did notice Abby last Sunday. How are things?"

Desmond glanced down at his leather loafers. "Abby insisted I move out last week."

"I was afraid of that." Pastor Waits shook his head, his eyes void of censure. "You know my offer of counseling still stands."

"I've tried to get Abby to agree, but..." Desmond grimaced and gripped the base of his neck.

Kinkaide, grappling with whether or not to speak, toyed with the zipper of his leather jacket.

"Actually, I'm going to take my girls home tonight and see if Abby will at least talk with me."

"I'm along for moral support," Kinkaide added with an uncertain smile.

The minister glanced up at Kinkaide and, for the first time, seemed to see him. Initially a puzzled frown crossed his face, then his eyes widened. "Kinkaide Franklin...are you the *pianist* Kinkaide Franklin?"

"In the flesh."

"Wow! So nice to meet you." Pastor Waits shook Kinkaide's hand all over again. "Desmond, I had no idea you knew—"

"I don't tell many people." Desmond chuckled. "I don't want to ruin my reputation or anything."

Kinkaide rolled his eyes as the pastor snickered. "Apparently the two of you have been friends awhile."

"Seems like ages," Kinkaide groaned.

Pastor Waits checked his watch. "It's time to start. They're going to send a posse for me if I don't head that way." He backed away and gave a friendly wave. "Come to the hearth room once you connect with Julie and Janie."

Desmond produced a "why not" shrug and glanced at Kinkaide for confirmation.

"Sure," Kinkaide said.

"We'll be there soon," Desmond affirmed.

Horace followed the twins down the hallway and was the last person to step into the gym, which throbbed with contemporary Christian music. The smell of basketballs, the squeak of sneakers on hardwood floors, the chatter of adolescence brought back more memories than he cared to deal with.

"Okay, guys, everybody find a seat," a female voice called over an unseen speaker. The group meandered to several rows of padded chairs sitting in front of a portable platform. Behind the podium stood a jeans-clad woman, about 30, who acted as if she were in charge.

After an examination of the whole gym, Horace noticed a door to the far left with a red exit sign above it. To the right, he saw another door that resembled a closet's entry. A glassed-in office protruded out between the closet door and the teen's gathering. The group's view of the closet was blocked. He cast a surreptitious glance toward the group, and his gaze locked with the group's leader. Her brows knotted, and Horace gulped.

Schooling his features into a decisive mask, Horace strode the few feet to the closet, opened the door, stepped inside, and shut it. The smell of cleaning supplies, dust, and fresh paint greeted him. Hopefully, the youth director would assume he was on an approved mission. He cringed and listened for approaching footsteps. The music, talking teens, and leader's voice through the speakers never abated. He glanced around the closet.

Might as well stay in here until the end, he decided. The closet provided a perfect hiding place.

He found and flipped the light switch, which verified he had entered a janitor's storage room. Behind him, a heavy-duty floor polisher stood among a collection of buckets, mops, and brooms. The unfinished shelves, lined with bottles of cleaning paraphernalia, also held a row of stained paint cans. One can, just above Horace's head, was open. A paint brush protruded from it, and the lid lay on a shelf nearby.

Horace stiffened. He retrieved the can, peered inside, gripped the brush handle and stirred the fluid paint. His attention moved past the paint, down to his feet, and to a bucket full of sudsy water. Horace replaced the paint can, bent, and inserted his index finger into the warm liquid. Stifling an oath, he straightened. For the first time, he perceived that several shelves were bare and sported a fresh coat of cream-colored paint. Horace ran a finger along a shelf and picked up a generous smudge of paint. He snapped off the light. Someone had just left the warm mop water and opened paint can. Someone who might return soon.

The music diminished. A woman's voice became prominent. Horace weighed his options. The best alternative might be to slip from the closet, hover close to the wall, then walk back into the hallway. Horace could easily wait in one of the empty rooms until the kids began trickling out of the gym.

What if the Casper twins use the exit on the far side of the gym?

Horace twisted the knob and inched open the door. He scrutinized the far exit and noted what he had missed during his first perusal—the words "Fire Escape Only" across the center of the door. He released a pent-up breath and closed the door. The handle produced a faint click, and he jumped. The click paled in the wake of a new crash of music and the raucous voices of energized youth.

Now's as good a time as any. He reopened the door and prepared to slink out of the gym. But the gym door, mere feet away, whipped open and two men stepped inside. Horace's eyes widened. His fingers gripped the doorknob. He held his breath, then shut the door.

Desmond Casper is here! What's he doing here? How can I tell the twins there's an emergency with their father if he's here? They won't go with me! The plan is ruined!

Horace slammed his palm against his forehead. In doing so, his fingers clobbered the base of the open paint bucket. The container tilted forward and belched forth a veil of cream-colored liquid. With a cringe, Horace held up his hands and closed his eyes. The paint splashed upon his hair and face, creating an odious mask. The paint tin clattered to the floor. He gasped and lunged backward as a foul taste assaulted his taste buds. The fumes sent a dizzy rush upon his brain, and he gulped for clean air. The closet door whipped open. Horace scrubbed unsteady fingers along heavy eyelids. Through a blur of paint clinging to droopy lashes he encountered two portly men dressed in janitors' khakis and holding soda cans. The two stared wide-eyed at Horace, then one blurted, "What are you doing in—"

With a grunt, Horace shoved past both men and bolted from the closet. As he lunged forward, his boot caught the handle of the mop bucket. The careening pail pitched forth an abundance of sudsy water. Horace slipped across the soapy liquid then sprawled forward. With a splat, his hands smashed upon the unyielding floor. His chin crashed against wood, and Horace's teeth ground into his tongue. The taste of blood mingled with paint, and his horrified holler ricocheted across the gym pulsating with music. Horace skidded to within feet of Desmond and his companion then scrambled to right himself.

"Are you okay?" Desmond asked, extending a hand.

Ignoring the proffered assistance, Horace struggled to his feet and bolted for the hall doorway.

"Hey, stop!" one janitor called. "Stop right now!"

Horace raced up the hallway, dripping paint and water with every step. He whizzed around the corner, smacked into an elderly lady, and knocked her over. A cascade of papers flew upward as pain-filled, feminine screams jolted his nerves.

"Stop now, you brute, or I'm calling the police!"

The janitor's voice faded as Horace, straining for every breath, dashed through the foyer and collided with the glass doors. They slammed open, and he ran into the darkness. With every step, the cold air sent a drying rush upon his damp clothing and his cheeks, laden with paint, began to tighten. Horace reached his vehicle, tumbled inside, crammed the keys into the ignition, and started the car. The engine came to life with a sputter. He slammed the Ford into reverse and sped from the parking lot. A last glance in his rearview mirror revealed the overweight janitors racing out of the church. Horace expelled a gush of air. *Not a chance for vehicle identification.*

The private detective steered toward I-30, where Lenora and Sara waited. The Holiday Inn loomed in the distance, yet he passed the appropriate exit, rubbed his paint-smeared fingers against his jeans, and reached for the cell phone. This recent fiasco must remain a secret! The hotel's sign dimmed in the distance. Horace determined to remove all vestiges of the paint before showing his face to either woman. With the fumes still tormenting him and his tongue swiftly swelling, he dialed the hotel and maneuvered the car around a string of slower vehicles. The signs clipped by on the lighted freeway as he asked for Lenora's room.

"Where are you?" she bit out as soon as he identified himself.

"Tonight's pwan was a wash." Horace used the most steely voice he could muster, despite his tongue's throbbing. Every time he opened his lips the taste of paint tainted his taste buds all the more. "Desmond showed up with a fwiend just before I was going to make a pway for the girls." He forced himself not to spit.

"What?" Lenora drilled.

"I said—"

"I heard you," she snapped. "And you better not be lying!"

"I'm not wying," Horace growled then grimaced as new paint seeped into his mouth. Never had he been so forceful with Lenora, but desperate situations required desperate measures.

"Are you okay? Your voice seems—"

"I'm fwine." He swallowed, his tongue throbbed, and he attempted to control his speech. "Must be the connecwion.

I'm going home. I've got another...probwem to deaw with. Can you take Sawa home?"

Lenora's meaningful pause gave Horace ample time to imagine her eyebrow's disdainful arch.

"Pwea—" He cleared his throat and forced himself to enunciate. "Please."

"Okay." The word came out as if it were wrenched from a throat tight with irritation. "But we're going to have to devise a new plan. And soon."

"Not tonight," Horace insisted. "We'w talk tomowow."

"Are you sure everything's okay?" Lenora demanded. "You don't sound like yourself. Are you hiding something from me?"

"No." Without giving her a chance to respond, he pressed the end button and tossed the cell phone onto the passenger seat. A shower of spit erupted from Horace, and he gagged. His eyes watered as he strained to maintain focus on the road.

You're nothin' but a crazy klutz! Victor Waggoner's life-long accusation blasted through Horace's mind and he groaned. Then he envisioned that million dollars and the paternal respect the money would have bought. The approaching Dallas skyline blazed with a shimmer of lights. Perhaps tonight's escapade wasn't as detrimental to the scheme as Horace had first thought. The paint, while proving to be rather displeasing, had completely concealed Horace's identity. He was still free to pursue the kidnapping. Free to forever obliterate his father's censure.

Twelve

Kinkaide knelt beside the petite Oriental lady with Desmond at his side. She looked as if she were well past the age where a fall was of little magnitude.

"Are you okay?" Kinkaide asked, laying a gentle hand on her shoulder as she fumbled to shove her skirt over her bony knees.

"I think I am," she said, groping to adjust her crooked glasses. "Who was that man? He had something all over his face."

"We have no idea," Desmond said. "But I'd say by the smell of things that he somehow got into some paint."

"Oh." She blinked. "You're Desmond Casper."

Desmond smiled. "Yes. And aren't you Mrs. Tang?"

"Yes."

"You teach the threes on Wednesday nights, don't you?"

She nodded and beamed. Mrs. Tang reached for Desmond's hand, and he and Kinkaide steadied her as she stood.

"There. I think I'll be fine."

The janitors returned from the foyer, their cheeks red. "We lost him," the shorter one said. His shirt bore the name Mark Fiest.

"I'm going to call the police," the older janitor remarked. "But first I'm going to see if anything's missing from the office or the closet." He trotted up the hallway.

"Are you okay, Mrs. Tang?" Fiest asked. The top of his bald head bore several pinpoints of paint.

"Yes…yes, I'm fine, thanks to these two gentlemen." She peered up at Kinkaide through thick glasses. "I don't believe I've met you."

"I'm just a friend of Desmond," Kinkaide said. "I don't live here."

Fiest began retrieving Mrs. Tang's scattered papers. The elderly lady fussed over the coloring pages and turned her attention to the janitor.

"Well, who knows what that was all about." Kinkaide dashed at a few soap bubbles clinging to the front of his twill slacks.

"Beats me." Desmond rubbed at the liquid that stained his all-weather jacket and edged up the hallway.

"Probably just a street person trying to get warm," Fiest said. "I'll call the police—just in case."

"I guess there's nothing more for us to do," Kinkaide said.

Desmond nodded toward the gym door. "Come on."

The two men entered the gym and found themselves the recipients of teenage scrutiny. The group had stopped singing in deference to the excitement at the back of the gym. With a shake of his head, Kinkaide sidestepped the water puddle and followed Desmond toward the restless group. They had progressed only a few feet when a duet of "Dad!" echoed across the gym. The identical twins broke away from the group, raced toward their father, and flung themselves into his arms.

"Wow! What a greeting!" The rhythmical cadence of his rich voice took on a doting undertone. "The last time I showed up at one of these gatherings you barely acknowledged my presence."

"We've missed you so much," Janie said, her braces flashing with every word.

"Are you coming back home tonight?" Julie asked. "Please say yes, oh please." Her dark, cropped hair distinguished her from her sister, who always preferred French braid corn-rows.

The hair was the only distinguishing factor that clued Kinkaide to their identities. The twins, indistinguishable in every other aspect, possessed their mother's wide-set, exotic eyes, their father's prominent nose, and the full lips of their African ancestors. Their skin, like flawless bronze, probably left them the envy of more than one of their female peers. While neither of the girls was a raging beauty, both promised to turn more heads than any father would be comfortable with, and both carried themselves with classy grace that spoke of a good upbringing.

Desmond, an arm around each daughter, pulled them close and exchanged a solemn gaze with his friend. Kinkaide shot a prayer heavenward. Hopefully, absence had made Abby's heart grow a bit fonder as well.

"I just wanted to let you guys know that I'm here, and I will take you home tonight if you'd like," Desmond said as the rowdy youth group grew more boisterous.

"Oh, sure." Julie tucked her bobbed hair behind her ear.

"Yes," Janie echoed. "We can leave now, if you like."

"Mom's at home," Julie said. "I'm sure she'd be glad to see you." A worried light flickered in the depths of her dark eyes. A light that begged for unity. A light that wrenched Kinkaide's heart.

Whew! Does Desmond have problems or what?

"Oh, Dad," Janie breathed, "when are you going to come back home? It's awful not having you there."

"Your mom and I have some things we need to work out," Desmond said, then bestowed lingering kisses on both their foreheads.

"Let's go now," the girls said in unison. They rushed back to their seats, grabbed their purses, and rejoined their father. Several of the kids observed their departure, but Janie and Julie were totally focused on their dad.

"We need to tell Frani you're leaving," Desmond said as they neared the youth director and Mr. Fiest.

"Frani, we're going home early—with Dad!" Julie called, and the youth director turned toward them.

"Sorry to disturb your service, Frani," Desmond said.

"No problem." The stocky youth director shrugged. "It's already been disturbed." She waved toward the pool of sudsy water.

The older janitor came out of the glassed-in office, and Kinkaide noted his badge bore the name Jeb Darr. "I've called the police," the worker snapped. "I don't think anything's missing. I can't imagine what that nut was doing in the closet. And how in the world he managed to get paint all over himself is beyond me."

"The hallway has drops of paint all over the place," Fiest said. "We're going to have to reclean the whole thing."

"So do you think it's safe to resume the service?" Frani asked.

"Yes, yes, go ahead." Jeb waved his beefy hand. "The nut's gone. By the looks of things, he ain't comin' back."

"See ya later, girls." Frani winked. They called an excited "goodbye," and Kinkaide followed them and Desmond out of the gym.

"Should we leave a note for your pastor?" Kinkaide asked as they entered the hallway. "We promised him we'd join the Bible study."

"Oh, right." Desmond stroked his thin mustache. "I completely forgot about that."

"Mrs. Waits is supposed to take us home, too," Janie said. "We need to let her know we're leaving early so she won't worry about us."

"Where's the pastor's office?" Kinkaide asked. "I could drop a note on his desk, if you like, and ask him to tell his wife that you're taking the girls home as well."

"Okay, sure. Keep following this hallway." Desmond pointed forward. "Pass the sanctuary. The hall wraps around the other side. His office is the third door on the right, after the last sanctuary door."

"Gotcha. You go on and get the girls in the car. I'll be out soon."

"Great. I'll pull the car around and be waiting out front." Desmond, arm-in-arm with his daughters, started toward the foyer then stopped. "Why not add a special prayer request on that note?"

With a smile, Kinkaide gave the thumbs-up sign and strode around the sanctuary. He soon found the door marked pastor's office and tentatively tapped on it. No one answered, so he opened the door and stepped into an ante-room that bore the faint smell of coffee. Shelves lined the walls. A copy machine claimed one corner. A small desk, burdened with a computer, fax machine, and printer, took up the center of the room.

Kinkaide stepped toward another door and peeked through the glass wall into what appeared to be the pastor's study. A massive oak desk sat in front of a floor-to-ceiling bookshelf, and a computer occupied a place on a table near the desk. Kinkaide turned the knob, but it didn't budge.

"Figures," he muttered then swiveled toward the secretary's desk. He grabbed the first pad and pen he saw, scribbled a brief message, then added, "P.S. Pray hard!" Kinkaide folded the yellow paper and wrote "Pastor Waits" on the outside. He taped the note to the office door and exited.

As the door closed behind him, Kinkaide glanced up to encounter a sizable bulletin board across the hallway he hadn't noticed upon entering. In the center of the board, a classy red poster snared his attention. "Shelby Canady in Concert" the gold-toned caption read. In the middle, a picture of the honey-haired Shelby with a gold cross behind her invited all to join the musician in praising God. The concert's dates and specifics were listed at the bottom.

From nowhere an explosion of guilt ricocheted through Kinkaide's midsection. Guilt and regret. Regret and memories. Memories of that day Shelby found Mel's photo on his piano....

"Who is this?" she had asked, her blue eyes wary as she read Mel's loving inscription across the bottom of the picture.

Kinkaide picked up the photo and examined his former fiancée. He hadn't intended for the singer to see the picture. He had planned for a smoother way to ease out of the relationship with as little pain as possible. "Her name is Melissa Moore." He hesitated then decided to simply state the truth. "We were once engaged."

"Oh?" Shelby crossed her arms. "And has she come back into your life?"

Kinkaide dared hold her gaze. A gaze that suggested she already knew the answer and didn't like it. "Not exactly."

"What does 'not exactly' mean?" she asked, drawing imaginary quotes around the words. "Either you're seeing her behind my back or you aren't."

"I'm not seeing her at the moment." He shrugged, then continued with the truth. "I think I'm still in love with her."

An ashen pall crept up Shelby's face. "What?" she gasped as droplets of crystal-like tears oozed onto her lashes.

Kinkaide paced across the spartan room. A room of uncomplicated lines with understated elegance. A room that bespoke his penchant for turning simplicity into a masterpiece—exemplified even in his music. His knees, decidedly unsteady, threatened to buckle beneath him. Kinkaide stopped pacing and plopped onto the edge of an over-stuffed, taupe sofa. He placed his elbows on his knees and leaned forward.

Shelby's soft footfalls stopped nearby. "But I thought one day, we would…"

Kinkaide stared at her thick-heeled shoes for several seconds then glanced up. Shelby's arms clutched her midsection, and she held herself as if she would collapse at any given moment.

"I thought maybe, too," Kinkaide affirmed. "But…" He stood and reached for her.

She backed away and waved him off.

"No…don't…don't…"

"I'm sorry, Shelby," Kinkaide said. "I never meant for you to…for this conversation to happen like this. I…I just can't seem to get her out of my head these last few weeks. It's like—it's almost like she's haunting me."

"Like I never have?" Shelby whispered, and the glistening tears splashed from burdened lashes to trickle down her fine-boned cheeks.

Kinkaide closed his eyes and shook his head. "I never once intended to hurt you. If I had known this was going to happen, I would have never asked you out the first time."

"Have you contacted her?"

"No."

"Then how do you know there's any hope for—"

"I don't. But it's time you knew the truth. I meant to hide that photo before you got here, but I was going to try to tell you today, anyway. It's just not fair to you for me to—"

"I'll tell you what's not fair!" Shelby ripped a dainty gold chain from her neck and hurled the diamond pendant at him. The necklace struck Kinkaide's chest and fell at his feet in a tiny, glittering heap. "It's not fair to lead a woman on and make her think—"

"But I never meant to lead you on. That was *not* my intention. *Ever!*" He shook his head. "You're the first woman I've even had a relationship with since her. I thought—I thought I was over her, but the more serious you and I became, the more I thought of her. I finally realized..." Kinkaide groaned. "I didn't mean for all this to happen this way, believe me. I meant to—"

"What? To let me down gently?" She snatched a strand of blonde hair away from her glossy lips. "And since when do you believe that a woman in love can be let down gently?" Shelby scoffed.

Helplessly, Kinkaide stared at her. Never had he felt so inept. Then he remembered the day Melissa handed him her engagement ring. That day had definitely topped this one.

The blurry red poster came into focus. Shelby's flawless face. The gold lettering. The cross in the background. The image of the woman he had rejected.

"Boy, do I know how to blow it with the fairer sex," he murmured. Briefly, he wondered about Shelby—how she was doing and if she still wanted to drop kick him through the nearest goalpost. "And maybe I deserve it," he whispered. *I should have never started a relationship with her. I don't even remember praying about it.* The golden cross relentlessly grabbed his focus. *I just liked what I saw and went after her. After all, she was a Christian, and she liked me right back.* "But what a mess that turned into," he whispered.

With a shake of his head, Kinkaide took several steps away until a new thought pierced his soul and stopped him in his tracks. *I never prayed about pursuing Mel again, either. I just knew what I wanted and went after her.* The realization struck him like a blow to the chest. The memory of those

Sunday morning moments in front of that cross at church plunged into his mind. *Love is patient, love is kind. It does not envy, it does not boast, it is not proud. It is not rude, it is not self-seeking.* Again, the poster's cross beckoned. Kinkaide pivoted and felt as if he were being tugged into the very center of that symbol of salvation.

Do I really love Mel or am I just in love with having what I want?

The question, unexpected and unyielding, bore upon him like a bolt of lightning, threatening to illuminate his soul's every flaw. Flaws Kinkaide preferred not to see. Flaws he needed to run from. He sprinted up the hallway.

Desmond awaited him.

Desmond had *serious* problems.

Desmond needed his support—*now*.

"I'm sorry, Detective Lightfoot, I've got some bad news," Sheriff Solomon said.

Jac's fingers tightened on the receiver, and she stared at the rumpled Rolodex card atop her desk.

"You were right in tracking the Wilson girl here to El Paso County. We picked up the lead you passed to us and found her."

"You found her." Jac's words reflected the numbness that swiftly spread across her soul.

"Yes. Or, well, we found her remains."

Rubbing her forehead, Jac groaned. The overstuffed bookcase across the room seemed to tilt. "Are you sure it's her. I mean...you haven't had time for DNA testing."

"There was a gold bracelet in the grave with the name Tammy Wilson on it. We have the perpetrator in custody. He's confessed that the motive was sexual assault, and..."

the sheriff's weighty pause heightened Jac's curiosity, "...he's her uncle."

"Oh, no," she breathed, and the chair opposite her desk swam in a pool of tears. Her stomach queasy, Jacquelyn spent the next ten minutes retrieving the details the parents would want to know. But the whole time, she wondered how she would inform them that a family member was most likely the kidnapper and killer. Her voice flat, she bid a final farewell then slammed the telephone receiver back on its cradle.

A vein of hot lava spewed from the bottom of her spirit. She snatched the answering system from the desk and hurled it across her office. The phone sailed only as far as the wall jack allowed then toppled to the floor. With a roar, Jac slammed her fist against her desk then dragged her arm across the top. Papers, pens, and family photos clattered to the floor. She whirled to kick her desk chair. It toppled backward with a rattle of wheels. Jac, her chest heaving, collapsed against the wall and pounded tight fists against hard wood until bullets of pain shot up her wrists.

"Why, why, why, oh God, why?" she sobbed, crumpling into a heap of whimpering humanity.

A hand touched her shoulder, and Jac went rigid. A large hand. A scaly hand. The hand of the dragon. As in her dreams, Jac shrank away from the fiend. Then she stopped and reminded herself she was no longer nine. She was no longer a victim like Tammy Wilson.

The primeval growl of a survivor erupted from her. Jac whirled on the dragon and went for his throat. The beast roared. She sprawled him upon her desk and prepared to...

"Jac! Jac! Stop! Stop it! Oh, Lord, tell her to stop! Stop, Jac! It's me...it's me, Donna!"

The detective eased her hold, and for the first time truly focused upon the one lying beneath her hands. "Donna?" she rasped, taking in the panicked hazel eyes of her middle-aged secretary. Jacquelyn backed away and gazed at her trembling hands.

Donna, her breathing unsteady, shook her head, rubbed her neck, and righted herself. "My word! What's gotten into you?"

Jac covered her face as harsh reality threatened to shove her over the edge. "Tammy Wilson...they found her." She lowered her hands and mutely observed the plump woman who had been as much a mother figure as a secretary.

"And..." Donna shoved a pin back into her sagging bun as if being attacked by her boss were all in a day's work.

"She's dead," Jac choked out. "They found her in El Paso County, where I lost the trail, and she was buried in her uncle's yard. They also suspect sexual assault."

With a moan, Donna placed her fingertips on her lips and shook her head.

"I've about had all I can stand. I can't take any more!" Jac determined to stay any new tears.

Donna blinked as if Jac were speaking Bulgarian.

A warm tingle, like the hot breath of a pernicious dragon, raced up Jac's spine. And the fiend's satisfied chuckle resonated from behind. Desperate to prove no dragon hovered near, Jacquelyn leaned against the wall.

Donna continued her blank-eyed stare. "I've never seen you like this before," she finally said. "And I'm not really certain what to say, but honestly, Jac, you really don't look good. I've noticed you've been kind of quiet the last few weeks, but I'm beginning to wonder if—"

As her knees weakened, Jac groped for the padded chair. She righted the chair then sank into it. "I don't think I can work for a while," Jac squeezed out, finally admitting what she had suspected for over a week. "Can you clear my schedule for a month—maybe two?"

"Yes. Yes, of course. Perhaps this is the time to call my nephew. Like I said, he'd make a great partner for you."

"Okay, call him," Jac rasped. "And—and while you're at it, call my friend Melissa Moore. Ask her if I can come visit for awhile."

"Isn't she the doctor?"

"Yes." Jac knitted her brows and strained to concentrate. "Good."

"P—please arrange the first flight tomorrow…um, one way. I've got to get out of here."

Something had to change in Jac's life or she was going to go crazy. The last two nights that detestable dragon had chased her until sunup. She had snatched only a couple hours sleep both nights. The idea of spending another night alone in her tiny apartment increased her anxiety tenfold. Thoughts of the dream hurled her mind into that dreaded sphere where the winged creature, his eyes ablaze with lust, awaited her. Once again she was a nine-year-old frozen upon the threshold of golden light with that fanged brute salivating over her.

Donna adjusted her double-knit vest and leaned against Jac's desk. "You've been working like a mad woman the whole five years I've been with you. And I don't remember a week when you got enough sleep."

Jac watched Donna's lips move, but she barely registered the words. Instead, a little girl's voice rang through her mind. *I don't want to know. Please. Please. No, I don't want to know. I don't. I don't.* Jac leaned forward and covered her face with her hands. A shower of sparkling light reached for her and Jac shrank from the revealing shafts.

No, no, don't! Don't, don't! No, please don't! Not again! Noooooooooooooo!

"Oh, God, help me," Jac groaned while a wave of nausea rushed up her throat. As if on cue, Donna's hand appeared attached to a trash can. Jac heaved, and with every retch the golden aura penetrated her resistance to illuminate a past where the dragon bore the image of a man. A man her parents had trusted. A man she had loved in her innocence.

Thirteen

Kinkaide followed Desmond and the twins onto the wrap-around porch that invited all to enter the spacious home on the outskirts of Richardson. The house, a showplace of country living, could have posed as the penultimate model for any number of magazines. Ironically, the family who owned the home was deteriorating—and fast. The stars, pinpoints of light in an inky sky, seemed as distant as Desmond's chances of a reconciliation.

Breathing a prayer, Kinkaide stepped past the beveled glass door and onto polished hardwood floors. The scent of mulberries and homemade cookies filled the foyer in a house that bore no evidence of the habitation of two teenagers. Kinkaide cast a surreptitious glance toward the formal dining room to the right and the den to the left. Abby Casper's philosophy of housekeeping hadn't changed a bit since Kinkaide first met her. She made certain the hired staff kept her home looking like a furniture store. Kinkaide hoped he didn't track in any dirt.

"Mom, we're home," the girls called in unison.

Abby, her plump face alight with a smile, walked through the dining room, toward the foyer. From where he stood, Kinkaide had the advantage of examining her without detection.

"Yes, I saw you drive up," Abby began, "and there's cookies in the—" She stepped from the dining room, focused on Desmond, and stopped. Her smile faded. Her dark eyes, shrouded in the dense fog of mourning, took on

131

the sharp edge of a rapier. "What are you doing here?" she snapped, never once noticing Kinkaide.

The twins' restless attempts to shed their coats ceased.

"I live here, remember?" Desmond softly challenged.

Kinkaide shifted his feet and produced a discreet cough. Abby cast a brief glimpse toward him, back to Desmond, then rested her attention on Kinkaide.

"Hello." Her eyes failed to reflect the faint smile.

"Hi." Kinkaide admired the tilt of Abby's large, dark eyes but appreciated even more the character of the woman within. Many women only dreamed of possessing the charm, grace, and dignity of Desmond's wife. Even though the years had added significant pounds to her big-boned frame, Abby carried herself like a queen. And for the first time since Desmond had shared his plight, Kinkaide wanted to thump his friend's head and demand to know why he had cheated on a woman like his Abby.

"Great to see you again," Kinkaide continued as Abby bestowed the typical southern hug granted to all close friends.

"You, too," Abby said, her voice tight.

Julie and Janie, hovering at the base of the massive stairway, took in the detail of every movement, as if thirsting for any hint that their father might be coming home for good.

"Can we talk, Abby?" Desmond asked.

She glanced toward her daughters then stared past Desmond.

"We *have* talked."

Desmond peered at Kinkaide with a pleading *do something* look in his eyes.

"Uh…" Kinkaide crammed his hands into his pleated slacks and verbalized the first words that came to mind. "I invited you, Desmond, and the girls on a cruise and—"

"A cruise! A cruise!" Julie and Janie exploded.

"And did you accept for us, Desmond?" Abby crossed her arms, and her elegant sweater swayed around her knees.

"Well…"

"Because, if you did, my answer is no. I told you, I want a di—" She cut herself short and looked at her frolicking twins. "The last thing I want right now is to go on a cruise," she leveled at him. "If you want to take Janie and Julie, that's your choice, but—"

"Abby, if you'll just listen to me." Desmond stepped toward her.

"I *have* listened." Abby's voice rose as she took a controlled step backward. "And I've heard all I want to hear."

The twins stilled, and the three adults simultaneously glanced toward them.

"Why don't you guys go check out the cookies?" Desmond suggested.

"Sounds like a plan to me," Kinkaide said, thrilled for any excuse to distance himself from the charged encounter.

He followed the girls toward the dining room. Kinkaide, not knowing what else to do, gave Desmond the thumbs-up sign behind Abby's back. In reality, he didn't much blame Abby for her negative behavior. She was probably handling this whole thing better than Kinkaide would if his spouse had been unfaithful.

And what if I were jilted? How would I handle that?

He stepped into the immaculate kitchen. Images of Melissa mingled with the blue plaid and geese motif. During those weeks after he had broken off their relationship, Kinkaide had almost called her a dozen times to do exactly what Desmond was doing….to plead for forgiveness…to beg her to come back. For Kinkaide's heart had bled with the impact of his own decision. A decision that even his mother frowned on. However, he had strengthened his resistance and stood by his choice. Once the ache wore off and the music opportunities exploded, he had lost touch with the part of himself that pined for Mel. After all, he had achieved what he set out to do—make a name for himself as a premier Christian pianist. The work that such a feat required gave little time for personal reflection.

He removed his leather jacket, draped it across a ladder-backed chair, and claimed a place at the knotty-pine table. Julie laid some peanut butter cookies in front of him, and Janie offered coffee. The girls, silent and alert, didn't press for conversation, and Kinkaide obliged them. With a sigh, he sank his teeth into the soft cookie and thoughtfully chewed.

As the rise and fall of voices reverberated from the entryway, Kinkaide continued his mental scenario. He placed himself in a church where he waited...and waited...and waited...until giving up all hope that Melissa would arrive. Then he imagined himself in his driveway with Melissa returning the engagement ring, sorrowfully shaking her head, and driving off into the sunset to make her dreams come true. Next, Kinkaide visualized six years later and his opening the front door of his ultramodern home to find Melissa on his doorstep.

If I were in Mel's shoes, I would probably be harder to get along with than she has been, he mused.

The folded white napkin in front of him bore nothing but crumbs, and Kinkaide didn't even remember eating the cookies. He sipped the steaming coffee, and a movement out of the corner of his eyes snared his attention.

"We're going up the back stairway to our room," Julie said and tucked a strand of bobbed hair behind her ear.

"And I refuse...that nothing has happened..." the volume of Abby's voice peaked then diminished to once more blend into indistinguishable dialogue.

"Come on." Janie pulled on her sister's coat sleeve then dashed her hand toward the corner of her eye.

"It'll be okay, girls," Kinkaide said and eyed the closed kitchen door. "Just hang in there and pray for them."

"Do you know what happened?" Julie asked. Janie stopped her urging and focused on Kinkaide. "Mom won't say. Neither will Dad. They both keep saying they're having problems. We heard Mom talking to an attorney yesterday, and," she gulped, "we're afraid—"

"Did one of them have an affair?" Janie prompted with candid scrutiny.

"Dad?" Julie added.

"I…" Kinkaide snatched the coffee mug, took a giant swallow of the unsweetened liquid, then reached for the sugar bowl. "I…I think you probably need to get the answers from your parents." He plopped two generous scoops of sugar into the coffee and vigorously stirred. With a splash, some of the hot liquid splattered onto his hand.

"I've told you over…again, Desmond, I don't…apologies. You should have thought of….before you ever…" Abby's rising voice supplied all the answers the girls needed.

"Come on, let's go on upstairs." Julie touched her sister's arm. Their weary eyes took on the tormented glaze of old women, wise with suffering.

"All I'm asking for is just one cruise, for pity's sake!" Desmond's frustrated yell preceded the sound of footsteps pounding up the main stairway.

In seconds, the kitchen door swung inward and Desmond, his face drawn, stepped inside. The twins hovered near the stove as if uncertain whether to run or cry. Their distressed father gripped his neck and hung his head. The silence pulsed with questions. Questions about their future. Questions no one voiced.

"I've decided I'm moving back in tonight," Desmond blurted.

Kinkaide, palms on the table, rose. "Does Abby know?"

"Yes. I told her. I didn't want to move to that hotel room in the first place."

The twins flung themselves into their father's arms and knocked him off balance. "Whoa!" he said as he stumbled into the stove.

"And is Abby okay with it?" Kinkaide asked.

"I'll go back to the hotel and get my things," Desmond said, sidestepping the question. He tightened his hold on his daughters and placed a kiss on each of their foreheads. "You're welcome to spend the night here, Kinkaide, or you can stay in my hotel room. I've paid for tonight."

"You're mighty quiet," Desmond said as he pulled under the luxury hotel's portico. The Mercedes' dash lights illuminated the car's interior and added to the glow cast by outside lamps. "Got something you want to say?"

Kinkaide shifted against supple leather, stroked his beard, and debated his options. At this point, brutal honesty might incite his friend's temper. When Desmond first told Kinkaide about the affair, he had been more concerned with the effects on his friend. Even though Kinkaide had fully realized that the sin was Desmond's, he had still lamented the family problems on Desmond's behalf. Yet seeing Abby and the shadows in her eyes, absorbing the twin's silent desperation, witnessing the family's agony, had sparked an unexpected flame of ire within Kinkaide. And the irritation had steadily grown since leaving the Casper household. By the time Desmond took the exit for the hotel, Kinkaide once again wanted to whack him on the head. And if he were Lawton, he'd have already told Desmond what an imbecile he was.

You've been an idiot, Lawton fashion seemed most appropriate. Nonetheless, Kinkaide stayed the words.

Desmond put the car into park and inspected Kinkaide. "You're mad at me, aren't you?" His right brow rose a fraction in a gesture Kinkaide had seen many times when his friend was miffed.

Kinkaide held his gaze and tapped the leather seat.

Desmond waved to the approaching bell attendant then rolled down his window. "Give us a minute," he clipped.

"Sure," the young man replied.

"I'm ready to go in if you are." Kinkaide grabbed the door release then checked the digital dash clock. "It's almost nine. I've decided to just drive back home tonight. I'm a little restless and not in the mood to sit in a hotel room."

"Okay, but that puts you getting home about midnight," Desmond said, his voice void of emotion.

"That's fine. I need time to think."

"You know, you're the last person I ever thought would judge me for this," Desmond said, his words measured.

"I'm not judging you." Kinkaide waved his hand. "Who said I was judging you?"

"Your eyes say it, man. Your eyes, that's who."

"Well, I was fine until I saw what this has done to Abby."

"You two always did have an admiration society going, didn't you?"

"I like her—a lot! Is that such a sin? I've always said that if I could choose an older sister, I'd choose Abby."

"So you want to rip the heart out of the man who's hurt your sister?"

"I didn't say that."

"Come on, Kinkaide! When are you going to be honest with me?"

"Okay, okay!" Kinkaide erupted. "Yes, I'm aggravated at you!" He pointed to his friend's chest. "It just didn't hit me until tonight—that's all."

"Do you think Abby should divorce me? That's what she wants, you know!" Kinkaide rubbed his eyes.

"No, no, no! I'm the one who suggested the cruise, remember? I've been praying, and I'll continue to pray, that the two of you can patch things up—for you and for those two girls of yours. It's just that—"

"You've all of a sudden decided I'm a selfish jerk." Desmond's hand balled on his knee.

"Nobody said that!"

"You know, my old grandmother had a saying for a situation like this," Desmond said with a smirk. "She used to say, 'This is like the pot calling the kettle black.'"

Kinkaide's legs stiffened. "Implying?"

"Let's just think a minute about what you did to Melissa Moore." The words, potent and weighted, stretched forth to grip Kinkaide in a vise of guilt.

A limousine pulled up beside the Mercedes, the bell attendant rushed forward, and another car's lights shone through the back.

"We need to get out." Kinkaide opened his door, stepped from the car, and slammed the door before Desmond replied.

He stalked into the hotel, and the classy lines of the brass-and-glass lounge did nothing to lighten his mood. Kinkaide waited by the marble-ensconced elevators while Desmond made arrangements to momentarily leave his car at the curb. Arms crossed, Kinkaide chose not to speak when his friend joined him.

The elevator door hissed open and a couple of femme fatales, replete with short skirts and long blonde hair, sashayed forth. The two men stepped aside and waited their turn to enter. Given the appreciative feminine observation, Kinkaide had little doubt that the women would grace him and Desmond with their company if they made but one move. He focused on the marblelike tile and entered the elevator with Desmond at his side.

The doors swished shut. He recalled those teenage years when he *had* made that one move more often than he wanted to remember. He had bucked against every boundary his parents tried to instill. A lithe man of 18 with his own wheels out to prove who knew what, Kinkaide hadn't been married, but his sin had been just as black as Desmond's.

By the time he was 20, Kinkaide had transcended those rebellious years and gotten down to business with God. At a summer revival he set aside the things of the flesh and secured a deep walk with His Savior. By the time college started the next fall, Kinkaide knew beyond doubt that the Lord was calling him to use his piano talents for His glory.

And I've gone and made a name for myself. The thought barged in from nowhere. Kinkaide, squirming with the implications, grappled for a means of diversion.

"I'm sorry, Desmond," he muttered as the elevator approached the seventh floor. "I don't know what got into me. You're right. I probably hurt Mel just as badly as you hurt Abby. I had no right—"

"You know what's funny about this whole thing?" The elevator stopped, and the door glided open.

"What?"

They walked out and trudged down the hallway lined with brass sconces.

"I've been just as aggravated at myself as you were," Desmond said. "Then I got teed off at you for being mad at me. Now that makes a lot of sense, doesn't it?"

Kinkaide slowed as they neared the room. "I don't know what got into me. Seeing Abby and the girls, and how upset they all are—it just…" He shrugged and the two stopped outside the door.

"I understand." Desmond placed a hand on his friend's shoulder and held his gaze. "It's quickly becoming a known fact that I *did* act like a jerk. A *stupid* jerk." Desmond's eyes stirred like deep pools of water invaded by a baneful sea monster.

"Well, I guess birds of a feather flock together, then, because I've spent my share of time in jerkville the last few years. I don't even know why Melissa is speaking to me."

Images of Shelby's shattered countenance increased Kinkaide's discomfort. "You, Lawton, and I might be in for a fun-filled trip all by ourselves."

A low chuckle accompanied clicks as Desmond inserted the card key and opened the door. "Who knows?" he speculated. "God just might work a miracle."

"Maybe," Kinkaide agreed, then a fresh thought struck him—something Lawton had said. *And maybe God could use a little help*, he mused as a new plan seized him.

Fourteen

Melissa checked her sporty Timex and noted that the scheduled conference call with her friends would occur in five minutes. She padded down her hallway and closed the guest room where Jacquelyn slept. Even though Jac had agreed that Saturday morning was a good time to talk with the sisters, Mel chose not to wake her. The private eye desperately needed sleep.

When Jac arrived Thursday evening, the dark circles under her eyes, unkempt hair, and fluctuating tears bespoke much of what Mel had begun to suspect. One of her dearest friends was on the brink of a nervous breakdown. After hours of interaction, Melissa had prescribed a mild tranquilizer for Jac, who in turn spent the last two days attempting to catch up on a month's sleep. Last night over e-mail, both Jac and Mel had agreed to a sister conference call. With Melissa's encouragement, Jacquelyn had decided to share her turbulent memories with her friends and beseech them for prayer and support.

Melissa grabbed the cordless phone from her nightstand, walked out to her patio, and received a welcoming snuffle from Bernie. Mel scratched his ear and reveled in the fresh spring air that tempted her to flit from one iris bloom to another and inhale nature's perfume. March had escorted in an early spring and transformed her backyard into an explosion of blooms. Lilies and roses, ferns and geraniums, apple, plum, and peach blossoms. Each dot of color across the yard created a surreal haven, a horticulturist's paradise, a work of art free of a restrictive canvass. She inhaled the sweetness, closed her eyes, then pondered Mother Nature's whimsical ways. Dubiously, Mel eyed the peach blossoms and hoped a seasonal frost didn't end her chances for fresh fruit.

The phone rang and she pressed the answer button while plopping onto a wooden park bench. "Melissa here," she said into the receiver.

The chorus of greetings attested to the presence of her five close friends: veterinarian Sonsee LeBlanc Delaney, domestic genius Victoria Roberts, pastor's wife Marilyn Douglas Langham, reporter Sammie Jones, and model Kim Lan Lowery O'Donnel. Their concern was unanimous.

"What's going on with Jac?" Sonsee voiced the group's concern.

"Is she on the phone, too?" Sammie asked, her Texas accent as heavy as ever.

"No, not right now." Melissa shifted as Bernie, standing beside her, laid his head in her lap. "She's still asleep. I didn't want to wake her."

"I've really been worried about her," Kim Lan said. "She's been posting a lot lately on our e-mail loop and then also e-mailing me privately. That's just not like her."

Mel chuckled. "She even called me a few times. I started getting suspicious as well." A bumblebee floated from his perch in the rose garden and hummed toward Mel. She swiped at the air, and he obliged with an altered path.

"She told me about two weeks ago that she'd been having some sort of recurring nightmare," Marilyn said.

"Was it the one about the dragon?" Sammie queried.

"Yes," Marilyn said. "It sounded like something out of *Twilight Zone.*"

"You can say that again," Victoria chimed in. Mel envisioned Victoria nodding her head in her solemn way.

"Or better yet, Edgar Allan Poe," Sammie added.

"Well," Melissa began, "I don't think Jac would mind my telling you. The best we can figure, she's been suppressing some really negative childhood memories for years. Then she started having that awful dream, and it got so bad she could hardly sleep. Anyway, the long and short of it is that she was molested by someone from the time she was 9 until she was about 12, the best we can put together. The memories are just now catching up with her, and the man's identity is hazy. Frankly, some of what she's told me will make you furious. If the moron isn't dead, I'm sorely tempted to perform a very special operation on him."

"Why don't you just be *honest* about your feelings?" Victoria said, the smile evident in her voice.

"Actually, if you want real honesty, I was expressing my thoughts a bit mildly," Mel countered. "And if you had seen the wreck Jac was when she got here, you'd probably feel the same. I've never seen her so weak."

"It's so hard to imagine Jac as anything but tough," Sonsee said.

"But don't you think this might be the reason she's been so tough all these years?" Marilyn asked. "I've learned through counseling people at church that often the ones who act the hardest are sometimes the ones who've been hurt the deepest."

"So you're saying that the whole thing with Jac was a cover-up?" Kim Lan asked.

"To keep people at a distance?" Victoria added.

"Yes, that's exactly what I mean," Marilyn answered, "especially men."

"I guess it worked," Sammie said. "I don't know a man alive that would cross her now. She'd take a karate chop at his nose before he knew what hit him."

"That's taekwondo," Mel corrected.

"Oh, yeah, like you're an expert," Sammie chided.

"All I know is that I don't want to be on the receiving end of any of it," Melissa shot back, and the group shared a burst of laughter.

"Think about it," Marilyn continued. "Jac has never really dated anyone and she says she's not interested—*ever*. Has anyone but me ever thought that was a little strange?"

"Actually, lately I've begun to think she's just smart." The dark tones in Sammie's voice reminded Melissa that the reporter never did answer her e-mail query concerning her marriage.

"Really?" Melissa added, her thoughts trailing to Kinkaide. "I've had a notion or two like that myself."

She shifted on the decorative bench. Bernie rolled his eyes as if to say, "How dare you disturb my position!" Melissa gave him a consolatory scratch behind the ears.

"Do you think Jac's going to be okay?" Kim Lan asked. "I've heard of women losing their minds over trauma like this."

"Yes, she's going to be fine." A cool breeze stirred the newborn leaves and shifted the wisps of hair around Mel's face. "Jac is a fighter, and I think she'll work through this. It's just going to take some time and lots of support from us. She's also arranged for a new partner to take on her cases for awhile. I've talked her into staying with me for a couple of months."

"She should be able to run interference between you and Kinkaide then," Sammie joked.

"So, how *are* things going with you and Kinkaide?" Sonsee asked.

From somewhere in the neighborhood, music erupted and Mel frowned. A voice that strongly resembled Elvis' began singing "Teddy Bear."

"Somebody's got their sound system up too loud," Melissa said. "Can any of you hear the Elvis music?"

"Listen y'all, she's got it bad," Kim Lan drawled in her fake southern accent. "She'll do anything to keep from talking about Kinkaide—even make up stories about Elvis music. Come on, Mel, we know your neighborhood. It's as quiet as a cemetery!"

"I thought everybody on your street was retired," Sonsee said.

"Forget the neighborhood. Tell us about Kinkaide," Victoria urged.

"There's really nothing to tell," Melissa said, then she recalled Kinkaide's Sunday visit. The engagement ring was still in the end table's drawer. But she decided not to mention the ring to her sisters—especially since she had placed the diamond on her finger last night before plopping it back into the drawer.

Soon "Teddy Bear" blurred into the melodious tones of "Love Me Tender," and Melissa stood. Bernie yawned in protest of losing his headrest. The music sounded as if it were coming from her neighbor's front yard, but that was crazy. The middle-aged couple who lived next door owned season tickets to the opera. Their musical taste, anything but pedestrian, certainly didn't encompass Elvis. Nonetheless, Mel walked toward the privacy fence.

"Hello, hello! Earth calling Melissa," Marilyn said.

"I'm here. I'm here," Mel answered. "I'm trying to see where the music's coming from." She tiptoed and strained to peer past the shoulder-high gate. But all she saw was the usual pecan tree that stood between her and the neighbors. Nothing seemed out of the ordinary. Still, "Love Me Tender," accompanied by a euphonious piano, continued to resonate in fluid rhythm.

"Has Kinkaide talked you into going on that trip yet?" Kim Lan prompted.

"A cruise and an excursion to Rome," Marilyn oozed. "Do you know how much I'd like to get away like that? You poor baby. I just can't believe that mean ol' man wants to take you on a cruise!"

"Give it a break, will ya?" Mel chided.

"You know, Mel, you ought to really consider going for Jac's sake," Victoria said. "Maybe she'd agree to go with you. Might do her some good."

"Hmm. I haven't thought of that." Melissa nibbled her bottom lip. While the sisters dissected Victoria's thoughtful observation, Mel, for the first time, contemplated such a venture. If Jac were to agree to go, that would place a whole new angle on the trip. Mel would be able to end Kinkaide's pressuring her while helping a friend in desperate need of some R and R.

A scene surged upon her mind. Kinkaide stood at an elegant ship's siderail awaiting Mel. Melissa, the ocean breeze caressing her cheeks, neared her former fiancé. Moonbeams rippled along the ocean wavelets like crushed diamonds sprinkled from heaven by an angel of love. Kinkaide opened his arms. She stepped into his warmth. He pulled her close and lowered his lips to hers.

A thrill shot through Mel's midsection before her spine could stiffen. She inserted her forefinger and thumb beneath her glasses and rubbed her eyes. *I can't start doing this to myself,* she scolded. *That only sets me up for more heartache.* Yet on the heels of her admonishment, the line of an age-old poem by Tennyson countered her claims: "Tis better to have loved and lost than never to have loved at all." *But I have loved and lost,* she argued with herself. And a place in her heart whispered that it longed for her to love all over again—even in the face of potential loss at the hands of the same man.

"You know, the thought of being on a moving ship makes me ill." Sonsee's injection was the first Mel had heard during the last few minutes. "Forget morning sickness! Whoever named this morning sickness must have never been pregnant. I'm sick *all* the time."

"That will pass," Victoria said in the tones of an older and wiser sister. "After about the fourth month, you'll be good as new."

"If I survive that long!" Sonsee said. She and her lifetime friend, Taylor Delaney, had pledged their love for one another during a tragic yet bonding event—the murder of Sonsee's father. Shortly after the killer had been captured, Sonsee and Taylor were married. After only a few months, God had blessed them with the promise of new life.

"Well, I'm nauseated with excitement," Kim Lan said. "Mick and I found out yesterday that we're scheduled to go get Khanh Ahn mid May." Kim Lan and her husband were returning to Vietnam to adopt a special-needs child the supermodel had fallen in love with during a humanitarian trip to her mother's homeland.

The sisters plunged into a new vein of conversation in honor of the expectant mothers, and the mysterious music continued to abound. While "Love Me Tender" blended into "Can't Help Falling in Love," Melissa decided to investigate the melodies' source through her front window. Just as she opened the patio door and stepped through, Jac, her short hair rumpled, emerged from the hallway.

"Did you hear the music?" she asked.

Mel covered the phone's mouthpiece. "Yes. I was coming to investigate."

"I already have. It woke me up, and I looked out the front window." Jac stretched then chuckled. "For a meek and mild pediatrician, you certainly live an exciting life, that's all I've got to say." She tightened the sash around her terrycloth robe and headed toward the kitchen. "There's a man with a beard out there—looks like Kinkaide Franklin. He's set up some sort of electronic piano in your front yard and is singing Elvis music."

"What!" Melissa, forgetting the telephone conversation, slammed her hand against her forehead.

The eruption of voices over the cordless phone left her staring at the receiver. Melissa rushed upon Jac, thrust the phone into her hands, and said, "It's the conference call. Tell them I—" She gulped. "Tell them—"

"I'll just tell 'em the truth." Jac raised her brows in that nononsense manner that usually ended any argument. "They'll get it out of you one way or the other. As far as they're concerned, you're the mouth of the south. They aren't going to let you hide a thing."

"Well, suit yourself." Mel hurried toward her front door. "No telling *what* the neighbors are thinking," she mumbled.

Her legs unsteady, she opened the front door and peered into the yard while "Can't Help Falling in Love" reverberated around the neighborhood. Kinkaide, his eyes closed, sang his heart and produced one of the best Elvis voices Mel had ever heard. He had sung Elvis songs to her the whole time they were dating, and she marveled at his mimicking ability. She'd never imagined the man would do such an outrageous thing.

She glanced around the manicured neighborhood, and her worst fears were confirmed. Several curious onlookers had emerged to explore the source of the sonorous music. Her face heating, Melissa scurried down the steps and neared the digital piano that shone in the morning sun like an ebony mirror. Kinkaide, dressed in a tuxedo replete with red bow tie, noticed her approach. A slow smile welcomed her, yet he never missed a word.

"What are you doing?" Melissa hissed, her fists clenched.

"I'm serenading you," he said while his fingers caressed the keys.

"Whatever for?" she whispered.

"Because I love you." Kinkaide's reckless wink reminded Mel of that moment during her nephew's dedication, and her traitorous mind replayed those manufactured moments near the ship's rail. A warm rush spread through her, and she struggled to hide the unexpected pleasure.

A movement from the corner of her eye drew her attention to the opera-loving neighbor's yard. Mr. Zanefield, dressed in housecoat and slippers, stepped from his porch and craned his neck toward Melissa's house.

"The whole neighborhood is watching you!" she admonished!

"Good! Maybe they'll enjoy the show." Kinkaide twirled on the swivel stool, and his coattails whirled outward. When his fingers impacted the keyboard, "Don't Be Cruel" resounded forth.

"You've got to stop," Mel demanded. "Somebody might turn you in for disturbing the peace."

"What a small price to pay," he said, still accompanied by the piano. "To get you to say yes."

"Yes to what?" Mel asked, her mind offering a list of options. A kiss? A date? The trip? Marriage?

"That you'll go on the cruise and to Rome, of course."

A scowling Mr. Zanefield neared and motioned to Mel. "Excuse me, Dr. Moore!" he barked and Melissa cringed. "This—this nonsense," he waved toward Kinkaide, "has awakened our grandbaby! *You're* the one who suggested we keep him for the weekend so his parents can get some rest. Well, his colic has made him scream all night!" Mr. Zanefield, bags under his eyes, rubbed a hand over his balding head as if he were prepared to rip out any hair that was left. "Please, *please* tell that man to stop!"

Kinkaide, never wavering his focus on Mel, shook his head. "Not a chance. I'm not stopping until you say yes." Without a pause, he then sang, "I don't want no other love. Baby it's still you I'm thinking of…"

Furtively, Mel peered around the neighborhood at the small audience that increased with every moment. She once again encountered the glowering Mr. Zanefield. Kinkaide, eyes closed, continued his singing, and Mel was tempted to cover his mouth with her hands.

"You've got to stop now!" she demanded, but he ignored her.

Mr. Zanefield shook his fist in the air. "If this nonsense doesn't stop in the next 30 seconds, I'm calling the police!" He lifted his wrist and coldly observed his watch.

As the seconds ticked by, Melissa imagined herself stepping aboard that giant boat. She envisioned the Aegean Sea. She visualized the Isle of Rhodes. She pondered the sights of Rome. And the whole time, Kinkaide—the man she feared, the man she loved—was at her side smiling in the sunshine.

Finally, Marilyn's teasing words mingled with Kinkaide's song: *You poor baby. I just can't believe that mean ol' man wants to take you on a cruise!*

Mr. Zanefield lowered his wrist. "That's it! I'm calling the authorities," he belched. Spine rigid, he stomped toward his front door.

It's just a trip! Get a grip! What's the harm in going on a cruise? Maybe Jac really would enjoy it. A trip like that would be good for her—and she'd be a good buffer!

"Okay, okay, I'll go with you!" Mel blurted. "Just—just stop it with the Elvis music!"

Kinkaide's fingers stilled, and the music came to an abrupt end.

"You will?" he blurted. "You mean, you mean you really will?"

Mr. Zanefield whirled around and faced them. "She said she would," he growled. "Now take your Romeo act inside so we can get the baby back to sleep."

"On the cruise? You mean, you'll go on the cruise?" Kinkaide babbled like a sixth grader just kissed by the school sweetheart.

"Yes!" Her toes curling, Mel fought the intrusion of that fabricated scene at the ship's rail. Yet the imagined moonbeams dancing upon the ocean like dazzling jewels bade her to relish every nuance of her illusory tryst.

As if Kinkaide transcended the realms of reality into Mel's fantasy, he stood, cupped her face in his hands, and placed his lips upon hers. Melissa's eyes bugged. She gasped. She stiffened. Then an old, familiar warmth crept up her back and weakened her limbs. Her eyes drowsed shut and she drank in the effects of Kinkaide's nearness. The faint sound of Mr. Zanefield's front door slamming barely registered, for Melissa had fallen headlong where she had pledged never again to tread.

Into the arms of Kinkaide Franklin.

Amid the waters of yesteryear's rapture.

Toward the glow of love, pure and bright.

Kinkaide lifted his face, and his dark eyes, incredulous and speculative, searched every crevice of Mel's soul. "I—I'm sorry," he stuttered. "I didn't plan that."

Melissa, her breathing unsteady, inched away and observed the piano. A glance at the numerous neighbors avidly watching heightened her discomfort. Her face heated, and she felt as if she were melting into a warm pool of chagrin and pleasure and dubiety.

"I've embarrassed you." Kinkaide reached for her hand and gave it a comforting squeeze.

She slipped her hand from his. "Whatever makes you think that singing Elvis music in my front yard at 8:30 in the morning and kissing me in front of the whole neighborhood would embarrass me?" Mel shook her head and swallowed against the lump in her throat. Her heart raced in panic. Panic and confusion. Confusion and ecstasy. "You haven't changed a bit, Kinkaide Franklin. Not one bit."

"Neither have you."

"Unless you count 15 pounds." Mel looked down at her new jeans, now size 12.

"That's just more to love."

"Kinkaide, I don't think—"

"I didn't mean to—"

"I'm not ready—just because we—"

"I understand. I know." He raised his hands, palms outward. "No more pushing. No more kissing. No more anything. I promise."

"Part of the reason I'm agreeing to go on the cruise is because of Jac." Melissa pointed toward her house and glanced over her shoulder. The living room drapes rustled, and she rolled her eyes. Undoubtedly her friends had pressured Jacquelyn into spying. On her own, Jac usually stayed out of everyone's personal business. She just inserted her nose where it counted—into solving cases.

"Jack?" Kinkaide's eyes widened and a thousand questions ricocheted between them.

"Jacquelyn Lightfoot. I believe you met her last fall at the airport. Remember? I was seeing her off on a flight."

"Ah, yes. You're talking about the detective. She's one of your 'sisters.'" The lines between his brows relaxed.

"Right. Well," Melissa crossed her arms, "she's really having a hard time right now, and I started thinking—actually, one of our other friends suggested—that a cruise would probably really do her good right now. So I was considering the option." Mel wasn't certain whether she was trying to convince Kinkaide or herself that Jac played a big role in her decision. "I haven't asked her yet, but I would want her to join us."

"No problem." Kinkaide inserted a hand into the pocket of his tuxedo pants. "I've invited my brother and another family who I'm friends with—Desmond Casper. He and his wife have been...they've been having problems. Yesterday, he told me she has agreed to go on the cruise. They have two teenage daughters as well, so there will be several of us. As far as I'm concerned, you can take that horse dog of yours if it makes you feel any better. I don't care just as long as *you* go."

Mel observed Kinkaide's black shoes that reflected the sunlight as brilliantly as did the piano. A knot formed in the pit of her stomach—knot encompassed in nervous queasiness that insisted Mel clarify her stance.

She dared encounter his velvet-brown gaze and stilled herself against the feeling of being enveloped in a fervid shroud of adoration. Kinkaide's focus trailed to her lips...and he might as well have kissed her all over again.

"Just because I'm going with you doesn't mean I—"

"I know." He stroked his beard. "I know." Yet an impish light glittered in his eyes. Kinkaide looked across the street as if he were afraid she might read his mind.

"Furthermore, I really wish you'd take that engagement ring back."

His attention snapped to her. "But it's yours."

"Not any more." Melissa fidgeted with the hem of her oversized oxford shirt. "And I would prefer—"

"Are you saying the ring repels you?"

"No, I didn't say—"

"Then does it attract you?"

The question hit her with hurricane force. She focused on a neighbor's golden cat trotting across her yard as she grappled for an honest yet concealing answer. "I'll go get the ring," she finally stated. But Mel had only taken a few steps when the muted notes of "Can't Help Falling in Love" blended with the birds' cheerful serenade. She stopped on the first porch step, and Kinkaide's mellifluous voice enveloped her heart. Nonetheless, Mel didn't dare turn around. Instead, she scurried into the house and rushed toward the end table.

"Your mom's on the phone." Jac, standing near the dining room, extended the cordless to Mel. "She beeped in on the conference call."

"Oh, good." Mel snatched the blue velvet box from the drawer and held up one finger. "This will give me an easy excuse to come back in. I've got to take this out to Kinkaide. Tell her I'll be right back."

"And what about the conference call?"

"Oh." Mel stopped and smiled. "Just tell them they've put you up to spying enough for one day."

Jac shook her head. "So you saw me?"

"I don't miss a beat." Melissa approached the front door.

"They forced me into it." Jac raised her hand. "Scout's honor."

"I believe you." Mel turned the knob and chuckled. "I'm just surprised a couple of them didn't crawl through the phone and spy themselves."

"Me, too." She rolled her eyes. "Oh, listen, before you go back outside, they've been talking about the sister reunion this summer. They wanted me to ask you where you wanted to have it."

"I don't have a clue right now. Just tell them we'll talk about it on the e-mail trail."

"Will do."

Melissa squared her shoulders and walked onto the lawn to lay the engagement ring on the piano. The music faded and Kinkaide stood, eyed the ring box, then challenged Mel with silent observation. For a second, she thought he might tell her he wasn't going to take the ring.

Then he scooped the box into his hand and flipped open the top. As if that one act opened a treasure chest full of remembrances, Mel recalled a bright spring day so like this one when the sun turned that diamond to fire. And Kinkaide...Kinkaide told her the flames in the ring paled in comparison to the ardor of his love.

Mel's throat tightened. "Mom's waiting on the phone." She inched backward. "I guess I'll—"

"We need to discuss details about the trip," he said, his eyes stirring with shadows. Shadows and memories. Memories and sweet torment.

"Yes, um, perhaps you should call me. We need to talk about—I haven't asked Jac yet, but I'm assuming she'll agree, and we need to arrange her ticket. And I guess there's lots of other details."

"Yes. We need to talk about a lot." He snapped the ring box shut and smiled. "I'll be calling."

Fifteen

Kinkaide relentlessly pounded on the front door of the familiar duplex. "Lawton, it's me! Open up!" he bellowed, then hammered again until the lock produced a round of telltale clicks.

"All right already," Lawton called from inside. "Hold your horses, will ya?" The door swung inward. "What's gotten into you? You'd think the sky was falling."

"No sky falling." Kinkaide grabbed his younger brother by the upper arms and planted a kiss on his forehead. "Melissa just agreed to go on the cruise!"

"Stop kissing me!" Lawton shoved against Kinkaide's shoulder. "I don't want your stinkin' germs."

Kinkaide bounded into the living room, doubled his fist, and jerked it toward him. "*Yes!*"

Lawton closed the door and turned to face his brother. "I really think you've finally lost it!" He shook his head and meandered toward the kitchen's open doorway.

"No! After eight months of chasing her, I'm just now getting it together! I can't believe it! You were right."

"Of course I was right. Not sure what about this time, but I'm always right. The sooner you figure that out, the better off we'll all be." He paused on the kitchen's threshold and pivoted to face his brother. The dark glasses that Lawton wore in public were absent and Kinkaide had clear view of clouded eyes in nystagmic motion. The stubble along his jaw attested that he had yet to shave—probably for two days.

"Since you're here, why don't you do something useful," Lawton said. "Mom visited a couple days ago and did some cooking. I can't figure out for the life of me what she's done with the black pepper."

"Sure." Kinkaide, still reeling with his good fortune, swept past Lawton and into the simple kitchen.

The duplex, only a year old, had been an answer to prayer for his younger brother. Tired of living at home, Lawton had prayed for the opportunity to be on his own. The new apartments, only two miles from the Franklins' home, proved close enough for Rosa Franklin to still assist her son while providing the independence Lawton desperately needed.

Kinkaide opened the oak cabinets and scanned the shelves. At last he spotted a pepper shaker tucked behind a box of oatmeal.

"Here it is, behind the oatmeal."

"Ah...I probably hid it from myself," Lawton said, extending his hand. "I had oatmeal yesterday morning. This morning, it's eggs." His smile reminded Kinkaide of a ravenous wolf.

"I haven't eaten yet, either. Mind cooking enough for both of us?"

"Hmmff. That figures. You just came to bum a meal." Lawton grabbed an egg from the nearby carton and cracked it into a crockery bowl sitting on the counter.

Kinkaide removed the constricting bow tie and tossed it on the glass dining table. Next he shed the tuxedo jacket and draped it on a chair.

Lawton slammed another egg against the bowl's rim, emptied it into the bowl, and tossed the shell into the sink.

"Do you remember your suggestion about serenading Melissa?"

"Of course."

"Well, I did it."

"This morning?"

"Yes. In her front yard. I took my digital piano over, plugged it into her outside plug, and sang Elvis songs to her."

"Ha!" Lawton threw back his head. "I love it! I love it! So I'm guessing by your reaction that the singing worked."

"It worked! She agreed to go!"

"Great!" Lawton wiped his hands on a dishtowel and shoved up the sleeves of his oversized sweater. He turned to face Kinkaide as if he were ready to do battle. "So does that mean I'm no longer invited?"

"No. I'm still planning on your going."

"Good." He nodded. "I was prepared to fight over that one. I've started looking forward to the cruise. It'll be my first, you know."

Kinkaide chuckled. "Mine, too, for that matter. It looks like there's going to be a whole bunch of us going."

"Really?" Lawton resumed his egg cracking.

"I invited my friend, Desmond Casper."

"He's the cat who owns those burger joints and speaks at men's conferences, right?"

"Yes. As of yesterday, he, his wife, and two daughters are going. Whew! That was a miracle and a half."

"Oh? Do tell." Lawton's tilted head bespoke his undying curiosity.

"Well, he and his wife are having all sorts of problems...as in Desmond had an affair." Kinkaide crinkled the corner of one of the paper napkins in the center of the table.

"Yikes!" Lawton, swiveling to face Kinkaide, opened his mouth then stopped himself. "Well, I was about to spew forth about the stupidity of that sort of thing, but I guess I've been as tempted as the next guy."

"Right. But you've somehow managed to resist—period. If anybody out there deserves to call Desmond stupid, it would be you."

"Nope. Doesn't work that way. But for the grace of God, there go I."

"You can say that again."

"But for the grace of God, there go I."

Kinkaide grabbed the napkin, wadded it, and hurled the missile at his brother's prominent nose. The napkin bounced off it and landed with a swoosh on the white tile.

"I guess you think you're really funny," Lawton said, his face impassive.

"Anyway, back to the *point,*" Kinkaide said.

"Yeah, yeah, yeah, your point." Lawton waved his hand and turned back to the eggs.

"Abby wants a divorce, and Desmond wants to rebuild the marriage. We were praying for a miracle."

"Looks like you got one." He opened a drawer and fished out an oversized fork.

"We got two, if you count Mel's agreeing to go. Oh, and she's also inviting a friend—Jacquelyn Lightfoot."

Lawton stilled. "Ever met her?"

"Yes. Several years ago, and then last summer as well."

"Is she single?"

"As far as I know."

"Christian?"

"I'm pretty sure. Who wants to know?" Kinkaide's smile softened his voice.

"Oh, you know, inquiring minds and all."

Shaking his head, Kinkaide eyed the pocket of his tuxedo jacket and slipped his fingers into the soft folds. The ring box fell into his hand, and he placed it on the table. "Well, I've told you the good news, now for the bad—Mel returned the old engagement ring that I left with her Sunday."

"So it's one step forward, two steps back?"

"Something like that." Kinkaide flipped open the ring box, peered at the modest solitaire, and pondered his options. He had been tempted to refuse the ring but decided not to push any harder. After all, Mel had agreed to go on the cruise and she had immensely enjoyed the kiss—if her reaction was anything to go by.

He stroked his beard and brushed a thumb along his lower lip. "Make that *two* steps forward, one back."

Lawton whipped the eggs with the large fork. "My, my, aren't we sounding like a satisfied pup," he teased. "Next thing you know, you *will* be howling at the moon! You're so love-sick, you don't even know—"

"You know what? I think I just added you to my prayer list." Kinkaide snapped the box shut and dropped it back into his suit pocket.

"Good. I need all the prayers I can get. Putting up with you is a full-time job." Lawton plunked a skillet atop his stove.

"I'm going to pray that you'll fall head over heels in love and that the lady won't give you the time of day. Then you'll see how it feels."

"Hey! I can live with the love part, but give me some grace. Pray that she'll fall at my feet or something."

"So..."

"Make yourself useful and get the margarine out of the fridge, would you?"

Kinkaide stood and opened the nearby refrigerator. "Now you're changing your tune. Last I heard you were saying you were fine just like you are." He grabbed a tub of oleo and set it on the counter near the stovetop.

"Well," Lawton's mouth turned down at the corners, "if the right woman came along, I'd certainly sit up and take notice." He flipped the gas burner on high, grabbed a spoon, opened the plastic container, and gouged out a clump of margarine. "Okay, I'll be honest."

"'Bout time." Kinkaide crossed his arms.

"Hmph." Lawton tapped the spoon against the side of the skillet. "I'm praying for a wife." The melted butter sizzled as if it were applauding his admission.

"No way! You?"

"Sure." He shrugged, and the neck of his sweater brushed the back of his dark hair. "Why not? I'm 33. It's time to settle down."

"Miracles never cease." Kinkaide moved the bowl of eggs closer to Lawton's hand. "But I'm not sure there's a woman out there ornery enough to take you on."

"We'll just see, won't we?"

"Yeah, I guess we'll just have to see." Kinkaide squeezed his brother's shoulder, and a lump formed in his throat. He was sorely tempted to mention just how fortunate the lady in question would be but decided to circumvent the mushy stuff. "Don't burn the eggs," he said instead as the smell of melting margarine tantalized his taste buds.

"Ahh, shut up and make the coffee."

Horace Waggoner stood in his tiny bathroom and peered into the mirror. His hair, once bushy with natural curl, now resembled a Q-Tip. According to the hairstylist, the only remedy to remove the remaining paint had been a generous dose of acetone. The acetone, while stripping the paint, had also lightened his hair from medium brown to a sick shade of sandy blond and given it the texture of a horse's tail. A flattop had seemed the only alternative. After shaping Horace's hair into the new style, the beautician had suggested bleaching the flattop in the way so many young men now preferred. In a moment of desperation, Horace had agreed. Now he wondered if he had been insane.

The bleached flattop that framed his fortyish face accented the bags under his eyes and gave his skin an odd, ashen hue. He checked his watch, picked up a comb, extended it toward his hair, then stopped. There was nothing to comb. *What will Sara and Lenora think?* Horace harbored no illusions about his looks and, therefore, had never been vain. After all, a skinny male with a protruding Adam's apple, long face, and Saint Bernard eyes wasn't any woman's dream man. Nonetheless, he wondered how he would explain his drastic change in appearance to his fiancée and Lenora. The truth would reveal his Wednesday night disaster. He had managed to avoid seeing either woman while he spent the last three days trying to remove the paint. Finally, Lenora had insisted the three of them meet today, so Horace had made an emergency trip to the beautician.

The doorbell buzzed, and he jumped. Horace dropped the comb in the sink and fumbled to retrieve it. In the process, he knocked over the opened mouthwash bottle. The cinnamon liquid splashed onto his sweatshirt then splattered on his shoes. Horace grasped the damp bottle, shoved it onto the cluttered sink, and grabbed the dank hand towel hanging near the shower. He smeared his hands on the towel then scrubbed at the spots on his shirt. The doorbell buzzed again, and Horace tossed the towel into the corner, atop a pile of dirty clothes. With the smell of cinnamon trailing him, he walked the short distance to the dingy apartment's doorway. He gripped the knob, braced himself, and whipped open the door.

Sara, her plump face alight with a smile, stood on the other side. Her smile stiffened and her eyes widened as she focused just above Horace's eyes.

"Hi," Horace said, trying to sound nonchalant. "Come on in. Lenora isn't here yet."

"I know. I was hoping to get here early so we could talk." Sara focused on his neck and bit her bottom lip. Mutely, she entered the apartment.

With a deep breath, Horace conjured up his courage. No sense in pretending the hair problem didn't exist. "I, uh, guess you n–noticed my hair." He closed the door and automatically turned the lock.

"No, I…well, I guess I *did* notice a–a slight change." She tugged the baggy sweater around her bulging midsection. Her eyebrows drawn, she dared observe his scalp once more.

Horace, attempting a lighthearted chuckle, rubbed the top of his head. "The last time it was this short, I was 12 and my dad made me get a burr cut for the summer. That was the last burr I ever got." The next year had been one of the few times when Horace successfully stood up to his father. He wanted his hair longer, like all his friends were wearing, and had made his desire known. Even then, if not for his mother's firm support, Horace wouldn't have been able to stand his ground.

"Well, I must say that it is, well, different." Sara, her dark eyes alight with a warm glow, produced a supportive smile, and something inside Horace uncoiled.

"Actually, I didn't plan this," he said, and the truth surged forth despite his previous vows of silence. "I accidentally got paint in my hair. By the time I tried to get it out with turpentine and the beautician used acetone, the color was a strange shade of blond and my hair was as wiry as a Brillo pad. The beautician suggested a flattop and the bleach job. There wasn't much else to do."

"Must have been a lot of paint." She deposited her purse in the worn green armchair. The questions, silent and weighted, spun between them.

Horace rubbed a hand along the back of his head and the short hair pricked his palm. He gazed at the hole in the worn shag carpet then back at Sara.

"Does this have anything to do with the reason you didn't want to get together last night?" her high-pitched tone, soft and nasally, urged his unreserved candor. She fidgeted with the strand of beads around her neck and her left eyelid twitched. The thick glasses did little to hide the worried glint in her eyes.

For the first time, Horace sensed that Sara might be concerned about the status of their relationship. When she called last night, his hair had been dripping with turpentine. He had been making one last effort to remove the rest of the paint. Looking back, he now realized that he had been somewhat brusque with her. His blunt adieu last night, added to his asking Lenora to take her home Wednesday evening, might very well have given Sara an uneasy moment or two.

"Actually, Sara..." Horace slumped onto the pea-green sofa and debated his options. He extended his legs and crossed them at the ankles, and his father's lifelong accusations draped across his shoulders like a rotting remnant of the past. *You're nothing but a stupid klutz! You can't do anything right! You don't even know how to hold a gun right! You don't have the guts of a man.* The paternal mantra swirled through his mind and left a cold knot in his chest.

"I was planning on repainting my bedroom," he said, his voice even as he studied his shoelaces. "And I had the paint sitting in the closet. The lid wasn't on good and I bumped it. The whole mess dumped all over me. I've been working for days to clean it all up." He waved his arm.

Sara settled beside him and laid a hand on his thigh. "Why didn't you say something? I'd have come and helped you."

"You're always doing so much for me." Horace stroked her face and dashed aside the trace of guilt that flitted through his conscience. "I felt like such a dunce, and I thought that this once I should deal with the problem on my own." He sighed. "If you have to know, I had turpentine in my hair last night when you called."

A giggle erupted from Sara, and she covered her lips with her fingertips. Smiling fondly, she rubbed the top of his hair. "It's not bad at all," she said. "Really."

Horace grabbed her hand and placed the palm against his lips. "You're an angel," he said.

"Lenora wants us to go to Rome," Sara blurted. Her eye twitched as she twisted a strand of her shoulder-length hair, forever frizzed on the ends.

"Why does Lenora think we need to go to Rome?" Horace asked.

"I learned that in about six weeks the Caspers are taking a three-day cruise to the Grecian Islands and then spending a couple of days in Rome." Sara fidgeted with a button on her sweater. "Lenora seems to think that we should make our move then. She's offering to pay your way on the cruise so you will have ample time to befriend the twins. By the time you get to Rome, Lenora and I will be there. We can nab the girls then. She said that if the girls feel like you're an acquaintance from the cruise, they might very easily walk off with you. The streets are supposed to be so complex that it would be the perfect setting for taking the two kids." Her glasses inched down her nose, and she pushed them up. "Lenora says that the beauty of arranging the kidnapping abroad is that once we get out of Italy, we can just disappear in Europe, and nobody will ever find us." A twinge of relief laced Sara's words.

"Yes, that works beautifully as long as we don't get caught." Horace rubbed his palms along his thighs. This whole thing was growing more intricate by the hour, and he mulled over the complications wrought by arranging a kidnapping overseas. "The only problem is how will the Caspers be able to pay the ransom? I know they won't carry two million dollars on a cruise."

"Desmond holds investments around the world," Sara said without blinking. "We'll just arrange for him to transfer money from his Swiss account to one Lenora opened. The beauty of Swiss accounts is that we can maintain our anonymity. Lenora and I can manage that part of the equation, if you'd lure the twins away."

"Is this why she insisted on a meeting today?"

"Yes."

The two shared a silent gaze loaded with speculation. Finally Sara spoke. "I think it's time you understand that Lenora isn't quite as smart as she thinks she is. I don't believe she's as tough as she wants us to believe, either. I've worked for her for two years, and…"

"And?"

"I've probably lifted about 1,000 dollars out of her purse." Sara's voice took on a hard thread that was foreign to Horace. "She never even knew it."

He stared at his fiancée. Never had Horace suspected Sara of such dishonesty. Then he reminded himself that she was as involved in this scheme as he was. *What's worse? Stealing a thousand bucks or kidnapping two teenagers?*

"Furthermore, when Desmond broke off their relationship, Lenora banged into her office and sobbed most of the afternoon. A woman as hard as she wants everyone to believe she is doesn't cry that long over losing a man. She just cuts her losses and moves on to the next one."

"Well, she's mean enough to kidnap the Casper twins."

"Yes." Sara glanced down at her hands, knotted in her lap. "She does have a vindictive side. But maybe that can be played to our advantage." Sara peered into Horace's eyes. "A million dollars is *a lot* of money." She nodded with each word.

"More than I've ever seen."

Sixteen

The first of May, Melissa scurried from one exam room to another. Her patient load had doubled this week due to a flu outbreak bred by the capricious spring weather. By six o'clock Friday, Mel felt as if she needed an eight-day cruise to the Grecian Islands. The trip, looming in just two weeks, had been a source of excitement for Jacquelyn who still fought daily for emotional equilibrium. As Jac's enthusiasm increased, so did Mel's, albeit with a measure of incertitude. Kinkaide's serenade episode and front-yard kiss had filled her dreams with all sorts of inviting images. Images she wasn't certain she was ready to embrace. Images that kindled the flames of longings held long at bay.

With the last prescription written and the final patient leaving for home, Melissa walked into the clinic's hallway and paused. She stopped long enough to rub her aching neck then cover her yawn. A movement to the left caught her attention, and Mel glanced toward the bench that sat in the hall's recessed alcove. A young blonde, lithe and graceful, stood. She bent to pick up her handbag as if she were preparing to leave. Mel thought she recalled seeing the lady there about midafternoon, but her memory was most likely inaccurate. The patient load had been so heavy, Melissa might have sidestepped a gorilla then promptly forgotten the hairy beast.

She ambled up the hall, bid her weary staff farewell, and stepped into her office. The tasteful decor, a blend of hunter green and burgundy, soothed her taut nerves as she meandered across the plush carpet toward the entertainment center. Without hesitation, Mel repeated the routine she had developed in the last few weeks. She inserted one of Kinkaide's CDs and awaited the first notes of "I Love You, Lord" to bathe her spirit in the worshipful tune that both relaxed and renewed.

Mel picked up the CD case lying nearby and admired Kinkaide's photo. Dressed in a tuxedo, he sat at an ebony grand piano, bent over the keyboard as if he were pouring his very soul into the music. Melissa stroked the cover, her fingertip resting upon his face. The tuxedo reminded her once more of the day he serenaded her, the day he kissed her. Of late, that day seldom wandered far from her musings.

A warm wash spread through her chest, and Mel bit her lip to stay the smile. Shortly after Mel agreed to the cruise, Kinkaide resigned to the inevitable and had returned to Nashville to resume his bookings. He kept in touch with an occasional phone call or e-mail. Otherwise, he backed off, as if he were afraid he might scare Mel out of going. However, he arrived back in the city yesterday and called to ask if he and Lawton might come over tonight. Kinkaide said he wanted to introduce Lawton to Jac as well as cover some final details about the trip. Mel discussed the visit with Jacquelyn, and the two women had agreed the meeting would be a good move. After all, the cruise and visit to Rome would result in their spending five days together. Jac even offered to cook Mexican food. Mel checked her watch. The men would be arriving in 30 minutes. She needed to wrap up the day and head home. Mel was looking forward to Kinkaide's presence more than she would ever admit—even to Jac.

She replaced the CD case and noted the one beside it—the one that no longer held a cover. That print of Kinkaide had suffered the consequences of her vengeance. Despite Mel's guarded anticipation about the cruise and pending visit, a surge of the old bitterness spread through her veins. And the questions, irritating and timeworn, wove a methodical incantation in her mind.

How do I know I can trust him this time?

Will he repeat the past?

Does he have a clue how deeply he hurt me?

Is there any way I can ever forgive him and put the past behind us?

Last night Mel had removed the old journal from the end table and flipped to the final entry. Once again, the bold scribbles had jumped out at her. A soft impression within her soul insisted that the Lord wanted to erase those black lines from the pages of her heart—if only she would relinquish her right to nurture the vindictive monster whose stagnant breath pulsated from the caverns of her heart. Yet releasing her right to bitterness proved a scary endeavor because the bitterness protected her with a shell so hardened, so thick, that no darts of pain could pierce her heart. But then, neither could love...

Last night's struggle had been so intense that Mel had dropped the journal on the end table and fled to her bedroom. Now she realized she hadn't put the journal back in the table's drawer. She must do that as soon as she arrived home.

A soft knock at her door instigated Mel's closing the entertainment center's glass panels. "Yes?" she called, assuming one of her staff members had a last-minute request. As the office door opened, Mel turned to encounter the attractive blonde she had noticed sitting in the hallway. The blue-eyed lady stirred a vaguely familiar cord within Mel, and she grappled to place a name with the fine-boned face.

The woman, never taking her gaze from Mel, closed the office door and hovered on the threshold as if she didn't exactly know what to say. "I—I guess you noticed me watching you all afternoon." She pulled a strand of straight hair away from her perfectly glossed lips.

Self-consciously Mel pushed up her glasses and wondered if she even had any lipstick left. "Actually, I noticed you a few minutes ago, but it's been so busy that I wasn't certain exactly how long you'd been sitting there. Is there something I can help you with?" She rested her hand on the top of her desk and tilted her head.

"You're playing his music," the woman's voice held a hollow note.

Mel's legs stiffened and she crossed her arms. The hair along the back of her neck prickled. She narrowed her eyes. "You mean Kinkaide Franklin's?"

"Yes. That's exactly who I mean. I guess I was wrong in assuming that you would recognize me. If I had realized you didn't know who I was, I probably wouldn't have followed you into your office. But I thought I owed you an explanation," she said, as if each word were being wrenched from her. "Allow me to introduce myself." She stepped forward and extended a hand. "I'm Shelby Canady."

Jacquelyn peered into the bathroom mirror and tucked her bobbed hair behind one ear. The other side hung chin-length and came to a fashionable point that swung forward when she moved. The new style had been Mel's idea, and Jac was trying to get used to the feminine "do." She usually just arranged a blunt cut below her ears and didn't worry about where it fell. But the last few months had found her concerned about her hair less and less and it had grown annoyingly long. Today's cut had given the ebony locks a new bounce and verve. Never having cared much for makeup, Jac eyed a tube of Mel's lipstick lying on the countertop, then dismissed the notion. No sense in pretending she was something she wasn't. Her bronze skin, black lashes, and full lips would just have to remain their natural hues. Besides, the hairdo was enough froufrou business for one day.

With a sigh, she turned off the bathroom light and walked toward the kitchen, from whence flowed an array of tantalizing smells. Jacquelyn never considered herself an accomplished chef, but she had long ago received the title "Queen of Mexican Food" from her six sisters. Just as she opened the oven to check the cheese-covered enchiladas, the doorbell rang. Jac glanced at her stainless steel watch. Kinkaide and his brother weren't due for another 25 minutes. She closed the oven and neared the front door. A quick look through the peephole confirmed that the guys were early.

Jac held her breath and examined Lawton. Last night Mel had cautiously mentioned that Lawton was blind, a bit outspoken, and somewhat endearing. She had failed to add that his dark hair, prominent nose, and high cheekbones made him just as attractive as his elder brother...or that the black glasses added an air of mystery. Jac moved her eye from the peephole, gripped the doorknob, and closed her eyes. Nobody had even hinted that tonight was anything more than a necessary precruise encounter, and Jac hoped for Lawton's sake he wasn't considering this visit some sort of date. The last six weeks of struggling with memories and fighting for her sanity had delivered enough pain to reinforce Jacquelyn's decision to never marry. She never again wanted a man to touch her in the ways the abuser had. The very idea engulfed her in a wave of nausea.

The doorbell rang again, and she twisted the knob. The only thing she knew to do was put on the usual no-nonsense persona that spoke volumes and kept most males where they belonged—at arm's length. By the time the cruise rolled around, Lawton would understand that Jac was only an incidental acquaintance—and nothing more. The vague idea flitted through her mind that Lawton might be just as disinterested in a new relationship as she was, and Jac hoped that proved true. She opened the door and produced a cautious greeting.

"Hi, Jac," Kinkaide said as the men stepped into the living room. "Kinkaide Franklin." The two shook hands. "We met briefly last summer at the airport."

"Yes, I remember."

"This is my brother, Lawton." Jac inserted her hand into his and acknowledged his presence with a reserved greeting. Lawton's warm grip intensified Jac's decision to remain aloof.

"We're early. Is Mel here?" Kinkaide's gaze hungrily roamed the classic living room and dining room.

"Not yet." Jac closed the door and focused on Kinkaide. "One of her nurses called for her about an hour ago and said she was running late. I expect her soon."

"Something smells great." Lawton rubbed a hand over the front of his ribbed sweater. "Mel says you're the queen of Mexican food. If the smell's anything to go by, I believe her." His dark glasses reflected the soft light of the lamp sitting on the end table. Jac experienced the uncanny sensation that Lawton might see more than she wanted him to.

She strengthened her invisible wall and spoke in a factual manner. "Well, Mexican food is about all I know how to cook, but according to my friends I've perfected the talent. Just don't ask me to bake a cake or anything. The results are enough to declare any kitchen a national disaster."

Lawton threw back his head. "Ha! I love it!" His generous smile revealed an even row of white teeth.

"You'd say you loved anything she said just as long as you got to eat," Kinkaide chided.

Lawton leaned toward Jac. "Don't listen to a word he says," he hissed, and his dark eyebrows rose above the glasses as if he and Jac were conspiring. "He's widely known as a pathological liar."

Kinkaide snorted. "The first time she sees you eat, she'll *know* who's lying."

Jac took a tiny step backward. *Endearing.* Mel had said that Lawton was somewhat endearing. She inched toward the dining room. Endearing wasn't on her agenda—now or ever. "Well, why don't you guys have a seat in the living room, and I'll put the finishing touches on dinner," she said, her voice more blunt than intended. "Mel should be here in a minute," she continued, attempting to soften her tones.

"Oh, sure," Lawton said. "We understand. Get back to work by all means! Personally, my life's goal is to never interrupt a chef—especially when I'm on the receiving end of the efforts."

Kinkaide reached for his brother's arm and tugged him toward the couch. "I think you better quit running your mouth while you're ahead, don't you?" He winked at Jac who retreated into the kitchen, gripped the counter, and took several deep breaths.

This was going to be a long cruise—really, really long. And Jacquelyn began to wonder if she were crazy for agreeing to go. But the plans were made, and she had allotted 4,000 dollars from her savings account in hopes that the trip would open a new dimension of healing within her ravaged heart. What if it had the opposite effect? Her legs shook and she squeezed the counter tightly.

Melissa, where are you?

Seventeen

Melissa's face chilled, and she mechanically shook hands with the well-known Christian singer. "Yes, I thought you looked familiar," she said, sounding trite even to herself. "But you're not in your element, and I'm so tired that I couldn't quite place you."

Shelby backed away, crossed her arms, and eyed Mel with a curious glimmer in her eyes. Her stylish jacket reaching to her knees perfectly complemented the floppy-legged pants. The singer looked as if she were ready to step onto a concert stage.

"I guess you're wondering why I'm here." Shelby's words held a melodious nuance that blended in rhythm with Kinkaide's piano solo.

"The thought *did* cross my mind," Melissa said with a faint smile that hid the fact that her knees quivered. So this was the woman Kinkaide had nearly married. She was everything Melissa was not: tall, thin, blonde, perfect makeup, blue eyes, drop-dead-gorgeous. When Mel considered the fact that God had not only made this woman stunning but also highly talented, she squelched the urge to dissolve into the carpet. What in the name of common sense could Kinkaide Franklin, pianist extraordinaire, see in Mel when he could have the likes of Shelby Canady?

"Actually, if I had known you didn't realize who I was, I would have left the clinic and not said anything. I guess since I've gotten this far, I might as well confess all," she said as if she were chewing a bitter weed.

"Oh?"

"Yes." Shelby focused on Mel's stethoscope hanging around her neck. "I actually came here today to meet the woman who stole Kinkaide from me."

Mel's eyes narrowed.

"But the longer I sat out there," Shelby pointed toward the hallway, "and watched you, the more I saw you were a woman of great integrity. And the Lord began to show me that I had no right to despise you the way I did." Shelby's voice broke, and she walked toward the windows lining the west wall. Her shoulders hunched, she gazed out the open blinds.

Melissa, her hands clammy, switched off the piano music. The resulting silence magnified Shelby's sniffles. *Blast you, Kinkaide Franklin!* The edict ricocheted through Mel's mind. The shattered woman before her reminded Mel of herself those first few months after Kinkaide walked out of her life. The man was still in the business of breaking hearts. Mel's spirit sagged as she recognized a startling reality. She had allowed herself to be teased onto the brink of another of his traps. Despite her better judgment, Mel had permitted Kinkaide's charm to worm its way into her heart and lull her defenses to sleep.

Shelby whirled to face Mel. "I'm sorry." She stood tall. "I had no intention of coming in here and crying like this. I just wanted to tell you that—that—I guess the Lord seems to be telling me that I must—must forgive you, and you have no idea how dreadfully sorry I am that I've been so vindictive toward you." Shelby waved her hand. "I can't believe I'm telling you all this," she rushed, her voice unsteady. "You had no idea I felt this way. We don't even know each other. This is beyond ridiculous. It's just that I had envisioned you as a horrible fiend of a woman who I would abhor upon sight. And I got here, and there you were, the epitome of everything anybody would admire and—"

"You have nothing to forgive me for." Melissa approached the singer and gripped her restless hands. "Kinkaide did what he did to you without any encouragement from me. He came to Oklahoma City without my invitation and spent several months…" Melissa trailed off and groped for words. "The man is 34 years old, and I think it's time for him to have a few lessons in life," she ground out. "You look like you feel just like I did the weeks after he jilted me."

"He *jilted* you?" Shelby gasped.

"Yes. He left me standing at the altar—*literally*."

Shelby's eyes, smudged with mascara, widened and fixed upon Mel as if she had suddenly sprouted antennae. "And I thought *I* had it bad."

"Oh, he's a sly one," Mel said, tapping her foot. "He'll make you feel like a million bucks then say, 'Oops, just kidding.'" She twisted her hand upward. And the bitter beast that hibernated deep within stirred from short-lived slumber. It lifted a head, pulsating with rage. *I was on the brink of letting him convince me,* Mel thought as wave upon wave of the old animosity crashed upon her. The closer the cruise grew, the more Mel had dwelt on the romantic potential of Kinkaide and a moonlit deck. She had begun to hope that this time he might be sincere in his commitment, that perhaps the old love would bind them in a new bond, that maybe she should beseech the Lord to repair their relationship.

Have I lost my mind? she thought. *If Kinkaide would rip out Shelby Canady's heart, what would stop him from changing his mind—again—about me?*

"You mean," Shelby dashed at a tear, "the two of you really aren't…"

"*No!*" Melissa doubled her fists at her side.

"But he told me he was still in love with you."

"That's what he told me, but right now I wouldn't trust that man's word enough to lead me out of a burning house."

Mel's face hardened, and her lips curled up. "I've managed to let him convince me to go on a cruise, but I'm about to make certain he understands that this trip means *nothing*," she said more to herself than to her visitor.

"But you still love him, don't you?" Shelby pushed a strand of blonde hair away from her damp cheek.

Blinking, Melissa crossed her arms, broke eye contact, and gazed upon the golden sky ablaze with the setting sunset. Across the street, the trees in the churchyard blocked her complete view of the sunset. Yet patches of light pierced through the gaps in the limbs laden with leaves.

"And I think..." Shelby gripped Mel's forearm, "...that you love him more than I ever have."

"Love has a funny way of turning sour," Mel spit out. "And once it's sour, there's not much that can sweeten it again." On impulse, she walked toward her entertainment center. Mel ejected the CD that had been playing, removed it, then opened the storage compartment's glass door. Mel plopped the disk into the case and scooped up the rest of Kinkaide's CDs.

"You know," she approached Shelby, "I have this gut feeling that the two of us could be good friends. I've admired your musical talent for years, and now that I've met you, I think you're a woman who lives what you sing."

"I do try."

"Here." Melissa extended the CDs.

Shelby, her brow wrinkling, took the proffered pile.

"Take these home with you. First, rip out all of his pictures one at a time and tear them into tiny bits. After that, stomp the CDs. Then forget you ever met the man. You don't deserve what he's done to you. There's a better man out there for you—someone who will cherish you the way you should be."

Shelby's eyes widened. She peered at the CDs, looked back at Mel, then slowly shook her head. Without a word, the singer walked to the cluttered desk and deposited the disks on the edge. "I don't think I could d—destroy his work l—like that."

Melissa gritted her teeth and concentrated on the patterns of light that dappled the wall behind her desk. Some elusive element within Shelby made Mel feel like a rotten ogre, but she was powerless to stop the perpetual flow of virulence that burst forth like a vein of sewage suppressed but never diluted.

The phone's shrill ring seemed the timer that announced the end of their meeting. The singer rushed forward, wrapped her arms around Mel for a brief, tight hug, then dashed from the office. The telephone continued its peel. Mel, her heart thudding, marched toward her desk, picked up the receiver, and announced her name.

"Mel, it's Jac," her friend's desperate whisper rasped over the line. "Are you coming home soon? They're here."

"Oh, Jac, I'm sorry." Mel rubbed her forehead then checked her watch to see that 6:30 had already arrived. "Yes. I'm leaving now. I've got stacks of work left," she eyed the pile of patient folders on her desk, "but I'll come back early in the morning." The two said their goodbyes, and Mel replaced the receiver. Squinting, she scrutinized the CDs on her desk's corner. "And when I get home, I've got something to do that can't wait until tomorrow."

Kinkaide directed Lawton to the couch, then he settled into an armchair. Quietly he gave Lawton a brief rundown of the layout of Mel's living room, dining room, and kitchen.

"Jac seems like a nice lady," Lawton said when Kinkaide had finished.

Blinking, Kinkaide groped for a response. Lawton seldom missed the undertow of any interaction. This time, either Lawton's hunger was clouding his judgment or Kinkaide himself had missed something. In his opinion, Jac Lightfoot, while certainly not rude, seemed too stiff to label nice.

"What's the matter? You don't agree?" Lawton turned his head toward Kinkaide and raised his chin as if he were straining to read his brother's mind.

"Well, she's not as nice as Melissa," he said with a slow grin.

Lawton shook his head. "You and your one-track mind. I hope you guys get married soon. Otherwise you're going to explode."

"Like I said, you're on my prayer list," Kinkaide teased. "It's going to happen to you one day, and I'm going to laugh!"

"Yeah, yeah, yeah. Shut up and tell me something important. Does she have a TV?"

"Of course."

"Turn it on, will ya? I want to catch the sports news."

Kinkaide obliged his brother then settled back into his seat. Normally the sports channel enthralled him as much as the next guy, but tonight his mind roamed in other directions. He perused the room and soaked up every detail as if he were absorbing Mel's very essence. Finally his attention rested upon the collection of flower photos hanging on the opposite wall. Kinkaide stood and approached the collage of pictures. These photos drew him into Mel's psyche as nothing else in the room. He drank in the images of the various blooms. Daisies, daffodils, irises, roses. Bluebonnets, spider lilies, geraniums. Dogwood and apple blossoms. Each seemed a different facet of Mel's beauty. Kinkaide rubbed his thumb against his fingertips. Her cheeks...once he had told her that her cheeks were as soft as rose petals.

His gaze settled upon the velvet red rose with diamond-like dew drops, and he frowned. Kinkaide ran his finger along the unsightly crack that marred the photo. A crack that wasn't there before. Something within him tensed and he turned around. Not looking back, he reclaimed his seat.

The sports news momentarily attracted him. But another item soon snared his attention. Once again, the TV commentators blurred into a jumble of voices as a sole book on the end table riveted his attention. A slender book. A leather-bound book. A book that at first glance resembled a Bible. But the longer Kinkaide observed it, the more he suspected the pages, bound in blue, held someone's deepest thoughts. Was that someone Melissa?

Kinkaide extended his hand toward the end table then stopped. If indeed the book were a journal, he had no right reading Mel's private thoughts. *But it might not be Mel's.* The practical thought proved motive enough for Kinkaide to wrap his fingers around the diary. The cover, pliable and worn, seemed to warm against his palm. A thread of caution wove a path across Kinkaide's soul.

Driven by a force he didn't question, Kinkaide dashed aside the premonition, opened the journal, and fingered the first page. Mel's distinctive scrawl leaped forth. Kinkaide devoured her hidden secrets like an addict. But amid the captivation, an unease crept from the center of his chest and trailed down his arms to penetrate his fingertips—a faint alarm, a tinge of anxiety, a conviction of duplicity.

Kinkaide prepared to snap the journal shut, but his fingers rifled across the middle and revealed an interesting page marred by black slashes. Frowning, Kinkaide observed the harsh scrabbles then flipped back to the previous page. The date indicated the day before their wedding. His fingers tightened their hold, and Kinkaide consumed the words that refused to relinquish his attention.

Personal

Well, this is the night before the big day. I can't wait to say I do. I know Kinkaide's love is forever. Every day our love grows and I can't wait to begin our new life together. I am a little nervous. Okay, I'm a lot nervous. This is a big step, a once-in-a-lifetime deal, the biggest day of my life.

Mom has called three times in the last hour. She wants to come down, but I insisted we'll be just fine. Kinkaide and I want this to be simple and private—just something between me and him. Honestly, I'm already a nervous wreck. Having Mom here would just make matters worse. I know she loves me, but at times I wonder if it's just too much!

I know Kinkaide's love is forever. He narrowed his eyes as the words pierced his conscience. *Yes, my love is forever, but I was too big a fool to see that,* he berated himself.

Practical

The button popped off my wedding dress. I've poked my index finger three times trying to sew it back on. Here I am, learning to sew-up patients and I can't even sew a button on. I've packed and repacked so many times I've lost count. The honeymoon has to be perfect, and I want to make sure I have all the right stuff together. I'm nervous about our first night together. Now I'm back to personal stuff. Oh well, my index finger is stinging, and the button still isn't on the dress.

I'm nervous about our first night together. Kinkaide smiled as his mind raced forward to what he hoped would soon be their wedding night. Nervous? A giddy delight spun through his midsection. Okay, maybe they'd *both* be a little nervous.

> **Spiritual**
> *I feel closer to God than I ever have. My father taught me that God is a fact. All I need to do is believe He exists because He does. But experiencing Kinkaide's love is opening a new realm for me. As mentioned yesterday, I've started a new Bible study—one Kinkaide and I plan to continue together after we're married. For the first time in my life, the Word of God is really coming to life for me. I've noticed that the New Testament talks about Christ as the bridegroom and the church as the bride. Yes, I believe that God is a fact, but I'm also beginning to sense a new dose of grace and love that I never really connected with before. Kinkaide has encouraged me in my spiritual growth. I thank God that He has put such a godly man in my life.*

Kinkaide's face went cold as he reread the final lines. He flipped to the next page and once again took in the ugly black slashes. The weblike lines sprang forth, entangled themselves around his heart, and constricted until every breath was cut short.

"How *dare* you!" Melissa's accusation ripped across his musings, and Kinkaide's head snapped up.

Eighteen

Melissa snatched the diary from Kinkaide. His fingers curled into his palms.

"This is my private journal. You have no right—no right to read this!" She shook the book between them.

"Uh-oh," Lawton drawled, turning the two syllable interjection into a verdict of guilt.

"Stay out of this!" Kinkaide's self-incrimination spewed onto his brother.

"I am. Believe me, I am." Lawton stood and felt his way toward the dining room entry. "I'm outa here. This time you've made too big a mess for even me to help clean up."

Kinkaide directed a scowl toward Lawton, but his self-disgust outweighed any irritation with his sibling.

"I'm sorry, Mel," he began, raising one hand. "I shouldn't have—"

"Oh, yes, I know." Her hazel eyes, as hard as flint, seemed to be marred by the diary's black slashes. "There's *a lot* you shouldn't have done!" She slammed the journal onto the end table, and it slapped against the dark wood with the finality of a judge's gavel. "But that never stopped you, did it?"

Standing, Kinkaide towered over her. Yet Mel, her cheeks flushed, didn't back down. Instead, she drew closer and glared into his face. The sweet smell of jasmine perfume mocked the moment's acerbity. In their college days, Kinkaide had pushed Mel a bit just to see if her mask of control would slip. At last he was witnessing her unrestrained rage.

"I've about decided you are the most selfish person I have ever met!" she snarled.

"Excuse me?" Kinkaide blinked.

"Guess who came to see me today?"

Grappling to regain his equilibrium, Kinkaide floundered for any hint of an answer.

"Shelby Canady." Melissa crossed her arms.

Eyes bugging, Kinkaide stared at Mel. "Shelby came to see you?" he croaked.

"Yes." A satisfied smirk twisted her lips. "She did." Mel raised her chin.

"Whatever for?"

"She came to face the person who took her man. The best I can gather, the poor woman has been in agony because she fell in love with you and you did to her exactly what you did to me. You *dumped* her!" Mel's voice cracked, and she stood on her toes then rocked back.

"Listen, Melissa!" Kinkaide barked, his jaw muscles tightening. "I ended the relationship with Shelby the best way I knew how." He raised his arms. "What was I supposed to do, continue on and pretend everything was hunky-dory with her when I couldn't stop thinking about you? Good grief!"

"Good grief yourself," Mel snapped. "Talking with Shelby has opened my eyes to much more than I ever knew."

"Exactly what all did she tell you?" Kinkaide's mind whirled with possibilities, yet he couldn't imagine Shelby being anything but honest. However, at this point the truth wasn't sitting very well.

"She explained why she had been sitting in my clinic hallway most of the afternoon. I think she originally came to chew me out, but wound up sharing her heart."

"That sounds like her." Kinkaide shook his head. "She always—"

"Sounds to me like she always does what's right—unlike *some* people!" Mel picked up the journal and crashed it against the end table again. The brass lamp's shade vibrated with the blow as a sports announcer's voice from the TV punctuated the moment: "...has scored more than 50 points in the last three games."

"From all I can gather, you did the same thing to her you did to me." Melissa snatched the remote control from the cherry coffee table and switched off the television.

The silence intensified the cold knot forming in the pit of Kinkaide's stomach. For the first time since he determined to win back Mel, their chances at reconciliation seemed irrevocably nonexistent. The years spanned in front of him. Years without Mel. Lonely years filled with nothing but memories. Memories and heartache. Heartache and regrets.

The pain in his stomach dissolved into nausea. Kinkaide turned his back on Mel and paced toward the wall. The flower photos loomed before him. The rose, covered in dew diamonds, clutched his focus. Kinkaide related more to the crack in the glass than the symbol of beauty.

"And what's to stop you from ripping my heart out all over again in a few months?" Some of the venom had seeped from her voice and an aching hollowness rang forth.

Kinkaide pivoted to face her. No words seemed adequate. He knew no means to convince her that this time he meant what he said. "I never intended to hurt Shelby." Kinkaide shook his head. "She's a great woman. If I had known things were going to turn out the way they did, I wouldn't have ever started that relationship."

"And who came before me, Kinkaide?" Mel crossed her arms. "Who else was there? I'm not stupid enough to believe Shelby and I are the only ones."

"You're the only ones since I—" Kinkaide gritted his teeth then cleared his throat. "Since I became a Christian."

"So this pattern was already set?" Her brow arched.

The knot in his stomach grew icy. Icy and unyielding. Unyielding and bitter. "I wouldn't exactly say that." Kinkaide's eye flinched, and his face hardened.

"What's that supposed to mean?"

"It's none of your business." He walked toward the front door. His jaw tight, he decided retreat was the only way to stop his ire from blowing into an inferno. The last thing he wanted to do was discuss those youthful years when he had trampled the values he now cherished. Mel's unrelenting accusations about present issues certainly irritated him, but dragging up a past he never planned to discuss jerked him close to the precipice of rage.

"Wait a minute," Mel demanded. "I'm not through."

Kinkaide swiveled to face her. "You'd better be quick," he growled.

Her malicious stance never altered. "I'm still going on this cruise because Jac has already agreed, and I really think she needs it. But understand one thing: I am not—*am not*—going as your date. Whatever was between us is over. Got it? *Over!*" She stomped her foot. "I don't trust you—not even that much." The rancorous words dripped with poison as she lifted her forefinger and thumb to measure a few centimeters.

"You know what, Dr. Melissa Moore?" Kinkaide snarled. He approached her and pointed his index finger within inches of her nose. "You might call me selfish, but you're more vindictive than I have *ever* been!"

Her hardened gaze never wavered, and Melissa remained a relentless pillar of acrimony.

Kinkaide felt as if his words bounced right off of her closed mind and hit him squarely in the face. "You're just like your mother!"

Mel's eyes held a glint of steel and her mouth hardened. An unearthly roar burst forth.

Without giving her time to release more ammunition, Kinkaide marched from the house, crawled into his Oldsmobile, and slammed the car door. The smell of new leather seemed to fuel his rage. Kinkaide cranked the engine, and Elvis' mellifluous voice flowed forth with "Can't Help Falling in Love." He jabbed his finger against the CD player's off button, slammed the car into gear, and sped up the street.

Only when he was three blocks away did Kinkaide remember Lawton. "Oh great," he said and pinched his bottom lip. He slowed the car, grabbed his cell phone, and punched the appropriate numbers. Lawton's phone rang only twice.

"Yo," Lawton said. "You forgot me, didn't you?" This time his brother's voice held no hint of mockery. Perhaps Lawton suspected that Kinkaide was past the point of good-nature-about his taunting.

"Yes," he said wearily, "I did."

"Don't worry about it. I'll get Jac to drive me home. I had just talked her into letting me sample an enchilada when you left. Maybe she'll let me get down to some serious eating."

Kinkaide grimaced and eyed a poodle on the sidewalk tugging its owner by a leash. Somewhere along the line, Lawton simply didn't catch Jac's rebuffing vibes. She was undoubtedly within hearing distance of the phone call, and Kinkaide could only imagine her expression.

"Are you sure she won't mind?" he prompted. "It's no problem for me to—"

"Why should she?" Lawton countered. "Just a minute. Let me ask." The sound of muffled voices floated across the line.

Kinkaide glanced in the rearview mirror to confirm there were no cars behind him. Releasing the brake, he allowed the car to creep forward.

"She says it's not a problem," Lawton said. "Hey, if all else fails, I'll call a taxi, okay?"

"What's gotten into you?" Kinkaide snapped. *Jac probably wishes you'd disappear, and for once you're clueless.* But he couldn't quite pull together the guts to voice such brutal honesty.

"I'm hungry, okay? And I don't have anything cooked at home."

"Well, we can go *out* for Mexican."

"Don't worry about me, I'll be okay," Lawton said, and his phone's weak beep announced the call's end.

"Well, that's just fine." Kinkaide shoved the phone back into the dash holder. "I just got chewed up and spit out. I guess you're bound and determined to have your turn."

As he steered through the Oklahoma City traffic, Kinkaide's death grip on the steering wheel relaxed. Finally he cooled enough to mull over Melissa's verbal attack without spiraling into a new whirlwind of fury. *I've about decided you are the most selfish person I have ever met...*On the heels of her irksome words, he contemplated his motivation in reading that journal. In the end, his desire to know Mel's thoughts had overruled his respect for her privacy. The observation functioned like a revealing shaft of blinding light that highlighted a flaw within Kinkaide he'd rather not see. In the hallway of Desmond's church, Kinkaide had resisted acknowledging the same flaw and sprinted toward assisting his friend. This evening the car held him captive. There was no place to run.

He shifted against fine leather and slowed to stop at a red light. The traffic whirred around him, but Kinkaide felt as if he were alone on a deserted island—completely alone—with his thoughts acting as an unrelenting bully. Lawton's humorous, although pointed, observation floated through his mind, *You know, for somebody who usually gets what he wants, you're really bombing big.*

Do I really love Mel, or am I just in love with having what I want? The question that had previously disturbed Kinkaide now left him reeling. And Mel's edict echoed through his mind like a chant of truth that refused to hush: *I've about decided you are the most selfish person I have ever met…you are the most selfish person I have ever met…the most selfish person I have ever met.*

"Stop it!" Kinkaide hollered and a honk blared from behind. The light, once red, glowed green. He pressed the accelerator and joined the line of cars ahead of him.

As if the moving car hurled him into another vein of thought, Kinkaide relived that day when Shelby found Mel's photo. He blasted himself anew for hurting the attractive singer.

"What a mess." He shook his head. "What a huge, huge mess."

With a groan, Kinkaide contemplated Shelby's confronting Melissa. Most people who met Shelby Canady found her sincere eyes inviting and friendly, her candid manner childlike in its purity. Her uncomplicated charm had attracted Kinkaide as much as her looks. Mel was probably no different from the rest of the people who admired Shelby. After the meeting between Shelby and Mel, Kinkaide undoubtedly came out looking worse than ever.

"If I'd just had the sense to pray about the relationship with Shelby," he muttered.

A familiar building loomed in the distance—a building Kinkaide had been heading for all along. He slowed and pulled into the parking lot, past a sign that read "Trinity Church of the Nazarene." The cross behind the pulpit tugged him, wooed him, beckoned him to finally set aside what *he* wanted and seek the Lord for *His* perfect will.

Kinkaide parked in the deserted lot and got out of the car. He headed toward the modern sanctuary's main doors and tugged on the handle. The glass door didn't budge. "Figures," he muttered and checked his watch. The hands, glowing through the dusk, announced that 7:30 had just slipped by. Kinkaide inserted his hands into the pockets of his pleated slacks and stared across the city's sprinkling of lights. The faint smell of burgers attested to a nearby fast-food restaurant.

Love is patient, love is kind. It does not envy, it does not boast, it is not proud. It is not rude, it is not self-seeking...

"Oh, Lord," Kinkaide breathed, "Mel is right. I *am* selfish. I've been nothing but selfish in this whole ordeal. I was selfish when I left her at the altar and went off to Nashville without her. I was even selfish when I serenaded her in her yard. I was willing to let that neighbor call the police in order to get what I wanted."

The words from Melissa's journal seemed a heavenly response to his prayer. *I'm also beginning to sense a new dose of grace and love that I never really connected with before. Kinkaide has encouraged me in my spiritual growth. I thank God for putting such a godly man in my life.*

With a sigh, Kinkaide leaned against the brick church and slid to the sidewalk. He propped his arm across his upright knee, pinched his lip, and pondered his plight. *When was the last time I lived up to what Mel's diary said?*

"Before Nashville," he said aloud. "Before I made a name *for myself.*" Kinkaide scrubbed his fingers through his beard. "Oh, God, help me," he breathed. "I've gotten so far from You. Here I am, a nationally recognized Christian pianist, for pity's sake, and I'm eaten up with myself. With me!" he slammed his fist against his chest. "I haven't given a flip about what's best for Mel—just what's best for *me!*" He pounded his fist against the unforgiving concrete. "Me! Me! Me! How could I really love her or anyone when I'm so in love with myself?" His lips contorted with the revolting admission.

Kinkaide set aside his glasses and rubbed his hands over his tense face. "Oh, Father," he whispered. "Give me what it takes to love her more than I love myself—enough to release her...forever." He pressed his forefinger and thumb against his eyes. "Also, if there's any way, please help Mel forgive me for jilting her."

He replaced his glasses and a sting erupted from the back of his hand. Kinkaide scrubbed at a fire ant then observed a trail of the tiny beasts marching near his leg. He stood, examined his hands and arms, then brushed at his slacks. His telling Mel she was just like her mother must have gone over like an infestation of fire ants.

"What a disaster. What an awful disaster."

The remaining weeks slipped by. Weeks in which Kinkaide sought the Lord. Weeks in which he struggled in dying to himself.

At long last, the dream of the cruise materialized into reality...

Nineteen

⌒

"I still can't believe Kinkaide told me I was just like my mother!" Melissa put the last touches to her lip gloss then swiveled to face her friend.

Jac, sitting on a cabin bunk, clipped her fingernail then eyed Mel. "Yes, I've heard that rumor," Jac's bland expression never changed.

"I've said that about six times since we boarded our first flight, haven't I?" Mel asked.

Jac shook her head and snapped the clippers into place. "No, I think it's more like eight. Let's see…" She held up her index finger. "When we were waiting for the plane in Oklahoma City." Finger number two shot up. "Right before we landed in New York." She held up a third finger. "After we checked into our hotel in Athens." Two more fingers rose. "Once while we were waiting to board the ship. Once after Kinkaide told you we were on the Venus Deck. Once after you sat by Kinkaide on the tour bus on Mykonos. And once right now." Jac examined her hands. "That's seven. I guess we were both wrong."

"But who's keeping track, right?" Mel chided.

"Actually, I could have missed a few times. Those are just the ones that come to mind." Jac smiled and stood. "I'm ready for dinner if you are."

"How do I look?" Mel asked, glancing over her white pantsuit. "I just hope we're not too casual."

"We're fine," Jac said, slipping into her red blazer. "They said tomorrow night's the dress-up night anyway. Don't worry about it. Kinkaide seems to have thrown in the towel over your relationship. He barely looked at you all day. I'm not certain he'd be impressed one way or the other."

"Who said anything about *him?*" Mel frowned.

"Oh, I don't know." Jac shrugged and examined her fingernails. "Seems there's this recurring echo since we started getting ready for dinner—but I could be imagining things." She rifled through her suitcase near her twin bed and pulled out a fingernail file.

"All this sea air is making you mischievous." Mel, delighted with Jac's lightheartedness, retrieved her purse-organizer from her neatly made bed. She glanced out the cabin's window that was framed in elegant drapes. The Aegean Sea, moon-kissed and glassy, extended toward the horizon. The brilliant day, ending with an evening stroll down the winding streets of the picturesque Isle of Mykonos, seemed a mockery to the ball of tension inside Mel. A ball of tension that had been steadily growing since the verbal confrontation with Kinkaide two weeks earlier.

Since then, every time her mother called, Mel relived Kinkaide's heated accusations. *You might call me selfish, but you're more vindictive than I have ever been. You're just like your mother!* Mel couldn't remember the number of times she had thought her mother was the most spiteful person she had ever met. Not only did Darla Moore try to control her daughters, she seldom forgot an offense. The last couple of weeks had been particularly difficult. Mel had finally scraped together the courage to confront her mom over her controlling tendencies—and the two conversations had not progressed well at all. Earlier in the week, Darla had even slammed down the phone in Mel's ear. That was the last time Mel had talked with her.

"So, do you think I'm like my mother?" Mel asked. She slung the strap of her purse over her shoulder and examined her friend.

Jacquelyn looked up from filing her nails, and the point of her bobbed hair swung against her cheek. "Well…I don't know her that well," she hedged.

"Come on, Lightfoot. Through the years you've met her several times and listened to me talk about her enough to make a call."

"Ummm…" Jac furiously filed her thumbnail.

"She threatened to disinherit me and never speak to me again last week when you were in Denver." Mel squinted and shook her head. "I'd never do anything like that. If I ever have a daughter, I want to be her best friend—not her dictator."

"Good grief. And I thought my mother was bad. I don't think she holds a candle to yours. Do you think she really means it?"

"Who knows?" She raised both hands. "This is the first time she's ever been so drastic. There was a time when I thought she'd never distance herself from me."

"Does your father know what she said?"

"I don't know. Mom has some old family money that, according to legal conditions, is supposed to go to her children when she dies. She has control over its direction." Mel sank onto the side of her bed and her shoulders drooped. While this cruise was already lifting Jac's spirits, the stress of dealing with Kinkaide while pondering her mother was having the opposite effect upon Mel—and they were only one day into the voyage.

"This is horrible, Mel. What caused her to say something like that?" Jac lowered herself to her bunk and scrutinized her friend.

"We got into a discussion over the cruise. I held off telling her I was going because I knew she'd get the wrong idea, and I didn't want her talking about it for weeks." Melissa adjusted her glasses. "She was thrilled about the cruise until I insisted there was no hope for Kinkaide and me.

"Then...get this..." Mel's fingers bunched tightly. "She told me that I was the most stubborn person she had ever met and that if I had any sense, I'd grab Kinkaide."

Jac nodded.

"That's when I told her I was tired of her trying to control me and that my life was mine, not hers. The conversation heated up from there. She denied ever having anything but my best interest in mind." Melissa yanked the zipper on her handbag. "I wound up telling her that if she couldn't talk to me without trying to manipulate me then to quit calling."

Whistling, Jac shook her head.

"That's when she said, 'No daughter of mine tells me not to call and gets away with it,'" Mel mimicked her mother's tone. "'You just might find out that I'll disinherit you and never speak to you again.'"

"Mel, why haven't you said something before now?" Jac gripped her hand.

Melissa held her friend's dark gaze. "I hated to burden you. You're going through some really bad stuff right now, and—"

"But it's not fair for me to lean on you and you not to lean on me," Jac said.

"You know what really bothers me?" Mel asked as if Jac hadn't spoken. "All my life I remember hearing my dad grouse that my mom is just like her mother. Anytime my mother hears that, she gets livid and denies it." The beds vibrated with the rhythm of the *Olympic Countess'* engines—a beat as predictable as the underlying currents that plagued her family.

"Do you think she's like your grandmother?"

"Well, a little, I guess. My grandmother died about ten years ago, but I remember she always asked too many questions. My father was forever aggravated because she was so nosy." Melissa stood and shouldered her bag once more.

"Needless to say, when Kinkaide told me I was just like my mother..." Mel left the rest unsaid.

Jacquelyn placed the fingernail file in the middle of her palm then slid her fingers to the base, flipped the file, and repeated the motion. The silence bespoke her hesitancy, and Mel's spirits ebbed.

"I am like my mom, aren't I?" she whispered.

"Not in a bad way, Mel," Jac said, her dark eyes imploring her friend. "It's just that—"

"My grandmother was always pushing for more information and trying to manipulate the situation. I remember her and my dad having arguments the whole time I was growing up." Melissa's focus trailed to the window, as if hoping it was a threshold to insight. "My mom does the same thing—except I think she's a little more vindictive than Grandma." The window blurred.

That vengeful ogre abiding in the caverns of Mel's heart stirred. It raised its head, and frenzied eyes burned red with disdain. For six years she had nourished the fiend with ample doses of negative memories. The number of nights she had lain awake and relived the day she returned Kinkaide's ring were too numerous to count. And with every recounting, her resentment festered tenfold.

"I even dreamed about laughing at Kinkaide when he came crawling back," Mel whispered.

"Excuse me?" Jac said.

She snapped her gaze to Jac. "I guess I am a little like my mother," she rasped. "After all, the sisters don't call me the mouth of the south for nothin' do they?" A corner of her mouth lifted, but Mel's heavy spirits didn't relish the attempt at humor.

Jacquelyn stood and placed a hand on Melissa's shoulder. "And we wouldn't want you any other way."

Sighing, Melissa nodded and followed her friend out of the cabin, up the ship's narrow hallway, and toward the elevator. Kinkaide, Lawton, and the Caspers were probably awaiting their arrival in the restaurant on the Apollo Deck. During their evening of sightseeing, Mel had managed to avoid Kinkaide except for the ride in the tour bus. However, after they came back on board, Lawton had insisted Jac and Mel join them for a late dinner.

Melissa gritted her teeth and counted the days until this trip was over. *Just two more days on the ship. One night in Athens. Two days and nights in Rome. And one day getting back home.* In six days, Mel would be back in Oklahoma City. Those six days loomed like an eternity.

"If you don't mind, Jac," Mel said as they paused beside an elevator trimmed in brass. "I want you to sit by Kinkaide. There's nothing left for us to say. The sooner this trip is over the better," she growled.

The elevator bell dinged, and Jac eyed her companion. "You really don't look so hot. You've even got dark circles under your eyes."

"Thanks for that report," Mel said with a fond smile. "With friends like you..." The elevator doors hissed open.

"Are you sure you don't want to call room service for dinner?" Without awaiting an answer, Jac stepped into the elevator, as if her offer were a token gesture at best.

"I'm not going to do that to you," Mel said. "You're enjoying this too much for us to hole up in the cabin."

"Well, okay, if you insist," Jac said with an impish smile. "This trip has already done me stacks of good. I haven't gotten away like this in years."

"How are you feeling about...things?" Mel and Jac hadn't discussed the issues of her past in several weeks. After Jac's emotional deluge those first few days of her visit, Mel hadn't pushed her friend into any uncomfortable conversations.

"Oh, I feel like I could kill the slime ball who hurt me." Jac's black eyes took on the glint of a vicious rottweiler. Her jaw muscles flexed, and she stabbed her finger against the button marked six. The door sighed shut, and a stifling oppression radiated from Jacquelyn. "I really would rather not talk about it until the trip is over," she ground out.

"I'm sorry," Mel said. "I shouldn't have—"

"It's not your fault." Jac tucked her hair behind her ear and looked down. One side of her hair swung forward, producing a barrier between her and Mel.

For once in her life, Mel wanted to rip out her own tongue. *My mother would have probably asked the same thing*, she accused. *When am I going to learn?*

Kinkaide glanced across the restaurant toward the main entry—still no sign of Melissa and Jac. His disappointment rose to a new level as he wondered if they had decided to order their meal in. The hum of eager diners, the exquisite blue carpet, the crystal goblets glistening in the light of chandeliers contradicted the pall of pressure that continually plagued their party of eight.

Abby Casper toyed with her white napkin, folded like a tent where her plate would eventually reside.

"I wonder what's on the menu tonight?" Desmond pointed the question toward his wife.

"Don't know," she bit out.

Kinkaide winced. When Desmond proclaimed that Abby had changed her mind about the trip, Kinkaide assumed that the two were making progress. However, he eventually discovered that Abby had been coerced into the cruise by her daughters. She had insisted upon separate cabins and treated Desmond with nothing more than cold civility since they'd left port.

Janie and Julie, as if intent upon denying their parents' plight, whispered between themselves then peered toward a young Athenian waiter dressed in a black tuxedo with gold trim. Abby followed their interaction and fondly smiled. An ever-present ache stirred her exotic eyes and tainted her motherly adoration. Kinkaide and Desmond exchanged a brief glance, and a veil of desperation settled upon them.

We're really enjoying this cruise, now, aren't we? Kinkaide mused, then snapped his napkin and placed it in his lap.

"Any sign of Jac and Melissa?" Lawton asked. He eased his fingers along the white tablecloth until he detected the water goblet.

"Not yet," Kinkaide said.

"Hope they don't change their minds." Lawton lifted the glass to his lips and took a swallow. "Jac seems really nice."

"I'm beginning to get the idea that you like her *a lot*," Kinkaide said, almost afraid of the answer.

"Well, she's…nice," Lawton replied. "We talked quite a bit on the plane."

During the flight from New York, Lawton had somehow landed in the seat beside Jacquelyn. Kinkaide possessed a blurred impression of the two carrying on an occasional conversation during the six-hour journey. Yet he wondered how much of Jac's cool politeness stemmed from good manners. She seemed far too frigid to sustain Lawton's perplexing interest. This evening, on the Isle of Mykonos, Jacquelyn had barely spoken to Lawton. Kinkaide, eyeing a waiter who carried a huge tray, marveled at his brother's growing fascination for the private detective.

"At least she's not trying to mother you," Kinkaide said, not certain what else to say—and that was an understatement. On the plane, Jac assisted Lawton with his carry-on luggage only when he almost pulled another passenger's briefcase out on top of him.

The waiter stopped at their table, and a waft of cream of strawberry soup teased Kinkaide's senses. The soup would prove a refreshing end to a stressful day. He cast a defeated glance toward the entryway, only to encounter Mel and Jac a few feet from the table.

"Hi," Jacquelyn said as the two approached.

She reached the table first and settled into the vacant chair beside Kinkaide. Mel, without even looking toward him, took the last seat between Lawton and Abby. Melissa had barely spoken to Kinkaide since they left Oklahoma City, and any notions he might have entertained about her warming to him dwindled to nonexistent. A strained hush settled upon the table as the waiter set a bowl of the exotic soup in front of each diner. From that point forth, the conversation endured short bursts, which usually erupted between the three women and Lawton and lasted but a few exchanges. By the time all the courses were served, Kinkaide was planning a swift retreat.

"I think I'm ready to hit the hot tub," Mel said.

"I'm in," Jac announced.

Mel turned to Abby. "Care to join us?"

"Sounds great," Abby said then looked at her daughters. "Do you two want to come?"

"Actually, we were wanting to go to the gift shop," Julie said.

"Do you mind?" Janie asked.

"No, that's okay with me," Abby said.

Desmond peered around the restaurant. "Do you think it's safe for them to be on their own?"

"Yes," Abby snapped. "We're on the Aegean Sea. Nobody knows us from Adam. Stop being so paranoid. They're 15! They can look out for themselves long enough to walk to the gift shop. At some point, you've got to let them grow up." She lifted her hand. "What can happen?"

"Okay, okay," Desmond shot back, and a line formed between his brows. Then, he glanced toward his daughters. "Be careful," he admonished.

"Could we have some money?" the two said in unison.

He rolled his eyes and reached for his billfold. "You two are going to be the cause of my financial doom."

Abby, her face a mask of steel, focused on her tea goblet.

Kinkaide swallowed his last bite of chocolate mousse. *Well, so much for our first dinner on the ship together,* he thought as the women and twins stood.

"Jac?" Lawton pushed back his chair and rose. "Can we talk a minute?"

She glanced toward Mel as if she were imploring her for a rescue.

"I'll meet you in the hot tub," Mel said.

The detective's eyes rounded and her lips pressed together. Mel responded with a slight shrug that said, *Tell him no, then.* She hesitated, and Jac remained silent. Mel darted a last glimpse toward Kinkaide. An intense glimpse full of speculation and sorrow.

Kinkaide didn't flinch. Instead, he broke eye contact and observed the candle, burning in the center of the table. The flame blurred through the glass globe, and he steeled himself against looking back at Melissa. He had vowed to stop pushing her, and with God as his helper, he'd stand by that vow. Not once had he so much as started a conversation with her since they left home. Their few verbal exchanges had been instigated by Melissa and concerned only necessary trip facts. If she ever did come around, it would be because she chose to, not because Kinkaide pressured her. While that decision had freed Kinkaide in one aspect, on another dimension, he panicked. The whole situation was now out of his control and in the hands of God and Mel. Never had Kinkaide felt so dependent upon his Creator and so vulnerable with the woman he loved.

Lawton gripped the back of Kinkaide's chair and neared Jac. He lightly grasped her upper arm and said, "There's supposed to be a Brazil Coffee Verandah somewhere on this deck. Think we could find it?"

Jacquelyn cast a final gaze toward Mel and Abby who companionably picked their way through the numerous tables. She looked back at Lawton, but this time her wary eyes, dark and haunted, barely softened.

Toying with his mousse spoon, Kinkaide blinked and scrutinized her.

"Okay, why not," she said. "The hot tub will be there tomorrow."

Kinkaide dropped the spoon.

Desmond rolled his eyes and scooted away from the table. Shaking his head, he watched Lawton and Jac as they walked toward the outer deck. "What's he got that we don't have?" Desmond drawled.

"Uh, the woman, I'd say."

"Aren't we a pair?" Desmond asked and dusted bread crumbs from the front of his cream-colored jacket.

"Yep. We might as well enjoy each other's company. Nobody else seems interested. Wanta take a walk on the top deck?" Kinkaide offered then stood. "I hear the moon is great up there."

"Okay, but if you try to get romantic, I'll shove you over-board." Desmond stood and stroked his thin mustache.

"Don't worry about me," Kinkaide shot back. "I've forgotten how to be romantic. And the way things are going, I can probably forget it for life." He adjusted his navy blazer and pushed his chair into place.

"We're really striking out big," Desmond said as the two friends wove their way through the sea of tables. "And I have a feeling that it's now or never for me and Abby. When she agreed to go on the cruise, I was really hoping she might be coming around. But right now, I'd say she's leaning toward never."

A cloud of depression descended upon the men as they took the lift toward the top deck. Kinkaide's prayer that God would give him the strength to completely release

Melissa had yet to be answered. Even though he had gained enough self-control to stop pushing her, Kinkaide continued to cling to Mel in his heart and hope that perhaps this cruise would work some sort of a miracle. So far, that hope had been smashed.

Twenty

Horace Waggoner stepped into the gift shop seconds after the Casper twins entered. He trailed them to a display of crystal fish and picked up a plate-sized angelfish as if he were enthralled.

"These are really pretty," the twin with the short hair said. Horace thought Lenora had told him she was Julie. "Dad would like one of these for the collection in his office."

"I was thinking of getting one for Mom, actually," Janie said. "She likes this sort of stuff, too." She reached for an angelfish and looked under the base. A faint gasp escaped her. "Maybe they'll have to get one for themselves."

Julie glanced at the price and giggled. "Dad really will think we're out to ruin him financially."

"Do you think they're going to split up?" Janie asked as she replaced the fish.

Glancing toward Horace, Julie tugged her sister away from the crystal display, toward the clothing. Horace, straining to hear the girls, continued to examine the various fish. During dinner he had scrutinized the Caspers. He didn't think there was any doubt that those two were heading for split city. Lenora had indeed wreaked havoc with that family.

And she's not finished, he thought. A swirl of guilt twined through his gut. He eyed the girls as they looked through a rack of shorts. Lenora and Sara both continued to say that nobody was going to get hurt in this ordeal. However, their ransom note, already written, threatens the twins' lives if the Caspers go to the police.

Horace replaced the angelfish and a shiver zipped down his spine. The eyes of the fish, tiny and bulging, bore into him as if the crystal replica fully understood his artifice. *What happens if Desmond goes to the police anyway? Will Lenora kill his children?* The spike-heeled vixen seemed to perpetually exist on the precipice of rage. One move over the edge, and she just might lose control. He wondered if she would eventually think that killing the girls would be the next best thing to killing the man who scorned her. *Once she gets them into her custody, can she be trusted to keep her word?*

Frowning, Horace stepped from the fish display and meandered toward the men's swimming trunks. He passed the twins and picked up a snatch of their conversation.

"Maybe if we talk to Mom and tell her how we feel," Janie said.

"Do you really think Dad had an affair? If he did..." Julie's eyes, wide and sincere, spoke her concern.

"I can't help it if he did," Janie said. "It's over now. It must be. I just don't want them to get a divorce."

Julie nodded. "Neither do I."

Horace pulled out a pair of swim trunks in octopus print and watched the girls as they wandered toward the scented soaps. Within a few minutes, they approached the clerk and laid several bars of soap on the brass-and-glass checkout counter. Horace, clutching his swim trunks, stopped behind them and awaited his turn to pay.

"That will be $7.49," the smiling clerk said.

Janie, fumbling with her purse, dropped a handful of change, and Horace seized the awaited opportunity. He chased down several quarters, retrieved them, and helped the twins gather the rest of the coins.

When he placed the money in Janie's hand, the twins both looked him square in the eyes without a glimmer of recognition. The minuscule doubt that occasionally plagued

Horace now fled. Ever since that park episode he wondered if the twins might recognize him.

"Thanks," Janie said.

"Any time," Horace replied and produced his most innocuous smile. By the time they got to Rome, he'd have earned their implicit trust. Leading them into Lenora and Sara's trap would prove an effortless endeavor.

But what if the Caspers involve the police, and Lenora really does kill them? The question bubbled up from a cesspool of concern fed by the steady drip of Horace's growing misgivings. If the Casper twins were murdered, he wasn't certain a million dollars would sufficiently ease his conscience. *Nobody's going to get hurt.* Sara's repeated claim now rang hollow. *Just suppose Lenora snaps?*

Horace meandered from the gift shop and watched the twins walk to a cabin about 20 feet down the hallway. An image of their lifeless forms, abandoned in a Rome hotel room, sprang upon him. Horace's stomach churned. He whipped around and marched toward the elevator. He had spent an hour before dinner in the bar on the Hera Deck. The whisky had taken the edge off his nerves and bequeathed him a renewed determination to not disappoint Sara. Perhaps another shot or two would remind him to maintain his focus on the original plan. A million bucks was a lot of money. And Sara's approval meant about as much to him as the money. When he was with Sara, the shackles of his father's scorn loosened. If the two took the million and disappeared, perhaps the past would sufficiently blur and Horace would finally experience peace.

Jac and Lawton settled at a table for two on the Brazil Coffee Verandah. The *Olympic Countess,* humming beneath them, sliced through the night, and the cool breeze both refreshed and teased the senses. The luminous disk rising upon an intangible canvas of night whispered of fantasies and bathed the dimly lit deck in a soft aura. The smell of the sea mingled with the mellow aroma of coffee seemed to fuse with the moonlight.

A thin, swarthy waiter holding a tray stopped by their table. "Would you care to order?" he asked, his words laced with a French accent.

"I'd like some decaf coffee," Lawton said.

"Me, too," Jac supplied.

"Do you have amaretto?" Lawton asked.

"Yes, of course," the waiter said. "Will that be two?"

Jac nodded and the waiter wisked away.

"Tell me what you see." Lawton placed an elbow on the table and leaned forward.

Jac pressed her back into the chair. Lawton's dark glasses, like the lustrous sea, reflected the moonlight and suggested the depths of a man with a heart the size of the sky. Jac, her pulse gently pounding, wondered how she managed to land herself in this situation.

Endearing. Mel said Lawton was endearing. Jac swallowed. *But I don't need endearing. Not now. Not ever.*

What if he tries to kiss me? the thought raced upon her, and Jac's palms moistened. But then she evaluated what she knew of Lawton so far and dismissed the illogical notion. They hadn't known each other nearly long enough, and Lawton didn't seem the type to push himself on a woman. Her stiff back relaxed a bit.

"Cat got your tongue?" he asked, and his lips tilted into a jocose grin. "Or have you silently deserted me and I'm talking to myself?"

"No. I–I'm still here," Jac said, then gazed toward the ocean. "The moon is full," she said. "The sea is slick—like a mirror. And the moonlight is seeping into the water. It's like there's this glow across the water—almost like phosphorous—as if the water is a sponge, soaking up the light."

"Oooh. And the detective is poetic. Do go on."

Jac's hands tightened in her lap, and her breath caught as a disturbing realization immersed her. She liked this man before her. She liked him a lot. Her heart hammered, and she was hurled into a whirlwind of conflicting emotions. On one level, Jac didn't want him to so much as hold her hand. On another level, she longed to step into his arms and relish the warmth of his ardor.

"Hello..." Lawton said.

"Well, there's not much more to tell... Uh, we have an umbrella over us."

"I figured that one."

"I guess there's the stars." Jac tilted her head toward the heavenly bodies and scanned the unending pinpoints of light.

"Ah, the stars," Lawton said. His voice, like a furtive nuance of the night, blended with the lapping of water along the ship's sides as he continued...

> Yes. I love the stars. I love them.
> I love the way they shine for the hand that created them.
> I love their magic—diamonds that dreams are made of.
> I love their unfathomable number, forever on fire to always inspire.
> Yes. I love the stars. I love them.
> Come with me. Come with me. We'll fly to the stars.
> We'll embrace them and soak up their splendor.
> We'll embrace them and forever blaze with His love.
>
> Yes. I love the stars. I love them.
> We are stars. We are stars.

> We are the carriers of light. The light of the universe.
> We twinkle forth with a message the world longs to
>   hear.
> Yes. He loves you. He loves all.
> Come with me. Come with me. Embrace this Giver
>   of Light.
> His jewel-like flame will transform dark night.
> Yes. I love the stars. I love them.

The words flowed over Jacquelyn like honey from a soul trapped in darkness but forever basking in light. "That was beautiful," she said. "Is it yours?"

"Yes." The word fell between them with a hint of reserve.

"What possessed you to go into computers when you can compose like that?"

"Well, I like to eat, for starters. The last I heard, the word 'starving' often prefixed many poets. Besides, I get a lot of reward out of empowering other blind people with their own computer systems. I love the travel. And I can still write poetry here and there."

An amazed smile began in Jac's soul and draped itself upon her countenance. The man in front of her had over-come a handicap with a success that few could boast. On top of that, he could write poetry to die for. The esteem that began a slow burn on the flight to Munich flared. "You know, it's amazing that you travel all over the States and you don't have a Seeing Eye dog," the warmth in Jac's voice spoke her approval.

"And the lady does know how to smile," he teased.

Jac's smile faltered. She intertwined her fingers and exam-ined the cluster of people two tables over.

"Actually, I went to mobility school in my younger years. That experience gave me the freedom to choose a dog or not. I decided a dog is a lot of trouble," Lawton said as if they hadn't skipped a beat in their conversation. "Besides, if

I had a dog, think of all the adventures I'd miss. Last hotel I stayed at in Mobile, Alabama, I went downstairs to the restaurant and wound up knocking over a sign right smack on top of a waitress." With a chuckle, he shook his head. "Actually, it was the restaurant's fault, not mine. The sign was placed right where I walked that morning."

"But aren't you ever scared when you're traveling?" The admiration that refused stifling seeped into her voice.

"What's to be scared of?" Lawton leaned back and crossed his arms. "My mom usually takes me to the airport and makes certain I get on the right plane."

"I guess that's always a plus," Jac interjected.

He snorted. "You got that one right. Nothing like getting on a plane to Indiana, only to find out you just landed in Montreal." The breeze teased his hair onto his forehead, and Jac figured he hadn't seen a barber in several months.

"Have you ever flown to the wrong place?"

"Not yet. Usually I'm nicely kept track of. The people I'm working for on each particular job are always waiting at the point of destination. And on the flight, the airline employees usually bend over backward to assist me. Then on the way home, Mom or Dad, or even sometimes my ornery brother, do the honors of seeing me to my apartment."

"So you live alone?" Jac, her amazement escalating, arched her brows.

"Yep. Don't most 33-year-old men?" A defensive edge entered his voice.

"Sorry. I guess—I'm sorry," Jac repeated. "I guess I've insulted you."

He sighed and dragged his fingers through the dark hair that touched his jacket collar. "No, I'm sorry," he said. "You didn't mean any harm."

"Actually, your whole life fascinates me," the admission sprang from Jacquelyn before she realized her intent. The last thing she needed to do was encourage Lawton. He

seemed interested in something deeper than mere friendship, and Jacquelyn was not. Period.

"I understand." And a veil of satisfaction settled upon his
face, as if he interpreted far more into Jac's comments than
she ever wished him to. "It's just that—I guess I'm a little
touchy at times. You know, I'm no different than any other
man, and well, there are times when people treat me like a
child. It gets really irritating, especially when that sort of
treatment comes from the opposite sex."

The waiter arrived with their coffee, and Jac welcomed
the interruption as much as the gourmet aroma. "Do you
like cream or sugar in yours?" she asked and prepared to
scoot the complimentary packets near his hand.

"No. I'm a *real* man," he teased. "I take mine straight."

"Then I must be a real man, too," Jac shot back.

"Ha!" Lawton threw back his head. "I love it!" He reached
for the mug of coffee and gingerly placed it to his lips. "So,
Jac Lightfoot, what are your plans for the Isle of Rhodes
tomorrow?"

Jacquelyn sipped the hot liquid and savored the rich taste.
"Well, I figured I'd just go with the flow of the tour and take
in the sights like I did on Mykonos today. I guess that's about
it."

"Want to be my eyes?" He fidgeted with a packet of sugar
lying on the table.

"Excuse me?"

"I need somebody to be my eyes. With all due respect,
Kinkaide was an awful tour guide today. He's so lovesick he
might as well have described everything in black and white.
I need somebody who'll tell me the sea is like a sponge,
soaking up phosphorous." He tilted his head as if he were
straining to absorb any sign from Jac.

Once again, she experienced the uncanny notion that he
saw straight into her eyes and right into her deepest
thoughts. She looked down and grappled for a means to

politely say no. Jac had taken this trip in hopes of escaping negative childhood memories about a man, not to create new ones—no matter how captivating the man in question might be. Picking up her mug, she took in a mouthful of the hot liquid.

"I promise not to bite," he said, "although I have been known to roll over and to speak—especially if the treat is particularly yummy."

A burst of unexpected laughter sprang upon Jac and the mouthful of coffee sputtered down her windpipe then out of her mouth.

"Mercy sakes, woman, you just gave me a shower," he said, swiping at his face and the sleeves of his blazer.

Amid a mixture of chuckles and coughs, Jac sponged his face and coat with a paper napkin. "Sorry," she said, and one of numerous barriers slipped from around her heart as new chortles rolled forth.

"It wasn't *that* funny," Lawton said through a snicker.

Jacquelyn gave a final dab to his hands, and he turned his fingers upward to twine them with hers. His gentle squeeze thrust all mirth from Jac and ushered in shock. Shock and delight. Delight and alarm. She stiffened, and he released his hold as quickly as the clasp began.

"So, whataya say?" he prompted. "If I promise not to bite…"

"N–no!" Jac blurted and she inched her chair backward. "I don't think…I–I–I'm really not—not interested in any kind of romantic—"

"Okay. Well, who said that had to be the goal?" He patted the table with both hands as if he were a drummer. "But the fact remains that Kinkaide *ain't* gonna be a good tour guide, and I plunked down four grand to take in some sights on this here voyage. Seeing as I have a…limitation in the eyeball area, I do need some eyes."

She swallowed and gazed toward the glowing sea. "Mel had really planned on our hanging together tomorrow."

"Hey, I don't mind hanging with Mel."

"Well…" The silence screamed Jac's reservations.

"So you'd just really rather not?" His smile held a tinge of regret, and Jacquelyn felt like the ogre of the century.

She attempted to harden her heart and replace that fallen barrier, but she couldn't seem to scrape together the resolve to do either. *Endearing.* But he was much more than that. Far more. Melissa understated his appeal—*drastically* understated his appeal. The man was more honest in a minute than most people were in a year. If Jac ever did develop a relationship, honesty would be one of her musts.

"You know, if you haven't already figured it out, you really intrigue me." He leaned back and cocked his head.

"Oh?"

"Mmm," he said and turned his face into the breeze. "And for once, I'm enjoying the chase." He flashed a daredevil grin toward her that revealed an even row of white teeth.

Jacquelyn stood and squelched the urge to bolt. "I'm not available for the catch," she stated, the edge back in her voice.

"So why'd you agree to come up here with me?" He waved his hand to encompass the verandah.

"I have no earthly idea," Jac muttered. "Temporary insanity," she added under her breath.

"Ha! That was a good one!"

"You're nuts," Jac barked.

"No, I'm not," he said. "And you know it. You're just scared, that's all."

"Scared of *what?*" She narrowed her eyes. "I'm not scared of a thing." Her voice held the thread of steel that had long since won the respect of male peers twice her size.

"I know…I know," Lawton said as if he were trying to soothe an overwrought feline. "I know."

He stood and Jacquelyn resisted the urge to walk away and leave him to find his own way back to his room. *I'm not scared!* she wanted to scream. *Except of that nightmare dragon.* The thought rushed upon her from nowhere and her stomach cramped. The last few weeks had proven that not only was she frightened of the dragon, Jac was also terrified that she was of no value. None. Just a piece of flesh that a man had used and tossed away. What would Lawton Franklin want with her once he found out her body had been squandered before?

"I'm ready to go back to my cabin," she said, her voice lifeless. "Is there someplace you'd like me to take you?"

"No." Lawton shook his head and settled back into his chair. "That's fine. I'm going to sit here for awhile."

"Okay, fine." Jacquelyn didn't doubt that the man was tenacious enough to find his way out of a cavern on the backside of Scandinavia. Without a backward glance she strode away. Yet she'd only taken two steps when his imploring voice mingled with the swish of the sea, "Come with me. Come with me. We'll fly to the stars."

Jacquelyn ducked her head and gritted her teeth. Her eyes blurred as she was rushed away. Stars weren't in her future. Not now. Not ever. They weren't even in her past. And she wouldn't know how to embrace one if it fell into her lap.

She paused beside the elevators. With her fingernails eating into her palms, she verbalized a fervid vow. "I won't exchange another word with that man," she whispered. "Not *one word!*"

Twenty-One

Closing her eyes, Melissa propped her head against the hot tub's rim.

"This is divine," Abby said.

"Mmm," Mel answered, and her body felt as if it were melting into the warm water. The hot tub, featured on the top deck, resided near the swimming pool. By a stroke of good fortune, the two women had found the tub empty. Furthermore, the late-night coolness deterred swimmers, and the pool area was relatively peaceful. However, numerous people hovered near the rails, and the faint sound of a Ping-Pong game attested to the recreation room's close vicinity.

"There's got to be at least a million stars up there," Abby commented.

Mel's eyes drowsed open. "Maybe two. And the moon…" She sighed. This moment was by far the most peaceful she had experienced since they left the U.S.

"I wish I could stay here forever," Abby mused. "Far away from problems, and—" The stately lady broke off, and Mel glanced at her. Kinkaide hadn't said much about the Caspers, but Melissa would hazard to guess the family, while exhibiting all the attributes of material success, was poverty stricken in relationships. Indeed, Melissa possessed a lifetime of experience observing a strained marriage. Her parents manifested similar friction. Mel wondered if perhaps the Caspers' rift went even deeper than her parents'. At least her mom and dad did exhibit some signs of affection.

"I've been married 20 years," Abby mused, as if she were reading Mel's mind. "And I guess the whole thing has just been a huge joke."

"Oh?" Mel said and squelched the barrage of questions that whirled through her. *What's the problem between the two of you? How long has it been going on? Are you thinking of getting a divorce?* But for once, Mel decided to curb her tongue. *Kinkaide would probably be proud of me*, she caustically thought. *I'm* not *acting like my mother!*

"Did Kinkaide tell you what happened?" Abby peered across the hot water. The wafts of steam, like apparitions from the past, danced between them and seemed to intensify the desperation in Abby's lovely eyes.

"No," Mel said. "There's not much Kinkaide *has* told me. We aren't exactly on the best of terms right now."

"So I gathered." Abby's full lips twisted into a wry smile.

Mel sighed. "I would hazard to guess that we could win the group award for the all-time most bummed-out cruisers."

Abby's laugh, rich and melodic, inspired a chortle from Mel.

After a weighted silence Abby blurted, "Desmond had an affair."

"Oh, really?" Once again, Melissa resisted the urge to live up to her "mouth of the south" status. Instead, she remained silent and allowed Abby to speak her mind in her own time. Apparently, the woman needed a confidant. Mel was more than willing to serve that role, but she wasn't certain she would have any of the right answers.

"Yes, an affair—with this *witch* in his office who looks like she just stepped off a Hollywood set." Abby sat upright. "I gave him two children and 20 years of my life." She looked down at her bulging figure. "No, I'm no longer a size 6. I'm not even a size 12 anymore, for that matter. But I—I loved him. I gave him the best years of my life, and he threw the whole thing in my face." Abby's voice resonated with gut-wrenching agony.

Melissa helplessly stared at her new friend. For once, she didn't have to hold her tongue. She truly had nothing to say.

"Now he thinks I'm supposed to just—just pretend the whole thing never happened and kiss and make up. He can't seem to see that he has destroyed me—it's like he's tried to kill me." She curled her fist atop her heart.

"I can only imagine," Mel said. She started to explain, but stopped herself. The last thing Abby needed to hear was Mel's woes over Kinkaide's jilting her. The poor woman had enough problems without listening to Mel's.

"I told him I want a divorce." Abby relaxed against the side of the hot tub, propped her head back, and closed her eyes. Yet her hardened features contradicted her languid pose.

"Have you prayed about that? I mean, if he's willing to start over…and…and what about how a divorce is going to affect your daughters?" This time the comment popped out before Mel could stop it, and she had no idea where that reference to prayer came from. She certainly didn't consider herself a prayer warrior.

Abby's head snapped up. "Are you sure you haven't been talking to Desmond?"

Mutely, Mel shook her head. "Actually, Jac and I have a really close friend who went through a divorce several years ago. Her husband had an affair. He was a pastor, of all things."

"Desmond was a Sunday school teacher and men's conference speaker," Abby bit out. "Seems this can happen to the best of them, doesn't it?"

"Anyway," Mel rushed, "I saw what the divorce did to Marilyn—my friend. Actually, her husband is the one who sought the divorce. She wanted to try to make the marriage work, but he just…" Mel shrugged and left the rest unsaid.

"I can guarantee that Desmond didn't *pray* about having that affair," Abby spewed as if Mel had never expounded about Marilyn.

Mel stirred in the warm water and observed the expanse of infinite sky. She hadn't prayed about her dogged determination to avoid Kinkaide either. *What right do I have to bring up prayer in the first place?* Those black lines in her journal seemed to appear in the sky—ugly scars against the breathtaking canvas of sparkling lights. Mel perceived similar scars festering with vengeance in the depths of Abby's eyes.

A sob erupted from Abby, and Mel instinctively scooted around the tub. Covering her face, Abby choked and pressed her fingers against her lips. "I don't—don't know why—why I'm getting emotional with all—all these people around." Her watery gaze skimmed the crowd.

"No one is noticing," Mel soothed as she stroked the grieving woman's shoulder. "I did the same thing when Kinkaide jilted me. There were times when I'd just burst into tears out of the clear blue. It's the craziest thing."

"Kinkaide *jilted* you?" Abby asked, scrubbing at her eyes with the base of her thumb.

"Six years ago," Mel said with resignation. "Six *long* years ago."

"But he still loves you," Abby said as if the statement were an undisputed fact.

"Or so he says." Mel looked down. "But he said that six years ago."

"Sister, I know how you feel," Abby said. "If you trusted him once and he ripped out your guts, what makes him think you're *ever* going to trust him again."

"You got it."

"I've thought all that." Her tears diminishing, Abby shook her head. The silence, companionable yet aching, meshed the new friends into a deepening understanding of the other's pain.

"But I've got to say," Mel mused, "I think your problem is worse than mine." She shook her head. "Yes, this is much, much worse. I can't imagine…"

A new sob escaped Abby, and Mel wished she could pluck the words from the air. Her good intentions at holding her tongue were crumbling into a dim memory. "I'm sorry," Mel said. "I shouldn't have—"

"It's not your fault," Abby gasped. "I don't seem to be handling this very well tonight. For some reason—for the first time since all this happened I'm beginning to have thoughts about maybe—just maybe—that I really should back off on the divorce." She swallowed. "I know I'm contradicting myself like crazy, but I'm so scared. You're right. I haven't prayed about all this like I should. But it's because—because I'm a–a–afraid. I think it would be easier to walk away than to tough it out and rebuild. I really do."

"Yes, I think you're right," Mel said, wondering if she were taking the coward's way out in her relationship with Kinkaide.

Two long shadows blocked out the deck lighting. Even before Mel looked up, she knew to whom the shadows belonged. As suspected, Desmond and Kinkaide peered into the hot tub.

"Hi," Kinkaide said.

"Hi," Mel responded.

"Abby?" Desmond called, his voice strained. "Can we talk? *Please?*"

A new round of sobs erupted from the distraught woman, and she covered her face. Mel and Kinkaide exchanged a wide-eyed stare, and Melissa wasted no time. She scrambled from the hot tub, grabbed her wrap, and handed Abby's wrap to Desmond.

"Come on, honey," Desmond crooned. "Let me help you out." His voice broke.

Sniffling, Abby stood and allowed her husband to assist her from the tub.

Mel inserted her feet into her slip-ons. By silent consensus, she and Kinkaide walked toward the stairway. Before turning the corner, Mel looked back at the couple, now clinging to each other.

"Maybe this is a new beginning for them," Kinkaide said as they neared the steps.

"Maybe," Mel agreed, "but they've got a long road ahead of them."

"Right. But most things that are worth fighting for are worth the road ahead. Don't you think?" Kinkaide paused on the top stair and touched Mel's arm.

She concentrated on the descending corridor, and her damp toes curled in her shoes.

"Mel...I—I think you have an apology coming from me. And this looks to me like as good a time as any to tell you how sorry I am about what happened a couple of weeks ago. That whole mess was my fault. I should have never read your journal."

Mel bit her bottom lip and demanded that her eyes not sting. One crying woman in one night was enough. A trite "it's okay" was on her lips, but Melissa wasn't certain that anything between them was okay.

"And if it will make you feel any better, I went to talk with Shelby last week."

Melissa gazed up at him. "You did?" she choked out.

"Yes." He sighed and gripped the base of his neck. "You know, when we broke off our relationship, I told her I was sorry, and well, I meant it. But I felt another apology might be in order."

"So you apologized *again?*"

He nodded. "And I think she's finally gotten some peace. It all boils down to the fact that I never even prayed about

that relationship. I just went with the flow and fell into it."
He slipped his hands into his pockets. "I've begun to realize
that I was totally out of the will of the Lord. Frankly, I think
Shelby has come to agree."

Kinkaide paused as if he were weighing his every word.
"You were right, you know. I have been selfish for a long
time—nothing but a selfish jerk."

Mel, having never expected this admission, once again
found herself in a rare moment—speechless utterly speechless.

"And I know I shouldn't have read that journal." He hesitated. "But I think it allowed me to see just how much I let
you down on a spiritual level. That last entry has haunted
me for two weeks. It seems that when I shut you out, you
shut God out." Kinkaide angled his head and narrowed his
eyes as if he were still trying to sort through all the facts.

Mel inserted her hand into the pocket of her pool wrap
and toyed with the oversized cabin key attached to a large,
plastic square. A dozen responses tumbled through her, but
she couldn't gather the presence of mind to verbalize even
one.

"Also…before I go, there's one more thing…I guess you
might have already figured out that I'm through pushing
you. I've come to the conclusion that regardless of what I
want, I'd rather see you happy without me than miserable
with me."

Her hand closed around the room key, and the notches
ate into her palm. "Thanks," she said and examined her
damp shoes. That explained his lack of communication
during the trip. Mel had indeed begun to wonder if, as Jac
said, Kinkaide had decided he no longer wanted a relationship. The notion had filled Mel with relief—relief and a
strange emptiness.

"Also," he descended a couple of stairs and looked back
up at her, "I'm sorry about what I said about your being like

your mother." His velvet-brown eyes, vulnerable and regretful, begged Mel to finally release the past. "And you probably have every right to struggle with being a little vindictive about this whole situation."

Despite her every attempt, Melissa could not look away.

"Do you think there's any way you could ever forgive me? Even if we aren't meant to be together, I—it would mean a lot to know that you've been able to put this whole mess behind you."

The vengeful monster within Mel emerged from the cesspool of bitterness. With clumps of mire dripping from scaly skin, it raised its head and hissed in Kinkaide's face. The fiend scorched him with flaming breath, laughed with glee, and mocked his sincerity. Yet this time, Mel didn't verbalize the beast's taunts. Instead, she covered her trembling lips with unsteady fingers and silently shook her head. "I don't know," she rasped. "I don't know."

With a resigned nod, Kinkaide walked down the rest of the stairs. His slumping shoulders appeared to be dragging a burden of guilt in their wake. Three times, Mel started after him and all three times the unforgiving monster bade her stop. She gripped the handrail and blinked against the tears.

Horace Waggoner staggered up the stairway and emerged onto a deck that looked vaguely familiar. Perhaps this level was where his room was located. His sense of direction, hazy and heavy, had failed him. Feeling as if he had been walking an eternity, Horace decided to sit down and rest. He swayed toward the pool and sprawled into a wooden chair.

He threw back his head and gazed upward. The moon, a soggy-looking sphere high in the sky, wouldn't stop wavering, so Horace placed his head in his hands as he rested his elbows on his knees. The taste of acrid whisky lingered on his tongue, and he couldn't remember exactly how many shots he had consumed. More than anything else, he longed for the comfort of his bed, but his room's location evaded him like an ancient mystery that defied explanation. Nonetheless, a ceaseless incantation demanded that he continue his search.

Horace stood and tottered forward. The nearby pool, a blue blear in his path, pulsated with an undetected rhythm. Horace swerved to avoid the body of water, but the depths tugged him forward with a force he could not deny. The resulting splash of cold water snatched his breath, and an alarmed gurgle erupted from his watery throat. His legs and feet churned, but the action seemed to encourage the water's unyielding grip. Horace sank beneath the surface and the water invaded his throat and nostrils as he fought his lungs' demand for air.

From out of nowhere, a pair of strong arms dragged him upward. Amid a round of sputters, Horace struggled for his next breath and detected the blurred image of dark skin and eyes. The rescuer hauled Horace to the shallow end where another set of hands awaited to assist in dragging him onto the tile. Hacking against the water in his windpipe, Horace strained to focus as the faces of two men swam in and out of view in sequence with the threats of a black pall. Just before the dark claimed victory, Horace grasped a vague recognition of the face hovering closest. A wet face whose eyes spoke depths of concern. A face that resembled the twins Lenora was going to murder.

Twenty-Two

"If you'll just move in closer together, I think I can get you all in the photo," the photographer said in his heavy French accent. The ship's cameraman, a pudgy youth, looked into the 35-millimeter camera and adjusted the lens.

Mel gritted her teeth and edged closer to the group. Kinkaide, only inches away, stood as rigid as the bronze deer perched atop the pedestals at Rhodes' port. The photo idea had been Desmond's. The group had converged upon the top deck at 9:00 to watch the ship pull into the port of Rhodes. Desmond seemed forever determined to mesh them together as "one big, happy crew." And this morning, he was more cheerful than he had been yet. For the first time, Abby and he were actually holding hands. Given Mel's deepening friendship with Abby, she didn't possess the heart to bow out of the photo—especially when Abby grabbed her hand and tugged her into the group. And when Mel joined the pose, she dragged Jac along with her.

"Great, great!" the photographer said. "This will be beautiful. Beautiful! I have got the windmills in the background." He pointed to the trio of stone windmills on the harbor's edge. The terra-cotta roofs reminded Mel of the pointed straw hats she saw the peasants wearing during last year's voyage to Vietnam. Before the photo, Jac and Mel had spent the last 15 minutes admiring the scenic harbor against an expanse of azure sky. For the first time since they began the cruise, Melissa had experienced a surge of expectation for the day's excursion. Despite the friction between her and

Kinkaide, she did love to travel. Rhodes, with its Old Town and New Town and rich mythical history, promised to be a tantalizing tour for a lover of adventure.

Just about the time Mel thought the young man would snap the shot, he lowered the camera and pointed to her. "Oh madame, madame, why so sad? Why so far away from the group? You must—must lean closer to your gentleman." He motioned for Melissa to move near Kinkaide and her legs went rigid.

"Just do what he says," Jac urged from behind.

Melissa decreased the distance until Kinkaide's arm brushed hers. As if the mere contact fueled a memory machine, she relived their last kiss—the morning Kinkaide had serenaded her. With his lips on hers, the years had peeled away and she was a young woman in her midtwenties, in love for the first time. How much different this cruise could have been if it were a honeymoon. The unexpected musing sent a searing flash through Mel's midsection.

"I am ready now. All smile!" the photographer said.

Melissa produced something that felt like a grimace. The camera flashed, the photographer lowered the camera, and she wasted no time in moving away.

"Beautiful!" The photographer kissed his fingers. "You may buy your photo from the bulletin board outside the purser's office."

She approached the railing and peered at Rhodes. The famous Old Town walls rose up amid palms and pines and reminded Mel of a rambling castle. According to the guidebook she and Jac read that morning, the medieval wall, eight feet thick, was built by the Knights of St. John and once surrounded the city. Now, New Town surrounded the muddled gray walls. Shortly, the call would come for them to disembark and board their tour bus.

Until then, the sights of Rhodes offered a perfect focal point for Mel. She'd even rather view the ship's engine room than look toward Kinkaide. After last night's conversation, she couldn't bring herself to encounter his searching, gentle eyes. She sensed his observation just as strongly as if he were standing next to her. Desperately trying to block out any awareness of him, she feigned interest in the azure water that phased into sapphire blue as it stretched toward the horizon.

The cool breeze, tinged with salt, stirred her oversized T-shirt and lifted wisps of hair away from Mel's cheeks. The zephyr seemed to beckon her to forgive Kinkaide. *But I can't,* she countered. After a long night of battling the covers, Mel decided that forgiving Kinkaide might not be an option. After six years of cohabitating with the unforgiving beast, its poison so penetrated Mel's veins that the death of the grievous monster might come only with the death of herself.

Mel turned to say something to Jacquelyn, only to discover that her friend had vanished. However, Abby neared and squeezed Mel's hand.

"Thanks so much for everything you said last night," she whispered.

Melissa looked into beautiful eyes that held a new sparkle, and she marveled at how one night had transformed Abby's features. Indeed, she looked five years younger.

"I'm not really sure what I said," Mel responded.

"You really encouraged me to do what I knew the Lord was asking me to do. I had been fighting His will about my marriage ever since Desmond told me about the affair." The breeze tugged at Abby's white gauzy jacket and tossed the collar against her neck. She adjusted the collar and tucked a stray strand of hair into the hair clip at the nape of her neck. "I'm not going to pretend that I've worked through everything. I still..." She swallowed. "I still think it's going to be awhile before I can trust Desmond on the level that I once trusted him."

"I can understand that." Mel followed Abby's gaze toward Desmond, who was dressed in khaki shorts and a polo shirt. He threw back his head and laughed at something Lawton and Kinkaide were saying. No woman alive could pretend that he, Kinkaide, or Lawton would lack for feminine appreciation. Although they weren't perfectly handsome, each possessed an aura of assurance that underscored their attractive masculinity. As if Kinkaide sensed Mel's appraisal, his attention darted straight to her. As Abby continued talking, Mel felt as if a shaft of electricity zipped through her midsection. She jerked her focus back to her friend.

"...not certain how long it will take to completely forgive him either," Abby said, and Mel grappled to piece together the words she had missed. "But I think we made a new start last night. We talked half the night. And frankly, I'm beginning to see that I haven't exactly been the perfect wife myself." She traced her index finger along the top of the railing, and Mel peered toward the cone-topped windmills. "Anyway," Abby squeezed Melissa hand, "I know I took advantage of your willing ear last night, and I just wanted to say thanks." She wrapped her arms around Mel's shoulders and the two women hugged.

"Any time," Mel said amid Abby's sniffles.

"Now!" Abby rubbed at her eyes. "Enough of that!" She glanced around the deck. "Where did my girls get off to? Desmond and I decided that we should make this a day for family. I hope you and Jac and the guys don't mind."

Melissa shook her head. "Oh no, that's fine. You four need some time alone." But inside, Mel wanted to groan. Her one hope for today had been that Abby and Desmond would serve as a buffer between her and Kinkaide. *Maybe we can get on different tour buses this time.*

Silently, Jac stole down the ship's stairway, all the while keeping an eye on the scrawny man she had noticed watching the Casper twins. His interest in the twins defied casual observation, and something about the man prickled the hair on the back of her neck.

On the Bridge Deck, he left the stairwell and stopped in front of the pair of elevators. Jac hovered in the stair hallway and waited until he boarded the elevator and the doors closed. She dashed for the stairway and raced to the next landing—the Hera Deck. The elevator continued its downward journey. Jacquelyn descended the subsequent flight of stairs and flattened herself against the wall by the stairwell. However, the elevator didn't stop on the Apollo Deck either. One flight of stairs later, the man repaid Jac's effort and disembarked on the Venus Deck.

Hands in his slacks pockets, head bent, the man meandered toward the main reception area where the passengers would leave for their tour of Rhodes. Jac mingled with the humming crowd, all the while keeping the man's locale in her line of vision. At the ornate cruise desk, she picked up one of the colorful brochures that featured Rhodes. By snatching a sentence here and there, she learned that the island they were about to explore was, according to Greek mythology, given to Helios from Zeus. Helios married Rhodes, the island nymph and daughter of Poseidon. Rhodes' beauty so ensnared Helios that he vowed to make the island as beautiful as his bride. However intriguing the ancient tale, it did little to distract Jac from her surveillance.

The man aimlessly wandered around the reception area spanned with royal blue carpet. He peered out one of the numerous windows that provided a breathtaking view of Rhodes. He toyed with a stack of brochures on the cruise desk, knocked them all onto the floor, replaced them, then wandered toward the gift shop. Jacquelyn followed him inside the shop. The man paused by a display of crystal fish then moved to the scented soaps and appeared to be in the throes of an uncustomary dilemma over whether or not to make a purchase. He exited without buying a thing. The swiftness of his gate, the tilt of his head, suggested that the decision had nothing to do with soap. All the more intrigued, Jac dogged him back to the elevators. However, when the door hissed open, the four Caspers exited with Kinkaide, Mel, and Lawton in their wake.

"Excuse me, Mr. Casper," the man called.

Desmond gazed toward the man and his eyes widened.

"Oh, hello," he said. "How are you?"

"I just wanted to thank you for last night. I wound up spending the night in the ship's hospital." His thin mouth turned down at the corners. The man extended his hand and peered at Desmond just as he had scrutinized that scented soap. The chandelier light did little to flatter the dark bags under his bulging eyes—bags that supported his next admission. "Seems I had a little too much to drink. You saved m–my life."

Jac, unobserved, hung on the edge of the crowd and sidled behind a lush potted plant that stretched toward the ceiling. She wasn't certain exactly what was going on, but she was sure the man was up to no good. Perhaps his artifice involved the Caspers, perhaps not. Whatever the scheme, a sixth sense warned Jacquelyn to absorb his every feature.

Finally, Horace moved away and Jac's friends neared the lobby. Mel, scanning the crowd, craned her neck and mumbled something to Abby. Jac stepped from behind the plant.

"There you are!" Mel bounded toward her. "I was beginning to think you jumped overboard or something."

Jac eyed Lawton, who seemed to be looking straight through her. She inwardly squirmed and regretted the way last night's conversation broke off. *But not enough to reverse my decision!* she thought. Forcing herself to dismiss Lawton, Jac greeted Melissa, then turned to Desmond. "Do you know that man?"

"Well, sort of," Desmond said. "I dragged him out of the pool last night."

Melissa raised her brows and looked at Abby.

"We were up on the pool deck talking for quite awhile after you left," Abby said. "About 12:30, that man wandered toward the pool and fell in."

"You certainly lead an exciting life," Lawton drawled. "That's all I've got to say. Next thing you know, you'll be helping some little ol' lady across the street in downtown Rhodes."

The group burst into short-lived laughter.

"Just ignore him, Desmond," Kinkaide said, rolling his eyes.

Jac squelched any signs of mirth before they began.

"Actually, I was hoping to help *three* ladies across every street." Desmond grabbed his wife's hand and extended his long arm to encompass his daughters.

The invitations to congregate with assigned tour guides began airing over the intercom six different times in six different languages: English, French, Japanese, German, Greek, and Spanish. Fleetingly, Jac wondered how long after the cruise she would expect every announcement she heard to be aired in so many languages. The last two days had certainly conditioned her for exactly that. She glanced over her shoulder to see the scrawny man disappear into the crowd.

"That man who spoke to you was watching your daughters up on the pool deck," Jac said.

"What?" Desmond's chin raised, and his shoulders grew rigid. His arm tightened around his daughters.

"That's why I left the deck. I followed him down here. He was watching Janie and Julie, and I wanted to see what he was up to."

"You know, he *does* look kind of familiar," Janie said and flipped her French braid over her shoulder.

"Wasn't he the man in the gift shop last night?" Julie asked. "You know, the one who helped us pick up your money."

"You saw him in the gift shop, too?" Desmond demanded, then scanned the crowd.

"Yes." Janie shook her head. "I'm sure that was him. Remember? He was looking at the crystal fish the same time we were."

"I don't have a good feeling about this," Abby said.

"Neither do I," Jac said. "That's why I followed him. His interest in the twins goes beyond casual observation."

"So what can we do about it?" Desmond asked.

"Actually, there's nothing *to do* at this point." Jac crossed her arms. "Legally, he has done nothing wrong. Helping a couple of teenagers pick up money and looking at them on the pool deck are not crimes."

"Maybe he was watching all of us because of what Desmond did for him," Lawton offered. "I mean, it could be that he was trying to figure out which man saved his life."

Kinkaide spoke up. "Maybe so. The twins do look a lot like you."

"Yes. And if I'm not mistaken, he did get a good look at me before he went unconscious," Desmond said.

"So maybe they just caught his eye because he was looking for you," Lawton finished.

"Then how did he know your name?" Jac asked. "Did you ever introduce yourself?"

"No." Desmond shook his head.

"And why didn't he say something to you on the pool deck? If he saw the girls, he had to have seen you. But he didn't approach you up there. Instead, he came down the elevator and meandered around down here." Jac frowned and considered Lawton's theory. "Actually, he *did* act like he was trying to make a decision. Maybe he spotted you on the top deck then deliberated about whether or not he should approach you. By the time you guys came down here, he may have very easily been going back up to find you. He was heading back to the elevators."

"I realize that concept was my idea," Lawton said. "But how would that answer his presence in the gift shop last night? And how did he know Desmond's name?"

"Maybe he asked the pool attendant." Abby tightly gripped Desmond's hand.

"Well, does the pool attendant know your name?" Jac asked.

"I don't know," Desmond said.

Janie wrapped her arms around her midsection. "This gives me the creeps."

"Me, too." Julie snuggled closer to her father.

"Okay," Desmond said, "let's not get wigged out over this. There's probably a perfectly logical explanation."

"Of course," Abby crooned, but a shadow of fear covered her words.

"I guess you know I'm a private eye. I hunt people down for a living." Jac slid her hand into the back pocket of her jeans. "Why don't we all stay together today on Rhodes?"

"Jac also has a black belt in taekwondo," Mel supplied.

"Mama Mia," Lawton mumbled.

Jacquelyn glowered at him, only to realize the gesture was lost...but not on Kinkaide. He chuckled and shook his head.

"What's so funny?" Lawton asked.

"Oh, nothing, nothing." Kinkaide rocked back on his heels and crossed his arms. "I'm just amazed that God is still in the business of answering prayers."

Jacquelyn ignored the brothers' private jokes. "I don't think there will be a problem. Really. We'll just sightsee together, and I'll keep my eyes peeled during the rest of the trip."

Mel nodded her agreement to Abby. "I think that's the smartest thing to do."

"Should we say anything to ship security?" Abby asked.

"What's there to say?" Jacquelyn raised her hand. "That the man Desmond dragged out of the pool last night helped the twins pick up some change then thanked Desmond for saving his life?"

Abby released a slow breath. "Yes, you're right," she said. "I just hope nothing comes of this."

"Believe me," Jac assured, "the first hint I have that something should be said to security, I'll be at their door."

"Okay." Desmond once again peered across the crowd. "But you girls are not leaving my sight for one minute." He turned to his daughters. "Got it?" They nodded.

Twenty-Three

The city of Rhodes proved to be everything the tourist package promised. For Kinkaide, the melding of medieval architecture, modern shops, and Greek history offered enough options to fill a week with meaningful exploration. Unfortunately, due to their time schedule, the group was allowed only one day.

By the time they embarked upon the Street of the Knights, Kinkaide decided to stay close to the Caspers. With Jac on one side, him on the other, and Desmond watching the crowd, Kinkaide figured the family was safe. Mel and his brother hung behind. Lawton, forever curious, rapped out questions about the scenery and Mel supplied the answers. As the cobblestone street crunched beneath his loafers, Kinkaide was relieved that Lawton had chosen another person for his eyes. Nonetheless, a twist of guilt followed the thought. But Kinkaide had been so distracted by Mel yesterday on Mykonos that he simply hadn't felt like describing any of the romantic island. As usual, Lawton didn't hide his opinion regarding Kinkaide's lack of details.

However, the Street of the Knights, constructed over an ancient pathway that led from the Acropolis of Rhodes to the port, proved a pleasing distraction. The various ornate inns lining the street had been constructed by numerous nations for the Knights of the Order of St. John. From the Street of the Knights, the tour guide led them to Ippiton Street and toward the reconstructed Palace of the Knights, built at the site of the ancient Temple of Helios.

Somehow, Kinkaide got separated from Jacquelyn and the Caspers and wound up falling in line behind Melissa and Lawton as they passed through one of the dome-shaped entries into the Palace of the knights. The statues of Greek gods, perched beneath the domes, seemed to warn Kinkaide that he should simply pass Mel and Lawton and resume his post with the Caspers. But once they entered the palace, the shafts of sunlight pouring through numerous windows high-lighted the red streaks in Mel's dark hair, and Kinkaide couldn't pull himself away from her. Amid the smell of aging stone and a sea of Gothic furniture, Mel and Lawton paused by one of the numerous intricately painted urns. As Lawton ran sensitive fingers over the work of art, Kinkaide stopped beside Mel.

"I think I heard the tour guide say these urns came from Japan," he said.

Mel jumped, covered her chest with her hand, and looked at him. "You scared me. I didn't know you were there."

"I'm omnipresent, remember?" Kinkaide flashed her the most charming smile he could muster. "Seems I've been accused of that lately."

Melissa ignored his reference to that day outside her clinic and turned to focus on the urn. She hadn't said a word to him all morning, and Kinkaide wondered if anything he said last night on the ship's stairway had affected her. Her shock over his apologizing to Shelby had softened her eyes. But today Kinkaide witnessed no signs that their conversation had in any way altered her determination to avoid him. Indeed, even when they were standing so close during that photo, she seemed as cool as if they were total strangers.

"Nice mosaics." He nodded toward the collection of pastel-colored mosaics against one wall, and Lawton lifted his fingers from the urn.

"Talk to me about those," he said as if he were bent on pulling Mel away from his brother.

Kinkaide scowled and watched as Mel led Lawton to a collection of early Christian scenes pieced together with stone near a number of Hellenistic and Roman mosaics. Hands in pockets, Kinkaide meandered toward Jac and the Caspers and followed them to the palace's upper floor.

Only when they exited, did Kinkaide see Mel and Lawton again. During the rest of the day, Kinkaide couldn't so much as snare a glance from Mel. Finally, at the end of the tour, he acquired Jacquelyn and Desmond's permission to strike out on his own. Kinkaide grabbed Lawton's arm and steered him away from the group, toward the jewelry stores on Socratous Street.

"Hey, what are you up to?" Lawton complained.

"I need a partner in crime," Kinkaide said. They wound their way up a narrow, shop-lined road. A blue canopy cast a cool shadow onto the street and blocked the unforgiving sun.

"No you don't," Lawton argued. "You've always been able to commit enough crimes on your own without a partner."

With smells of pasta and garlic wafting from the nearby Alexis Restaurant, Kinkaide steered Lawton into the Alexander Shop. The tour guide said the high-quality jewelry shop offered the best in European design.

"Where are we?" Lawton asked as the door sighed behind them and they stepped into cool air that smelled of rare perfume. "There for a minute, my nose said we were heading for a restaurant. But this is no restaurant."

"No. The restaurant is nearby. This is a jewelry store," Kinkaide said, gazing around the modern shop.

"Hmmm, not a bad choice," Lawton said.

Kinkaide shot his brother a surprised stare.

"I was thinking of trying to get something for Jacquelyn while we were on the island."

"Why?"

"Well, I think that's obvious, don't you?"

Kinkaide nudged Lawton across the oriental rug toward a glass jewelry case. "Fill me in on the details," he said. Now might be a good time to warn his brother about Jacquelyn's lack of interest.

Lawton gripped the edge of the wood-trimmed jewelry case. "What's the matter? Are you *blind?*" he challenged.

"No!" Kinkaide glowered at his brother. Even though she and Lawton spent time on the coffee verandah last night, today Jacquelyn seemed more distant and cold than she had yet. "But for the first time in your life, I'm beginning to wonder if you've lost all sense of…of whatever it is you rely on that makes you see!"

"What's that supposed to mean?" Lawton demanded, and his voice carried across the various display cases.

A clerk glanced up from finalizing a transaction with another pair of customers. "I'll be right with you," she said in perfect English.

"Keep your voice down," Kinkaide admonished. "I'd prefer that half of Rhodes doesn't overhear our conversation."

Lawton shook his head. "So tell me what's so wrong with my buying Jac a piece of jewelry? I really think the lady likes me." His voice lowered. "Besides, you know I've been praying for the right woman to enter my life. I'm not saying for sure that Jac is the one. We haven't known each other long enough, and I've still got some praying to do, but I do have my suspicions—especially since the Lord hasn't even hinted that I should back off."

"Lawton…" Kinkaide looked into a polished glass case. An array of precious stones, nestled against blue velvet, winked up at him. For the last several days his protective instincts had prohibited him from blurting the truth to Lawton. He hated to hurt his younger brother, but the longer he put off the inevitable, the more deeply Lawton might be injured.

"I know Jac fascinates you, but—"

"I think that's apparent."

"But...but I really don't think she's interested. When she looks at you, she's as cold as the walls of the Palace of the Knights." Kinkaide waved his hand to encompass the expanse of the stylish jewelry shop. "I just hate to see you waste your money on her. This shop is one of the finest on the island, and I figure the prices—"

"So why are we here?" Lawton's dark brows rose over the top of his black glasses.

"Because I was thinking about seeing if I could find something for Melissa," Kinkaide explained.

"Ha!" Lawton's white teeth flashed as an explosion of resounding guffaws burst forth.

The swarthy clerk walked toward them, and Kinkaide crammed his hands into his pleated shorts and glowered.

"*Who's* wasting money?" Lawton mocked. "That woman wishes you'd drop off the face of the earth."

"I don't think so," Kinkaide growled as the attendant stopped behind the case.

"The only thing that's wrong with Jac is that she's scared," Lawton said as if he were the sage of romance. "Melissa, on the other hand, is downright hard as diamonds when it comes to you. I've about decided you don't stand a chance."

"Thanks for your encouragement," Kinkaide drawled. *But what do you know? You weren't there last night on the ship's stairway...or the day I kissed her on the lawn.*

"Yes, and thanks for *your* encouragement, too," Lawton shot back. Then he directed his attention toward the attendant. "Do you happen to have anything with stars on it?" he asked, never missing a beat.

"Oh, yes," the clerk said. "We have a wonderful collection of platinum and gold link bracelets that have different charms you can choose from."

"Sounds like a winner," Lawton said. "Would you do the honors of leading me there?"

"Of course." The smiling woman, probably in her mid-thirties, rounded the counter and took Lawton's outstretched hand. As they were walking away, Lawton said, "Where are you from, anyway? I didn't expect to hear such precise English here."

"Actually, I'm from Boston," she replied. "Ten years ago, I visited here to rediscover my roots and decided to stay." The two continued their amiable chatter as they spanned the jewelry shop.

Kinkaide shook his head. *Lawton, you think you could charm your way around the world*, he thought. *I just hope Jacquelyn doesn't throw that bracelet back in your face.*

He eyed the variety of jewelry that filled the cases, and a mixture of anticipation and dread filled him. Lawton's reaction to his wanting to purchase something for Mel was more appropriate than Kinkaide dared admit. Jacquelyn wasn't the only one who might throw the gift back. Last night he'd told Mel he was through pushing her, and he meant it. Nonetheless, he still wanted to present her with a special, no-strings-attached gift—something that in years to come would instigate happy memories of Rhodes and, perhaps, of what they once shared. Even if Mel never agreed to marry him, Kinkaide still wished to witness her pleasure when she opened the gift.

Kinkaide hungrily gazed upon the rows and rows of jewelry—not even certain what he wanted to purchase. One by one, he dismissed every necklace, bracelet, and strand of pearls. Stone by stone, he rejected every ring—until he encountered an exquisite ruby set in a swirl of tiny diamonds perched in the middle of an octagonal glass display in the store's center. The dark-red stone and dewlike diamonds glistened in the case's light. Kinkaide thought of the picture of the rose in Mel's living room. This ring would be perfect on her finger.

By five o'clock, Mel's feet ached despite her well-cushioned walking shoes. She longed for a place to relax. Fortunately, the tour guide arranged for them to eat dinner on the balcony of an upscale restaurant that offered fresh fish, lobster, and pasta. Mel couldn't seem to get enough of the Greek salad and heavenly bread, crispy on the outside and soft on the inside. After dinner she relaxed on the balcony and soaked in a breathtaking view of the harbor, with an aqua ocean against a sky the color of bluebonnets.

With a tinge of regret, Melissa left behind the narrow streets spotted with motorcycles. She bid farewell to the palms and pines and exotic waterfalls. On the way to the tour bus, the guide allowed them a few last moments to linger by the wall of Old Town. Mel stepped onto the stone bridge that crossed what used to be a moat. Now the moat was covered in spongy grass the color of emeralds. The ocean breeze lifted Mel's hair from her neck, and she closed her eyes and inhaled the smells of old stone and fresh foliage.

"Did you get a shot of any bougainvillea?" Kinkaide asked from beside her.

Mel jumped and spun to face him. "That's the second time today you've sneaked up on me," she said.

"Sorry." Kinkaide's smile flashed in the sunset's radiant beams. "Both times were unintentional." He placed his forearms atop the stone bridge, and leaned forward. "Hard to believe this once was a moat, isn't it?" He cut a glance at her from the corner of his eyes, and Mel stifled the flutter of her heart.

Today had been an exercise in self-discipline. The whole time she escorted Lawton, Mel had forever been tempted to stare at Kinkaide. Last night's conversation on the stairway continued to reverberate through her mind, and for the first time Mel began to wish she could somehow erase all that had passed between them. But those years of heartache refused to vanish.

Mel turned toward the moat. Bougainvillea. He had asked her about bougainvillea. Or was the last thing he mentioned the moat?

"There's some bougainvillea right there." Kinkaide pointed toward the top of the stone wall. A vine with blooms the color of pomegranate seeds crept across the top. "That would make a great shot. You could hang it beside that rose."

"Yes." Mel raised her 35 millimeter camera and zoomed in on the flower. Even though she had already taken numerous shots of bougainvillea, she didn't resist Kinkaide's suggestion. She accomplished the exact focus and pressed the button. The camera flashed, and Melissa lowered it.

A chorus of high-pitched bird songs christened the moment. Mel leaned against the bridge and feigned a relaxed pose. But inside she wanted to run for fear of what she might say. As the day wore on, so the old flames seemed to burn ever brighter. The minutes stretched. Mel felt Kinkaide's appraisal and sensed an unspoken message hanging between them.

"Speaking of that rose, Mel, I found something that—"

"There you two are," Jacquelyn called from the bridge's edge. "We're waiting for you."

Mel glanced toward Jac. The dark circles under her eyes attested to her stress, yet Jac's smile bespoke her enjoyment of Rhodes.

"We can't stay here forever you know!"

Kinkaide swiveled to face Jac and casually waved as if he had no intention of budging.

Mel's toes curled. She glanced from Jacquelyn to Kinkaide, and back to Jac, whose lips formed a silent and significant "O." A rust of heat assaulted Mel's cheeks, and she bolted from Kinkaide. She needed rest. Rest and time—time to reconstruct her crumbling defenses.

Twenty-Four

As Melissa boarded the *Olympic Countess,* the ship took on the aura of home. With great anticipation, she looked forward to a quiet evening with Jacquelyn, another soak in the hot tub, and eventually the soft folds of her bed. After Mel accompanied Jac to verify that the Caspers were safely in their quarters, the two women headed for their narrow cabin.

"Well, I didn't see one sign of that man the whole day," Jac said as she flopped onto her narrow cot.

"Good." Mel slipped off her walking shoes and dropped her shopping bags filled with clothing, pottery, and even a brooch for her mother. Mel had purchased the pin with a mix of emotions. On one hand, she wanted to do everything in her power to mend their differences. On the other hand, she didn't want her mom to think she was bending to her control. *But she's still my mother,* Mel thought as she stretched onto the bunk and tugged the drape cord. The paisley drapes danced open, and Mel basked in the shaft of evening sun that cast a soft illumination upon the dimly lit room. Peace filled her heart. Perhaps the gift would ease the tension between them. Her mind wandered.

"Do you really think that man's a threat?" She mused.

Jac moved her pillow to the bed's foot and plopped onto it so she could observe her friend.

"Who's to say? I just didn't have a good feeling about him this morning."

"And what are your feelings about Lawton?" Mel asked with a smile. By the time she got to the room last night, Jac was already asleep, and the day had given them little time to discuss yesterday's activities. "Frankly, I was surprised that you went to the coffee verandah with him last night."

"So was I," Jac said, broodingly eyeing the dresser near her bunk.

"I think that he's, well, I think he's more interested in you than you know."

"Maybe I see more than *you* know," Jac said with reserve. "But I'm not interested."

"Because he's blind?"

"His being blind has nothing to do with it. As a matter of fact..." Jac trailed off and punched her pillow. "His accomplishments amaze me." She raised herself up on one elbow. "It's just fascinating the way he travels all over the States the way he does."

"Yes. When Kinkaide and I were together before, I always looked forward to being with Lawton. He usually kept me laughing."

"He's a poet, you know," Jac said, and her dark eyes, once wary, sparkled.

"Oh?" *And maybe you like him far more than you want to admit,* Mel thought. "Today on Rhodes, he asked several questions about you. I wasn't exactly sure what all to tell him." Melissa sat up in the bed, propped the pillows against the headboard, and leaned against them. "I didn't know what you wanted him to know."

"Such as?"

"Oh, you know, the typical stuff...if you owned a dog, if I thought his being blind in any way deterred you, why you think you need to act so tough when you're really a softy..."

"Excuse me?" Jac's full lips pressed together.

"Hey, I didn't ask the questions." Mel held up her hand with the palm facing Jac. "I'm just telling you what the man said, okay?"

"Let's talk about something else." Jac ground out and flopped back on her bed. "Like maybe you and Kinkaide," she challenged. "What was going on at that bridge?"

"I don't want to talk about it," Mell muttered and shrank away from the memory.

Jac produced a disgruntled, "Figures."

Attempting to change her vein of thought, Mel leveled a calculating glance toward Jac then sat up and looked out the window. The sun melted into the horizon, a blaze of orange against an expanse of rippling blue. "I think I'm going up to the pool deck for another soak in the hot tub. I'd like to take in the sunset from up there."

"Suit yourself," Jacquelyn muttered, her dark complexion clouded with ire.

"Listen, there's no need for you to get all miffed at me." Mel swung her feet to the floor.

"Well, what did you tell him?" Jac demanded, an accusatory edge to her voice. "If I know you, the mouth of the south, you probably filled him in on all the juicy details of—" She cut herself off.

Melissa stood. "Don't do this, Lightfoot," she growled. "You know good and well that I wouldn't tell Lawton or anybody else what you've confided in me." Mel's face heated. She flung her suitcase onto the bed, unzipped it, and flipped up the lid. She snatched her swimsuit, marched to the tiny bathroom, and slammed the door.

The knob rattled and the door burst open. "I don't want you telling him stuff—period," Jac snarled. "I don't want him to know if I have a dog or a stinkin' goldfish or if I give one flip whether he's blind or not. Got it?"

"Go back to your bed, Jac," Mel blurted and the whole time she wished she could somehow stop herself. "Go back to your emotional shell!" Her mouth's eruptions worsened. "And go back to your lonely existence. The world will move on without you—so will Lawton." She slung the swimsuit onto the bathroom counter. "And if it's any consolation, I didn't tell him a thing except that you don't own a pet. I hope that isn't some kind of national security secret. Now are you happy?" With a pointed glare, Mel shoved the door closed and turned the lock. She stripped, donned her one-piece suit, and yanked her terrycloth wrap from the hook by the shower.

The second she opened the door, Jac stopped her pacing and scowled at Mel. "You are really a fine friend, aren't you?" she snapped. "If you'd been through what *I've* been through," she stabbed her index finger at the center of her chest, "you'd be in a shell, too! What do *you* know about having nightmares where you're chased all night by a dragon that wants to eat you alive? What do *you* know about the dread I have of trying to tell a man like Lawton that I haven't been a virgin for a long, long time—" Jac choked and a childlike cry escaped, yet she hardened her face. "Don't hurl sanctimonious diagnoses at me until you have been where I've been. When you have, then we'll talk!"

"Jac, I wasn't the one that started all this. You did," Mel stated and shrugged into the pool wrap. "All I was trying to do was answer your question and tell you what Lawton asked about you." She forced her voice into even tones and this time was able to control her tongue against doing more damage. "I'm going up to the hot tub." Melissa padded the short distance to their door, gripped the knob, and pivoted back to her friend.

Jacquelyn stood in the center of the room, her back to Mel, her slender shoulders hunched, her face stubbornly facing the window.

"And I shouldn't have said what I did about your shell," Mel said, a gentle thread in her voice. "I'd probably be in a shell, too, if I were you." She opened the door, stepped into the hallway, and walked toward the elevators. With every foot she progressed, her legs quivered more violently.

Oh, Father, help her, Mel groaned, and she was struck with the sincerity and fervor of her prayer.

Horace sank deeper into the corner booth and swirled the trace of whisky in the tiny glass. He grabbed the bottle of Chivas Regal, sloshed another shot of the amber liquid into the glass, then gazed across the 9 Muses Lounge. He'd spent most of the afternoon here. Drinking. Staring. Thinking. After he'd downed a couple of shots of scotch, Horace ordered a whole bottle. That was two hours and five shots ago.

Now the lounge's royal-blue floor tilted while the dark wood furnishings never budged. The smell of vanilla pipe tobacco mingled with the scent of floral candles and induced a twist of nausea that pushed against his throat. Horace closed his eyes and tried to forget the reason he started drinking in the first place. But the image of the dead Casper twins sprawled in a cheap Rome hotel room wouldn't relinquish its grip on his mind. Last night he'd almost drank beyond the point of caring about those corpses. Then he forgot where his room was. One near drowning was enough for a cruise. Horace laid his room key on the table. Although the key blurred in and out of focus, he confirmed that he still knew his cabin number and deck.

"Apollo Deck, number eighth," he slurred. "Go down the elevavor, up the righth hall, room is on—on the righth." Horace nodded. Last night he had been so drunk he had gone up in the elevator instead of down. When he landed on the Bridge Deck, he just took the steps up to the Ouranos Deck and ultimately fell into the pool. He dashed the last gulp of the honey-colored liquid down his throat and set the glass on the table. The aftertaste of vanilla and butterscotch lingered on his tongue. In one hand, Horace scooped up the oversized key attached to the large plastic card, in the other he grasped the corked bottle of Chivas.

"I'll just finith you off in my room." He gripped the table and stood on swaying legs. "Then—then maybe I can forgeth." He tottered from the lounge and toward the elevators.

Even with the haze of alcohol blurring his mind, Horace felt as if he were gripped by Zeus and Prometheus—both warring for the right to influence his choice.

"Apollo Deck, number eighth," he repeated as the elevators came into view. "Go down—down," he held up the whisky bottle, "*down,* up the hall, room is on the—on the righth." Horace pushed the button with the arrow pointing toward the floor.

Choices...these choices whirled upon him like a tempest bent on ravishing the sea. A mixture of uncontrollable thoughts jumbled through him. *How can I kidnap the daughters of the man who saved my life? What will Sara do if I pull out? What will Lenora do? What if Lenora really does kill the twins? How can I kidnap those girls when their father saved my life?*

The elevator bell dinged, the light above the elevator lit up the number seven, and Horace stepped into the cubicle. He knitted his brows and scrutinized the buttons. "Go down," he admonished himself. "Down, down, down. I'm—I'm on se–seven. I go to—go to six." He pushed the button marked six.

This morning, Horace had debated whether to thank Desmond for dragging him out of the pool. The very gesture seemed insane: *Thanks for saving my life, and by the way, I'll be kidnapping your daughters in Rome.* But Horace had finally decided that the decent thing was to express his thanks. The incongruity of doing this in light of planning a crime left Horace wanting to rip out what was left of his hair.

The elevator halted. The door hissed open. Horace stumbled out. "T–to the righth. U–up the hallway," he muttered and managed to stagger up the hall. "Num—" He burped and the pungent taste of scotch burned his tongue. "Number eighth," he finished, and his room came into view. "Number—number eighth," he repeated and scrutinized the bleary gold number to affirm he had the right room.

After several attempts, Horace managed to insert the key into the lock and fumble his way into his cabin. He collapsed on the first bunk and let the bottle fall to the floor. The setting sun blazed through the window and seemed to ignite within Horace an immediate and irrevocable certainty.

"I can't—I can't," he groaned. "Sara, I'm sorry, b–but—I–I can't." Horace closed his eyes as a new peace swept upon him like morning mist across the face of the deep. He begged for sleep, but a new round of problems thundered through his intoxication. Horace sat up, swung his feet around, and placed his head in his hands. *If I don't, will Lenora and Sara still go through with it?* Horace reached for the Chivas Regal and pulled out the cork. *And can I let them?*

Twenty-Five

Kinkaide settled at a small, round table in the Stella Piano Lounge and ordered an appetizer. The pianist, perched behind an ebony grand piano, played a collection of old, soft favorites, and Kinkaide's fingers flexed against the highly polished table. The votive candle in the table's center stubbornly flickered despite the diminishing wax. The flame was just as tenacious as his love for Mel—forever burning regardless of her lack of interest.

With a sigh, he gazed out the porthole at his elbow. The setting sun, now half out of sight, spilled forth unfathomable radiance upon the expanse of the glassy sea. The evening sky, as blue as the water, fused with the ocean on the distant horizon. Kinkaide wondered if he and Mel would ever be united as one. Today she hadn't given him so much as an encouraging smile, even when he had talked with her.

He removed the white leather box from his shirt pocket and dropped it beside the small plate of stuffed crab. *What possessed me to buy this?* He snapped open the ring box and eyed the two-carat ruby surrounded by a swirl of diamonds in a setting of gold. The ruby winked up at him as if it were a snatch of fire against white velvet. The impulse purchase mocked his foolish heart. He had almost conjured up the courage to give the ring to Mel when they were on the moat bridge, but she raced from him as if he were a cyclops. In his present state of mind, Kinkaide figured that if he gave Mel the exquisite ring she'd probably throw it back in his face—or worse, toss it overboard. *Lawton's was right. When it comes to me, Melissa is as hard as diamonds.*

He snapped the box shut and dropped it back into his shirt pocket. Kinkaide finished off his savory snack, downed a cola, and stood. Stifling a yawn, he eyed the blonde pianist in the corner. She gracefully trailed her fingers over the keys, ended one love song, and eased into another. Once again Kinkaide's fingers flexed, and he rubbed his forefinger and thumb together. The only thing he missed on this cruise, besides Melissa, was his music.

He meandered from the lounge and neared the open deck. The pool glistened in the diminishing sunlight, and a waft of chlorine mingled with the scent of the sea. Kinkaide's thoughts wandered to last night, when he and Desmond had spotted Mel and Abby in the hot tub.

He glanced toward the hot tub and stopped. One woman, her back to him, claimed the tub. A woman with dark hair exactly the shade of Mel's. She propped her head against the rim, and Kinkaide continued walking until he was parallel with her profile. His jaw tightened as he encountered the indubitable profile of the woman he loved. Kinkaide adjusted his annoying glasses and the ring box stirred in his pocket.

He removed the box, snapped it open, and the winking ruby issued a dare. His mind spinning, Kinkaide closed the box and dropped it back into his pocket. His thumb grazed his fingers, his eyes narrowed, and he stared at the doorway to the piano lounge. His thoughts raced on, hurling him into a spontaneous scheme that took on a life of its own. Without another glimpse of Mel, he strode back the way he came and resisted examining his motives. Close scrutiny just might reveal a compromise of his "hands off" vow.

Melissa watched the last rays of light dissolve into the sea. As the horizon gradually darkened and the hidden stars sneaked upon the sky one by one, her eyes slid shut. She teetered on the brink of dreamland when a tap on her shoulder jolted her back into the real world.

"Excuse me, madame." A rich-timbered male voice penetrated her drowsiness.

She looked up into the face of a smiling attendant. "This note is for you," he said, his French accent making the simple statement sound like a marriage proposal.

With a yawn, Mel took the slip of paper and sat up in the warm water. As she flipped open the folded missive, she wondered if Jac had sent her a note. Then she dismissed the thought—Jacquelyn was too aggravated to be sending notes. The block letters, scrawled in the middle of the paper, did nothing to indicate the messenger's identity. The letter simply read, "Come to the Stella Piano Lounge."

Melissa, now fully awake, twisted to observe the other end of the ship. The doorway to the piano lounge loomed in the distance, and an occasional snatch of notes drifting on the breeze revealed a pianist at work. Melissa looked back at the message then eyed her pool wrap. She wondered if the request were from an acquaintance or from a male passenger making a pass. She bit her bottom lip and studied the note.

Jac would probably ball up the note and toss it into the first trash can she came to, Mel thought. But Mel wasn't Jac. She stepped from the hot tub, and the evening breeze sent a shiver across her limbs. Melissa dried off with a nearby towel, then wrapped the terrycloth robe around herself. Slipping her feet into the canvas shoes, she once again eyed the note. If a strange man were on the other end of this venture, she'd tell him to get lost then march back to her cabin.

Mom would have to find out who was behind the note or she would explode. "I'm just too much like my mother for my own good," she mumbled. Mel walked across the tile surrounding the hot tub and pool. When her shoes encountered the wooden deck, she stopped. *What if Kinkaide sent the note?* She closed her eyes and pondered the possibilities. If the note *were* from Kinkaide… Melissa chewed her bottom lip and didn't know whether to hasten toward the lounge or race for her room. All day, she had battled the urge to slip her arm through his. Those moments over the moat had almost cost Mel her dignity.

Last night's ardent apology created a new respect for this man who had jilted her. He had certainly done a lot of growing since they were first engaged. Whether she was ever able to completely forgive him or not, Mel sensed that with his new maturity he might make somebody a good husband one day.

"I doubt it will ever be me, but…" Mel walked toward the lounge. If Kinkaide were the person waiting to meet her, she would decide what to do once she got there.

Arms crossed, Kinkaide stood in the shadows near the piano. He strained to see the lounge's entry, and a simmering dread bubbled in his gut. Ten minutes had lapsed since he sent the note. The whole scheme was farfetched, at best, but he depended upon Mel's undying curiosity to propel the plan forward. If she didn't come, he had nothing to lose. Nothing…except a romantic interlude that just might influence her heart. He cupped his chin in his hand and stroked his beard. His vows of backing off the relationship taunted him, and an unexpected wad of panic thickened his throat. He had told Mel only last night that he was not going to pressure her anymore. This little encounter was anything but relaxed and casual.

Okay, Lord, Kinkaide breathed, *I've jumped into something spontaneous here. If I'm in over my head, just prevent Mel from coming. Otherwise…*

A movement at the entryway stopped Kinkaide's breathing. Mel stepped over the threshold, extended the note to the host, and surreptitiously glanced around the lounge. Along with the pianist, he had shared his scheme with the lounge host and the pool attendant. Each had been thrilled with the idea. Indeed, Kinkaide sensed each of them cheering him on.

Melissa pulled her wrap snugly around her, glanced at the other patrons, fully dressed, and exchanged a furtive whisper with the host. With a smile, the host laid an assuring hand on her arm, led her to an empty table, and pointed toward the piano.

Kinkaide stepped from behind the plant and neared the pianist.

"She's here," he whispered.

With a smile, the musician brought the tune to a graceful close, slipped from the bench, and Kinkaide claimed the seat. Never looking at Melissa, he began the first strands of "Can't Help Falling in Love." With the introduction completed, he raised his gaze to hers and began singing the love song he had planned for their wedding.

Her eyes wide, her mouth half open, Mel perched on the edge of her chair. She didn't move. And neither did anyone else in the lounge. Everyone fixed their attention upon Kinkaide. However, the others paled into a blur while Melissa's image grew more vivid with every passing word. Never had Kinkaide so put his heart into a song. *Never.*

The votive candles in the center of the tables seemed to flare in sequence with the rhythm of the music. Kinkaide's heart pounded twice the pace of the tempo, and his palms produced a thin film of sweat. Nonetheless, the piano continued spilling forth the heart of its master, as if the music were composed by angels.

By the time the final note flowed from his fingertips, a tear trickled down Mel's cheek. Kinkaide didn't know whether to shout or worry. She might be crying because she was overwrought with love, or the tears might stem from the bitterness eating up her heart.

When Kinkaide stood, applause exploded from the patrons. After a slight bow, he descended the piano platform and approached Mel. Kinkaide lingered beside her table and pondered her reaction to the next phase of this outrageous plan. Nevertheless, he pressed forward. The hush across the lounge sent a quiver down his spine as he extended his hand.

Her watery eyes held his, and the panic mixed with amazement suggested that she teetered on the precipice of irrevocably denying him. Her fingers knotted atop the table, then Melissa slowly extended her hand to his. Kinkaide sensed a collective sigh from the silent onlookers. Her fingers trembled against his, and Kinkaide tightened his hold on her hand. Gently he tugged her to her feet and escorted her from the lounge, onto the deck, and toward a private niche.

Melissa, feeling as if she were trapped in a dream, followed Kinkaide until he stopped at the rail. Laughter flowed up from the decks below. A soft love song wafted from the Stella Piano Lounge, and the water gushed and swooshed as the boat swished through the night. The moon, low on the horizon, bathed the ocean in a luminous wash that heightened the fantasy atmosphere.

Kinkaide, his dark eyes stirring with love, stroked Mel's cheek and a spray of tingles threatened to bring her to her knees. "You're beautiful," he whispered. "So beautiful." Kinkaide brushed wisps of hair away from her face, and Mel's senses reeled.

For a brief time she was caught in the moment, caught in the love radiating from Kinkaide. Gradually, common sense bore in upon the tryst, and a battery of questions sent a lump to her throat. *What am I doing out here with him? Have I lost my mind? Nothing has changed. I still don't trust him. I don't!*

Mel stiffened and inched away. "Kinkaide, I don't think..." The denial came out like a weak plea. She cleared her throat and forced her voice into a firm tone. "I don't think—"

"Would you let me have this time, Mel?" he asked. "Just this one brief moment? Tomorrow is the last day of the cruise. Then we're off to Athens and Rome and that's it." He shook his head. "I might not see you again for years, and I..." His gaze faltered, and Mel forced herself to peer at the stars shimmering like gold dust against a silken sky. Yet the stars gave her no courage to break away. Instead, they beckoned her to grant Kinkaide his wish.

Just one moment. That's all he's asking...just one. Mel's focus, as if controlled by a holy force, drifted from the glistening skies and back to Kinkaide.

His eyes widened and his hands encompassed hers. The sea, the wind, the moon, the stars all blurred, and Mel saw Kinkaide—and him alone. The years peeled away. They were sitting in his parents' front yard about to experience their very first kiss....Kinkaide grazed his thumb along the line of her jaw, cupped her face in his hands, and lowered his head to hers. Yet he stopped within inches of her lips, and his eyes stirred with unspoken questions.

Melissa, her heart thudding, knew that one little move would stop the kiss. But his hold on her heart nullified every attempt at resistance. The claims of not trusting him were consumed by the bond of the past, by the love they once shared, by the love that had never died. Mel gazed at his mouth. With a sharp intake of air, he pressed his lips against hers. Kinkaide's arms slipped around his love, and she swayed in the impact of his embrace. The minutes, fraught with turmoil and ecstasy, lulled Mel into pools of longing. Longing and love. Love and sweet release.

At last the kiss subsided, and Kinkaide propped his forehead against hers. "I have something for you." One arm remained around her as he reached into the pocket of his cotton shirt. His fingers shaking, he pulled out a small leather box. Mel swallowed against the tremor in her throat. He flipped open the lid, and a brilliant ruby, as breathtaking as the stars, winked up at her.

"Oh, Kinkaide," Mel breathed. She looked from the ring to him and back to the ring.

"No strings attached," he said. "I saw it today at one of the shops in Rhodes and couldn't get away without buying it for you. I know how much you like rubies." He paused. "It reminded me a little of the photo of the rose in your living room. You know, the red one with the dew that looks like diamonds?"

"Yes, I know." A mist of tears blurred the jewel, and Mel labored to breathe. She shook her head and covered her lips with unsteady fingers. "I can't," she whispered. "I…" Mel looked into his eyes and was struck speechless by the aching love spilling forth.

"Last night I told you I wouldn't pressure you anymore." He observed the ring. "I guess we can all safely say I've blown that claim." One corner of his mouth lifted. "Really," he shook his head, "I don't want to shove the ring off on you, but I *would* like you to have it—if for nothing more, as a token of…"

Melissa gripped the nearby rail and the purring of the engine seemed the whirring of her own mind. Before Shelby arrived in her office, Mel had imagined a moment just like this one. She peered across a sea covered in a diamond-dust sparkle as enchanting as she ever dreamed—as enchanting as the man before her.

The ring box snapped shut, and Kinkaide nudged it into her free hand. Without looking at him, Mel wrapped her fingers around the box and the leather warmed with her touch.

"Take the ruby for now," he urged. "If you decide later to return it, I won't make a scene. I promise."

Mel searched Kinkaide's soul, and the breeze whispered something he said last night. *I've come to the conclusion that regardless of what I want I'd rather see you happy without me than miserable with me.* The old Kinkaide would have never said that. He also wouldn't have apologized to Shelby a second time.

"But if you decide to keep the ring..." he lifted the hand that clutched the box, her left hand, "...and if by chance I see the ring here..." Never taking his gaze from hers, he pressed his lips against the finger that once bore the first engagement ring. The rest remained unsaid.

As Kinkaide straightened, Mel tugged her hand from his. The scaly monster of vengeance crawled from the caverns of her heart and urged her to shove the ring in his face. But, as with last night, Melissa chose not to heed the creature's prompting. Instead, she pivoted to face the sea, and her grip on the ring box tightened.

"I don't know what to say," she whispered.

"Well, I guess this is a historical moment," he softly teased.

A smile tugged at her mouth. Mel darted him a coy glance, then looked into the water and bit her lip.

Kinkaide placed his forearms on the railing and leaned forward. "So...how 'bout them Red Sox," he quipped.

The two shared a laugh. "You and Lawton are so much alike," Mel said, recalling Lawton's exact words the day she and Kinkaide talked in the church.

"Except I sometimes think he's got more sense in the tip of his pinkie than I've got in my whole brain," Kinkaide drawled.

On a whim, Mel opened the leather box. The exquisite ruby bade her to slip the ring on. She stroked the fiery stone yet denied the ruby's summons.

"Do you like it—at least a little?" Kinkaide asked.

"Mmm. I think I'd have to be dead not to like it."

A pleased pause punctuated the moment.

"But..." Mel hesitated.

"Ah, the inevitable but," Kinkaide chided. "*But* you just want to be friends, right? The words every guy dreads hearing."

"No," Mel said and grappled with a means to express her problem.

As if he sensed her dilemma, Kinkaide remained silent, respectfully silent.

At last, she decided to state her thoughts and hoped her verbal wanderings made sense. "You said something last night that was true."

Kinkaide shifted his position and faced her, yet Mel continued to observe the moon-touched sea. "You said that when you jilted me, I shut God out. And, well, that was true. I've spent the last six years going to church every Sunday but deep inside I'm cold." Fleetingly, Mel wondered if the vengeful monster within thrived in the cold.

"You shouldn't blame God for what I did, Mel," Kinkaide said. "I was acting like a selfish jerk. I was so focused on what I wanted that I couldn't see a thing except my side of things."

"But even so, you *did* help me grow spiritually before..." She pivoted to face him. "You weren't all bad during our early years."

"Nice to hear you say that." Kinkaide's smile lit his features. "I had begun to think I must have been way worse than I remembered."

"Also, I don't think I ever really blamed God." Mel examined the leather box and rubbed her thumb across the top. "It's just that, I guess my pain and all those messy emotions somehow stunted my spiritual growth. I thought about this a lot last night." She stifled a yawn. "Subsequently, I didn't sleep well."

"Good." The grin increased.

She rolled her eyes.

"Maybe you'll sleep even worse tonight."

"Would you stop?" she admonished. "I'm trying to be serious. I've got a problem here."

Kinkaide laid his hand on her shoulder. All banter fell into the ship's frothy wake. Mel opened her mouth to explain then frowned. *This is insane! This is worse than insane! I'm about to ask the man I can't trust to tell me how I'm supposed to forgive him.* The block of unyielding ice ensconced in the center of her heart grew colder. Her fingers tapped against the leather box.

"Melissa?" Kinkaide prompted.

"I..." Mel gulped. "I need some time to think," she blurted—then bolted. She hurried across the pool deck, down the stairs, and took the elevator to the Venus Deck. Melissa stumbled into her cabin, her chest heaving from the rush of physical exertion.

Jac looked up from a mystery novel. Her face impassive, she observed Mel then went back to her reading.

Mel looked down. The white leather box still claimed the hollow of her hand. As if the box were burning her, she dropped it onto the small dresser near Jacquelyn's bed. The private detective observed the box, then Mel, and once more resumed her reading.

Without a word, Melissa snatched her pajamas from her suitcase and padded to the bathroom. She changed into her pj's, washed her face, brushed her teeth, and plopped onto her bed. The box beckoned her to slide the ruby onto her ring finger—her *left* ring finger.

"I'm sorry," Jacquelyn said without looking up from her book.

"Me, too." Mel's tension eased.

"I seem to have some emotional problems going on," Jac said, her voice void of inflections.

"Don't we all," Mel said with a grimace. "At least a little."
At least. That's an understatement. There's nothing "least" about this unforgiving monster that's eaten up my heart.

"Kinkaide gave you a ring?" Jac asked.

"How'd you know?"

"That's a ring box. What else is in a ring box? And you look like you've been talking to him." Jac shut her book and watched Mel, a humorous gleam in her eyes.

Mel squinted. "How can you tell?"

Jacquelyn chuckled. "You have that harassed look you only get when you've been with him, that's all."

"It's not funny," Mel snapped then softened her tone. The last thing she needed to do was pick another fight with Jac. "You can look at it." She pointed toward the box.

Swinging her legs to the floor, Jac snatched the box and snapped it open. A gasp erupted from her. "This is the mother of all rubies!"

Mel nodded.

Her eyes round, Jacquelyn stared at her friend. "Is it an engagement ring?"

"Only if I want it to be." Mel scooted down and pulled the covers under her chin.

"So do you want it to be?"

"I can't. Not with…" Mel trailed off. *Not with this lump of ice in my heart. Oh, Lord, what am I going to do?*

Twenty-Six

That desperate plea for heavenward help awakened Mel to the true needs of her heart. She could no longer deny the desire to reunite with Kinkaide. The yearning blazed just as brilliantly as the stars shone during that heart-melting kiss. But despite the longing, Mel knew beyond any doubt that she couldn't forgive Kinkaide in her own power. And for the first time, she acknowledged her destitute spiritual condition. By the time the ship pulled into port and the group checked into their Athens hotel rooms, Mel arrived at a sickening conclusion. That vengeful monster had not only taken over her heart, but it also had leeched all spiritual strength from her.

While Jacquelyn showered, Mel dug out her Bible from the bottom of her suitcase. She had thrown it in as a last-minute thought and hadn't opened the pages since the trip began. Clutching the book to her chest, she stepped onto the balcony, slid the glass door closed, and leaned against the ebony iron railing. She peered past the green-shuttered houses and businesses that lined the street, toward the Parthenon on the Acropolis, only minutes from her hotel room. The multicolumned structure, once built in honor of the Greek goddess Athena, now crumbled bit by bit as the years eroded what once had been a work of brilliant architecture.

Just like my relationship with Jesus, Mel thought. A tear trickled down her cheek, and she wondered if she could ever go back to the time before those harsh marks in her journal.

"What's up, girlfriend?" the cheerful voice floated across the Athens traffic.

Mel glanced over to see Abby Casper on the next-door balcony. The smile lighting Abby's smooth, dark face seemed as cheerful as the blue railings and red staircases they had seen in Rhodes. Mel sighed. If only she could take steps toward the peace that Abby was beginning to experience.

"How are you and Desmond?" Mel asked.

"Okay." Abby glanced down at her diamond-studded wedding band and twisted it. The stones glittered in the afternoon sunshine, and Mel thought of the ruby ring stowed in the side pocket of her suitcase. Not once had she placed it on her finger. No matter how the stones beckoned and how her heart pined, Mel had resisted wearing the symbol of love. Every time she thought of sliding the ring on her finger, fresh panic seized her soul.

"Everything isn't perfect," Abby added. "I still get angry when I think about..." she trailed off and gazed toward the Parthenon. "But I'm committed now to trying to repair what we've lost. After a lot of talking, I'm also fully accepting the fact that I've not exactly been the best spouse myself. I really believe Desmond is sincere, otherwise I would have hopped the first plane out of here." Abby's gauze housedress rustled in the warm breeze as if she were a monarch fluttering rust-colored wings.

Mel leaned into the railing. With the smell of seafood tantalizing her senses, she wished she could bid the sun to bequeath her Abby's courage. "How can you do it?" Mel asked. "I mean...I'm just now realizing I need to forgive Kinkaide, and it's been six years since he left me at the altar. You seem to have so much more resilience than I ever dreamed of." Mel clutched the Bible.

Abby gazed toward the sky, void of clouds. "All I can figure is that it's from obeying the Lord. Once I told God I'd go back into my marriage, He overflowed my heart with the assurance of His approval and enough strength to get me through. I'm not going to say that these past few days have been easy, or that I think the next months will be. But then, doing God's will isn't always easy." She gripped the rail and peered into Mel's eyes. "I just know that I'm in His will and that He's holding me up. But then, you're the one who encouraged me to stay in my marriage, remember?" Her head tilted, she scrutinized Mel.

"Sometimes, it's easier to preach a sermon than to live it," Melissa admitted.

"Been there." Abby chuckled. "Last year, I encouraged a friend to stay in a marriage that was on the rocks. I found out that it's a whole lot easier to give advice than to swallow it."

After a comfortable pause, Abby looked back toward the Acropolis. "You know, Mars Hill is just on the other side of the Parthenon."

"Yes, I overheard them talking about that in the lobby." Actually, Kinkaide and Lawton had tried to get her and Jac to toss their luggage into their rooms and clamber up the hill with them.

"Desmond and the girls and I have been thinking about climbing it. The steps are supposed to be straight up and slippery like polished glass. The hotel clerk said you have to come down on your bottom, step by step, or you'll slide right off. Want to join us?"

"Sounds like paradise." Mel rolled her eyes.

Abby chuckled and glanced down at her plump frame. "I just hope I don't go bouncing down."

"You'll do fine," Mel assured.

"Well, I wouldn't miss it. You know, that's the hill where Paul spoke about moving and living in Christ. I was looking out the window thinking about how he was right next to the Parthenon when he talked about all the stone gods in Athens."

Mel fanned the pages of her Bible until she came to Acts. "What chapter in Acts?" she asked.

"Seventeen, I think."

"Hmm...seventeen." Melissa mumbled as she flipped pages.

"I really wish you and Jacquelyn would join us. Besides, we'd feel safer if Jac was with us. Desmond hasn't really relaxed since she spotted that man watching the girls."

"Have you noticed him since?" Mel's toes curled in her shoes.

"No. We haven't seen anything of him." Abby tucked a strand of hair into the clasp at her neck.

"Good."

"I'm hoping the whole thing was just a meaningless incident. The closer we get to going home, the more I believe that."

"I hope so, too." Mel found Acts 17.

"Well, I'll have Desmond call your room when we're ready to leave just in case you change your mind," Abby said. "I need to change into walking shorts."

"Okay," Mel called as Abby eased back through the sliding glass door. Melissa scanned the chapter until she arrived at the passage marked "Sermon on Mars Hill." She devoured Paul's words...words that were spoken two thousand years ago on the exact spot where Mel would soon stand.

When she came to the passage that Abby mentioned, Mel paused to ponder the message that wove an uncomfortable web around her heart. "For in him we live and move and have our being." She peered toward the Parthenon, a crumbling monument to a false goddess against a blue-white sky. Mel realized that years had passed since she lived and moved in Christ. Instead, she had built a monument to herself in the center of her heart and burned the incense of unforgiveness to a monster that lurked among the pillars.

"I've been too tangled up in myself and my pain to really live in Christ. Fresh tears trickled down her cheeks. On the skirts of that admission, the accusation she hurled at Kinkaide pierced her mind like a verbal spike: *I've about decided you are the most selfish person I have ever met.* Mel groaned and buried her face in the pages of her Bible soon dampened by her tears of repentance.

Horace paced the Rome hotel room a couple of blocks from the famous Fountain of Trevi. Sara and Lenora would be here within minutes. Neither of them suspected Horace's agenda. The room's cream-colored walls closed in on him as he debated how to explain his decision. Hopefully Sara would listen to reason. Lenora, on the other hand, might explode. Horace stiffened his resolve. If Lenora detonated, she just might find out that he could erupt as well.

Horace approached the window and yanked the curtain cord. The heavy drapes, covered with baroque flowers, wobbled to a halt. He grabbed the sides of the windowframe and glared upon the weblike streets of Rome. Motorcycles zipped in and out of traffic. Cars determined to seize the right-of-way honked and bullied their way forward. Every direction he gazed, Greek mythology and ancient Roman structures imprinted the city. People were everywhere. The painters...the street vendors...the sightseers. Just as Sara predicted, Rome was the perfect place for a kidnapping.

Horace whirled from the window and reached for the bottle of cheap red wine he had bought before entering the hotel. He sloshed a mouthful down his throat and followed that with another. While the tart liquid would in no way deliver the fire of scotch, Horace convinced himself he needed the boost for courage to face the stressful task before him.

He set the bottle on the windowsill and peered up from his second-floor room. The buildings along the narrow street made him feel as if he were a speck in the center of a canyon. A very deep canyon. A canyon full of quicksand. Quicksand and vipers. Vipers and desperation.

A determined rap on his door sent a shock up Horace's back. He jumped and hurried away from the window, only to stumble over the suitcase at the end of the double bed. Horace lunged forward, and his palms slammed into the short-piled carpet. He groaned at the resulting burn and rolled to his side to pound the floor with his fist. Horace set his lips as his father's derisive laughter echoed in his mind. Self-disgust burned a trail through his gut. But this time he shoved his father's voice from his mind. The world moved forward—regardless of what his dad thought of him. Horace had a future—a future he did *not* want to spend in prison. He pushed against the floor and stood. Another rap bespoke Lenora's impatience. Horace whipped open the door, and Lenora and Sara swept in.

"Hi," Sara said, her large brown eyes flashing. "Looks like this is it."

Horace paused for a brief embrace then closed the door.

"I missed you," Sara whispered.

Horace hesitated then returned the endearment. His obsession with kidnapping had left him precious little time to ponder Sara's absence.

Lenora, dressed in the typical slinky pantsuit, sidestepped the suitcase, paced toward the window, then whirled to face him. "When should we make the move?" she demanded.

"The Caspers aren't here yet," Horace explained. He removed his keys from his jeans pocket and jiggled them.

"When will they be here?" Lenora snapped.

"Tomorrow."

"Lenora and I were thinking that we should arrange the kidnapping as soon as they start sightseeing," Sara said. Her frizzed hair framed her flushed cheeks.

Horace narrowed his eyes. Sara, more animated than ever, seemed to be enjoying this whole ordeal. *Maybe she's not the woman I thought I was falling in love with.*

"I think we need to take advantage of their being disoriented," Lenora said. "Horace, by now the girls should trust you. You can call them away from the crowd. Sara and I will be ready with the car. When we pop open the back door, you shove the girls in and crawl in after them." Lenora fumbled through her purse and pulled out her silver cigarette case. She yanked a long, brown smoke from the case.

"I think we're all a little giddy." Sara settled onto the end of the bed. "Just think, in a couple of days we'll be rich!"

"Actually…" Horace walked toward the window and gripped the bottle of wine. He gulped another mouthful and deposited the bottle back on the windowsill. The blinding sunshine, caressing the ancient stone structures along the streets, did as little to boost his courage as did the wine.

"Actually?" Lenora prompted.

Horace pivoted from the window and clenched his fists. "I really think we shouldn't go through with the kidnapping." His gaze implored Sara.

"What?" Sara demanded as she jumped to her feet.

"I told you from the start he wouldn't follow through," Lenora snarled.

Sara placed her fists on her hips. Her skirt swirled around her ankles as she approached Horace. "You can't back out now!" she commanded. "The whole plan is almost complete."

"Yes, I can, and I will," Horace said. For once, his voice never wavered and his determination increased with every word.

As Sara's cheeks grew bright red, Horace reflected upon his yearlong relationship with her. From the time they met in the shadowed corner of that Dallas bar, he never once remembered her being anything but domineering. And Horace wondered if he might very well have found a female version of his father. While Sara had never verbally scorned him, she had certainly maintained the upper hand in their relationship. Horace had meekly gone along with her because having a woman around made him feel important.

"I told you! I told you!" Lenora yelled. She inhaled on the brown cigarette and an acrid haze surrounded her flawless face.

"Oh, shut up!" Sara spun on her partner. "And don't start getting too pushy," she snarled. "I still have enough dirt on you to put you away."

Horace glanced from Lenora to Sara and back to Lenora. The day they met in Lenora's apartment, he sensed an undercurrent of animosity between the women. An undercurrent now rushing to the surface.

The lithe beauty underwent a metamorphosis before his eyes. Hatred—raw, seething hatred—transformed her features into a monsterlike mask. Her lips curled away from teeth, glistening white.

"Listen, you fat devil," she growled, "you used that same threat to force me into going in with this imbecile of a detective." She waved her hand toward Horace. "And I *refuse* to let you continue to call the shots."

Horace frowned. There was obviously more going on than he thought..

Lenora drew deeply on her cigarette and lowered her face to within inches of Sara's. "And if you ever—*ever* mention the embezzlement again, I'll kill you. Got it, peaches?" The room seemed to darken with the utterance of her every word, and she blew a smoke cloud smack into Sara's face.

Sara sputtered and stumbled backward.

The inky evil flowing through Lenora's eyes left no doubt about her intent. Furthermore, Horace was doubly sure that Lenora would kill the Casper twins if she was given half a chance. His manipulative fiancée had twined their fates with a fire-breathing gorgon.

"And you—you spineless excuse of a detective," she accused. "You *will not* bail out! I've paid your way here, and I'll make sure you don't see another birthday if you don't go through with the plan. *Understand?*"

Horace glanced down at his suitcase and shuffled his feet. "I got it."

Twenty-Seven

Melissa thought the descent on Mars Hill had been precarious, but nothing on the trip so far matched her present state of circumstances. The road from the airport into Rome, though weaving across rolling green mountains and fertile fields, contained a swarm of demon drivers. Little cars that looked like igloo doghouses on wheels swerved in and out of traffic and dared anyone to question their right to hog the road. One driver of a doghouse car actually slammed on his brakes as a "punishment" to their van driver for tailgating. Mel clutched her handbag and took in a lungful of air.

"This reminds me of traffic in Vietnam!" Mel exclaimed.

"You've been to Vietnam?" Kinkaide turned around in the seat in front of her and stared at her. Mel held his gaze. She hadn't expected Kinkaide's direct question and given the impact of his observation, she couldn't exactly remember what he had asked anyway. Since that encounter on the deck of the ship, Mel had kept her distance. Even on the plane to Rome, when her seat was next to his, Mel surreptitiously switched seats with Jac—who was thrilled to avoid sitting by Lawton.

"Are you going to answer him?" Lawton prompted. "Inquiring minds and all that."

"Uh...yes...yes...uh...Vietnam. I stayed in Saigon and Can Tho last year. Sonsee, Kim Lan, and I all went on a mission trip to help at an orphanage and old folks' home." Another doghouse whizzed around them, and Mel scrunched down in her seat.

"Kim Lan wound up marrying the trip's coordinator," Jacquelyn drawled.

"Would that we all were so lucky," Lawton shot over his shoulder then laughed at his own joke.

"You're nuts," Mel fondly teased.

"Yeah, and you love it," Lawton quipped.

"So, tell us about Vietnam," Kinkaide said.

Abby and Desmond, two seats up, swiveled and observed Mel.

The driver slammed on his brakes and muttered an oath.

"Mamma Mia," Lawton muttered as they were thrown against their seat belts.

"You're experiencing Vietnam traffic!" Mel exclaimed, her midsection aching from the pressure of the seat belt. "The trip was an adventure. There's so much to tell—"

"Wow, that was close!" Desmond gasped as yet another car cut in front of them. As the passengers hung on for dear life conversation died. Interest in Vietnam faded in the face of surviving the present ordeal.

When the van finally pulled into the parking lot of the Hotel dei Mellini, Mel squelched the urge to fall from the van and kiss the sidewalk. The ambiance of the exquisite hotel, situated near the Tiber River, snatched all memories of traffic from Mel's mind.

"Welcome to Roma," the Italian doorman oozed as Mel swept through the double glass doors, up the steps, and into a lounge. As plush as their cruise ship had been, the burgundy sofas with gold pillows, wood-and-glass tables, and comfortable arm chairs situated on tiled and parquet floors beckoned tourists to embrace the city of Rome.

I'm embracing! Mel thought while she and Jac arranged their check-in. Soft piano music drifted from the hotel's small restaurant, and the smell of bruschetta tempted her taste-buds. Mel guessed that she had probably gained five pounds this week, but what fun pounds they had been!

A smiling attendant dressed in a black suit loaded their luggage onto a cart and motioned to them. "If you'll follow me," he said with a slight bow.

"Whew! Do all Italians of male persuasion have eyes like that?" Jac whispered while the attendant preceded them.

"What's the matter with you?" Mel teased. "Is the city of romance making you go soft?"

"There's nothing soft about recognizing *the truth*, sister." Jac's dark eyes flashed with a glimmer Mel hadn't seen since their college years. And Mel stayed the impulse to hug her friend. This trip had definitely done her good.

"Melissa, wait!" Kinkaide's determined footsteps followed his voice.

She stopped abruptly, then motioned toward the attendant who was swiftly approaching the elevator. He didn't see her, and Jacquelyn stepped forward to intercept him.

Mel turned to face Kinkaide. In short, the last couple of days had been one large spiritual crisis for her. Melissa looked into the eyes of the man who had once encouraged her to a deeper walk with God, and her heart twisted with an aching love she longed to express. If only...if only she could finally come to the end of herself and release the past into the hands of the Lord. *If only.* Those two little words embodied years of struggle.

"Mel?" Kinkaide's voice and his searching gaze were proof of a man hopelessly in love.

"Did you—did you want something?" she rasped.

"We were just talking." He pointed toward the Caspers and Lawton, who were arranging to have their luggage taken to their rooms. "We've decided to walk to the Spanish Steps and see one of Bernini's fountains and the Fountain of Trevi. We'll meet in the lobby in about 15 minutes. Do you and Jac want to join us?" Since that kiss, Kinkaide had honored the silent wall Mel had erected between them. Now the pleading shimmer in his eyes reminded her of his request of just one moment on the deck of the ship.

She looked toward Jac, who shrugged. "Might as well," she said, then cast a wary glance toward Lawton.

"Okay." Mel nodded. "We'll be back down in about 15 minutes."

Kinkaide produced a smile warm enough to melt the North Pole. "You know what they say about the Fountain of Trevi, don't you?"

"No."

"If you toss in one coin, you'll come back to Rome. Toss in two coins, and you'll come back and fall in love with a Roman. Toss in three coins, and you'll come back to Rome and get married." The impish light in his eyes sent a zip through Mel's stomach.

Lawton and Abby neared from behind. "I'm planning to toss in three coins myself."

"We'll just be keeping our coins," Jac said as she grabbed Mel's arm and tugged her into the open elevator. "Good grief, woman," Jacquelyn whispered. "Some of us are ready to get to our rooms." The attendant followed with the luggage cart, and the doors closed.

"This place ain't too shabby," Mel quipped.

"You're starting to sound like Lawton," Jacquelyn accused.

"In Kim Lan's immortal words, 'Honey, you got it bad,'" Mel drawled with a fake southern accent so like their friend's feigned cadence.

"What are you implying?" Jac demanded.

"Lawton," Mel simply stated. "That's what I'm implying."

"Not a chance. *Not a chance!*" Jac's hardened features dared Mel to push another inch. "Look, I've stayed out of whatever this on-again, off-again thing is with you and Kinkaide..." She left the rest unsaid.

"Okay, okay," Mel raised her hands. "I'm sorry. Let's don't get into it again."

"I'm sorry, too," Jac said and sighed. "Really." She squeezed Mel's fingers.

Horace trailed the Caspers toward the Spanish Steps. He dodged in and out of the never-ending stream of pedestrians. The harried streets proved a haven for petty thieves… and kidnappers. The plan had been laid. Now it was in motion. Behind him, Lenora and Sara crept along in a rented car. Outside the Hotel dei Mellini, the three of them had awaited the Caspers' arrival then continued to tarry in hopes that the group would exit the hotel. Their patience paid off. The first opportunity that arose, Horace was to divert the Casper twins and enable Lenora to shove them into the back of the car. She had a .38 Special that would encourage the girls to obey without a noise.

He followed the group through the angular streets lined with ancient buildings sporting ornate stonework. Yet the open cafes, the painters, the musicians flaunting their talent were lost on Horace. As he glimpsed a cross perched atop a distant church, an unexpected peace enveloped him.

Melissa, soaking in the aura of Rome, hung toward the back of the group. A couple of times Kinkaide paused, glanced over his shoulder, and made eye contact, as if his sole interest were her safety. He then resumed his stroll. They had been repeatedly warned about pickpockets, and neither Mel, Jac, Abby, nor the twins carried a handbag. Instead, they each used the money belts that fit beneath their casual clothing. Furthermore, all cameras were secured around their wrists.

Amid the sea of motor scooters, a horse-drawn open carriage meandered along the street. Mel raised her 35-millimeter camera and snapped a shot. The couple ensconced in the leather seat were oblivious to anyone except each other. The sound of an accordion floated from an outside cafe. Mel slowed even more to enjoy the trio of men who sang, of all things, "Moon River" to a blushing table of American women. Mel stopped by an olive-skinned painter who sat in front of his easel. He smiled and winked, and Mel scurried ahead to find her group and discovered the Spanish Steps were in front of her.

The multitiered stone steps stretched upward as a monument to Spain—a special thanks from Italy for support during military crises. A few palm trees dotted the sides of the scenic memorial and offered a splash of green against a cobalt-blue sky. Mel raised her camera to take a shot then realized the cream-colored building at the top of the steps was actually a church. She lowered her camera and eyed the place of worship graced with stained-glass windows. The twin towers stretched skyward, and a cross, posed atop a tall, stone pedestal rose in front of the belfries. That cross tugged Mel forward, urged her to inspect the inside of the church. Mel snapped her photo then nudged Jac.

"I'm going into the church for awhile, in case anybody misses me." She glanced toward Kinkaide who chatted with the Caspers and Lawton. "And I'd really like to be alone."

"Sure," Jac said, and Mel shot her an appreciative grin as she started up the steps—all 137 of them!

Mel wove her way toward the church and, at last, stepped through the entry. Her eyes, accustomed to the blinding sunshine, struggled to adjust to the dimmer light. Although the building was not air-conditioned, the stone floor and walls offered cooler temperatures that relieved the heat of the city. The hushed whispering, the scent of candles, the aura of rest plunged Mel into a spirit of worship. She paused on the threshold and absorbed the milieu of the Catholic sanctuary. The ceiling, painted in biblical scenes, summoned all who looked upward to meditate upon the things of God. The dark, wooden pews told of countless others who had sought the Lord in the hushed atmosphere.

Mel moved forward and noted the eight-foot iron gate, about a third of the way down the aisle. The gate's door bore a padlock that prohibited visitors from approaching the altar, which was covered in red cloth and surrounded by icons. Although the altar beckoned, Mel settled into a pew. She placed her hands on the back of the pew in front of her and rested her forehead on her hands.

Since her trip up Mars Hill, Mel had been drinking in the words of Paul. Not only did she meditate anew upon living and moving and being in Christ, she also read and reread Paul's words from Galatians—words that unfolded in her heart as she waited upon the Lord: *"I have been crucified with Christ and I no longer live, but Christ lives in me."* Like a shaft of light straight from heaven, Mel recognized a sickening fact. While she had spent her whole life in church, while she had often parroted biblical concepts, while she had confessed Christ as her Savior, she could never say there had been a time when she had truly died to herself. Paul's claim of "I die daily" for Christ had never crossed Mel's lips. Instead, her motto had been "Melissa Moore lives and lives for herself and dictates her own life."

And that was exactly where her mother was.

She looked toward the altar. Near the center stood a statue of the Savior, His arms extended outward, nail scars in His hands. "Oh, Jesus," Mel moaned. She felt as if He whispered, *In order to get rid of that monster of unforgiveness, you're going to have to relinquish your rights—all of them—to Me. Let Me be your sole reason for living.*

Tears streaming down her cheeks, Mel began softly singing "He Is Lord." And with each word, the same notes from Kinkaide's recent CD echoed through her mind. She began the song again, and this time she closed her eyes and lifted the melody toward heaven as a prayer of repentance, a prayer of commitment, a prayer of praise.

That heinous beast in the caverns of her soul shrieked and gasped for air. Indeed, it stumbled forward and fell before shrinking from existence. With the tune reverberating through her mind, Mel breathed deeply and reveled in the freedom that descended upon her. No more tension. No more need to retaliate. No more bitterness. Nothing, but a flood of heavenly peace. Peace and love. Love and forgiveness. Christ's radical forgiveness extended to Mel, allowing her to extend it to others—including Kinkaide Franklin.

Mel removed her glasses and placed them on the pew beside her. She fumbled underneath her oversized T-shirt until she grasped the zipper of her money pouch. Sliding the zipper around she retrieved a tissue and swiped at her cheeks. Blinking against the retreating tears, she reached into the pouch and pulled out a small leather box. Without questioning her motives, Mel had obeyed the silent urge to place the ring in her money pouch before leaving the hotel room. She opened the box, lifted the golden ring, and slipped the fiery stone upon her left ring finger. The symbol of love fit perfectly.

Someone settled onto the pew beside her, and Mel scooted over. Expecting to encounter a stranger, she glanced up. But the man who joined her had soft brown eyes that caressed her tearstained cheeks then focused on the ruby, glimmering in a nest of dewlike diamonds.

Twenty-Eight

*

"Oh, Kinkaide!" Mel whispered, then she flung herself toward him.

Taken aback, he encircled her trembling shoulders with his arms and reveled in the clean scent of her wispy hair. The church seemed to spin in a haze of disbelief as he grappled for equilibrium. "Wow! I just came in to tell you we are heading back down to see Bernini's Baraccia Fountain," he said.

"I've been such a fool," she sputtered as if he'd never uttered a word. "I'm so sorry I said you were selfish. I've been just as selfish as you ever were. And—and you—were right! I *am* like my mother. Just like her! All I ever think about is what *I* want!"

"Ah, Mel." Kinkaide laid his cheek atop her head and stroked her hair. "I should have never said that about your mother. That was so unfair of me to say you're like her. But I—I—" He swallowed and decided to admit the ugly truth. "I was just trying to find a way to jab you. I knew that would really get to you. Those were words that should have never—*never* been spoken."

"I've been praying," Mel said, her words muffled against his cotton shirt. "The last few days have been a time of personal purging. But really, I think I've been leading up to it for quite some time. I've been so stubborn." Mel's voice broke. "I'm so sorry for everything," she squeaked out.

"Me, too." Kinkaide sighed. "Me, too."

As the minutes rocked on, Kinkaide regained his equilibrium and restrained himself from snatching the opportunity to seal Mel into a commitment. When he sat down beside her, she had just been placing that ruby on her finger. Even though the sight of the ring sent a thrill through him, even though she was doing exactly what he suggested a few nights ago when he kissed her left ring finger, even though he had flagrantly flirted with her near the elevators that very day, Kinkaide could not allow her to make a commitment to marriage on the skirts of such an emotional and spiritual upheaval.

He loosened the hug and rested his hands on her shoulders. With a sniffle, Mel pulled away and peered upward. This time no shadows tainted her hazel eyes. Where the thorns of bitterness once dwelt, now blazed fragrant flowers of love. Love and promise. Promise and hope.

"I think it's fairly safe to say that by now you know how I feel about you." One edge of Kinkaide's lips tilted up.

"Yes." She smiled.

"So I don't want you to think that what I'm about to say is any reflection upon my love. I love you, Mel. I love you with my whole heart. But..." His gaze trailed to her lips, touched with earth-toned gloss. Another urge heated his veins. Clearing his throat, Kinkaide backed away and forced himself to maintain control. "But I told you the other night on the cruise that I'd rather you be happy without me than miserable with me."

"But—" Mel held up her hand and stuttered as if she were wrestling for the right words.

Kinkaide grasped her hand, and she quieted. He placed her palm against his and admired the ruby's flaming splendor. Gently, he tugged the ring from Mel's finger, turned her palm upward, and placed the precious stone in the center. Kinkaide wrapped her fingers around the ring then covered her hand with his.

Mel shook her head and covered her lips with trembling fingers.

"I want you to take your time. I don't want there to be any regrets. None. I've kicked myself for kissing you the other night. I should have stayed by my pledge to keep my hands off. I guess I blew that, but I'm not going to blow this. This is just too big. Please...keep the ring. Think the whole thing over, and when you're sure—absolutely sure—I'll still be here."

"But I—"

Kinkaide rose.

"But...but..."

His heart pounding, Kinkaide leaned forward and kissed her forehead then did the hardest thing he had ever done in his life. He completely took his hands off the situation, placed it in the hands of God, and stepped away.

Horace mingled with the crowd and followed the Caspers as they meandered away from the Spanish Steps and walked toward a line of stores. He narrowed his eyes and scrutinized Lenora and Sara in the gray sedan. They cruised about 100 feet behind the twins, and Lenora craned her neck, as if in search of him.

He smiled, gripped his camera, and snapped several shots of the sedan, making certain the Casper twins were included in the photo. He double-checked the zipper on his short's front pocket. Horace had worn the shorts with the zippers today for the sole purpose of hiding the microcassette recorder. While waiting in front of the Casper's hotel, he had recorded enough information from the mouths of both Lenora and Sara to attest to their culpability. A few pictures would seal their doom.

Once again, Lenora leaned out, and Horace remained hidden in the sea of people. If Lenora proved true to her nature, she would eventually get tired of waiting on him, decide he had messed up again, and try to nab the girls on her own.

The twins paused beside a man selling stuffed poodles on a leash. The dogs yelped then did a backward flip, and the twins laughed. Their parents, unaware that the girls had stopped, continued hand-in-hand toward an elegant antique shop. The gray car pulled away from the line of motorcycles and stopped at the curb inches away from the twins.

Kinkaide trotted down the Spanish Steps and neared Lawton, who amiably chatted with Jac. Yet she peered toward the church as if she were silently beseeching Mel to appear.

"I'm ready to head to the fountain if you are, Lawton." Kinkaide nudged his brother's arm.

"That's fine," Jacquelyn said. "I'll go get Mel. We'll be there soon."

"Okay, just be careful."

Jac tilted her head and tucked one side of her hair behind her ear. "We're big girls. We can take care of ourselves."

"Yes, I believe you can," Lawton derided under his breath.

"Did she finally get to you?" Kinkaide asked as they descended the stairs.

"Let's not talk about it right now," Lawton said.

In silence, Kinkaide steered his brother back down the Spanish Steps, toward Bernini's Barcaccia Fountain where they would reunite with the Caspers. As they wove in and out of the crowd, Kinkaide vacillated between saying "I told you so" and extending a heart full of sympathy toward his younger brother. Then his mind roved to Melissa, and all thoughts for his brother's problems vanished.

"What took you so long with Mel?" Lawton asked as if he had read Kinkaide's mind. "Did she throw herself into your arms, beg your forgiveness, and pledge her undying love?" he teased.

"Actually, yes." He eyed Lawton.

"What!"

Kinkaide caught sight of the Casper twins beside a man with some stuffed poodles. Near the curb, he noticed a car stop and the passenger door open. A tall, dark woman stepped out. The sunglasses and floppy hat did little to hide her exquisite beauty. With a trench coat draped loosely across her shoulders, she opened the back door then turned toward the twins. A snatch of black steel glimmered from within the coat's hidden folds.

Kinkaide tensed and shoved Lawton toward a dress shop's display window. "Stay here. I'm coming back!"

"Hey! What's going on?" Lawton yelped.

The woman glanced around then issued an order to the twins. They straightened from perusing the toy dog and another customer snared the vendor's attention. Wide-eyed, both twins observed the woman. The girls looked down the center of the trench coat to the snubnosed .38 special.

With a primeval roar, Kinkaide sprang forward, grabbed the woman, and threw her to the sidewalk. His right knee ground into unforgiving pavement as the two landed amid thuds and grunts. Another man clambered over Kinkaide and crawled into the front seat to latch onto the driver. An eruption of screams multiplied throughout the crowd. Kinkaide, straddling the heaving woman, gripped her flailing wrist and slammed it against concrete. The gun clattered from her grasp, and her angry accusations mingled with the crowd's screaming.

"Janie! Julie!" Desmond's panicked cry cut through the raucous moment. "Janie! Julie! Where are you?" He broke through the restless crowd with Abby in his wake.

The woman squirmed beneath Kinkaide and screeched like a rabid cat. Her sunglasses slipped down her nose and lodged across her full, red-stained mouth.

Kinkaide, maintaining his hold on the writhing woman, peered up at his friend. "This is Lenora, isn't it?" he asked. He knew the answer before the stricken Desmond ever nodded, and his mind reeled with his friend's plight.

"You traitor!" a female voice screamed from the car's interior. "You stinkin' traitor! We *trusted* you!"

The man's deep-voiced reply was cut off by the sound of sirens.

"Come on, girls." Abby drew her distraught daughters into her arms as she eyed Lenora with blatant distaste.

"Oh, God, help me!" Desmond fell to his knees beside Lenora. "What have I done?" He cradled his head in his hands and dug stiff fingers through springy hair. "I have been a fool's fool!" he bellowed.

Two policemen rushed upon the scene now surrounded by a huddle of curious onlookers. They fired out rapid Italian, and Kinkaide shook his head. He possessed precious little knowledge of his grandmother's native language. They switched to English. Kinkaide succinctly answered their questions and relinquished his post. One of the policemen took control of Lenora.

Desmond remained on his knees, staring at the exotic beauty as a police officer hauled her to her feet. A trail of tears dripped from his chin, yet he never blinked.

"Desmond." Abby laid a hand on her husband's shoulder. He turned to press her palm against his lips.

"I'm so sorry, Abby!" he groaned. "So, so sorry."

"Why don't you just shut up," Lenora hissed, struggling against the officer's attempts to handcuff her. "I hate you! Do you understand?" She choked on a sob, and her face distorted with the force of her vengeance. *"I hate you!"*

The other man dragged the protesting, plump female from the car and plunked her on the sidewalk where Lenora once lay. Her oversized frame encountered the concrete with a force that wrenched a wince from Kinkaide.

"It's you," Desmond gasped, gaping at the bug-eyed man he'd once saved.

"You traitor," the woman shrieked again as she struggled against toppling over.

"Didn't I tell you, Sara?" Horace nodded toward Desmond. "He saved my life."

Twenty-Nine

That night, Kinkaide stepped into the hotel bathroom's marble shower and turned on the water as hot as he could stand it. He twisted the showerhead to the massage setting and allowed the heat and force to penetrate his tense muscles. He, Lawton, and the Caspers had spent the afternoon at the police station. They grabbed dinner on the run, and Kinkaide was now ready for an early night.

"What a way to spend the first day in Rome," he muttered and closed his eyes. Bernini's Fountain and the Fountain of Trevi would have to wait until tomorrow.

Now that all details of the arrests and charges were behind him, images of Melissa bore upon his mind. A giddy smile broke across his face, and he prayed that the afternoon on her own had given her time to seal her decision.

At last, Kinkaide turned off the water and grabbed one of the fluffy white towels from the marble counter. He had barely shrugged into one of the complimentary hotel robes when Lawton's knock sounded against the bathroom door. Without awaiting an answer, his brother shoved open the door and a waft of cool air swirled through the steam and blew against Kinkaide's legs.

"Hey, lover boy, this note came for you. I've been waiting on you to get your lazy self out of the shower." Lawton extended an envelope. "I never signed on to be your postman, by the way," he grumbled.

"You're just jealous because you didn't get a note." Kinkaide grabbed the envelope and read his name in block print. *Could it be from Mel?*

286

"In your dreams." Lawton crossed his arms and leaned against the bathroom doorway. "I've never been jealous of you a day in my life."

"Yeah, yeah, yeah." Kinkaide ripped open the envelope and read the simple message, also written in block letters. "Come to the eighth floor." The giddy grin returned as he dashed a comb through his wet hair.

"So are you going to tell me what it says?" Lawton demanded.

"None of your business," Kinkaide teased.

"Listen, your business is my business and my business is my business." Lawton pointed to his chest. "The sooner you figure that out, the better off we'll be."

Kinkaide swept past his brother, toward his suitcase on the end of one of the twin-sized beds. CNN blared from the large television perched on a shelf across the room. Kinkaide switched it off.

"I was listening to that," Lawton protested.

"Okay." Kinkaide flipped the television back on. "You're going to be by yourself anyway. You'll need the company."

"And where are you going?" Lawton measured his steps until he reached one of the leather armchairs near a cherry wood desk.

"To the eighth floor—at least that's what the note says." Kinkaide pulled out a pair of pleated shorts and a polo shirt.

Lawton slumped in the chair and lifted his chin. With the absence of the black glasses, Kinkaide had a clear view of cloudy eyes constantly in motion. "I guess the note's from Mel?"

"I guess." Kinkaide's broad smile melted into his words as he tossed aside the robe and began to dress.

"Do you have to sound so pleased about it? Have some respect, will ya?"

"You never did tell me what happened with Jac this afternoon." Kinkaide tugged the shirt over his head.

"She gave me the 'I ain't interested' spiel."

I tried to tell you, Kinkaide thought, but he stopped himself before voicing the words.

"But you know what?" Lawton placed his forearm along the table and leaned forward. "I don't believe her."

Kinkaide stifled a groan as he stepped into leather sandals. "So what are you going to do with that platinum bracelet you bought?"

"Give it to her anyway," he claimed.

Mom would probably appreciate it more. Once again Kinkaide stifled the words. Then he thought of his pursuit of Mel. She had been far more adamant about her lack of availability than Jacquelyn Lightfoot. Furthermore, Lawton wasn't any more apt to give up than Kinkaide.

"Well, you never know." Kinkaide stepped toward his brother and gripped his shoulder. "Give her a few months, and you just might badger her into a relationship."

"Ha!" Lawton threw back his head and laughed.

"I'm outta here," Kinkaide said.

"Okay, sure. Just leave me with CNN to keep me warm while you go off to some rendezvous on top of the hotel." Lawton waved his hand at Kinkaide as if he were at the epitome of disgust.

"Well, it's a tough job, but..."

"...somebody's gotta do it," the brothers finished in unison.

"Get outta here," Lawton commanded through a smile.

Melissa paced across the terrace and checked her watch for the third time in three minutes. She'd sent the note to Kinkaide 30 minutes ago!

What if he doesn't come? the thought barged in upon her mind with another on its heels. *What if he backs out of the whole commitment—again?*

Mel stopped beside one of the umbrella-covered tables and gripped the cushioned chair. She stared at the Night-Blooming Jasmine that covered one wall and emitted a heady perfume. The flowers seemed to reassure her that Kinkaide was simply delayed. Surely some logical reason prohibited him from an immediate appearance. The selfless love he displayed in the chapel came from a heart that had pledged its faith to her—and her alone.

The door to the terrace opened, and Kinkaide walked into the night. He paused as if he were a connoisseur savoring the beauty of a rare work of art. Melissa's heart palpitated, and she swallowed against her tightening throat.

"Hi," she whispered.

"Hi." Kinkaide approached and took her hand.

"Your hair's wet." Mel touched the damp curls at the nape of his neck.

"I was in the shower."

"So that's what took you so long."

"Hmm." Kinkaide pulled her into his arms, and Mel reveled in the warmth she had missed for six long years. Her heart whispered that she had at long last come home.

"I've been thinking..." she said.

"Yes, I know."

Mel looked up at the stars glittering like Fourth of July sparklers against a silky sky. Kinkaide swayed her to the soft violin music floating from the street.

"And..." Mel backed away and drew the white ring box from her slacks pocket.

A flash of panic ripped through Kinkaide's eyes.

"I want *you* to place the ring on my finger," Mel whispered.

"Don't scare me like that, woman!" he growled. Kinkaide flipped open the box, extracted the ruby and diamonds, and wasted no time slipping the ring onto her hand. "Now it's sealed." He kissed her finger. "No turning back."

"No turning back." Melissa slipped her arms around his neck as his lips claimed hers for a brief, powerful kiss that shook the terrace.

Kinkaide backed away and stroked her hair with unsteady fingers. "Okay, enough of *that*," he teased and Mel joined him in mutual giggles.

The evening breeze swirled around the terrace and the smell of jasmine increased tenfold. Mel rested her head against Kinkaide's chest and relished his strong heart's steady rhythm. He took a breath as if he were going to speak, but no words came forth.

"There's something we need to talk about," he finally blurted, as if the subject were tainted with the most odious of auras.

"Oh?" Mel raised her head.

"In the middle of that big fight we had, you asked me something that I didn't want to answer." Kinkaide distanced himself from her and approached the terrace's edge.

Mel joined him and looked upon the city sparkling with a million lights that rivaled the star-studded sky. She gripped the terrace rail and sensed exactly where this conversation was leading. Part of her dreaded the knowledge, but another part of her respected Kinkaide for having the courage to admit the truth.

"You asked me who else there had been before you." The words came out as if wrenched from his soul. "I would love to tell you that—that—what Lawton will be able to tell his wife—but I can't." He gripped his neck. "If you think I was selfish by the time we were engaged, you should have known me before I met the Lord." Kinkaide shook his head. "I've regretted the choices I made a million times, but never as much as tonight."

"There's nothing you can do about it now." Mel wrapped both her hands around his forearm. "God has forgiven you, and so have I."

A tear, glimmering as if it fell from the heavens, trickled down the side of Kinkaide's prominent nose. "I only wish that I had had enough sense to—"

"God has forgiven you," Mel repeated, "and so have I. So have I—for everything."

Kinkaide draped an arm around her shoulders and tugged her close. He bestowed a gentle kiss on her forehead and whispered in her ear, "Would you marry me this week, Mel? Here in Rome?"

Melissa pulled away and stared at him. "Are you serious?"

"As serious as I've ever been in my life."

"But—but what about the time it takes to have all the paperwork approved and—"

"I already checked into all that," he said with an impish grin.

"Oh, you did, did you?" Mel placed a hand on her hip. "And exactly when did you do all this checking?"

Kinkaide deliberately turned down the corners of his mouth. "Before we left for the cruise. You know, just in case my miracle came through."

"So what did you find out?" The eager question sprang forth with a life of its own.

"There's actually a company here in Italy that will arrange all the paperwork for us. It's quite simple and legal. The processing takes a couple of days. Of course, we'd have to change our plane tickets and go home later. Can your practice survive without you for another week?"

A warm assurance crept from Mel's spirit and filled her whole being. "I think so," she said, stroking his beard. "I think they'll do just fine."

Thirty

～

"Excuse me! Would somebody please tell me where the package tape is?" Mel stood in the walkway between the dining room and living room. Mounds of boxes cluttered her home. Her six dearest friends glanced up from their packing endeavors.

"We forfeit our sister reunion to help you pack, and all you can do is gripe about the tape," Sonsee teased. She flipped her auburn ponytail and flopped the top of her box in place. "I could use the tape, too."

"Better let Sonsee have it first. She's pregnant, remember, and is getting more bossy by the hour!" Jac wrapped a sheet of newspaper around a vase and laid it in a box.

"Hey, you!" Sonsee stood and punched Jac in the arm. "I'll take you on any day!" Her oversized T-shirt bloomed out in the front.

"Did somebody say tape?" Kim Lan held up a roll. She sat at the dining table covered with a sea of photos. For once, the Asian supermodel was without a trace of makeup. Last month she and her husband, Mick, traveled to Vietnam to adopt their new son, Khanh Ahn. Kim Lan had mentioned that life hadn't been the same since. Mel even noticed that the elegant model arrived with a broken fingernail. Motherhood certainly produced its casualties.

Admittedly, none of the sisters looked their best. The moving endeavor was taking its toll. Melissa stepped toward Kim and grasped the tape. "Thanks." She handed it to

Sonsee. While she waited, Mel crossed her arms and leaned against the doorway to silently observe her friends.

Marilyn Langham, her blonde hair as disheveled as Mel's, moved toward the kitchen. "I'm starting on the dishes," she announced.

"I'll help!" Sammie Jones, shirttail out, traipsed after Marilyn.

"Count me in," Victoria Roberts called. The soft folds of her curly hair were pulled away from her face with a headband Mel recognized from her own bathroom.

With a chuckle, she shook her head as an appreciative warmth sent a sting to her eyes.

"Hey, babe." Kinkaide approached from the hallway and placed an arm around Mel's waist. He brushed her lips with his for a brief peck.

"You two cut that out!" Sonsee teased.

Mel grabbed Kinkaide and planted her lips against his. Several cheers went up from the friends.

"Wow! I just came in to ask for packaging tape," Kinkaide said, his eyes wide.

"That seems to be an epidemic." Kim Lan closed the lid of her box.

Sonsee extended the tape to Kinkaide. "Consider it on loan," Mel said, "*I* need it back." He took the roll and disappeared into the hallway.

"Ouch!" Kim held up her index finger. "I just broke *another* nail!"

"Somebody report her to the modeling police," Jac quipped, then moved toward the dining table.

Kim Lan playfully glared at her.

"Looks like you could use some help," Jac said. She scooped up an empty box and plopped it atop the table. "Mel's got enough framed photos to start her own studio."

"Okay, you can leave off the judgment calls any day now." Mel eased up the hallway to find Kinkaide in her bedroom packing her computer.

The phone rang, and she cringed. He glanced up. "Think that's your mother again?"

Mel stared at him. "I don't know, but I don't want to talk to her. She's driving me nuts about this move."

"So let the machine pick up."

"Marilyn already packed my machine."

Without a word, Kinkaide reached for the receiver and said hello. "It's her," he mouthed and a long silence followed. "Yes. I understand....I know. Yes...I can only imagine... Well, Mel and I have decided that this is the best move for both of us." Kinkaide adjusted his glasses then stroked his beard. "No, I'm afraid she can't come to the phone right now."

Mel sank onto the end of the unmade bed and grappled with the guilt that always ensued if she avoided her mother. While Darla Moore had been ecstatic about Mel and Kinkaide's marriage, she had been devastated that her daughter would actually sell her practice and her home and move to Nashville. *You're part of the reason we made this choice*, Mel thought.

All her adult life, Mel had expected her mom to behave like a person with a fairly logical thought process. Finally she was beginning to see that that expectation would probably never be met. While Darla could certainly function in the real world, her step was slightly out of rhythm. Darla had been attentive and loving in Mel's childhood, but now... Melissa dearly loved her mom. While she would always be there for her, Mel also knew that moving to Nashville would grant her a peace her mom would never allow if they lived in the same town.

"Okay, okay, I'll tell her....Goodbye," Kinkaide said. He sat beside Mel and placed an assuring arm around her shoulders. "She was crying," he said simply.

"Yes. She was crying this morning, too. I feel so sorry for her, but at the same time..." Mel sighed.

"We've got to carve out a life for ourselves, Mel." Kinkaide squeezed her shoulder. "You'll still be there for her. It's not like we're moving to the moon or anything."

"I know—and this *is* the right move." Mel leaned into Kinkaide's warmth and absently stared at the bare wall. "But I still feel a little guilty."

"Well, that's what she wants, you know."

"You're right." Mel nodded and smiled up at her husband. She placed a hand upon his chest as Kinkaide drew her close for an assuring hug. For the first time, she noticed a slender white box tucked in Kinkaide's shirt pocket. "What's this?" she asked.

"Oh!" Kinkaide slammed the heel of his hand against his forehead. "I almost forgot. Lawton would *kill* me!" He removed the box. "This is for Jac."

"From Lawton?" Mel's eyes widened.

"Yes. He got it for her the same time I bought your ring. I mentioned that Jac was going to be here today, and he asked me to pass it on. He's in Michigan or he'd have given it to her himself."

"What is it?" Mel queried.

"Your curiosity is going to be your downfall." With a fond smile, Kinkaide opened the hinged leather box.

Mel gasped at the platinum link bracelet within. Three star charms hung from the bracelet, and she pondered their significance.

"Do you think she'll keep it?" Kinkaide asked.

"I don't know."

"Honestly, I think Lawton was a little scared to give it to her in person. He said she basically gave him the brush off. The poor guy was afraid she might throw it back in his face."

"Mmm." Mel fingered the gleaming bracelet. "I think she really likes him, Kinkaide."

"You sound like Lawton. He's convinced of it but doesn't seem to know exactly how to get around her defenses."

"She's got those for sure," Mel said.

"Well, we Franklin men know how to break those down, don't we?" He snapped the box shut and tugged Mel backward until she flopped next to him on the bed. Mel squealed, and he playfully growled before covering her mouth with his.

"What happened to the tape?" Jac's voice floated from the doorway. "Oh, good grief, you're at it again," she mumbled.

Mel squirmed away from Kinkaide and sat up. "Sorry," she said with a grin.

"That's okay," Jacquelyn said, entering the room. "After all this is *your* house and you *are* married, but I would think that given the workload you'd have the decency to at least contribute to the task." She winked.

"With friends like you..." Kinkaide left the rest unsaid and extended the white box toward Jac.

"What's this?" she asked suspiciously.

"Just a little something from Lawton." Kinkaide nonchalantly approached the computer system and resumed his packing.

Jacquelyn looked at Mel. "This box is similar to the one your ring came in."

"Yes, I guess it is." Melissa grabbed an empty carton from near the dresser, opened a drawer, and dumped her socks into the box.

Eyes narrowed, Jac held the gift as if she were teetering on the brink of returning it without sneaking a peek. Finally, Jacquelyn snapped open the box. She glared at the bracelet and blurted, "Lawton and his stars." She snapped the box shut, tossed it onto the dresser, and turned to leave. But Jac barely took three steps before whirling back around and snatching the gift. Without a backward glance, she stomped from the bedroom.

Kinkaide held up the tape. "She forgot this," he said.

Author's Note

Dear Reader,

I hope you enjoyed interacting with the couples in this book. As with any marriage or potential marriage, Melissa and Kinkaide, Abby and Desmond each faced tough situations that needed to be bathed in unconditional love and forgiveness.

Like these two couples, my husband and I have needed to exercise heavy doses of understanding and love to make our marriage work. Daniel and I got married when we were 19 and 23, respectively, and we have now been married for more than 18 years!

The beauty of getting married young is that you get to grow up together, and eventually there's a deep bond that grows from having survived those youthful years as one. The drawback of a young marriage involves all the things you put each other through until you grow up.

Neither Daniel nor I have ever had an affair. However, we have each had our moments of immaturity and struggled with forgiveness. And there have been times when I have felt as if we were like Horace Waggoner—flopping around on a floor covered by sudsy water. All marriages go through these relational rapids.

Whether a couple marries young or waits until later in life, there will still be issues to face, forgiveness to extend, and love to grow into. According to Gary Smalley in *Love Is a Decision,* we women are the relationship monitors of our marriage. Does your marriage need work?

If you need to forgive, forgive.

If you need to love unconditionally, love unconditionally.

If you need to repent, repent.

God has extended His grace and mercy to you. Extend it to your spouse. We can do all things, we can overcome all obstacles, we can initiate healing, intimacy, and reconciliation through Him who gives us strength.

In Christ,

Debra White Smith

P.S. By the way, the engaging character of Lawton Franklin is based on a friend of mine. Everything about Lawton is lived daily by Rob, who embraces life more fully than many sighted folks. I hope you look forward to his and Jac's story, coming next, as much as I look forward to writing it!

Debra White Smith

Like Melissa Moore, award-winning author Debra White Smith proudly lives up to her well-earned title as the "mouth of the south." She has been dubbed the garage sale queen and would rather go fishing than shopping, despite the fact that she holds a stuffy M.A. in English. She enjoys writing both fiction and nonfiction and, since 1997, has had more than 400,000 books in print. Her fiction books include: *Second Chances, The Awakening,* and *A Shelter in the Storm.* Her nonfiction books include: *More Than Rubies: Becoming a Woman of Godly Influence,* and *The Harder I Laugh, the Deeper I Hurt.*

Debra is often featured on radio across North America and cohosts a Sunday-morning radio show in her hometown. She speaks across the nation and particularly enjoys stopping in at airport ice-cream parlors—especially if they serve German chocolate. Debra lives in small-town America with her wonderful husband of 18-plus years and two adorable children.

by *Debra White Smith*

The Seven Sisters series follows the intriguing lives, romances, and adventures of seven friends.

Second Chances

Marilyn Douglas Thatcher's happy life as a minister's wife turns upside down when her husband leaves her for another woman. Marilyn begins to piece together a new life with her four-year-old daughter, Brooke...a life that doesn't include a husband or God. When Marilyn meets her charming new neighbor, Joshua Langham, her heart begins to awaken. But when she learns that Joshua is a pastor, she determines to cut off all contact with him. She will not lose her heart again.

Joshua is also trying to make a new life of his own, one free from his sinful past. But when a former acquaintance begins to send him mysterious letters, Joshua realizes that his secret—and his life—are in danger. *Second Chances* is a tender story of redemption, forgiveness, and the healing power of God's love.

The Awakening

Supermodel Kim Lan Lowery has it all: exquisite beauty, wealth, an engagement to famous heartthrob Ted Curry, a close circle of friends, and a budding faith that seldom interferes with her plans. When a secret admirer begins to send flowers and love notes, Kim is flattered by the special attention. But as the letters become more possessive, warning signals flash. When an unusual opportunity to escape the mysterious gift-giver arises, Kim Lan jumps at the chance.

Joining a mission outreach to Vietnam, Kim's high-profile status conflicts with coordinator Mick O'Donnel's vision for a quiet, sincere offer of aid. Sparks fly between Kim and Mick as their lifestyles clash, their values collide, and they battle a deep undercurrent of passion. When the secret gifts and notes start appearing again, it's apparent that her "secret admirer" isn't very far away. In desperation she turns to the only person in Vietnam she can trust...or can she?

A Shelter in the Storm

An old southern mansion. A deadly game of cat and mouse. A love that refuses to surrender. When Sonsee LeBlanc realized she was in love with longtime friend Taylor Delaney, discouragement gripped her heart. Taylor had made it clear that romance was not in his plans—and never would be. Struggling to find peace, Sonsee relinquishes her heart and her future to the Lord. But then her father is killed and Taylor is the prime suspect...

As the search for the murderer intensifies, Sonsee enters a maze of betrayal and greed that leads to a hidden key, a secret chamber, and a long-held family secret. When the killer makes a desperate move, Sonsee faces the ultimate challenge...and discovers God's protection and the freedom to love.